Helena: An Odyssey

A novel

Carolyn Taylor-Watts

To angela,

Best wishes to you &
cheers!

Carolyn Nov. 14

The author gratefully acknowledges the support of the Ontario Council for the arts.

LIBRARY AND ARCHIVES CANADA CATALOGUING IN PUBLICATION

Taylor-Watts, Carolyn
Helena: an Odyssey / Carolyn Taylor-Watts

Type of Book: Historical Fiction
Myth-Obsession-Greco-Turkish War- Deportation-Toronto-Hair

ISBN :9781502708526

Cover Design: Stephen Yeates
Author Photo: James Lynch
Website design: Susan Dineen

www.CarolynTaylorWatts.com

Other books by the author, written under the name *Carolyn Matthews*:

Non Fiction:

Heroic Rescues at Sea: True Stories of the Canadian Coast Guard, Nimbus Publishing, Halifax, Canada, 2002. Global Television based their series, "***The Guard***" on these stories.

To the Rescue: True Stories of Tragedy and Survival, Dundurn Press, Toronto, 2005.

True Stories of Rescue and Survival: Canada's Unknown Heroes, Dundurn Press, Toronto, 2008, a young adult book nominated by Doubleday Canada as their Book-of-the-Month Club pick.

To Kiki Kostakyriakos (Kontoni) who provided the inspiration
for this book

And to Cameron, Rachel, and Lindsay.

Chapter 1

Toronto, 1994 -1995

Georgia:

Mom and I don't talk much in the mornings before she goes to work, but today at the kitchen table, without looking up, she starts muttering about her mother in Greece, like, "Your *Yia Yia*'s gone back to living in the past, moaning and groaning about everything she lost. I say to her, you're lucky you got to keep your life, like a lot of other people didn't ..." Then she just trails off and stares into her coffee cup.

Ha, my chance at last to find out more about our mostly unmentionable past so immediately I jump in with, "So who did set the fire that started it all? What did happen to the rest of our family and why doesn't anyone ever talk about them?"

"Eh?" Mom jerks up her head. Confusion comes over her, like she had no idea what I was talking about.

Damn. Too much of a leap, too early in the morning. I watch as she drains her coffee, as she gets up and sweeps crumbs from the table.

"Who was responsible for all that?" I persist. "*Yia Yia* said our family lost everything when they fled the fire ..."

"Georgie, see the hands on the clock? I'm late for work already. And don't ask your *Yia Yia* questions about the past, it's best for her not to dwell on it - or any of us for that matter."

"Another time then Mom? I really truly want to know." She doesn't answer but I catch a fleeting, hunted kind of expression on her face as she fixes her hair in the hall mirror. In that moment I understand that while she might want to forget all that stuff, whatever it was, she can't.

Months later I'm sitting on my unmade bed remembering that exchange, thinking about my weird family –"Obsessed," my sister Amalia says. Helena, our Mom, rushed off to Greece a month ago. We've heard nothing from her since except she's coming home today. It's to do with our forebears in Greece and Turkey, I think. There's a mystery about them, something sad, even shocking. When I inherited my sister's bedroom I heard things through the walls. Once I tried to talk to her about it.

"Mom talks to herself at night about our ancestor called Yiannis," I said. "I hear her cry out for a Stephan."

Amalia had dropped in and was at the kitchen table leafing through an old *Hello* magazine. "Yeah," she said, "I used to hear her go on about the old fogies. But it's history Georgie, all gone and done. People should forget what happened way back."

"What happened? Do you know something you're not telling me? Has Mom got a terrible secret?"

"Sure she does. Who doesn't? Of course I don't know. Maybe this Stephan's a missing boyfriend over there. Or an ancestor's ghost haunting her ..."

"Malia!"

"What an innocent you are Georgie." Amalia continues to flip the magazine's pages. "Let Mom sort it out. Let it go."

I try, but can't. I keep thinking that if I can just get to the bottom of whatever the mystery is, all our lives might be easier. Hey, I might even be different.

It's around five o'clock when I hear the door open, footsteps in the hall, the thump of a bag on the floor. I call out hello and jump up, expecting any minute Mom will come into my room. Damn, I should have cleaned it up. But she walks right past, into her room, and shuts the door. Creaky silence follows. I think about following her in, decide she needs space, and instead go into the kitchen to start cooking supper.

Dad comes up from the basement. He's in old jeans and a coffee-stained shirt: no dressing up for his wife's return there. He plants himself on the living room couch among a pile of Greek newspapers. After a few moments he looks at me and raises his brows in inquiry.

I shake my head and continue preparing dinner. When it's ready I call out to Mom, but her door remains shut. As the night clicks on and still she doesn't come out, I get worried and appeal to Dad: "Shouldn't you go in and see if she's okay?"

He lumbers up from the couch and goes in, only to come out, frowning, a few moments later. "She's hiding under the bed clothes Georgie, she won't talk to me. Something's happened over there." From the expression on his face I think he might actually care. But immediately he rubs his hands and asks about dinner.

There's no sign of Mom next morning so I go off to my job at Book City. Late afternoon I come home to find her still shut off in her bedroom. Really worried now I call up my sister and say, "Malia, you better get over here, Mom's acting weird. You know how to talk to her."

"Georgie, you're such a baby. Can't you learn to do things by yourself? I'm busy. Mom can take care of herself."

"Wait! She won't get up. She won't even talk to me!"

Amalia cuts me off, but I have a feeling that she'll come anyway, if only out of curiosity.

She blows in the door about nine, walks straight through the hall without taking her boots off, and into Mom's bedroom. She switches on the light and yanks at the window shades.

"Well Mom," her voice booms out the open door, "you meet a ghost or something? A dead lover reached from the grave and tried to grab you?"

From the doorway I hear only an unintelligible sound from under the duvet, then nothing.

Amalia pauses by Mom's bed, then walks about the room. She straightens the portrait of a crucified Christ on the wall, rearranges snapshots of our family in Greece on the dresser. It's when she turns and looks me over with her judgmental stare that waves of old inferiority wash over me. I'm still trying to find a smart-ass thing to say when I hear Dad's footsteps clump up the basement stairs. Amalia hears him too and flies from the room. Next thing the front door bangs.

Rubbing my tight neck muscles, I walk away and into my bedroom.

Through the wall that night I hear Mom again, talking to her *Voices*, 'Thoughts that clatter about in my brain,' she once explained. I hear the name Stephan. Faithful. Stephan (again). I never forgot … I was coming to you. Something about a person called Yiannis, and a promise.

3

I've learned a bit about Yiannis over the years of course, and about Stephan in more recent times, but now as I sit hugging my knees to my chin I wonder what on earth my beautiful, excitable mother Helena has been hiding from us.

Two days later she's up, makes coffee, and gets ready for work. Whew. But she's dressed herself in black. The mother I know is flamboyant, like a peacock. This is weird. I follow her into the tiny hall.

"Mom, are you okay? Did something happen over there? You've haven't said – anything." She's fixing her hair in the mirror and I can tell she's been crying. In fact she looks terrible, all stiff and broken up.

"Something always happens." She looks at me through the mirror, and I look back into a pair of hollow eyes. She starts muttering about being very busy, then in a voice that holds accusation, says, "You? Got any work today?"

"Yes, a shift from ten this morning till four. Can't you get help if you're so busy?"

"Why don't you help me in the salon if you're not so busy?"

Hair. Toe nails. Finger nails. Make-up. I hate all that stupid beauty stuff. I can't work with her anyway since we're opposites in just about everything. Suddenly it occurs to me that she might mean it this time so I have to tell her, now, what I've always really wanted to do. The words just fall out of my mouth:

"Mom, I know you think I spend too much time in my room scribbling, as you call it, but, well, I want to study literature. Seriously, I want to be a writer." I look straight into the red-rimmed eyes in the mirror. "So now you know."

"Write?" Her head jerks around. "Whatever for, what about? You're nineteen and think you'll get somewhere making up little stories? You should get proper life. Get some ambition and be more like your sister."

I hate it when she compares me with Amalia, but right now I don't care, she's scaring me. Maybe she thinks she'll pass whatever it is onto me. I step back and draw my dressing gown tight about me.

"Our family's got secrets you're not telling me about Mom," I say, "some kind of tragedy." I rush on, even though that hunted look creeps up her face. "Something happened to you in Greece. You talk in your sleep about a Stephan. A person called Yiannis and a promise. Mom, why can't you just tell me? Why don't you ever talk to me?"

She starts for the door and I hurry after her. I lay a hand on her arm but she shakes it off. "Really Mom, we can sort it out together."

She grabs her purse and keeps on walking. A pulse throbs in my left temple. I have to get to work. I should eat something first but am suddenly not hungry. That's a good thing: after the way Amalia looked at me the other night, after Mom compared us, I feel even worse about being overweight – and whatever else my family thinks about me. It doesn't matter that Dad ignores me, that Amalia dismisses me, but it does hurt that Mom won't talk to me.

Every day now Mom goes to her salon, but she's changed. I continue working my shifts in a bookstore, at home move about in air that feels thick. Sleepless some nights, I conjure up cataclysmic deeds my forebears might have done, tragedies that hit them. Who's this Yiannis? What promise? When Mom's not around I get on the phone to my *Yia Yia* in Greece. *Yia Yia* refuses to talk about Stephan but does tell me bits about our family's origins in Turkey, about this Yiannis Kouvalis who imposed a burden on his descendants.

Belief that something momentous is about to unfold swells within me as the days pass and I must hurry to learn what it is. Maybe the consequences of this burden and promise are still echoing across the generations.

I'm not to know when I begin my research that it will take me through Greek-Turkish wars, a burning city, an exchange of ethnic populations and into fairy tales and myth. I'm not to know I'm to be the chronicler of powerful and tragic love stories. I'll make it my mother Helena's story, I think, and in it I'll call her Helena, but not to her face of course. I'll have to imagine what I don't know, and so I begin this Yiannis person from long ago.

***

5

Chapter 2

Anatolia, Turkey, 1908

The air lay very still that late afternoon, the world hushed into somnolence by the heat. Adam draped his lanky form beneath an oleander bush, his long, thin fingers curled over the spine of a book. He watched bee-eaters buzz about him, green and yellow, their breasts the colour of the Aegean Sea. He filled his head with birdsong; pushed himself further into the dark earth – *his* earth. Here lay the bones of his ancestors stretching across the centuries: warriors, horsemen, peasant farmers. Here also powerful armies trod, St Paul, the prophets of great religions, central Asian nomads riding the steppes to conquer it.

At a clamour of voices he looked up, to catch sight of his father and mother in kitchen doorway. Both were looking at him, probably talking about him, and he shrank further into the shade.

"Got to get the boy out of school and put him to work." Adam heard the irritation in his father's voice across the baked dirt yard. "Explain to me how learning Anatolian history will make our family rich, eh? Reading Turkish poetry? A waste of time."

"Yianni, our boy needs to learn." His mother Georgia's voice soothed. "He wants to know things … about Christian, Muslim and Jewish people and all the tribes that lived here a long time ago. It will make him wise, you'll see, and the world can always use wise men."

Adam heard his father mutter as he withdrew inside the darkened house.

Adam knew the image he portrayed: an indolent first-born son in a shirt stained with wild raspberries. Books in his lap. His nostrils flared to absorb the perfumes of trees and earth. He shifted his position and caught sight of his brother Spiros digging in the potato patch, his movements quick and angry. Adam saw his brother's shirt all wet with sweat, that his straight black hair almost covered his eyes, and guiltily recalled his mother admonishing him: *Spiros, you must look to Adam and learn to be gentle.*

Next thing Spiros' shadow fell across him, his brother reaching for his book.

"Teach me what you know," he begged, and at the snapping of his fingers Adam knew he hated having to ask.

"Looks like you lost a fight with one of the goats." He smiled up at his brother.

Spiros glanced at his torn shirt, the many scratches on his hands, and pointed at the book. "What do you read this stuff for?"

"Well, since you ask, it tells me the history of Anatolia – our history."

"What do you care? You want to be a teacher? A priest?"

"A teacher," Adam said. "I want to know things and one day teach them."

"You know Papa won't let you stay in school."

Adam saw the prickling anger rise that he had seen that morning. His brother had followed him into the schoolroom. In the doorway the bowed figure of the scribe stood stroking his grey-streaked beard and rubbing the side of his nose. When Adam offered him a flower, the teacher's mouth stretched slightly; cadaverous hands reached up and patted Adam's springy curls. He knew he would not likely be in trouble that morning. He saw Spiros coming up behind him. In imitation, he offered up his best smile, in his pudgy hands the gift of a wild iris. The scribe thumped his flat black hair and pushed him away.

Adam felt his hands being grabbed, heard Spiros begging, "Come on, the weeding's all finished, let's do something."

"Like what?"

Sudden childish laughter trilling from the orchard made them both look up to see their younger brother Nikos shimmying up the linden tree by the gate. His twin Basil stood at its foot, his mouth hanging open. From high in the branches Nikos aimed an apricot into it. The squishy fruit bounced off the boy's nose and in a mock faint, he shrieked and fell backwards.

Adam laughed. He looked at Spiros, in time to catch the expression of naked longing he'd seen before. What exactly was his brother looking for?

"Come *on*, do something." Spiros' slant eyes begged.

"I suppose. But didn't you want me to help you learn to read?" Reluctantly Adam sat up.

"Reading, reading, reading. You better watch it or your eyes will fall out."

"The book – can I have it back?"

Adam sat up on hearing footsteps on the hard-baked path. Their father Yiannis appeared, muttering about sunflowers needing to be staked and olives to be picked and how was he to do better than the neighbours when he had such damn lazy sons. He stopped before Adam and kicked his book through the long grass. "You think your reading will feed this family? That history will make us rich? *Get up*."

Adam often puzzled over his father's changing moods toward him. "Let him have books," he declared on hearing him read aloud to his brothers and sisters. "The apothecary's son in the village can read and so can my boy."

After this, Adam would sometimes catch sight of his father pretending not to see his mother trudge the path to the Old Silk Road to barter books for him from passing traders; would pretend not to see Adam's face brimming with pleasure in the sunshine of a thousand summer days, and in his books. But when frost killed the fruit, when summer rains rotted the wheat, Adam hid them.

Reluctantly he joined Spiros in the potato patch. In the early evening, while Spiros hovered about their father who was muttering over the accounts, Adam returned outdoors, straining to hear voices in the wind: mixed tongues from Asia. Plaintive Pontic voices from the Black Sea. Sing-song tones from the beautiful Aegean coast. Above all, warm breezes laughing all the way from the Mediterranean Sea.

***

Late the following Saturday Adam headed for the kitchen with his arms full of vegetables. His mother dozed in her chair by the door. He was about to slide past her when he heard wheels dragging on the rough path up to the house, and looked back.

Oh, strangers! He tapped his mother on the shoulder.

8

She straightened in her chair and smiled up at him. "My dear boy…"

"Mama, wake up. We've got visitors."

Georgia's smile faded as she looked at two men in strange costume pulling a handcart up the slope. Each wore flowing beards, long waistcoats over trim black trousers. The one who had pulled the cart stood with shoulders hunched, sweat running down his face.

"Mama, who are the strange people?" The twins had appeared. One grabbed his mother's hands and pulled her onto the baked dirt courtyard that served as a living room in the summer. Georgia faltered before the visitors, then whispered to the twins, "Go - quickly. Find some refreshments for our visitors."

The twins returned with cool drinks, flat bread and cheese and set it before the strange men. Adam hurried to place chairs for them.

"We've come to talk to your husband," said one in an unfamiliar dialect.

Georgia looked faint and Adam hastened to say, "Don't worry Mama, I'm sure he must be on his way home by now." Or he might not be. Each Wednesday his father went early to the small village over the hills to play backgammon. On his return, he rested in the wilderness awhile to smoke his hookah pipe.

"Please take some refreshments." His mother's voice squeaked. "I'll go at once and find my husband." Her enormous figure moved clumsily toward the orchard and Adam excused himself to run after her. Neither spoke as they walked a path through the trees that would take them over a stretch of flat land toward distant hills. Adam saw disappointment settling in his mother's face and knew the reason: his father always returned after his weekly visit full of local news, his mood mellow. He would not like the visitors' intrusion, and for his wife the evening was spoiled.

The pine trees cast long shadows as the clipped figure of Yiannis came through them. Adam smelled peppery oregano and thyme on his clothes as his father drew close. He hung back, watching as his mother gently brushed pine needles from her husband's rough brown jacket.

"A fine thing to sit up in the hills in the dusk," he greeted her. "I watched the sun turning church steeples into gold, and minarets too." Then he frowned. "Tomorrow we must go to the mosque and give prayers for our neighbour's little one."

Georgia dipped her head in acknowledgement. Adam stepped forward to tell him of the strangers. Yiannis' thin frame tightened and without a word he strode toward the side of his home, Adam alongside, Georgia hastening after them.

On bare ground that sloped from the kitchen door stood a cart stacked with books, the angular forms of two men standing stiffly beside it. Adam saw his father's eyes flick over the flowing beards, their odd clothes; saw his muscles tensed further.

After a formal exchange of pleasantries one of the scholars said, "Your families are Karamanli Greeks descended from Byzantium, but you have forgotten who you are. You have mixed yourselves up with the Muslim Turk and lost your Christian faith. In plain words, you have become like the Turk."

Turk? Adam felt puzzled. Their Muslim friends called themselves Ottomans or Osmanlis. To call one a Turk was to insult him. Occasionally a Muslim might call a Christian a dog or infidel, but it was always said in good nature.

"You write with Greek symbols, but you speak the Turkish." The scholar's voice had become faintly accusing. "We intend to set up schools for your children so they can properly learn their Greek language."

More school? Adam saw the younger children's puzzled expressions and knew the twins would never be confined in a schoolroom. Who would pick the fruit, tend the vegetables, the animals. Who would milk the goats?

The strangers departed, leaving their books and a promise to return. That evening when dinner was over and the older girls had put the smaller children to bed, Georgia dropped heavily into her chair by the door to watch the night's darkness gather up the day.

Adam came upon her when her chin had reached her chest and he slipped off to check on the children for her. Stepping into the long, airless room where his brothers and sisters slept on cots lined up against each wall, he was surprised to find them asleep, all tucked up under the watchful eyes of Christ on his cross. He paused in the doorway, a warm glow coursing through him – for them, for the earth's rhythms, for the constancy of life and for his place in it. And for his mother. In some part of him he understood that she accepted, like all the generations of women before her, that she would live close the earth and be tied to it, to endless cycles of pregnancy and birth. It was all as infinite, as timeless as the land itself.

His father: he would run into future epochs if he could. But maybe not: he was king of his tiny universe right here in the land of his forebears. Adam had seen him, irritable at first, then nodding when the visitors declared him descended from the ancients, nodding when they said a father's duty was to have his family practice their proper religion, to learn their Greek history. "Adam must be the one to learn it all," he'd said.

Adam awoke next day to a soft rain, to his mother moving tiredly about the kitchen.

"I'll get the water for you," he said, picking up a bucket and heading for the communal well.

"*Merhaba*," he said, smiling at the Muslim neighbour.

"*Merhaba.*" The neighbour frowned and turned her head slightly. Another young woman on the dirt path ignored him. In the days that followed Adam saw doubt clouding once friendly faces; noticed fewer Muslims entering Christian churches. He knew then that they had heard about the strangers and their message.

"A tribal distinction has been made," he told his mother, frowning. "We've co-existed across the centuries. What a shame to come and disturb it now."

***

The Greek scholars were not to be the last of the family's visitors. One late spring day, Yiannis walked about his orchard picking at shrivelled white grapes on the vines. A cruel winter had passed, followed by a slow blossoming out of the cold earth. The world lay silent as though holding its breath. He walked the twisting path toward to the Old Silk Road and, at its intersection, leaned against a lone poplar tree to watch heavily-laden camels pass by, trying to guess at the wealth they carried to the coast. Gold, silks, jewels and spices, no doubt enough to make someone a very big fortune.

He jumped as a figure sprang off a bullock-drawn wagon and walked towards him – another wandering Greek carrying books about the ancients? But it was a modern-looking man wearing smooth black trousers, smart waistcoat and Latin sash who approached. When within a few feet of him, Yiannis recognized his brother Vasilis from Konya. The short, swarthy man held out his arms for an embrace, stepped back and raked his eyes over the shabby form of his older brother.

"Times are tough, Yianni?"

Yiannis grunted. He might own the largest property surrounding the town of Boldavin, but over the centuries his few acres of wheat, sunflowers, a small orchard and vegetable garden had been repeatedly divided for sons, grandsons and great grandsons. The land was no longer enough.

"I've got news." Vasilis' voice cut into Yiannis' brooding. "Invite me home to meet your sons and we'll talk about the future. Your oldest boy – what age?"

"Thirteen, fourteen." Familiar conflicting emotions arose at the mention of Adam and Yiannis stomped on a shrivelled grape. "Got to get him into factory work to earn a wage, like in your carpet business. As you say, times are not easy."

After a formal meal, Yiannis took his brother into the orchard out of earshot of the family. Vasilis' words punctuated the enveloping darkness. Next morning he departed as abruptly as he'd come, trailing words over his shoulder, "Send for me, or come when you decide."

"*Daxi*. I'll wait for a sign."

Vasilis walked away leaving Yiannis on the dirt path rolling new words on his tongue: *Wealth. Influence. Titles.* Other words too: *Turks are restless and rising up.*

In the following days his lone figure stood among the wheat, as motionless as a tree on a windless day, his eyes scanning the horizon. Knots formed biliously in his stomach and tightened the muscles across his shoulders. One evening he ordered his family early to the dinner table, a slight smile twitching his lips as they swarmed to it. Not because of his many children, that too, but because of the table. After Vasilis' news he'd felt driven to raise the family's way of living – at once. No more sitting on the dirt floor for meals. Clattering upright at the head of its rough-hewn surface, he raised both hands to command silence. Nine chattering children, girls on one side, boys on the other, sat quietly erect and darted fleeting glances at their father. The patriarch cleared his throat.

"My brother tells me the Kouvalis family was once rich and powerful in the land of ancient Caesarea. This is the cradle of civilization, as all of you should know. Now you can see what we've come to, poor farmers on lands that were ours. Time for us to do something about it and have all people know our great name: Jews, Christians, Muslims – everyone."

He shot his words, bullet-like, into the hush. "We owned buildings in Constantinople and part of this great plateau. Enough of being poor, we will take back what is ours!" As his fist pounded the table, nine inscrutable faces remained fixed on his. Yiannis, ranging his eyes over his many children, was astonished yet again that from his very loins had issued these little people: Adam a rising young god, but not always, damn him. Light-skinned Maria with her mother's golden hair. Nikos with his tilted Tartar-like eyes, and Basil with ice-blue Circassian ones. Second-born Spiros? Yiannis turned from him, to find his wife's eyes resting on his.

"So, this is what's making you sweat and lie awake," she said to him afterwards, her voice gentle. "Why don't you talk to me?"

Yiannis wavered. He wanted to, but remained mute for so long that she moved from the table, arranged herself comfortably in a wooden chair by the kitchen door, and shooed away chickens scratching at her feet. Tilting her head, she listened to birds settling in the trees. When she lifted her eyes to the horizon it was to an early evening so clear she could almost see the lone poplar tree near the main road; see the grand panorama of the plains. Dotted among the wheat fields moved speck-like figures in bright-striped trousers and white shawls. Turkish nomads and goat-hair tents. Shepherds watching small flocks on a distant horizon. They were scenes gentle and timeless, and Georgia wondered if her husband really wanted any of this to change.

In the days that followed Yiannis' mind seethed. His head ached. Hunger gnawed in his belly. His moods shifted as quickly as flitting birds and nothing pleased him. He was harsh to his children, but never his wife. His eyes narrowed to slits as he stomped over his estate, his boots kicking at crooked fences. He walked more often the grassy path to the Old Silk Road, listening as passing merchants spoke of an infidel city called Smyrna on the Aegean Coast.

One late afternoon he caught sight of Adam back under the oleander bush. He spat. The boy might be good to look upon; he might have a smile that could light up a subterranean passage, as his wife once said, but must it

13

be him the gods intended to lift the family out of poverty and insignificance? "Aghh!" he said, and spat again.

"Yianni?" Georgia was plucking apricots from low-hanging branches nearby. "What is it?"

"That damned big boy of yours. All his life he walks in a dream backwards into the past. Never does he think about the future. Never does he get any ambition."

Ambition? Georgia rolled the word on her tongue. "But what should he do?"

"Same as that boy." Yiannis pointed at Spiros in the orchard mending a broken fence, and as though aware of the focus on him, Spiros looked up. He wiped his bleeding hands on his threadbare shirt, dropped his tools and walked toward them. Coming close, he locked eyes on his father. "Time for inspection yet?"

"Inspection? What's the matter with you, boy?" Yiannis could see his son was angry, and vaguely discomforted, remembered his recent decision to line up his children each evening for inspection. One day he had a smile for them. The next, harsh nasal commands and a clip to Spiros' ear – yes, he realized, it was always Spiros. Sometimes he slapped Nikos' shoulder, barked an order that he change his shirt. Georgia murmuring that he had no other. Maria smiling up at him, her springing golden hair falling over her eyes and not a word to her.

"Why don't you let *me* go to my uncle? Why don't you? " Spiros was hopping from one foot to the other, his eyes hot and angry.

"No. Not you." Yiannis' discomfort turned quickly to irritation. "It's for the oldest son to do these things."

"You must look to your brother, Spiros." Georgia added softly. "You see how gentle he is, how he studies his books to become wise."

Yiannis filled his pipe and studied his second-born son. Right now the boy's lips had formed a thin, tight line. He did most of the work, tried to understand the account book. He sheltered the stock in winter. Maybe he was being unfair to him. But look at him. And as Yiannis looked, comprehension dawned: his son reminded him of Mongol hordes, wild Turkmen mingled with Phrygians, Armenians and Persians, maybe a whole mongrel mix. He reminded him of himself. Who was he, Yiannis, anyway but part of a conquered people born to servitude, people half-literate and poor? He looked again at Spiros, to see an expression of envy cross his face as he watched his twin brothers laughing under the trees, their arms and legs in a tangle.

***

Again Yiannis trekked to the main road when rumour told that another *caravansary* would soon be passing from the East, and waited impatiently under shelter of the poplar tree. It was not until late afternoon he saw dust rising, and straggling lines of men and camels coming into view. They halted for rest and water, Yiannis pressing them for news of the fabled city of Smyrna.

"Greeks do most of the business there," said a weathered old man with a blade of grass between his front teeth.

"A new Byzantium," offered a boy who hid from the sun beneath a bullock cart. "A glorious Greece just like before. Any fellow can get rich in a place like that."

As Yiannis walked home he held visions of silk, gold and precious stones pouring into a polyglot city; saw vessels from around the world carrying exotic foodstuffs from the Near and Far East; glittering merchandize from Italy, Spain and France. How could he get there? He made plans, and discarded them. '*The past has flown away ... I am alone in a wide desert, listening to echoes of strange noises.*'

From a carpet salesman he learned of the rise of the Onassis family from Moutalasski, Karamanli Greeks like themselves. How, after arriving on the coast they had amassed a fortune and risen in the city's political circles. That Socrates helped direct the affairs of the *Rum Mileti*, a community of Greeks inside Turkey. If this poor Onassis family could do this, then the Kouvalis sons could do the same and better. *Daxi!*

That evening he stretched to his tallest at the dinner table, his voice calm with the certainty of his decision. "God has given me a sign," he announced. "I will be taking my two oldest sons to the glorious city of Smyrna where we will buy and sell gold and silks and build up a big fortune."

A smothered cry burst from Georgia but he cut her off. "The devil roams," he said. "God is asleep. It's a poor harvest we have suffered and our animals are hungry." He coughed and spat. "We leave the day after tomorrow."

All about them life stilled, and into its hush came Spiros' voice. "Papa, how do you know about the gold and the silks?"

"The railways, boy. To the north and east the lines run out from Smyrna. They've opened up the great wealth of the Ottoman Empire to all the Western nations. Maybe you're clever enough to know what this means: now we too can trade with both West and East."

He looked into the eager eyes of his second son. "This family," he said, "will become important in this place because the *Fates* have decreed it."

"Yes Papa." Spiros pumped his arms.

"Must we go?" Adam's voice was plaintive. "Papa, this is our home. Mama, tell him we can't leave you."

"Papa, you say!" Yiannis lowered his brows. "A family must live in dignity, but where is the dignity without money? Your brothers would cut off an arm to see this ancient city. Maybe, stupid boy, you read all these books and still don't know your history. Before the first millennium of our Lord, the Greeks lived up and down the coast of the eastern Mediterranean. It was a civilization that came before Athens itself, part of the Ionia when this name meant to the world everything fashionable and enlightened. The Greeks made it so, the ones who run the business of Smyrna. Never forget: We are also these Greeks."

Silence filtered about the table. Yiannis did not look at his wife. Such plans were unheard of; she would think they might never come home. The children too. When all fixed their eyes on him Yiannis held a sudden vision of himself: rock-like, intense and deliberate. Heavy brows. Thick red lips at odds with the rest of him. Dimly he knew that to his children he appeared solid, dependable, unmovable. The world might change all about them: camels giving way to cars. Carts and donkeys to tractors. Hand-watering to commercial irrigation systems. But he, their father, like the rock beneath his feet, would never change. Well, damn it, they were wrong.

"Mama, *Mama*." Adam was speaking, gently lifting his mother's chin. Yiannis saw the pale skin above her upper lip, the darkness of night under her eyes. He saw Adam brush a hand over his mother's hair, rest his long, tapered fingers on her shoulder. Each looked at the other. Adam bent to whisper to her and Yiannis caught some of it … *don't be afraid of life changing because this is already a hard one for you.* He heard rough emotion in his son's voice as he added, *"Who cares about wealth and reputation in the old days? Why should my father decide the fate of a whole family?"* Yiannis turned away.

"Whatever happens," Adam added aloud into a dull silence, "I'll come back to you, Mama. I'll look after you always."

That night, when Georgia cried in her sleep, Yiannis clumsily cradled her. He thought about his sons: Spiros already agitating to get to this shining city on the Aegean Sea. Adam? Yiannis could not read him. He could not know that in awful prophecy, the boy dreamed he saw the ancient metropolis of Phrygia erupting, a city eventually consumed by a Lydian civilization. Dreamed he saw Hittites crossing the plain, powerful and civilized, but bringing destruction in their wake.

***

Chapter 3

Anatolia, 1908 - 1909

The air hung heavily the morning of the departure, blue-black clouds dipping low. Adam slunk low on his stool at the table watching his mother serve breakfast to her husband, to him, and to Spiros. She spoke not a word. He saw the younger children hanging about, eyes darting from one parent to the other. Heard Maria stifling giggles as she looked at her father's moustache splattered with yogurt, at Spiros devouring flat bread covered in feta cheese and washing it down with a mug of strong tea.

He ate nothing at all. He'd gathered his small sack of possessions and stood with his mother on the sloping path outside the kitchen door. He leaned against her rough brown tunic full of baby smells, of the garlic, sweat and smoke. Memories rushed at him, the tumultuous years when babies arrived every year but still his Mama found time to read to him about shallow plains and large salt lakes, about the trajectory of moon and stars. She would smile at him, tell him his eyes were the colour of the forest, sometimes a tobacco leaf in full ripeness. Sometimes he'd wrapped himself in the folds of her clothes to listen for the rumble rising up in her belly when she laughed.

When older, he read old Greek-Turkish folk tales to her, and stories about Turkic tribes from Central Asia.

"Anatolians just like us," he exulted. "We live here too, Mama, in the ancient land between Persia and the Aegean Sea, best place on the earth."

"But a harsh land it is," she said, "remember this when you're missing it."

The two stood apart from the Kouvalis tribe, limbs entwining, until Adam, aware of a hush, of many pairs of eyes on him, moved away from his mother's embrace. He promised her he would get rich and buy her fine linens. He'd look for a wife exactly like her, and bring her home.

"No, *chryso mou,* your father will find you a wife in the usual Greek tradition. A woman who comes from the earth and knows its seasons. She will hear your music and see the beauty of the steppe. She will not look like me ..."

Her voice trailed away as her eyes flitted over her body as though examining it.

And Adam saw his mother as though for the first time: the near-toothless mouth, skin mottled and burned by sun and wind; the bulging fat of her arms, her thighs, her belly. He felt an ache form behind his eyes but once more she was drawing him close, whispering that if he did as his father wished and worked hard, he might become rich. He could pursue his dreams of university, read books, and perhaps become a professor.

Yiannis stepped between them, looked up into his wife's eyes. "Your brothers will look after you," he said. "When our grown sons are rich and established in the great city, I'll be home with you always." Turning his back, he strode down the path to the road, not another word nor gesture to her, but Adam saw him slip a hand to his eyes to wipe away a tear.

***

"In 1909, a skeletal middle-aged man and his two oldest sons left the spreading fields and rocks of their ancestral home, taking only their knowledge of farming, and one of them, some book learning and a head filled with poems and songs of Anatolia. They headed for the city of Smyrna on the coast of Asia Minor."

Adam, shielding his eyes against the sun, mentally recorded their departure as he walked the Old Silk Route where once the feet of Alexander, of Tamerlane, Genghis Khan and the Crusaders had tramped. Turning, squinting, he gained a last glimpse of his mother who towered above roses and sunflowers as she watched him retreat, surely more than six feet of him and not yet fifteen years.

The three travelled by wagon using large pack-saddles called *havats.* As rock cliff gave way to fertile plain, as distance separated him from his ancestral land, Adam stored up images: his child-like self, flitting over hills and plains. Adults drinking *ouzo* beneath cypress trees. His mother as a large troll guarding her cave. He heard the tinkling sounds of the *kahve,* goats bleating on the hills, Mama calling her children to supper. Memories flitted of cool nights after the sun dipped below the horizon, children lulled to sleep by the sweet-sad sounds of a *saz.* Adults eating and drinking long after midnight, Adam peeping out a curtain-less window on a moonlit night to watch an intoxicated Uncle Mitsi dance the *Zeybekiko.*

"Mama, what is the strange dance Uncle was doing last night?" he had asked next morning.

"Shh, you should not be looking!" Assuming an important voice his mother added, "This is the dance of the Eagle. Its name comes from a non-Turkish tribe called the *Zeybeks.* Brigands they were, a thorn in the side of the Turkish Government."

Memory of the night he saw his mother belly dance warmed Adam's thoughts. He'd rushed to her, flung his childish arms about her legs, only to be put straight back to bed.

He was not to know that these, and other memories, would become the recurring theme of his own children's bedtime stories. That long after his early death, his wife Eleni would continue to tell them to her children and grandchildren, and even the great grandchildren Adam would never know.

***

Georgia

I'm one of those children! A huge desire to know more about him floods over me. My mind races: I'll phone up my *Yia Yia* in Greece – when Mom's not around. And my uncle Alekos in Athens.

About my mother Helena: she's still acting weird. Like throwing out her sexiest clothes: black lacy things, some clingy see-through stuff and a pair of spiked-heeled shoes too – I saw them in the garbage bin. She won't answer when I ask what's going on. "Not that music!" she shouts when I turn on the radio. "Turn off the T.V!" And she sits staring into space, tolerating only wailing Greek *rebetika* music as background noise. She's been cleaning the house in a fury too, and started going to church. Amalia says she won't even bother coming back to visit until our Mom gets her act together. Aunt Thalia doesn't come much anymore either.

Right now I need money for phone calls. At Book City next afternoon I approach my boss Terry and ask if I can get extra shifts. He's at his desk wearing what I call his bus driver red checked shirt, his face dipping close over a pile of computer print-outs.

"I love it here," I say unnecessarily. "And, well, I need the extra money."

He looks up shortsightedly at me and runs stubby fingers through his hair. "Pretty chipped up about something today, aren't you? Still working on that Greek thing?"

"I'm in Turkey right now," I say, delighted that he's remembered. "Can I get any extra shifts?"

"See what I can do – here, you might be interested in this." He takes a hard-cover book from his desk and hands it to me.

'History of the Ottoman Empire between 1700 and 1950.'

"Oh, thank you!" I hesitate, and rush to give him a hug.

And so begins my juggling of five shifts each week, two of them 12 hours, plus finding times to be alone in the house to make phone calls. *Yia Yia* loves to tell me what she knows, and Uncle Alekos fills in bits and pieces. I study my new history text. I let my imagination loose.

***

Chapter 4

Smyrna 1910 – 1914

After uncounted days and weeks, Yiannis and his sons at last reached the hills overlooking Smyrna. Exhausted, sunburned and dirty, each leaned against a walled road that would take them to into it, silent as they gazed at a glistening blue-green sea with ships dotted upon it.

The mighty Aegean Ocean: Yiannis crossed himself before fumbling for a cigarette. Spiros, yelling, danced frenziedly on his feet and pointed at the scene below.

Adam alone remained motionless as he stared over dense throngs of people, over donkeys, camels, motorcars; at railway lines snaking along the waterfront, and trains shunting them. Railways have opened up the world to commerce, his father had said, and these trains must whistle to the far corners of continents.

Spiros had grabbed Adam's hand. "What do you say, brother?" He continued his jig on the road. "We'll be rich as kings in this place before many moons have crossed the sky, filthy rich I tell you!"

Adam frowned at his brother's rapacious expression. Turning away, he gazed over hills and valleys, over red and orange-tiled, flat-roofed houses, smoke rising from their many chimneys. With the sun glinting on domes, mosques and churches that rose above the sea, words came to him: '*Happy is the man...who, before dying, has the good fortune to sail the Aegean Sea.*' Across the ocean lay Greece ... Greece ... and he wondered then if his forefathers had ever set foot there. But this city, surely it held some of the world's great culture and history. Imagination soaring, he saw beggars, gods and kings alike cloaked in crimson robes. He heard music floating, church bells tolling for the faithful while the archangel flitted among the clouds. Above it all, Mount Pagus smiled benevolently upon a place not yet concerned about an impending world war and entirely unaware of its future destruction. His sudden vision then was of himself, his brother and father crammed among the city's teeming numbers, all seeking to make a fortune. He understood his father ached for recognition and would not be happy until his sons were among the city's elite. *We arise from an old, noble Hellenistic family from central Anatolia,* he would say. *Before that, from Constantinople, from Byzantium itself. Through no fault of our own we have become poor* ... Adam's thoughts clattered among new dreams: himself among the city's intelligentsia, discussing great and noble things: history, philosophy and ancient affairs.

He trailed his father and brother down a spiraling stone road that took them to the city's waterfront. The sun touched the tops of grey stone buildings on its evening slide into the sea. Crushed in a narrow alley, he felt blinded by a collision of colours: black frockcoats, red fezzes, green turbans, embroidered hats and cloaks. He blocked his ears against noise from steam engines, ships' horns, yelling merchants and barking dogs, all of it painful after the hush of the plateau. A steam engine belched black smoke about him and he lost sight of Yiannis and Spiros.

Coming upon them again he saw his father attempting to speak with ragged boys who shouted in strange tongues. One looked up briefly and Adam's breath stopped in his lungs. Within the boy's ice-blue eyes lurked an expression of adult cunning. Strange words ran out of his mouth. What the devil was he saying? The second urchin's eyes, the colour of copper coins, stared rudely at his father before he turned away.

"Panagia!" He heard his father swear. Squeezing through the crowds to get to him, Adam was struck by the insignificant, diminished figure of him. Of his brother too.

The three walked on, past grey concrete slabs, a clock tower, a fountain around which gathered a knot of old men. Not knowing what else to do, they kept on walking, past Romanesque-like buildings bearing the names Customs House, Post Office, Trading House, all just steps from the waterfront. Then came formal, stately-looking mansions, white-washed villas, and further along the bay, quaint fishermen's cottages.

"Papa." Adam pointed to rough-hewn two-storied wooden dwellings lining an alleyway. "Maybe here is a place we can afford," and stepping around flea-bitten dogs, blocking his nose against the stench of sewage, he headed to it.

***

Adam remembered his first weeks and months in Smyrna as a time of aching hunger and raw survival. Of feeling adrift, bereft and anonymous. Shell-shocked by crowds and noise. Of suffering under his father's voice:

"Adam, stop dreaming. Get up, get up! Not a minute to waste. Pay attention! *Panagia!* How much? Too much! I get a deal another place. Adam, stop dreaming and wake up! Watch my cunning when I buy."

A day came when Yiannis ordered him to stand behind a rickety table that had become the family's stall while he took Spiros with him to hunt for bargain-priced produce. Adam leaned his thin frame against the table. He felt tired, sunburned, detached and dispirited. It was while he was scanning the crowds for sight of his father and brother that a sack fell from a camel and split open. Apricots scattered over the cobblestones. He crawled on his belly under vendors' stalls to grab the fallen fruit. His hand grasped another and he looked up, and into the eyes of his father. Not a word was said but that evening each emptied their pockets of ripe apricots. It constituted their evening meal.

Yiannis' small fund and line of credit were rapidly depleting. His smoking increased. He ate little of the meals Spiros prepared. One evening he sat on the steps of his apartment, turning indoors only when the sun had completed its boastful slide into the sea. "Tomorrow you bargain for raw tobacco leaves," he said suddenly. "Learn how to strip, age, and package them yourselves. And learn it fast."

When disbelief widened both sons' eyes he shouted, "Just do it!" He made another gamble: with the last of his funds he purchased figs, dates and olives, arranging them on his stall at half the price he'd paid. Merchants' eyes' bulged, and they bought all he had. Purchasing further stocks on limited credit, he raised his prices marginally over the following days. As the months passed, his reputation was secured as a vendor with good prices, but still his ragged and hungry sons piled discarded vegetables and fruit on their evening dinner plates. In the markets Yiannis heard Spiros' hoarse voice barking, 'How much? Not enough. I get a better price

24

another place.' He nodded to him. He heard his own voice, almost in unison with his son's: *quotas, quantities, quality, delivery times.*

Adam, when ordered to stand behind the family stall, heard the clink of coins, saw on pale faces and swarthy ones expressions of greed, anger, excitement. Who were these people? Where were they from? Later, as he wandered in the sun, images of ancient Persians came to him. Bright stone-work and pottery, surely the work of little people from the Anatolian Plateau? Aromas of cakes and pastries made him think, not of cloaked Armenians, but the busy hands of small people baking in 400-year-old communal ovens underground. He saw, not Greeks pulling laden carts into the city, but Mongol tribes thundering west across the plain. In his imagination, wild Turkmen replaced hook-nosed fellows selling corn, wheat, raisins and olives.

A string of curses stung his ear as a sack of figs scattered over the cobblestones. It was not urchin hands reaching for them, but his brothers' pudgy fingers plucking grapes from the vines: dirty hands, baby hands, his own bearing scars from the country where his forebears lay buried. The images collided and collapsed one upon the other until Adam was lost among the epochs of history.

"Open your eyes." His father's rasping voice brought him sharply to the present. "Pay attention!"

***

The family developed a ritual: long before daylight Yiannis rose early, walked to the door of the flat, coughed, spat, and returned to splash his face in cold water. He pulled on his one pair of trousers, buttoned a faded shirt and smoothed the ends of his moustache. After brewing Turkish coffee he ordered his sons out of bed. Long before the sun emerged above the horizon the trio was on their way to the markets. "Don't forget about the different languages," he ordered. "Talk to a man in his tongue as well as him and you get the better bargain. Learn when to be angry and when to be accommodating, you understand?"

His sons dipped their heads in acknowledgement.

Twice each Sunday he took his sons to worship, St. Polycarp in the morning and the Greek Orthodox church *Ayia Fotini* in the evening.

Adam reflected how quickly his father had become absorbed in the life of the city, almost as though born to it, as though he had no history, no wife, no children. How could he forget all that?

"Pay attention! You dreaming again." He longed to block his father's voice, but heard it, even in his dreams: *"Panagia! Filthy scoundrel!"* With foreboding he witnessed his father's increased smoking, coughing and swearing. As he trailed him to their small stall in an alley off Front Street, he picked up tins of biscuits, chocolates and lemon drops from England; ran his fingers over shining fabrics from the Orient and carpets from the Anatolian interior. He felt jostled, crowded, overwhelmed. Spiros was beside him. Then he was gone. Adam looked after him. His brother was sharp, like a stick in the desert. He whistled when he wasn't bartering. He'd taken to clicking his tongue when he haggled and the swift pace of his deal-making made Adam's head ache.

"How much? Too much! I get a better deal another place." Spiros again. Adam saw how quickly his swarthy form had darkened under a furious sun. How his eyes narrowed to mere slits when he laughed. He cursed, and fellow merchants soon dubbed him *The Furies.*

"Take it from me, Adam," he exulted, "I'll be a king in this place before many suns have crossed the sky. But you: you say, 'begging your pardon' and smile at a fellow cheating you. Better you swear and walk away." He looked at Adam under the untidy locks of his hair.

"Sometimes I wonder if we came from the same parents."

Adam smiled gently at the brother who was all elbows, knees, and furious energy, but Spiros' look was sharp. Before he turned away, Adam saw expressions of wonder, pity – and surely not – contempt? Discomforted, he turned his thoughts to his mother.

"Dear Mama," he wrote,

"A letter to you from your first-born son, so you know we are well, and to tell you what we do in the city. Papa dreams of having a stall in a covered market called the Bedesten and chatters to Spiros about how much to pay for it, and about prices and turnover. Every day I go with them and try to learn the business, but get distracted. You should hear the music of mandolins, the opera, at eventide the chimes and dirges and chants to mingle with it all.

Mama, this is to make you smile: When the sun sets the maids come out from hotels to sweep the dusty promenade. They set out chairs for the rich people to sit on so they can talk and watch the dying sun. Papa, of course, dreams that one day we will be among them and get invited to special functions in the famous Kraemer Hotel.

One day Spiros and I walked through the prosperous Armenian section to find out what they sell, our eyes popping at women wearing embroidered hats and cloaks and swinging skirts. Everywhere were cauldrons of sweetmeats and fish. We went to the poorer Jewish part – and the Turkish area is also poor. But the Europeans and Levantines are very rich, and Americans too. Some of their men drive motorcars. Sadly, more and more I go alone to look at all this because Spiros won't stop working.

So much swearing and cursing here, but most of it in strange tongues (Papa tells us we must learn all the languages, but not the swearing.) Old men sit under arches and sell postcards, religious relics and prayer beads. Old women sit outside too, but under a fountain away from the noon-day sun. All of them smoke. Some of them beg, and the children too. You'll be pleased to hear Greeks do most of the city's business. They also help to run it..."

Adam did not tell his mother about the nights when an exhausted Yiannis ordered his sons to go somewhere – to the cinema, to a tea garden – while he took to his bed.

On these evenings Adam and Spiros wandered, Adam sniffing the salty air, smiling at small boys and stray dogs, listening to ancient bells ringing, to the clank of carts, horns and motor cars. In a café one evening, old Sufi poems came to him and he quoted them aloud:

"Come, let us be friends for once,
Let us make life easy on us,
Let us be lovers and loved ones,
The earth shall be left to no one.
We should all live the good life here,
Because nobody will live on."

"What kind of nonsense are you talking, man?"

The weight of a sudden silence in the café grew and chilled. Adam saw faces turned to him puzzled, bored, some hostile, and a vein throbbed in his temple. "It's ... it's Shabistaris' old poem," he said. "*The Secret Rose Garden.* Spiros, tell them, tell them it's what we learned at home." He turned anxious eyes on his brother but the chair where Spiros had been sitting was empty. He'd already headed out into the night.

***

Georgia

Adam! He's definitely my kind of guy and already I'm infatuated with him. A sudden thought strikes me: am I creating some likeness to myself? The thought elates me and I'm still warmed by the feeling when I open the door to an insistent knock.

"You." My old high school friend Jeff's hand is still raised. He's smiling, looking at me with his clean bright eyes. Reluctantly I ask him to come in, and while I'm making coffee I'm thinking, I do want a boyfriend. I'm nineteen and have never had love, or anything passing for it. I want it! But not from Jeff. My fantasy lover has always had large soulful eyes that I can fall into, and keep falling. I saw eyes like that once in snapshot, a young man smiling shyly into a camera.

"This was on your dresser," I told my mother Helena when I saw it. "Who is he? A relative?"

She snatched the photo from me. "You been snooping in my room?"

"It says something on the back but I can't make it out."

"Nobody you know. Don't you ever snoop in here again."

"Want to come to a movie?" Jeff has gulped his coffee. His smile is hopeful and I'm saying yes, better than being home with Helena in her strange moods.

Chapter 5

Smyrna 1914-1915

One evening a letter arrived postmarked the Anatolian village where Yiannis had played backgammon, written by the apothecary. Yiannis, closing a hand over it, snapped. "An abomination that a stranger must send the family's news."

"Papa, the letter?" Adam read aloud news of summer rains and a poor apricot harvest. About goats trampling the gardens and Mama's broken toes. The city's glamour dimmed as familiar images crowded: his mother in a ragged, tent-like cloak, teeth missing, skin roughened by the sun. A centuries-old way of life moving slowly over wide spaces where prices and profits scarcely existed.

Night deepened. The letter had been passed around a second time, but Yiannis continued to finger it.

Adam saw that Spiros was upset by the news - probably also because he could not read and write. He watched his brother as he abandoned the account book he'd been studying and thumped angrily over the apartment's floorboards. Hair fell in his eyes and breadcrumbs stuck to the hairs on his chest where his shirt was unbuttoned.

"But I'm good at numbers! He said and his voice boomed loud in the apartment's emptiness. "Something else, Papa: we're making damned good money now and should have a few comforts."

"Shouldn't we send any spare money to Mama?" Adam asked.

Spiros cracked his fingers and ignored him. He picked up an orange and sucked noisily on it, spat, then wiped sticky fingers on his shirt.

"Adam," Yiannis said suddenly, but with his eyes on Spiros, "You will be the guardian of the manners of this family. See to it your brother doesn't do that in front of important people – any people."

"Do what?"

"You will charm customers with your good manners," Yiannis continued addressing Adam, "so everybody knows our family comes from the upper class. Tell them we're rising up to our rightful place in the world. Already I see how you charm the girls. Now you must learn to speak knowledgeably to those Onassis fellows."

"Onassis? But what ... what should I say?" Adam noticed his brother's deepening frown and quickly looked away.

"*What*, you say? You, the one who sticks his nose in the books, make it up. Tell them our tobacco comes from the best and most ancient places in the world and we prepare it with our own hands. Let those Levantine people know our family descends from Greek Byzantium, show them you understand history, politics – everything that's important."

Adam turned from the intensity in his father's eyes, from anger in his brother's. *Everything that's important.* From the window, all he saw was his mother's face, her ragged bulk among the sunflowers.

***

A year passed. Profits accumulated, but Yiannis was in a hurry and it was not fast enough. The family had made no social or political contacts. The family stall was too small; not close enough to the central markets and it was time to risk renting space in the coveted Bedesten, and to get occasional help.

"Go find that young fellow Unal with his rickshaw," he ordered now. "He looks honest enough."

"He's a Turk," Spiros said.

"He knows all the languages," Adam said, "like you."

Spiros gave a half bow.

"Get off and offer him a deal." Yiannis continued ripping open bales of textiles.

Unal was found on the waterfront with his rickshaw. When offered part-time employment hauling produce from rail carts and ships, his moon-like face widened in a smile, and he bowed.

"I'm strong," he said, flexing his bicep muscles, "and I know how to fight."

"We don't need you to fight," Adam said, "at least not yet."

In the heart of Smyrna's old covered market known as the *bedesten* Yiannis enlarged his export-import business. On credit he purchased a stall measuring twelve feet across, behind it, an unpainted wooden structure as his warehouse, a canvas stretching above.

"Spiros, paint it bright orange," he ordered. "Make it stand out. Adam, write the name Kouvalis across the top – big letters. Right now, watch our stuff with sharp eyes like an urchin boy. Use your charm to sell. Spiros, first get down to that ship just come in."

But Adam forgot the stall and struck up conversations with tourists, bent down to play with children, helped elderly women to seats in the shade. He inquired about a man's family, conversed with Italians about Italy, with Russians the little he knew of their history. Paying a drachma for a book of Shabistaris' poetry, he slipped it in his pocket. As the sun dipped low over the sea, as the crowds thinned out, he looked at last at his stall. Horrified, he saw that little had been left on it. Wildly he stared about him. Grinning boys slipped by. Adjacent merchants shrugged and spread their hands. Then came Yiannis, pushing through merchants and shoppers, his eyes lighting up at the sight of the family's half-empty tables.

"Ah my boy, good, good. How much?"

"Papa, I don't know … some of it must have been stolen when I wasn't looking."

***

Adam, with much to make up for, hauled produce from the railways and pier alongside Unal, sorted and labelled in the new warehouse. One brisk autumn day he straightened his back and ranged his eyes over the harbor and its ships, towards the city's rooftops and a distant Mount Pagus. Suddenly, across a soft blue sky flitted a smiling archangel Michael, gone in a split second. The sky changed, and red-streaked clouds dipped close enough to hit him. Adam opened his mouth to scream, but no sound emerged. Whatever could it mean? He shut his eyes. On reopening them, he saw the chaotic world of commerce still pulsing. Sacks of figs. Balls of raw opium. Stacks of animal hides. Carvings, statues, and religious icons from the Middle East and Russia. The exuberance of it all roused him out of his superstition, but the sense of having been visited by other-worldly life lingered. Looking for his brother, he saw in his place a hook-nosed, swarthy-skinned fellow who swore as he hawked.

"Spiros!" Adam cried out. "Where are you?"

"Over here." Spiros looked surprised. "What's wrong?"

"N... nothing." Adam headed for the harbor.

Spiros looked after him, irritation rising. His brother should at least make some effort. Why should he look after old people and children and dogs while he himself did all the work? *But you enjoy this; it's all you want to do,* a small voice said inside him. *It gives you lots of social opportunities.*

"For what?" Spiros asked aloud.

Women. *Women.* A thought hit him, something about a saying - *you cut your success according to your stature.* That was it - his stature. He had to raise his eyes to meet those of most of the other merchants. Damn, that's not what the saying meant surely. But in truth, he knew he was nothing but a short, stick-like, ugly fellow. His spirits plummeted. Suddenly within his line of vision a vaguely familiar face intruded – a scoundrel, no doubt. Wait, it was none other than Socrates Onassis. One of his brothers too, and the kid Aristotle. All were hawking tobacco, silk carpets, furs, and sticky figs.

"See who's right next door?" Spiros pointed as he whispered to his father.

"Of course. I say a plague on them." Yiannis said this with rare good cheer.

"This was a fine move of yours Papa." Spiros hopped from one foot to the other. "The Fates are smiling ... *Panagia!* When you rented this place, did you know the Onassis family was right next door?"

"Is your father is a stupid man?"

"Ha!" Spiros laughed. "So, we do exactly like them, but give a better price. We say we have better quality. Onassis, they're nobodies but think they own the city already. The Kouvalis family will beat them yet."

Yiannis nodded, and Spiros' spirits soared.

"Where's your brother?" Yiannis asked a moment later, and Spiros shrugged.

At six came the call to Moslems for prayer. Many merchants closed their stalls, but still came no sight of Adam. Only when the sun's slow slide into the sea spread orange flames over it did his elder son appear.

From the doorway Adam saw Spiros in the kitchen preparing rice and fish for dinner. Saw his father in the apartment's one armchair, newspapers in his lap and a cigarette burning between his fingers. Adam recognized the anger coiled inside his body and knew where it was directed. He hid a string of books behind his back.

"Stupid boy, still dreaming?" Yiannis hissed without looking up. "Wandering the city, writing your poetry? You made any deals? What, nothing at all?" He got up, walked to a small cupboard above the stove, took out a large enamel jar and shook it. "Nothing to add? Then why do I give you anything from it?"

Adam walked boldly through the doorway. Drunk from music at a waterfront bar, and from wine consumed, in his mind the gods of Dionysus and Bacchus had fused. He looked at his father and said, "You know Papa, Smyrna is the most cosmopolitan city in the East and got built by the Amazons. Some people say it was Tantalus himself. Look around and see how it bursts with the bloom of a hundred flowers. Listen and you'll hear the beautiful music of Vivaldi and Brahms. Surely a man's duty is to enjoy these things while he's alive?" *Pleasure should never be neglected ... making money not to be confused with enjoyment.*

"What? You going to drop dead any minute?" Spiros slapped his chest in mock horror.

"The time for flowers and music is not now," Yiannis snapped back his invariable answer. "You want people to know who you are in this great city yet still you walk like a sleeper. You think money will fall into your hands while you read your books and smell the honeysuckle? I warn you again, I'll send for one of your brothers to do the work you don't do. I tell you both, and devils take me if I'm not successful, the Kouvalis name will be more famous than Onassis."

"A man's duty is to enjoy the world all about him," Adam persisted. "And it's a Greek world, Papa."

"That's what *you* think." Spiros threw a newspaper onto the floor. "It still belongs to the Turk, whatever you say."

33

"It's a Greek city," Adam insisted. "The churches are Orthodox. Ships fly the Greek flag. It's Greeks who send caravans from the East and the wine from Italy."

"They might have the upper hand right now," Yiannis said, "but no man – *no man* – knows of a day when he needs to protect the things God has given him."

Adam shrank back as though to ward off a blow, then moved to the window that gave a glimpse of the waterfront.

"Look!" He said. "Hotel maids are setting out the chairs. Papa, you and Spiros are getting to be prosperous merchants and can sit with the upper classes to watch the sunset."

"First I got to do the day's accounts," he heard Spiros say, and turned to see the naked longing on his brother's face he'd seen it before. He's still looking for Papa's acknowledgement he thought with sudden insight Even if he gets it he'll never be satisfied. He'll keep on looking for all this life. In spite of his father's harsh words to him, Adam knew he enjoyed advantages as first-born son, and with this new knowledge, felt somehow he had betrayed his brother.

He became aware of his father staring at him, heard him muttering, and picked up some of his words … never make a businessman … charming manners might make a good impression and like to a gentleman born … thinks himself guardian of the poor…"

"What's the use in all that?" Yiannis spoke aloud. "Damn everything to hell! You." He coughed and pointed a bony forefinger at Adam. "Maybe you should get off to the countryside and look for local produce. You can write your damned poetry there *and I won't have to know.*" He pulled at his moustache. "Maybe … yes, maybe you can write some fine poetry stuff if you can and show it to the intelligentsia. Maybe that way you'll get yourself noticed by the people that count. Ah, and soon I must find you a wife from this class." He sank in his chair as though profoundly fatigued.

Into the following silence Adam said, "Papa, will we go walking the promenade and meet our neighbours?"

"Never mind the walking and the talking, *I* don't go, I'm tired. Too many people on the promenade. Too much noise. Too many cars."

Adam looked at Spiros. Motor cars were very few among the donkeys and camels. But the next minute Yiannis was climbing stiffly to his feet and ordering Spiros to add up how much profit they'd earned today, then to forget the books. "Adam," he barked, "you serve the dinner. Tonight we are the upper class. What sweets do we have that we can offer our neighbours?"

Yiannis' bent form wheeled crookedly along the waterfront, his eyes peeled for sight of Rahmi Bey, the city's Turkish governor who often strolled about in frockcoat and carried a silver cane. For sight of the Onassis brothers, or any who held influence in the *Ethnic Armeni*. If he chanced upon them, he'd ask straight out that his sons be given a chance in this organization trying to build a Greek state inside Asia Minor. To hell with his thick-accented Turkish-Greek, to hell with his rough manners, he would not rest – or return to Anatolia – until his sons were members; until he had enough money to send all his children to school to properly learn to read and write.

The last rays of the sun sparkled on the glass of hookah pipes and brushed the walls of trading houses with an orange glow. Adam, trailing after Spiros, heard him whistle to the Bouzouki tunes spilling from music halls and Ragtime from waterfront clubs. Saw his father continuing to scan the crowds for sight of anyone holding political power.

"You, keep learning the manner of the upper classes." Adam jumped at his father's sharp voice in his ear. "You have the charm. When you talk, make a man feel important, a woman to dream. Learn how to use it. Get us respected."

Adam, warmed by the rare praise, waited to hear his words for Spiros.

It did not come, and Adam saw jealousy flame his brother's cheeks. This was all wrong. He, Adam did little of the work. He made no money. He wandered to the sea to dream of Greece and other faraway countries. All the while Spiros hunted and bargained; shut himself in the dank apartment to balance expenditures with profits made.

His right arm was being yanked, Spiros pulling him ahead of their father.

"It's not fair," Spiros burst out. "Lazy, that's you Adam. You think reading books will put food in your mouth. If Papa and I don't make money, you starve." Angry red blotches appeared on his face.

"What if I don't want so much money?" a surprised Adam said. "What will you do with yours? – keep making more?"

"I'm going to be a big international trader, make a fortune, get a big house on the edge of the sea, maybe in a rich suburb. I want a motor car ... and a position in government. A wife and children, of course."

"Money alone won't buy you a government position," Adam said mildly. "If you want to get into politics you must study and read history."

"Then I'd have no money, like you. Without a big house and a big bank account, who would notice *en apospore* like me?" Spiros stopped to catch glimpse of himself reflected in the window of a trading house. His shoulders slumped.

"You're not ugly," Adam said softly. "That boy Aristotle Onassis is. He's a weird, squat kind of fellow but see the attention he gets, and all the girls, even though he's only thirteen." His brother, he thought, was just another oddly put together man among the races of the world where nobody was odd.

"I'm not ugly?" Spiros stared up at Adam, and Adam guessed at his complicated feelings: love for him wrapped up with jealousy and inferiority over their stark physical differences. Adam, towering over his brother, now hunched his shoulders. He ran his fingers through his hair, hair that curled like the petals of an oleander flower, his mother once said.

As though guessing his thoughts, Spiros raised a hand to run it through his own. It was dry, like flattened wheat, and Adam saw bitterness return to his face.

"You know what?" Lightly Adam punched his brother's shoulder. "You're damned good at making money."

A slight smile dimmed Spiros' angry expression and he said, "Don't you care nothing about getting rich?"

"Well, I just don't like having to make it. I like looking at the past to find out where people come from, especially the ancient Hellenes." Earnestness crept into his voice. "Aren't you at all curious about the tribes that once raced across the Anatolian Plateau and the people who made this city what it is?"

"No. I only care about now, and the future. Anyway, know what the merchants say? I'm a worker going for success. You, they just shake their heads." He lit a cigarette, inhaled, and blew a ring of smoke in the air. "So - your turn: what do *you* dream about?"

"Like you, a wife and children someday," Adam said. "The years beyond, I don't know... I don't know."

"You must see some kind of future."

The past has flown away. The coming month and year do not exist. You are asleep and your vision is a dream.

The Poet's words coiled in his head, and Adam shook it. "I don't like to look too far in to it," he said.

Chatter and song wrapped about them. Yiannis, behind, continued to walk stiffly, bowing and smiling as was the custom. The great clock on the Konak tower chimed. Ragtime music spilled over the quay. Forgetting his quarrel with his brother Adam smiled as he offered squares of coconut cake to passing neighbours.

"I think you should come play with me," a young female voice said in his ear. Adam jumped. The diminutive figure of a woman stood at his elbow. She laughed and fluttered and tossed her yellow hair. In reflexive gesture, Adam raised a hand to smooth his own wayward curls. He looked at her briefly then averted his eyes. The scantily clad American woman tapped her spiked heels impatiently on the pavement as she blew a ring of smoke.

"Not tonight," he said, flushing, avoiding his brother's scowl, and walked on.

***

Chapter 6

Smyrna, 1914 -1915

Spiros was in the flat's tiny kitchen preparing *mucver* for supper, his thoughts spinning along the lines of last night's conversation. We're making money now and getting comfortable, but it's not enough for Papa. Nothing ever will be until he gets Adam into that Greek organization, the *Ethniki Ameni.* Not he, Spiros, for governor. He was just *andraas koinos enas* − no class. His tongue felt thick in his mouth. He bit it and swore softly so he wouldn't wake his Papa in the next room. Papa was not feeling well, and getting worse. Spiros thought that business in the city was killing him, or disappointment that he and his sons had not yet been recognized in governing circles. Or − Spiros held his breath at his next thought: maybe it was about the war engulfing the European continent, Turkey taking one side and Greece the other.

He was hungry, but the zucchini was still cooking. He opened cupboards randomly, his stubby fingers plucking at boxes of biscuits, packets of dried apricots and raisins. He reached for the bottle of *raki,* poured a shot, added water, and sat looking at posters of the Athens acropolis that Adam had picked up and stuck on the walls. He walked to the window and caught sight of his brother pacing the quay. What's the matter with the dreamer now? We got to talk about Papa.

Adam, striding alongside the tramway lines, raised a fist at a cawing magpie atop a nearby building. His worried thoughts, like those of Spiros,' were also about his father. Not half a century in years, he was old before his time. Once he'd walked as the powerful patriarch of a large family, even as a king. In all his growing years Adam rarely remembered him raising his voice. To induce terror in his children he had only to lower his eyebrows or tighten his lips. In Smyrna he'd been shoved aside, treated like a nobody: a simple Turkish-Greek like countless others. He scarcely ate, or slept. He smoked too much. He was being consumed before their very eyes for some crazy idea of redeeming a family's reputation. For the sake of this dream would he cut his life short?

Adam stared up at the teeming slopes of the city. All life is ephemeral. Wealth and reputations and great deeds, here for a moment, then gone as though they'd never been. Slowly, dispiritedly, he returned to the apartment.

"We got to do something about Papa," Spiros whispered as he came through the door. "We should try to get him home to Mama - you tell him."

A reluctant Adam entered his father's narrow bedroom. Its walls were bare, the only furniture a wooden bed where he lay. The air was stuffy. Adam wrenched open the one small window, only to wrinkle his nose at putrid whiffs rising up from the alley. Clearing his throat he said, "Papa, I … we … think it's time for you to go home to see the family. One of us will go with you."

Yiannis turned red-rimmed eyes on him, and with a sharp voice said, "I'll go to the place where I was born when my sons are part of this city's important people. Then bring another son, and another, into the family business. You will take a wife, Adam, a woman from a rich Levantine family that owns factories and wields power. Then, I tell you, our name will be famous again, like the name Onassis is already."

The name respected. Spiros was right: their father's obsession was consuming him.

"Papa, we can't be sure our family was once rich and important." Adam added under his breath, *"Who cares if it was? Each person or family should create their own importance − if they must."* His thoughts tumbled, one after another, that all great families rise and fall, almost to a rhythm. And that was the way it had always been. He must try again, and as he began to speak, Yiannis jerked himself upright and yelled, "Just shut up!" He stared at his sons with flinty eyes. "The future of our family is right here, in this city. I tell you this now, I tell you tomorrow, and the next day too. You will remember my words!" Abruptly he turned his head away but not before Adam saw a tear slipping down his cheek.

Spiros walked from the bedroom doorway to the east-facing window. Adam joined him. They knew that a dozen or more ships from Italy, France and the Near East would be lying at anchor awaiting their turn to unload.

"For how much longer?" Adam said. War was being raged on the continents all about, but had touched little on the city. Not yet. The people said it was because of their clever governor, Rahmi Bey who refused to follow orders from the powerful Young Turks in Constantinople.

"Listen, someone's knocking."

"The devil gets them!" But Yiannis' voice was hoarse.

Adam opened the heavy door to their apartment. A half-grown boy stood on the step, an envelope in his fingers.

"I hand deliver it for a price," he said, his hand outstretched.

Adam opened the letters, and stared. "Papa. Papa!" We've got an invitation. It says:

To Mr. Yiannis Kouvalis and his sons Adam and Spiros: Please join us for an evening with the governor. Kraemer Hotel, tonight, 7 PM sharp."

"Last minute, isn't it?" Yiannis frowned, but a flush spread over his cheeks.

"Who cares?" Spiros pulled his good trousers from a hook on the wall.

In the bedroom, a dizzying transformation took place. Yiannis hauled himself out of bed and hobbled to the bathroom. When he emerged shaky and sputtering, he struggled into black trousers with red braces and his one good white shirt. "Get dressed," he snapped. "Polish your shoes. Get your jackets."

Invitations had occasionally arrived for the family to attend social functions with the governor, and in haste, new suits had been purchased and shoes polished. Adam greased his hair while Spiros cleaned and filed his nails. As always, Yiannis enjoined Adam to use his manners to make a good impression

***

Cigar smoke curled in the air of the splendid Kramer hotel ballroom. Wine and ouzo flowed. Late in the evening attention centred on the Onassis family, on Socrates' son Aristotle, who, yet so young, worked the crowds with surprising sophistication. Spiros saw the disdain he showed to those he felt were competing with him. Knew that he had already developed a reputation as a womanizer, and felt astonished that this short, bushy-browed, rather ugly fellow should attract beauties from the wealthy classes.

"Papa," Spiros began as the three walked home near two in the morning. "What was all the whispering in the corner with Socrates Onassis and his brothers? – fighting up the coast? Will it get to the city?"

"All nonsense," Yiannis snapped. "Forget the war talk."

"B … but it comes closer all the time." Spiros stuttered his anxiety and Adam laid a hand on his arm.

"Don't worry, it won't touch Smyrna," he said and cocked his head as church bells chimed, together with the call of Moslems to prayer. He glanced up toward the shrine of St. Polycarp, at a city ranged over the slopes of old hills. And as he looked, mansion roofs, church spires, the domes of mosques, all collided into one giant image. His skin prickled, and as though to reassure himself, added, "Papa is right. Nothing's going to happen here."

"Good evening." A young woman looked up at Adam and his blood leaped at sudden memories of the innocent-looking girls he'd passed recently near the Parthenon. Then he remembered his father was looking for a wealthy European bride for him; his mother, a country girl in Anatolia. He crossed himself.

Once home and unable to sleep, he wrote:

Dear Mama:

At last Papa gets what he wants and we go to social functions now. Sometimes to meetings with the governor, and with the city's wealthy patrons. For this we buy smart suits and new shoes. Poor Spiros: he has trouble with his big hands, and his fingers with blisters and his nails broken. But you should see – still he curls his moustache exactly like Papa. For me, I am always squashing down my hair with grease.

Papa says he trusts me to make a good impression and that I must use my best manners. When first we came to Smyrna, he said how we must learn all the languages, like when we speak to the English, they must think we are also English, and the same for the Italian, the Spanish and the Turk. So, we go to the splendid ballroom of the Kraemer Hotel where all the important people gather to talk about what might happen if fighting comes closer.

41

Helena: An Odyssey

Papa says the Turks have put themselves on the wrong side of the war and they're grumbling about it, is all. Good news that our clever governor has kept us out of it – for now – and a very good thing he ignores orders from Constantinople to close the Levantines' factories because they employ about half the people here.

"It is our first night at the hotel, hard to breathe in the ballroom for all the cigar smoke. So much noise, and drinking that loosens the tongues. Papa finds himself talking to Socrates Onassis who mutters about one of us getting invited into the Ethniki Ameni. One day, the fellow says.

Afterward, Papa huffs about The Onassis, as he calls them. Just a bastard Turkish family from the poor provinces of Kayseri, they cover up their ignorance with a bit of Greek culture learned in the city. We might come from the same place, he says, but descend from an ancient, glorious family and one day will out-do these Onassis; we'll climb Smyrna's social ladder to the very top.

Aristotle – he's only a boy but his attitude makes Spiros upset because he looks down on people he thinks not his equal. 'A plague on him,' Spiros swears. They call him Ari, and already he's got a reputation as a chaser of women. Surprising that a short, bushy-browed and, well, an ugly fellow gets the rich girls and local beauties buzzing around him ... "

Mama, not all the people there are Greek, but the Greek influence is everywhere, and getting more all the time."

He looked at the last sentence, not understanding why he'd written it only that in his mind the idea of Greece had been growing and growing.

***

Chapter 7

Toronto

Georgia

I see my great uncles almost like a comic show, and think how cruel was fate to put them side by side. Gifts to one and none for the other. But that wasn't quite true. Spiros had energy. He had ambition, loyalty, and a strong sense of duty. They were brothers living, loving and suffering together. Not exactly Cain and Abel, nor Jacob and Esau, but balanced in ancient dual: Was one to live, and the other to die?

Then I think about myself and my sister Amalia, how she, like Adam, got the good looks and personality that earned our parents' favour. But she wants too much, takes anything she can get any way she can. And I? Like Adam, I dream among books (how writing about him consoles me!) I live in other worlds. I cohabit with the ancients.

Right now I'm smack in the middle of history. Ideas clamour and gather like thickets in my brain, even when I'm sorting books and making sales. But I'm also preoccupied by my mother Helena and the change in her since she got home from Greece. Sorrow still clings to her, I can almost touch it, and still she's wearing black. Our whole house feels creepy, like everything in it is on hold. Then there's Dad who hangs around in the living room making comments about the news. Getting no answer, he retreats to his basement.

Christmas passes in a confusion of people dropping in; a perfunctory dinner I cook. When Aunt Thalia and Uncle Kostas stop by, I whisper to them, "You were there with Mom in Greece (I call her Mom to the family) so you must know what happened."

Uncle Kostas's face closes up. Aunt Thalia, when she gets a chance, whispers, "I'll talk to you some other time."

One night at the end of January, I come home to find Helena at the kitchen table warming her hands around a coffee cup. The place is spotless and smells of cleaning stuff. Since her return she's increased her habits of scrubbing and reorganizing the house. When she hears me, she jerks her head up and gives me a kind of measuring look so I figure that maybe I'm next on her clean-up list.

"You like selling old books?" she says, "any money in it? No, anybody can see. You go clack clacking on your computer all hours and your room such a mess." She gets up, walks into my room, and starts picking up stuff off the floor. "You're a mess too, and sometimes I ask myself what man will take notice of you ... who's this Jeff who keeps phoning?"

"Huh? Nobody. Just some guy."

She stares. "Where are the stories you write? What do you do with them?" She's still reorganizing my stuff, and feeling guilty I take my clothes out of her hands. I start smoothing and straightening my room, then wait for what next.

But her shoulders slump and she seems to fold up. Pity washes over me, and driven to try and give comfort, I move toward her, tentatively putting an arm about her shoulders.

"Mom, I'll try harder," I say to the blank face, "really I will."

She remains trance-like for some moments. Then abruptly snapping back into the present she steps away from me, and totally out of the blue says, "Look, if you come with me to the salon, I'll pay you to wash hair and tidy up. Then you go buy yourself new clothes; do something with yourself."

Oh! Astonished, but wanting to please her, and in some vague way make up for whatever happened to her in Greece, reluctantly I agree.

Two days later we head to the subway, and her salon.

We walk down Yonge Street dirty with old snow, past business people and the homeless. Vaguely I notice the gaudy streamers fluttering above *The House of Lords*, large-canvas water colour prints hanging in *Robert's Gallery*. Suddenly she says into the chilly air, "Hair: this is my business, but you know what? It's all vanity."

She stops and turns me to face her. "What do you think, Georgie? Painting yourself up and getting a fancy hair style? After it, you think you are beautiful, or more important or better than somebody else? Maybe it makes you for a little while something you are not. Where is the glory in doing this?" A cold wind blows her scarf across her face. She grabs it and continues almost under her breath: "When I'm only thirteen my *Yia Yia* tells me I have big dreams and talent; that it's for me to keep the promise."

Promise? My skin begins to prickle. "Mom," I say carefully, "you've never told me any of this. If you did —if you do — I could write it all down for you." I take hold of her arm but she doesn't notice; she hasn't even heard me. Now we're at the salon. She stands for a moment under the sign that says, 'Kouvalis Beauty Salon,' then walks in, and down the length of it, giving orders for this and that to be cleaned up, straightened, put away.

Inside are the beauty makers as I call them: Bonnie, skinny Isabel and Silent Sylvia, all as astonished to see me as I am to be there. They love Helena, but are surprised at this change in her and jump to do as she orders.

My dislike of all the beauty stuff washes over me again but I've got my laptop, and when not busy I can get back to my books and my research. In a chair at the back where colour is done, I absorb the atmosphere, the chatter, the voice of Greek singer Grigoris Bithiksi bouncing off the blood red walls, but softly now or Helena will switch it off. I can't keep my eyes off those walls either, for there is Lady Godiva still streaming through the primeval forests I helped paint on them.

My new routine looks like this: shifts at Book City. Research at the Reference Library. Talks with Aunt Thalia. Phone calls to my *Yia Yia* in Greece, but only when Helena's not around since we still tiptoe around each other. When I ask about this promise thing, she looks away and changes the subject. I work in her salon washing hair, sweeping floors, folding towels and organizing the product shelves. When finished I resurrect my forebears, bury myself in that other time and place; I think about the stories we tell ourselves and the universal truths that attach to many of them.

In the periphery of my consciousness I hear Helena's fretful voice: "What little story are you writing now? You should go out, make some friends."

***

Chapter 8

Smyrna, April, 1915

Spiros, pulling on his jacket to go out, saw his father emerging from his room tucking his one good shirt into a pair brown trousers.

"Papa ...?"

"Appointments, boy. Not your business." Yiannis tugged at his shirt collar.

"It's about the war, isn't it, Those German guns, you think they're going to blast that British ship out of the water? I'm coming too."

"A plague on the war. And a plague on you if you don't stop jabbering. This is my private business."

Spiros stood indecisively in the doorway rubbing his hands, saw his father raise heavy-lidded eyes to Adam who leaned against the window, a coffee cup in his hand.

"You Adam? His voice was sharp. "The sun comes up and our warehouse still closed? Damn big fool." He bent to struggle with his shoe-laces. "Maybe you go to the country, like I told you before," he said at last, "see what the peasants do, get off to someplace and search out produce and handcraft. Write your damned poetry, and make it good."

Spiros choked on his last swallow of strong black tea. His black eyes snapped. "I think we should forget about these little bits and pieces, Papa," he said, his voice bold. "We should go for the gold and silver and silks."

"Never spurn the small stuff," Yiannis warned, "thread and linen and Benjamin, pepper and marjoram – the flower sellers will buy it."

Spiros stared, then turned and ran down the steps to the alley. Adam looked after him, caught glimpse of him striding along the waterfront, his red shirt at odds with the gloom of the morning. His father followed.

About to leave the apartment himself, Adam glanced around it - cold, bare, *soulless*. Whether or not his father meant what he'd said, he felt conflicted; Spiros would interpret this as favoritism, that he, Adam, was shirking. He hesitated. He should follow Spiros to the markets. But his feet took him north along the quay to *Alsancak*. Without further thought he rented a wagon that would take him east into the country.

The country: remembered fragrances washed over him, the shape of clouds, bird songs, small creatures running about his feet. His pleasure provoked further guilt when he thought of Spiros − all furious energy and a cauldron of irritable gestures and his slant eyes filled with pain or passion or glee. He thinks I'm lazy, but still getting privileges. He should hate me. Maybe he does. But he wouldn't want to go to the country. He lives for outsmarting another man and getting the better of him because it makes him feel bigger. And some of what he does is to impress Papa, but Papa doesn't notice.

Adam's thoughts lifted as he travelled toward orchards that lay beyond wealthy suburban Bournabat. He sniffed the earth's fragrance, felt its particular somnolence as sharp relief from the markets' chaos. Relief too from the talk of war, the pervasive uncertainty that was hanging over the city. Vaguely he wondered at his refusal to engage in conversations about a war spreading over a continent, about the fighting in Anatolia and up the coast of Asia Minor where many non-Turks were being chased from their homes. Pushing these thoughts aside he jumped off the cart and began strolling the vineyards, the ground crunching softly under his feet. Ripe olives. Tall wet grass. Rich brown earth saturated with the blood and tears of fallen men, to bloom now with the swelling fragrance of honeysuckle and wild roses; trees heavy with old blossoms and ripe fruit.

The early morning sun had fingered its way through the trees to dry up the remnants of the night's dewfall. Distant mountains in purple majesty, and smaller hills, inscrutable, rose beyond a line of trees that hummed with fruit pickers, young women colourfully veiled against the rising sun. Adam walked toward a scattering of houses on a hillside and sat on a tree stump beside a shed. Pulling pencil and paper from his pocket, he thought to capture what he saw, but felt distracted. What were those figures doing on the hillside? He got up and crossed the rough ground toward them, to see young women digging and moving stones.

He pitied them, and feeling vaguely ashamed, returned to the olive grove. He saw a woman, just a girl really, under the far tree near a stone wall. Saw her rivers of hair, a golden arm reaching to pluck the fruit from a tree, the lines of her body wrapped with bright colours. An unfamiliar sensation logged in his chest, and surprised, he held his hands against it.

Conscious of his scrutiny, the girl half turned to look at him. Adam saw a singular, breathtaking beauty: eyes as burnished sunflowers, a mouth that curved in fleeting smiles. Hastily she pulled the scarf that hung about her shoulders over her hair as Adam moved closer. He reached to pluck fruit from the tree above her, to drop them into her basket. He continued this, neither of them speaking, and the afternoon drifted to its close.

"Do tell me your name," he said as she picked up her basket to join other fruit pickers heading toward a distant shed.

"Eleni," she whispered, not looking at him.

"You work here every day?"

"*Ne*. Mostly yes."

"Then you live somewhere around here?"

"My father herds goats and sheep up there." Eleni pointed to a distant bunching of smaller hills. "Sometimes I work in other orchards. I ... go to school when there's enough money." Eleni half-turned her head.

"Will you come tomorrow?" Adam studied her profile: the slope of her forehead, small straight nose, the lift of her chin, the bright robe that hid her body. At the question, fleetingly she turned golden eyes to him and long afterward he revisited the sensations that hit him: trees moving, and the ground beneath his feet, the earth's perfume smothering him.

Eleni gave him a sideways smile, picked up her basket and walked away.

***

"Papa, business in the country might be good." Adam sat across form his father and brother under the shade of an almond tree near the fountain where old men played cards. Small dogs chased each other. An urchin boy cursed as he tripped over them.

"What sort of business?"

Adam fumbled in his string bag and pulled out a jar. "Marmalade," he said. "The best you can get. Have a taste."

Spiros dipped a finger in it. Yiannis frowned. "Manners, boy!"

Both father and son agreed it had a fine flavour. If purchased cheaply and in quantity, it might yield some profit.

In the following weeks, Adam repeated his visits to the olive grove, lingering as Eleni worked and flicked golden eyes at him. He picked fruit with her, his eyes on the smooth skin of her arms, her shoulders. Her hair: in time he would dare to wrap its strands around his fingers. Urgently he talked to her but she did not answer. Until one day she whispered, "A girl is not supposed to talk to strange men." Hesitating, she added, "Come to my house. You can meet my father and sisters."

Back in the city, Adam only smiled when asked about his visit.

"You got to have something to show for it," Spiros warned when he was about to slip away for a second time that week. "Whatever Papa said he'll be mad – *madder* – if you just go there to write poetry. He'll say, what else, boy, what the hell are you doing there? A wonder he hasn't already. Something else: you better pay attention to what's going on. There's a war, you know."

"So you keep telling me."

Jumping off the donkey cart one early evening after another visit to the country, Adam walked slowly along Rue Parallele from the Customs House and headed slowly toward the *bedesten* through crowds of Muslims gathering around the *Hisar* Mosque. He passed the foot of the clock tower as it chimed the hour of six. In the outer harbour he saw four war ships from Britain, France and Italy swinging at anchor. Gulls swooped furiously against a darkening sky. Angry voices shot toward him. Trams on the pier rail lines stood idle. Hearing the word *Armenian* repeated, he remembered the whispered rumours, and as always, mentally brushed them aside. He came across Spiros at the corner of Otella Street, his brother's eyes following a speck droning over the bay.

"See that?" Spiros pointed. "You think the pilot's touring the harbour for fun?"

"Stop worrying so much." Adam slipped an arm about his brother's shoulders and grinned at him. "You always see the worst but nothing serious will happen, you'll see."

"What the hell's the matter with you?" Spiros pulled away. With trembling fingers he lit a cigarette. "You: dreaming, dreaming, dreaming and nothing bad ever happening and everyone smiling and no one fighting. Take a look, stupid, there's a war!"

"But nothing's happening here." Adam's voice faded at his brother's anger, "See, the factories stay open, merchants are trading and everyone's got work. Anyway, governor Bey vows to protect us, and because of him we're *not* at war."

"Not yet. But you must be both blind and stupid not to notice that not much comes in on the ships anymore." Spiros dragged on his cigarette. "Heard the ugly talk about Armenians – no? Are you deaf? You hear about the Zeybeks getting close to the city?"

"Talk, talk. It's all exaggerated."

"Well, believe it. What's with you? The Greek army is pushing into the Anatolian interior and the Turks are fighting back and trying to get rid of all non-Turks from the country ..."

His words ran on but Adam stopped listening. He put a hand to his face as though to brush away words and messages he'd blocked: Armenians being marched into the desert and left to die. Young men shot at the edge of the city on orders from Constantinople. *Evict them all from their homes. Get rid of them.* They hammered in his brain. He couldn't see, damn it, couldn't see, and didn't want to. Conversation from the evening before came back to him, Yiannis quoting fellows from McAndrew's and Forbes Liquorice Company who had seen these things with their own eyes. "Read the news for yourself," he'd said as he tossed Adam a folded Greek newspaper.

"... then they come for the women and children," he read.

Adam had felt sickness rising. At this moment on the Konak he glimpsed his father on a wooden bench near a water fountain under the shadow of the clock tower.

"Better go join him." Spiros' voice jolted him into the present. In silence the brothers pushed through shoppers, merchants and loiterers, among animals, wagons, and an occasional motorcar. Spiros slid onto the seat alongside his father and immediately lit a cigarette.

Adam noticed his father's prized black waistcoat with its gold thread lying folded beside him and wondered again why his father refused to say where he'd been. He saw his brother's smoke rise to mingle with his father's, two pairs of braces glint in the dying sun. Ill-at-ease, he remained aloof until startled by Spiros jumping and pointing skyward. Adam followed his gaze, straining to see two black specks that loomed larger as they sped toward the city. Dipping low near the waterfront they headed toward Mount Pagus then turned to the Turkish quarter. The aircraft veered away and disappeared from sight. As the chatter about him subsided, Adam heard a bare-foot beggar mutter in his ear, and automatically slid a hand in his pocket to drop a coin into the boy's palm.

"Papa," he said with urgency, "there's something I have to tell you," but Spiros interrupted.

"Now, big brother, got your brains working yet? No war, you say? But forget that: *I'm* the one's got something to say." His fingers drummed the seat. He opened his mouth to speak, hesitated and closed it again. "Doesn't matter," he said.

Adam stared. His tongue felt thick in his throat. "Well, what *I* was going to tell you is ... is that I want to get married."

Yiannis turned quickly away from the strange green light in his son's eyes and his jaw dipped at a dangerous angle. Tendons bounced in his neck. The word "Ha!" shot from lips that had formed into a savage line. "And where did you find this woman? In the country with the sheep and the goats, the daughter of a goat-herd? A Turkish peasant girl on the wrong side of the war?" A snort came up from his throat. "Stupid boy. Forget you ever met her. She does not exist. You go do this thing while your father humbles himself before wealthy families to find a wife for you, for both of you. Humbug. Humbug." He spat.

Adam's hands twitched and he shifted his weight from one foot to the other. His brief defiance had ebbed. In conciliatory tones he said, "Papa, wealthy people marry only into their own families and would never look at me."

"If a man has many daughters he'll marry the younger ones to merchants like you, *if* anyone can call you that."

Adam swallowed. His eyes followed a dark cloud as it drifted toward Mount. Pagus.

"Eleni, she's a beautiful innocent Greek girl, and I love her." His voice was scarcely more than a whisper. "It's not that we – I – have nothing. We have enough money ..."

"To support a little goatherd eh? Alliances, stupid boy! You do not marry for love. Who told you such nonsense?

"So ..." Spiros' voice sputtered. That explained why his father had been wearing his gold-trimmed jacket. It also explained Adam's sun-drenched face and dirty clothes when he returned to the city: he'd been helping a little goatherd in the fields. He would take a woman like *that* for a wife. Realizing his own chances had just diminished, fury shot through him.

"So," he yelled, "you've been hustling a girl in the country. Mother of Jesus are you a fool!"

He got up and strode back and forth along the nearby tram tracks, only to jump at a burst of gunfire. He pointed to flames shooting into the sky, his body twitching as though pierced. But when he turned back, his voice held triumph.

"So, you want any more proof we're at war? Wait, what's this?" Like snow falling, paper floated from planes that had earlier raced toward them. Spiros grabbed one, a brochure bearing Britain's Royal Coat of Arms. His mouth twisted as he thrust it at Adam and said, "You read it."

Adam read that such raids would occur as long as German aggression continued.

"See, I told you," Spiros said, "Turkish-German aggression is true, and so are the stories about the Armenians being hunted out of their homes and deported."

Adam stumbled away and over the railway lines. Was his life to end before it really got started? The thought entered swiftly as he returned to his father, fear sliding up his belly.

"Obviously things are serious," he said, opening his palms in a gesture of conciliation. "But surely our governor will protect us and put a stop to ... I mean he's got a lot of influence. Papa, truly I've met the girl I want to marry. She's an angel. When she smiles it's like the air is filled with perfume. When she laughs I hear goat bells tinkling on a mountainside. She ...." He broke off at the contempt in his father's eyes, at the mirth replacing anger in Spiros'.

"Papa, I had something to tell you too." Spiros said. "But never mind, what my brother forgets is when a man looks into the face of his bride he sees only the sacred and mysterious face of Aphrodite. One day he'll discover the real face of his angel and then the poetry won't be falling so fast out of his mouth." With a mirthless laugh he got up and tap-danced in a circle. The face he turned to Adam had changed, the frequent half-mocking, good-natured expression hardened.

Yiannis picked up his jacket, rapidly changing expressions flitting across a sun-darkened face. The fingers of his right hand crushed one of the printed leaflets.

"So," he said. "I dress up and call on rich merchants with daughters. I'm about to close to a deal with a senior *politico* to marry my son to his daughter. And this ignorant son goes chasing a little goatherd in the country. I forbid you to marry her." His eyes bulged with rage.

When at last he spoke, Adam's voice wobbled with both fear and defiance. "The woman who will be my wife is Eleni. One day soon I'll bring her to meet you." He sloped away and headed for the pier, incoherent thoughts tumbling: for the first time in his life he had defied his father, freed himself from his expectations. He had grown up at last. And so thinking, he walked away, and toward the pier.

***

Chapter 9

Smyrna, 1916

Spiros eyes were almost shut as he watched his brother leave. He looked then at the crumpled form of his father: how small, tattered, how insignificant he seemed, and decided he could not tell him right now that he too hoped to marry. Alone with his thoughts, he strode the quay, staring over grey-green swells of the sea and the vessels studding it; at a purple dusk casting long-fingered shadows. A peal of laughter made him turn to see governor Rahmi Bey among his fellow ministers in Costi's waterfront café, smoking and drinking in the warm evening air. Desperately he wanted to be among them. Brooding, he watched the governor point towards the British destroyer *Euralis* riding at anchor. Edging closer, he picked up words about British shelling of the city's fortifications; saw ministers pointing at fireworks that lit up the sky. Some muttered warnings that Spiros couldn't hear and he cursed again that he could not afford the expensive waterfront bars but still had to crowd with the poor on the quay.

His thoughts returned to the woman he wanted for his bride and he rehearsed what he would tell his father. *Not from an old Levantine family, they won't pass an eye over me anyway, but Greek merchants that got rich trading in Europe and Africa. Papa, she'll help put money in our pockets.* His mind shifted to Adam and his little goatherd, as he called her, and aloud he swore, "Damn you, Adam. You've gone and ruined my chances, damn you again! Where the hell are you anyway?"

Adam still walked the water's edge, his chaotic thoughts diverted only by gunfire. Stupid war, for two years it had been fought on the European continent and north in Asia Minor, but had touched little on the city. Well, he'd ignore all the rumours. He would write odes to his beloved Eleni and soon would marry her. His heart beat fast within his chest.

"Turkey was stupid to have aligned herself with the Germans, with Greeks on the other side." Spiros had caught up with him. "The war's monstrous and getting worse all the time."

Adam argued that people still went to the opera. Wealthy Levantine families in the villages still met for afternoon tea the way they always had, kept up their tennis games, socials and balls.

"What about those rich European women on *Blvd Aliotti?* Get a look at their faces in the windows; you think people line up outside theological schools for fun? Those wretches at the soup kitchen ...?" Spiros picked up a newspaper and sank onto a nearby bench. He looked at it, then angrily crumpled it. "We should go back to Papa," he said. "It's not right to walk away from him. Go and make your peace."

"I can try." Reluctantly Adam walked toward his father. Spiros followed. Adam's shadow fell upon the shrivelled figure still seated on the bench, and fear washed over him at his father's fragility, guilt for having flouted him. Words ran out his mouth about Eleni being clever and bringing her to the city and one day taking her to Anatolia.

Slowly Yiannis filled his pipe. When at last he lifted his eyes it was to look, not on Adam, but on Spiros, a look that leapt with sudden hope, only to fade as quickly as it had come. Adam knew Spiros saw it, that he understood its message. With a useless gesture his brother smoothed his moustache, tucked his shirt into his draw-string trousers, flicked hair from his eyes. Yiannis turned to Adam then. His mouth opened and closed. His shoulders rose and fell. It was an old man who got up and walked away.

***

Over the following months an excited, anxious Adam planned for his wedding. He rented a tiny flat that jutted into the alley close to the old one. One warm spring day he set out to meet Eleni's family, and to bring her to the city.

Eleni stood waiting among long grass that grew to the door of her family's leaning wooden home. A simple dress fell to her ankles. In her hair she wore flowers, daisies in a chain about her wrists, but the bright smile she held for Adam dimmed at the sight of his shabby clothes.

Eleni's father joined her. Wiping a hand across his whiskered chin, he admonished his daughter always to behave like a lady and to give her husband many sons. Extending the grubby hand, he wished Adam good health and success at making money. Two of Eleni's sisters looked at her with empty faces, but in the eldest girl's eyes jealousy sparked, and she turned her back.

As his rented wagon pulled away over the rough ground, Adam said, "Look, turn round, wave to your family."

But Eleni would not look, could not give thought to her sisters without stirrings of guilt, knowing they were doomed to repeat the harsh rhythms of their lives until their end. She strained with every fibre of her being toward a future heaped with elegance and riches that would stretch to endless epochs. And so a frantic dance jerked her heart, her breath, her brain.

As she so worried and dreamed, a war was being waged throughout Europe and in Turkey all about her. Out of the ashes of the Ottoman Empire a new one was emerging, and as Eleni rode into Smyrna, its governor sat biting his nails as he studied yet another document from Constantinople repeating an earlier order. Close down the Europeans' factories. Remove all the Levantines from positions of power.

Vaguely she listened to Adam talking about her father and sisters, her dead mother, and how at first how she might miss life among hills, trees and wide open spaces, about centuries-old paths among the stones.

"I don't have to think about that anymore," she said.

Adam said nothing.

They entered the waterfront from its north end and continued along the quay, their wagon among many donkeys and carts and the occasional motor car. Eleni remained unmoved as they bumped along alleyways teeming with boys and chickens and dogs; among buyers, sellers and people strolling. When at last they reached the covered markets of the *bedesten*, she cried out to the driver to stop and sprang from the wagon.

She flitted, randomly fingering objects, her voice trilling above the din. Picking up a bolt of silk, she draped herself with it. "Adam, maybe one day I can have a dress made with this? It's so very beautiful." She dropped the bolt and skipped to other stalls, her eyes falling on stacks of rawhide, trinkets, vegetables and spices.

Adam remained in the wagon, a collision of feelings hitting him, and only long afterward would he acknowledge that within Eleni there was little poetry, little imagination to soar with his. It's of no account, he told himself: his dreams would become hers, and wasn't she the source of them anyway? After all, her body and spirit had been formed on slopes and in forests where once mighty armies had marched, where, dreaming or dozing, they'd been shaded by the same olive groves that had given her family sustenance. Didn't he love the whole image of her? The thrust of her shoulders, the lift of her chin, the movement of her hands in the air when she talked. Within her rough accents he heard a mingling of many tribal voices from the Anatolian Plateau.

Returned to the wagon, Eleni spoke in a voice that had become sulky, "Adam, I haven't been to school. I don't know how to talk properly. You and your brother and father are gentlemen" – *even if you don't wear gentlemen's clothes* – "What will they think when they see me? How can I be your wife when I'm not a lady?"

"Don't worry about my family. And I'll teach you all you need to know." While Adam's tones were cheerful, his shoulders tightened. But Eleni was smiling once more, and Adam could not know it was at an old memory of her father taking her into Smyrna's wealthy suburb of Bournabat when he delivered vegetables. There she had seen mansions, spires rising against Mount Pagus. Gardens blooming over stonewalls. Beautiful women holding tea cups in the shade of old trees. And it was there she had dreamed of becoming one of them.

"Those ladies, Adam, they're the wives of rich men like you, and I'm not ..." Her sulky tones returned as she pointed to strolling women wearing fitted jackets with embroidered skirts. Women wearing hats on coiffed hair, women chatting and laughing, careless in their confidence.

Adam saw her shaft of uncertainty and in a gentle voice said, "Eleni, can't you see? I'm not rich, and I don't want you to be like them."

"What do you want me to be?"

"Like you are right now, the same."

"But you're a businessman, you must have money." Adam saw her looking over the clothes he wore and understood she believed he wore them only when in the country, that in the city he would dress differently. The tightness across his shoulders spread to his neck.

"When I become your wife," she was saying. 'I will have to have the right manners and when we're rich enough, some nice clothes – see, like that lady ..."

"You don't need clothes like that," Adam interrupted without looking. "To me you're already the most glamorous lady in all of Smyrna."

As he spoke, fragments of past conversations came to him, words he'd let float by unabsorbed: Eleni chattering about shoes and clothes, about servants in the house and men working in the gardens.

The knots in his shoulders deepened.

***

They had reached the heart of the old *bedesten* and stopped before an orange-coloured wooden frame that receded to a warehouse-like structure behind. At the sight of *Kouvalis Trading* painted in black lettering across its roof, Adam found himself thrust back into the business of buying and selling and his father's voice constantly drilling: *Mind the manners. Study our country's history. Understand its politics. Get the best prices ... the better bargain ...*He closed his eyes, opening them to the life pulsing all about him: alleyways jostling with merchants and shoppers calling for prices. Small boys swearing as their feet slipped on fallen fruit.

"Spiros?" Adam spied him on hands and knees at the far end of the stall. He heard Eleni's breath catch in her throat. Saw her astonishment as she stared at a small man in a stained brown shirt, at his chipped and bleeding hands, his smudged, gnome-like face and lank hair half-covering his eyes. Her eyes widened when he put down a hammer to tighten the string that held up his trousers.

"Been fixing the stall leg over there," he said, "someone kicked it." He pushed back his hair and looked at the tiny woman in white clinging to Adam. "So, your little peasant girl." He gave a mocking bow in Eleni's direction and turned his back. "Papa," he said to a bent little man emerging from the warehouse, "Adam's brought his little goatherd to meet you."

Adam saw Eleni's expression change to disbelief at this scruffy spectre dragging a bulging sack. He followed her eyes, watching as his father straightened and peered at her, giant eyebrows reaching a row of sun blisters at his hair-line. Sweat dripped from his nose onto his chin.

"We're a poor family, didn't Adam tell you?" Spiros' voice mocked. "You'll be working harder in the city than ever you did in the country, you might even go hungry – want to change your mind?" He stared at her openly and Adam saw Eleni smile. Of course she would know she was pretty, he thought. How many times had he told her so as he kissed her small round face, her pink lips, run a finger over her high arched brows? At this moment she lowered her head from Spiros' stare, to frown at the rough skin of her own hands, her fingers with their broken nails. Tucking stray wisps of hair inside her scarf, she turned from Spiros, back to his father.

Yiannis had sliced open the sack he'd been dragging and now scooped figs from it, methodically arranging them on tables. Minutes passed before he looked again at Eleni.

"So: the peasant girl." He folded his arms tightly as though to control the bitterest of his many disappointments. No words left his mouth, and after some moments he returned to sorting figs. When at last he turned to Adam, he jabbed a finger. "The best hope for the Kouvalis family was for you to make a good marriage. What will that girl bring as her dowry? A sheep? A goat? With this she thinks to marry my first-born son? She's nothing but a skinny string of bones. You: I go humbling myself before important people to find you a bride – ah, damn, damn, damn you boy!" His cheeks wobbled. He emitted a groan that stopped passing merchants and shoppers alike. To Eleni he said, "A little shepherdess, eh? Can you count the buttons on your dress? Make intelligent conversation with wives of politicians about our country's history? Know anything about the war, or even know which side you're on? – *gomoto!*" His face and neck burned a furious red and he swore again.

Adam saw Eleni shaking, the flush that stained her face, and moved to draw her close. Again Yiannis jabbed his forefinger. "Will she help you make political alliances? Get you a step up Smyrna's social ladder? Damn big fool! Born with no sense. Got yourself stuck in a poetry book and know nothing at all!" He sputtered into silence.

As merchants began gathering about them, Adam finally spoke up. "Her name is Eleni, Papa, and she *will* be my wife." Sweat formed on his upper lip. He shifted his feet. "Her family is poor, as you say, but like ours, as you often remind us, hers also might have been important a long time ago."

"If you marry this woman," Yiannis' voice rang across the cobblestones, "you live on your own and earn what you can. I divide up the money in the jar and give you one third. After this, I no longer hold any responsibility for you, or for this woman."

Adam glanced down at Eleni and caught a gleam in her eyes – a calculating look? After a startled intake of breath, he said nothing.

***

At the edge of the Aegean Sea, Adam betrothed himself to his Nereid, his maid of the olive grove. It was a simple ceremony. In the picturesque Church of St. John near Alsancak, not in the magnificent church of St. Polycarp as he had once dreamed, he towered above his tiny bride in her thin white dress, his face bright as a midsummer sky. Yiannis refused to attend, leaving Spiros as the lone witness – "No, my father and sisters can't come," was all Eleni said of her own family. Adam understood and felt sorry for her, for them.

After a brief, unremarkable ceremony, he twined his wife's Eleni's arm in his and led her down the sloping alley to the flat that half jutted like an elbow into the alley. Oblivious to her sharp little *oh oh* sounds and dodging refuse and dog excrement, he carried her up the wooden steps where, at a window giving a fragmented view of the harbour, the newly-weds stood hand in hand, gazing at a sun that burned orange over the sea. Without warning, a black cloud thrust rudely in front of it to blot its glow. Adam started. A feeling of foreboding twisted in his chest and he flicked a hand as though to brush it away. A bewildered Eleni clung to him.

***

Chapter 10

Smyrna, 1916

In the weeks and months that followed their wedding, Eleni's moods fluctuated between extravagant love, anger and confusion. One moment she would fling her arms about Adam, the next, sit humbly at his feet. Anxious about cooking him good meals, she asked for more money to buy what she needed. Repeatedly she lifted her hands to examine her nails. One late autumn evening as the two sat on a stone bench watching the setting sun, she gave a small cry and thrust both hands behind her back.

"Whatever is it, *chryso mou*?"

"It's just ... my nails are broken. How can I be a lady?"

Adam stopped her words with a kiss, picked up a hand and tenderly rubbed her fingers with his own. "You're already a lady," he said, "beautiful inside and out. These little things mean nothing and you must not care about them."

The very gentleness in his voice brought tears to Eleni's eyes and she kissed the hand that held hers. For a time she forgot about beautiful clothes, maids and houses by the sea; about Adam's father and brother, this man awakened in her feelings she'd but fleetingly imagined, heard whispered from women's lips in the orchards. Fairy tales, she'd thought, dreams belonging to rich people in sunlit gardens. She remembered her yearnings, even as a child, for a fate different from her sisters who toiled over spinning looms, scrubbed clothes, milked goats; sisters who would be forced into marriage with a coarse fellow grabbing drunkenly at her. Who would work from sunrise to sunset lifting stones, stoking fires, pounding *nigella* seeds. The face Eleni raised to Adam held a chaotic mix of love and gratitude, enormous relief at the escape from her fate, even if it was into a poorer one than she'd imagined.

Now ever more anxious to build a good home, she set out to make the most of little things and in a short time the walls of the flat shone freshly scrubbed. Its wooden floors gleamed. Over a table Eleni draped a cheap colourful cloth, on a wobbling cabinet, a cup of purple flowers.

One morning, her hair decorated with flowers, she slipped outdoors, stepped around strewn garbage, and avoiding stray dogs, wandered toward the Kordon. There she gazed at the city's architecture, at church mosaics depicting faces of saints she'd learned about at school. Another day she ventured as far as the *bedesten,* fastening her eyes on Turkish merchants selling gold and diamonds and trinkets. She hesitated, then walked right up to them and smiled prettily. Three sun-darkened, darkly dressed merchants hid their surprise at the lone woman approaching and bowed, and was their custom. One hurried to offer her tea: *we give you a good deal because now we are friends.* But Eleni's sudden boldness soon fled, and thanking them for their time, she got up and hastened home.

"I don't like you going to markets unless I'm with you," Adam said that night while Eleni was cooking.

"But I just like to look at the church mosaics," she protested. "I walk past the *bedesten* on my way to the Church of *Ayia Fotini."* Busily she continued clattering dishes.

Adam, watching her, recalled his own feelings when first seeing caravans from the East filled with exotic fabrics, food, spices, opium; on hearing church bells summoning the faithful, women hastening toward it with arms full of candles. He got up and opened the window facing west that gave a tiny view of the waterfront. A whiff of dead fish hit him, then the aroma of coffee. Past his line of vision walked a woman in cross-gartered stockings jiggling coins in her goat-hide belt. Soon writers and artists would be strolling; wealthy merchants' wives tapping high heels on the cobblestones as they headed to the new Kraemer Hotel. *Wealthy merchants?* One day he might be considered one, but would he want Eleni to be like these wives?

Eleni's voice was in his ear and he heard words about plays and concerts and sitting among the wealthy in waterside cafes in the evenings.

Something about dresses and how Bournabat women send for theirs from Paris and London.

"You can have a new dress from anywhere in the world when I have the money," Adam promised, but still he struggled with images of his wife walking about the city unaccompanied by a man. And why would he not want her to wear fashionable clothes – *if he could afford them?* to make him proud at dinner tables and balls? He recalled how intently she watched and listened, how quickly she copied the manners and deportment of women around her in the few social situations they'd attended. How she lowered her head and smiled sweetly, not answering to anything she didn't understand.

His muddled thoughts were further complicated on receiving a letter from home. After reading it, old images rolled, one after another and another: dark earth and pine forests, wild thyme and oregano; a splendid sun, endless skies and distant mountains. Images of his mother too, her huge comforting folds full of babies' smells, her rough skin and blistered hands. With heartache he compared her to Eleni, his wisp of sunlight, her breath as a lemon flower, her hair swishing like the tides of the Aegean. His mother had so little. Eleni wanted so much. Upset, angry, he tossed the comparisons aside.

Forced now to think about money, about quotas, quality and prices, he made efforts to shout, beg and argue like Spiros when buying and selling. Evenings saw him bend over lists of expected expenses against income. But he was often distracted by Eleni's chattering that ran like a film in his brain: *a house by the sea. Maids. Pretty clothes.* The knots in his shoulder muscles deepened.

"Why choose her, you damn fool? And why so much hurry to marry?" Spiros said. The two were at their warehouse hiding under an awning from the mid-day sun. "Why set your damn fool eyes on a peasant girl when you got all those rich city ones making eyes at you?" His eyes slanted almost shut against the glare of sky and sea.

Adam found no words to express that Eleni represented primal things of the earth: soft swells of hills and sky and changing seasons. The perfumes of trees. Soaring of hawks. Echoes of butterfly wings. He could not explain his sense that time was slipping away so fast that he might run out of it.

"What about money? You sell almost nothing."

Adam spread his hands. "I have my share from Papa," he said, and smiled suddenly at his brother. "And you can see, I'm trying be more like you."

***

On a late spring day, having finishing unloading merchandize, Adam straightened and stretched his aching muscles. A figure in white caught his eye, only to disappear among merchants and shoppers. Loath to resume his back-breaking work, he chatted to old women, bent to pet stray dogs. He sold nothing. Suddenly the figure in white was at his side.

"Smile, Adam," Eleni whispered, "charm your customers and they'll buy more from you." Before her astonished husband could speak she made a deal of her own. Holding up a bolt of silk to reflect the shifting sunlight, she draped it over one shoulder.

"See how this fairy-like fabric sings to the senses and makes the wearer to look beautiful." Adam saw how her trilling tones stopped passing shoppers. He watched as she pirouetted and spun the cloth about her. Shoppers fingered it. "How much do you want?"

"Aphrodite herself would sweep down from heaven to find something like this." Eleni's hands fluttered beneath the cloth. "She would pay any price. You tell me what it is worth to you."

Adam stiffened. He saw Spiros gape. "You should not be doing this," he whispered. "Your job is to make our apartment into a comfortable and proper place for us, and for all the children to come."

Eleni raised golden eyes to him. That night she teased him, covered him with hot frantic kisses. She fluttered before him, a butterfly. He moved as though to capture it, only to touch her arm humbly.

In the following weeks he made no comment when she sauntered to the markets, concluded a deal, and left. Knowing he could no longer depend on his father and brother, he must accept his wife as a trading partner.

"What you selling, man?" A broad-faced Turk fingered a stack of books on one corner of Adam's stall.

"Wisdom." Adam smiled. "Books to understand how one man cheats another so he can better feed his family. And because he does, he takes food from the mouths of that man's family."

He saw Spiros staring at him, and an image of himself came to him: a sloping form beside the warehouse, a stack of books on his stall, one open in his hand. He could almost hear his brother's voice: *Wake up Adam, wake up. For that shameless shepherdess of yours you'll need all the money in the world.* He watched as Spiros struck a bargain on his behalf. But this flicker of old solidarity soon turned to irritation when the two talked about the war.

"You got to listen." Spiros' voice was filled with anxiety. "Everything's rushing to Hell. When you get together with our damned politicians, ask them. Ask them what's going to happen."

"Don't worry yourself about the war," Adam said lightly, but a frown creased his brow.

***

Adam sat slouched at the kitchen table, poring over an account book. Glancing up, he saw Eleni at the window watching rain lash the panes. She moved to lean over him, to run her eyes over the page. Without comment she walked away, and he knew then that something was brewing in that head of hers. In the days that followed he caught sight of her wandering about the pier and chatting with merchants.

"Whatever are you doing?" he asked, mystified. She only smiled and shrugged.

One evening while drying dishes, she said in an off-hand voice, "Adam, merchants can't afford losses like you see sometimes. These big strong men, they cry over what they lose. Their carpets and animal hides get torn and dirty. Bags split open and everything is lost in the sea. Their families go hungry. Isn't there a way they can insure their stuff?"

Adam's head jerked up. "So that's what you've been doing at the pier! Did I ever tell you you're a clever woman?" But Adam's mind was also confused at this muddling of wifely roles. Eleni continued clattering dishes and said nothing further.

"Insurance, man? Damned good idea!' Spiros punched the air. "You being the clever brother, you go look into it, see how we can get started."

"It was Eleni ..." Adam began, but Spiros had already gone. Over the following months Adam saw Eleni cast furtive glances at the account book, saw her smile, and knew why. Profits were slowly accruing in a column headed, "Cargo Insurance: Rail. Wagon," profits that in time would bring increased wealth to both families.

"Will it last?" Adam stood alongside Spiros as the brothers picked through overripe fruit. Only sporadically did he allow his mind to turn to the war. Newspapers reported that it was creeping closer. How long could governor Rahmi Bey resist orders coming from Constantinople? What would happen if he refused their orders to close the Levantines factories?

"What about Mama and the family?" he asked aloud. Spiros said nothing and Adam continued sorting and stacking merchandize. Dark grey clouds hung low and the air that blew from the sea felt damp. Abruptly he straightened his aching back. "Look, we know nothing about what's happening to them. I'm going home to see."

Spiros stared. Yiannis, resting under the awning covering their tables, said, "A fool idea. It's not safe."

"One of us needs to go." Adam's voice held a mix of apology and defiance. "We've had no letters for some time and I'd really like to take Eleni there and maybe Spiros will look after my business while I'm gone and…"

Yiannis walked away before Adam ran out of breath. It was then he realized his father had scarcely acknowledged him since his marriage, that he'd ruptured the existing fundamental relationship between them, even if it had been one of ambivalence. First-born, a gift from the gods at the waning of the old century, he'd represented hope for the restoration of some ancient family status. All he'd done was to flout and disappoint. In the following nights of restless sleep, he agonized. He'd done what he'd done, was in new territory where the rules were not known. But one thing he knew: he was finding favour among the political elite and surely his father would see this. Surely he would see Eleni's cleverness, and maybe it would cancel out what he had done in marrying her.

"Papa," he said, hesitating in his father's bedroom doorway, "why don't you come to Anatolia with us?"

"Yes, Papa." Spiros came up behind him. "Mama will be missing you, and all the family."

So, he's got his own agenda, Adam thought.

"Let the devil take you both – and you too!" Yiannis looked at Eleni hovering. He moved restlessly in his bed. "Not safe," he said. "The damned

Turks are roaming, getting rid of the non- Turks and pushing them into the Anatolian desert. Is your wife," as he continued to call Eleni without ever looking at her, "fit to travel the distance? She's nothing but a skinny bag of bones."

A spark lit Eleni's eyes, but she said nothing.

"Eleni is strong. See how she works …"

"Indeed." A gleam suddenly entered Yiannis' eyes. "I will say this: it is your wife who has all the ambition. It is your wife who puts money in your pocket. Ha, I know what she wants: all the fine clothes so she can walk about and pretend she's a lady. Yes indeed."

"You should go, Papa," Adam heard his brother saying, "it's gotta be safe enough. Take Unal with you, the fellow's a Greek, a Turk – whatever you tell him to be. Adam, use your tongue like the Turk. Get a third-class rail ticket and no one'll bother you. I'll look after the business, and … I might just get married myself."

***

Chapter 11

Anatolia, April, 1916

Against the advice of fellow merchants, Adam set out to travel part way across a vast Anatolian plateau. Deportation of Christians from coastal Asia Minor continued sporadically, but the Russian army, having extending itself in late 1915 in Eastern Anatolia, remained subdued. The family would travel by third-class rail on the Smyrna-Cassaba line that ended in the mountain city of Afyon. After that they would take a wagon. Unal, a tribal Turk from the Afyon region, would accompany them to act as their spokesman, or bodyguard, if necessary.

In late May, Adam, wearing a turban, led Yiannis and a pregnant Eleni into a third-class overcrowded carriage in *Alsancak*. Unal, wearing ragged pants tied with string, a faded shirt and coarse cotton jacket, elbowed throngs of peasants aside, searching for a seat for his *omorfya,* his princess, as he called Eleni. Inspired, he lifted her onto a large luggage rack above where she sat squeezed between sacks. Next he looked for Yiannis, away from babies and animals. Yanking a young man from his seat he said, "Give it up," and pushed Yiannis into it. The train rumbled from the station. Unal and Adam sat on their upturned bags on the floor.

The carriage air was fetid with smells of sweat, spiced food and smoke. Yiannis, coughing and spitting, drew a cloth from his pocket and wiped his mouth. Adam wanted to whisper that he had spit on his chin, but could not, the relationship had never allowed such intimacy, and certainly did not now. He looked at the faces about him, at the shapes of noses and chins, of hair lines and foreheads, the build, the colouring. Who were they? Greeks and Turks of course, some Armenians and Kurds – maybe an intermingling of all. Perhaps they didn't know themselves and didn't care. Well, because of the war, now they had to.

The railway followed parts of the Great Silk Route, along shallow plains, with mists fingering mountains valleys.

"Can you see from there?" he asked Eleni, "look." Eleni craned her head, to see dry riverbeds lined by poplar trees, small villages shrinking under an already hot sun. In the distance, pack-horse drivers and bullock carts; an unpainted wagon trundling a dirt road flying a crescent flag – "Turkish *posta*," Unal announced.

Varied shades of the earth slid by; harvest gold, purple-shaded mountains, pink, grey and white rock. To the west, wheat fields rolled away to the horizon, relieved only by low hills, dots scattered on them – "Roaming herds of goats and sheep," Adam called up to her. "Quick, look at this." From her perch, Eleni saw two figures – husband and wife? – ploughing a field using a tree trunk pulled by two cows; saw Yurak nomads and a scattering of tents. All of it reminded her of her own humble origins; of her father's advice to the daughter who wanted to go to school: *marry a man who is about to rise up in the world. One who will teach you how to behave like a lady.*

Adam stood for long periods gazing out the windows, smiled as he glimpsed wild flowers when the train slowed: hollyhocks, anemones and peonies among the asphodel. On distant hills he saw figures on horseback, Circassians probably, a hardy race of horsemen. The long line of figures moved so slowly as to not move at all. Then he saw they were driving ragged lines of men before them; that they might not be Circassian after all.

"Turkish soldiers, they're driving those men into the Syrian Desert," Unal whispered, and Adam, horrified, understood that most would die long before they got there. His skin prickled and he felt cold. The train slowed as it approached a local *Kahve,* near Usak, where passengers spilled out, clamouring around cay-sellers offering sweet tea from large samovars and ragged men offering cool water. Adam helped his father off the train. A Turkish peasant stood at Yiannis' elbow, speaking rapidly. Yiannis shook his head.

"He sees your tired eyes and hears you cough," Unal whispered. "He wants to bind your head for you and wash your feet. This is how he gives hospitality. It is the very best in the world and if you refuse, he will think of you as a graceless person." To Adam he said, "We should stay in the *hanuri* here tonight, your Papa will feel better after the rest."

Adam, striding the wooden platform, gave a sudden, urgent yell. "Get back on the train. Get on the train. Look − look over there!" His hand shook as he pointed north. Through the shimmering haze he saw the horsemen leaving the line of refugees and galloping toward them.

"Get inside!" Adam's voice rose.

Jamming themselves back into the carriages, passengers crouched, listening to horses hooves thudding the ground, closer ... closer. Although many seats were now empty, Unal had hoisted Eleni back up onto the luggage rack. Adam pulled the turban further over his forehead. One hand slipped into his jacket pocket, his fingers curling around a string of worry beads. Fleeting thoughts were that while Yiannis would not interest Turkish military men, they might throw him off the train like a piece of garbage and leave him to die. Eleni remained hidden. Unal was a Turk. He himself? His heart contracted painfully.

A few stragglers still wandered outside the railway carriages in the early afternoon sun, even after the train's engine bellowed and sent up a puff of smoke. The soldiers galloped closer, their horses' hooves clipping across the far end of the wooden platform. Menace hung in the carriage like a weight and shouts snapped the air. The stragglers continued to wander, in spite of orders to remain where they were, to raise their hands. Were they confused - or just stupid? Adam's thoughts were cut off as gunshots erupted. He broke out in a sweat and crouched on the floor. Screaming erupted all about him. He saw Unal's large frightened eyes fixed on him.

"Move the damn train, move it," he yelled. A sudden hush fell and he risked a peek out the window. Shocked, he saw that all the stragglers had fallen, their corpses kicked about like bags of litter. His right hand frantically squeezed his worry beads. A stench of vomit filled the carriage and he blocked his nose; curses and pleas begged of the Almighty.

As the horsemen clattered alongside the carriages, the train's engine coughed. It belched black smoke, but still did not move. Adam raised his head from his knees and risked another glimpse out the window. His eyes stared straight into those of a soldier, smartly dressed among his ragged companions. Something glinted in the sun. He saw the fellow's silver belt buckle, read the words, *Sultan's Soldier* in German imprinted on it. *Sultan?*

His rigid stance suggested to Adam he'd had German training. A dozen red-faced men on sweating horses cantered alongside him and Adam fell back to the floor. As bile rose up in his throat, his irrelevant thought was: *a man is most a man when he's mounted on a horse.*

"All passengers will get off the train," the Sultan Soldier commanded. No one moved. Hearing the click of rifle safety catches, passengers screamed, Eleni's voice added to a crescendo of other horrified voices. Still not a person stirred. The smell of vomit grew.

"Move the train! Move, *move!*" Adam, cursing under his breath, felt a sudden jolt, and another. In agonizing slowness the train chugged along its platform. He risked another look. The horsemen aimed their rifles straight at the carriage windows. Shots were fired. There was an explosion of shattered glass followed by curdling cries. The train continued sliding and quickly gathered speed. With furious shouts the horsemen galloped after it. Adam's last look was at a knot of tiny figures about to be swallowed up in a billow of smoke.

Silence lingering from fright held in the carriage for many moments. Eleni moaned and begged to be lifted from the baggage rack. Yiannis hardly stirred.

To Adam it felt like an hour passed, with only low moans, crying and whispered entreaties heard. He huddled with Eleni, and thinking to distract them from fear, from the stench of vomit, he commented on the odd houses they passed. Words ran out of his mouth about animals living alongside their owners. About the hayricks piled on roofs for feeding them in winter, about the animals providing dung for fires and both living close to keep each other warm.

"It gets so cold then?" Eleni tightened her shawl.

"You grew up in a mild climate," Adam said. "It can get extremely cold here, especially when winds blow, and snow drifts through the Eastern passes."

The train soon entered the plain that lay between Mountains *Sultandag* and *Emirdag*, close now to *Afyon*.

"Rich agricultural land beyond," Adam said, "a place of opium and buffalo cream." A dreamy glow appeared in his eyes.

"Eh, we're almost home?" Yiannis, awaking from a prolonged stupor, pulled himself upright. "Eh, the train doesn't take us to *Boldavin* ..." and he began grumbling about damn fool governments who should finish what they start.

The group of four left the train at the *Afyon* station and end of the line. They were met by Yiannis' younger brother Zevio in a horse-drawn wagon.

"It's a long way yet," Adam said apologetically to Eleni, but she was gazing with delight at the city of *Afyon* that lay cradled in a steep mountain valley, many of its houses painted in bright colours. Adam gave a worried glance at his father, turned to Unal, a request on his tongue, but the young man's eyes held a strange gleam. "This is where I stop," he said in tones of finality. "I go on now to *Aksehir* to pay my respects to *Nasreddin.*"

Nasreddin?" Adam jumped.

"His statue – they built one for him in the town. They say his spirit is everywhere there and I stay for it to come to me."

"Oh!" Longing flickered briefly in Adam's eyes but he could not stop here, not now, and he signalled Zevio to continue. By wagon, the family skirted the western edge of Cappadocia and the beginning of an odd rocky landscape. To the south rolled shimmering wheat fields.

"Not far now from *Boldavin*, soon we'll be seeing Mama." The joy in Adam's voice awoke the dozing Yiannis, and he grunted. "Eleni – look! See if you can make out a path with a poplar tree at the end of it. If you can, we're almost home."

Eleni peered into the distance. "I can't see anything," she said, "only a small tree –oh, now I can see some houses."

When clouds of dust from their wagon settled, both looked at a home apart from the others with trees and earth all about it. Ragged gardens sloped to a small vineyard.

"I'm going to meet your mother," said Eleni in a small voice, "but I feel ragged and dirty."

Adam only hugged her.

Not long after they had passed the lonely tree, he heard shouts and children's laughter; saw a cluster of people under a tent in the orchard. A country festival, he thought, his heart swelling. Maybe he and Eleni could stay for a while and celebrate someone's name day, a saint.

Retrieving himself into the present, he saw with astonishment new flowerbeds with borders, smooth grass covering the dirt courtyard. Chattering children of all ages came laughing about them, only to fall silent, as they would at strangers. Dogs licked around their feet and somewhere in the orchard, a goat bleated.

Adam's eyes were on his Mama in the doorway. He gave a shout and ran toward her.

Georgia had arisen from her chair in the sun and now wobbled precariously as she walked. "Ah my boy, my boy…" But when she turned to her husband, loud exclamations burst from her.

"Eh, eh," she cried, "What have you done to your father in the infidel city?" She stooped toward Yiannis and smothered him in her arms. Tears trickled down the valleys of her face and she rocked back and forth on her heels. Adam felt wetness in his own eyes as he watched his father briefly cling to her. His face had softened with a gentle expression Adam rarely saw. Georgia gave orders for her husband to be fed with soup and put to rest in the matrimonial bed. It was only then did she embrace her son.

"Mama, the flowerbeds, the new fences …"

"The twins," Georgia's face crinkled in a smile, "they took up carp fishing in the *Aksarcay* River. Basil cuts rushes and sells bundles of it. But," her face altered, "they are so much changed. You talk to them, Adam. But where is your beautiful wife?" She looked around, to see Eleni hiding herself in a corner near the fireplace.

"Ah, *chryso mou, chryso mou!*" She turned and crushed her daughter-in-law to her, exclaiming in dismay over the rabbit-like bones.

"Don't worry Mama, she'll grow to be more like you. Already she's with our child." Adam looked with love at Eleni who smiled, but Adam could see she had no words to answer her mother-in-law.

Eleni, that night, tossed in her bed, gazing at walls hung with stylized figures of the saints carved in wood; at icons of Christ draped in Turkish clothes. She listened to the *kahve* and to the murmur of male voices below her window.

Papa is not well. His lungs are hurting. The Turks, they call your city the infidel Smyrna … our daughters are Greek and now they cannot go to the local schools. We get a notice from the Government and it says it cannot guarantee our safety. Times of trouble are coming. We are Greeks, and the Young Turks are taking over. What shall we do, what shall we do?

In the days that followed, white-clad, her hair in long braids, Eleni walked about the wandering home, marveling at the immensity of Mama reclining in her chair as she ruled her large family. Children clattered about her, swung from trees in the orchard, played hide-and-seek in the vegetable gardens.

She could tell older members of the family felt threatened. They spoke of the many Greeks who had packed up a centuries-old way of life, and carrying what they could on mules and carts, began a trek to the coast. She saw Yiannis forced to relax, how he cast frequent quick glances at his wife, his eyes full of tenderness. Whenever she came near heatted her shoulder and thought how much he must have missed her.

Eleni moved close to catch what sixteen-year-old twins Basil and Nikos were saying to their father.

"Not long after you left," Basil's blue eyes large with anxiety, "some people came looking for descendants of the ancient Hellenes who lived in Anatolia ..."

"Ha, the teachers from Athens," Yiannis remembered.

"They said we must take back our land from the Turk," Nikos added. "We must learn proper Greek because it's the language of our forefathers; we must remember our Orthodox religion. Then they came back to open little schools."

"They took our books away." Basil's voice rose with his eyebrows. "We must not write in the Turkish, even if we use Greek symbols. Then they showed Greek people in the village stores how to be money lenders and bank managers to the Turks." He raised his eyebrows higher as though still surprised at these astonishing developments. "The store keeper is told to offer one hundred per cent credit and hold Turkish lands as security. This is how Greeks can get back all the lands stolen by the infidel."

Under her breath Eleni said, "Surely these lands by right belong to the Turk."

"Well, well." Yiannis smiled suddenly. "My twins have learned to take life seriously at last." He was silent a moment, then added, "But the Turks have always been our friends. We lived together through all the generations and now it's all to change? No good will come of it."

"The priests said we must show off our Christian faith." Basil opened his palms of his hands. "This way we can unite all Greeks across Anatolia – and everywhere else too, all of us into one big Greek empire. A return to Byzantium, they said."

"Byzantium, eh? A fool's game," Yiannis said. "Greeks and Turks, all of us will pay a price."

"But then the Turks came." Basil's voice dropped. "In the night they crept in to steal from us and frighten us away. Tell me Papa, where are we supposed to go?"

"So, the danger already falls." Yiannis' chin sank into his whiskery chest. When darkness gathered about home and orchards, he got to his feet, shuffled to the kitchen door to peer into the gloom. Eleni followed him. Only restless birds and wind rustling the trees disturbed the ancient quiet of the steppe. Yiannis turned and saw her, Adam behind her in a tiny circle of light.

"Get back to Smyrna at once." His voice was loud in the room. "You work, work to make yours the biggest import-export business in Smyrna. Basil and Nikos can go too, in a while." He broke off in a harsh fit of coughing, after it, adding in a diminished voice, "Son, buy all the gold you can. Store it up against the bad times coming."

"Bad times?" Eleni whispered, and Yiannis cast a withering glance at her.

"We hear rumours from passing merchants." Basil and Nikos had joined them, Basil twisting his hands. "They say Germans and Turks are occupying Smyrna."

"All the talk is of German and Turkish aggression." Nikos said, and kicked a chair.

Yes, a little bit of difficulty." Yiannis, still in the doorway, hunched himself against a blackening sky. "A problem when Greece puts herself on the side of the Turks' enemies ..." he broke off as lightning streaked overhead. He withdrew and shut the door.

"... Britain, France, Italy," piped up a childish voice. "We learn it in our school."

"Yes, yes, who does not know these things? I ask my clever sons to find an answer to this: if the Turks get the upper hand, what will happen to Hellenistic Greeks who've lived here all the centuries?"

"I suppose, Papa," Adam said gently, "we've been living all this time in the land of the Turk. Why can't we all ..." Thunder cracking overhead and cut off his words.

"At sunrise you start for the city." Yiannis infused his voice with old authority. "I'll stay here and look after my family against the infidels."

The world next morning had been robbed of all colour and washed lifeless. Children's voices ceased. No bird song, no barking dogs disturbed the eerie quiet. Gently Adam disengaged his weeping Mama; hovered uncertainly about his father. Rigid in his chair by the stove, Yiannis remained with his eyes fixed on the grey walls of his house, reaching up with stained fingers briefly to touch his son only when he was about to leave. He nodded slightly at Eleni and turned back to the wall.

Dressed as Turkish peasants, Adam and Eleni climbed into an unpainted wagon that would take them to the train that would carry them across Anatolia. The once golden wheat fields lay dull under an indifferent sky. Trees twisted into grotesque forms in the wind.

***

Chapter 12

Smyrna, 1916 - 1917

The grand sweep of the Steppe gave way to rugged mountains and valleys, to rows of marching hills, and to the purplish-green peaks encircling Smyrna. From the station they hired a wagon, and as it neared the flat of the quay, Eleni gave a cry: "Look, Adam! The boys are wearing the Turkish Fez, and armbands with the star and crescent."

Adam's mood plummeted. He must find Spiros at once. Hurrying his wagon along the waterfront to the old apartment, he raced up the stairs, rattled on the door and opened it. He stared. A Turkish rug graced the living room floor. Prints of hills and flowers decorated the walls and a large bronze pitcher sat on a sideboard.

There was Spiros, hair neatly parted, eyebrows smoothed, dressed in pressed pants with tucked-in shirt. Instead of embracing his brother he opened the bedroom door saying, "I want you to meet my bride, Maria." A smile lit up his often somber face.

Ha, Adam thought, after all his evenings in brothels, he's besotted with a plain and bulky merchant's daughter. When Maria moved, the odour of cheap soap scattered in the air about her. Spiros' cracked hands constantly caressed her, his face creasing into sharp lines only when he spoke of British raids, of bombs on residential areas of the city. Maria gently interrupted him to suggest Adam invite Eleni to join in refreshments.

"Thank you," Adam said, "but only if we don't talk about the war."

"She doesn't even know there is a war." Spiros' eyes held old mockery, and Maria, surprised, said, "But she'll have to now with the bombing raids all over."

The raids reminded Adam, and all Smyrna's citizens, that war encircled them. A war that forced the city's larger Greek population to pay homage to a Turkish government controlling it, a population trying to pretend no war existed. Wealthy patrons still crowded the opera house. Lively music spilled from bars and cafes. In the villages, tea parties were catered even as aerial dog-fights occurred between German and British airplanes, even as British bombing raids continued.

Spiros told Adam he'd heard that German General Otto Leman von Sanders was being billeted in Karatassis up the coast near the Onassis family mansion. Everyone was paying lip service to the occupying army; giving prayers for King and Queen in Greek churches, and for the safety of Greeks everywhere.

"You know what that Aristotle said? Why are we praying for the enemy?" Spiros laughed in derision. "That family, they're not real Greeks. They know nothing."

But Adam saw that into his brother's face had crept a softened look; that the corners of his mouth crinkled upwards. He seemed to have grown taller. And vague thoughts flitted that this had happened since their father had left the city. Another idea chased this one: Spiros no longer competed with Adam for his favour but enjoyed partnership with him. He was not to know that Spiros held images of his twin brothers Nikos and Basil in Anatolia and believed that he and Adam now might live as lives as intertwined as they did. It was just Eleni ... he must tell him that it was through her they were making profits insuring cargo and caravan.

Eleni gave birth soon after their return, a tiny boy they named Alekos. The year rolled on: ships steaming into Smyrna's harbour bearing merchandise from Italy, the Middle East, Bulgaria, and Russia. Long days were spent in the market. Spiros' rasping voice arguing, bargaining. The brothers carrying goods in sweltering heat to their warehouse. They seldom spoke from the time the sun rose, crossed the sky, and began its slow descent. Nothing existed but this; no one knew if business would continue, and life as they knew it.

In the following year Eleni gave birth to twin girls, Melina and Christina. Only a few months afterward, she was back at the warehouse leaving the children in the care of a nanny. Bending over Adam, her voice running softly like water over stones, she whispered, "*Do it like this, Adam: How much? Too much! I get a better deal another place. Quantity? Quality – I don't know – not good enough. Give me a better price.*"

Humbly Adam tried to imitate her and surprised himself at times with successes. Each evening he returned to his apartment and shut out the world. Its near-empty rooms echoed with music scratching from old recordings of mandolin and flute. Quietly he purchased an occasional gold piece on credit, to be saved up for the villa on the waterfront Eleni wanted, one day a boat. Big dreams, but better to have them than not. Awake sometimes in the small hours of the night, he marvelled as he watched his wife smiling in her dreams, her body, pregnant once more, rising up through the sheet that covered it: *A woman full of devotion and tenderness; I have a little money now, some nobility in the eyes of the people, yet I feel I have nothing until she comes to me.*

Adam was not to know that Eleni dreamed waking and sleeping, not always of him, but of beautiful clothes, a house in a wealthy village, elegant social functions to which she would be invited. He had no knowledge of her efforts to banish frequent nightmares where she was returned to the country digging stones under a relentless sun. Having dirty hands, broken nails. He saw her checking and polishing her nails again and again.

As the year trundled on, imports dwindled; fewer came in on the tides and fewer still by road and rail. Merchants grew restless. Rumours flew. Sleepless sometimes when a full moon stared down from a star-studded sky, Adam got out of bed and followed mournful music from one local cafe to another, sometimes to the place where steam engines shunted, or to the edge of the fast-emptying Armenian quarter. There he sat beneath an almond tree, inhaling the aroma of freshly-baked bread that mingled with the perfumes of the night. The city was surely heaven itself, home to all the races of the world with more than half of them Greek, all living harmoniously across centuries. Surely nothing could happen to it?

***

Chapter 13

Smyrna, 1918.

1917: worst year of the war on the Continent. Adam's heart lifted on hearing this, because the war had scarcely touched the city and surely would not now. 1917 rolled into 1918. One early winter morning he leaned toward Spiros over a stack of animal hides. "We're thinking of moving to a suburb, like Bournabat." He tossed the words carelessly in the air. "The times are still uncertain and we'll be safer in the suburbs."

"What? You damn fool! You don't got money for a house in Bournabat." Incredulity darkened Spiros' eyes. "Ha, Eleni's pushing for this."

"Well, it's the little ones really. Here they'll see too much."

"You don't got the money," Spiros repeated, not pausing in stacking carpets. "Bournabat's only for rich Levantines."

"Armenians too, and Jews and Turks. Not everyone lives in a mansion. Anyway, I thought you'd be the first to want something better, even if it's just to keep up with the Onassis clan."

"Listen Adam, you can't *afford* it. Oh! You think we'll move too? Ha, forget that!"

"It's also because Eleni ..." his voice trailed away. How could he explain her ambition to become a proper lady and mingle with old wealthy Levantine families? Adam abandoned his forced cheerfulness. "Look, she's expecting me. Let's finish up here, go home and have a drink."

Along the edge of a darkening sea, past the hulk of grey buildings facing it, the brothers walked, and into Adam's small apartment. As he poured two shots of *ouzo* Adam glanced toward a half-closed bedroom door through which floated Eleni's voice crooning to her babies. "Don't mention the war," he said. "Women don't understand it and should let men worry about it."

"Damned fool, whatever sort of world are you living in? My Maria knows what's going on. You got the problem, you don't tell your wife nothing, so why don't you? Doesn't she want to know?" *Or is she too stupid?* Spiros clicked his tongue.

"I tell her what she needs to know." Adam's smile vanished and his voice bounced roughly off the room's pale walls.

"*Daxi.*" Spiros banged down his glass and prepared to leave just as Adam's twin daughters crawled out of the bedroom. Adam picked up the twin with hair that sprang wildly about her head. "Melina, go back to your mother," he ordered, and as though comprehending, the child crawled away.

"We'll be safer in the suburbs," he insisted. "The Allies are close to winning the war, but what if the Turk turns …?" his voice trailed away.

"Ha! You paying attention to the war at last. So, you got no faith in the Greek army and the Allies?

"I think the Turks might be plotting their revenge even as we speak."

"Let the devil take them all to Hell!"

Eleni walked into the living room then, baby Christina under her arm. "Always the war talk. Adam, you promised me we'd move to Bournabat." She tossed her silky hair over a buttoned-up blouse and frowned at her fingernails.

Spiros looked under his brow at Adam and muttered, "You damn well can't afford it, but you, little goat-herd …" Aloud he said, "Safer in Bournabat?" and cracked his knuckles. "Dear sister-in-law, just last week a couple of locals got kidnapped by the Turks."

"Stop doing that!"

"What?"

"Cracking your ugly bones." Eleni spun around and headed to the bedroom.

"Yes, I heard about that," Adam said, embarrassed. "But suppose you were a Turk being threatened with your city or a part of your country being taken over by Greeks − or anyone - what would you do?"

"Don't ask me about the bloody Turks! The only decent one I know is Rahmi Bey. Venizelos? Damn prime minister's still holding onto his grand vision of a super Greek state: three oceans and the shores of three continents. Got stars in his eyes, that one. He says the Allies will support him but you think for a minute the Turk will lie down when he loses a chunk of his country? No damned way. Venizelos is either greedy or crazy. He sees ships in the harbor and most flying the Greek flag. He knows the Greeks run the city's business. Confident he is, too confident." Spiros crossed himself again and stared gloomily into his empty beer mug.

***

Chapter 14

Toronto, 1994

Georgia

Bournabat? The lush village that lay six miles west of the city centre now called Bornova. I take myself wandering this about-to-be-lost paradise, its leafy boulevards, and turreted, gabled mansions. I stroll among the Levantines enthroned in their rose-coloured arbours, in lavender day rooms, in gilt-embroidered bedrooms, all of it much too manicured for my taste.

The lights in the Reference library blink off and on signalling closing time and I walk out onto a crowded, dishevelled Yonge Street. It throbs with energy and the wild, crazy ambitions of its entrepreneurs – much more to my style. With my mind so clattering I head south toward the darkened Kouvalis Salon, preferring it over home, over Helena harping on about my room, my clothes, my life. Across the street the *Panasonic* Theatre lights shine blue on the pavement. Pinpoints of light come from *Roberts Gallery*, but *The House of Lords* is darkly shuttered. I unlock the salon door and peer into the dim space. Spooky. In my mind the chairs are filled. The ghostly figures of Bonnie, Silent Sylvia and Isabel comb and tease and lacquer. Wailing *rebetika* music creeps from the walls. Plunking myself at Helena's desk, I'm about to open up my laptop when I hear tapping on the door. "Who is it?" I jump up in alarm and peer through the bay window. My old high school friend Jeff is standing in a yellow circle of light. "Oh, you."

'Young man shows clean lines, is decisive and precise.' Mentally I write his advertisement for a dating site, and sigh. "Why are you … are you following me?"

"At the Reference library," Jeff smiles his clean, shy smile, "I saw you leaving and thought we could get a drink."

'Thin and tidy, hands by his sides, hair parted carefully in the middle.' As I look at him I get a snapshot image of myself and wonder again at his persistence. Must be to do with opposites attracting, like lean and clean and clear of complications against large, messy and unfathomable. I look up briefly at him, hear myself sigh as I say, "Sorry, "got to work, got a deadline for a project. I'm not here, not really."

No, I'm just anxious to get back to Smyrna and board a train for Bournabat.

At home, I push open the door, to see Helena – and Dad! – sitting across from each other. It looks like they've been doing some serious talking. They're not smiling, but the air about them feels uncharged for once. Helena looks up at me, about to speak, but I slide past them to my room, and to my other life...

***

Chapter 15

Bournabat

Adam and Spiros walked briskly along the quay on a late August afternoon toward the railway station in *Alsancak*, colonial-style swept and polished. A steam-powered train would take them to their new homes in Bournabat. Men in bowler hats, pressed suits, and starched shirts greeted each other as they entered the train. Spiros hopped along the line of carriages, swung himself into one marked first class, and sank into a reclining chair. He grinned in satisfaction at the carpeted floor, at the incandescent lighting above. "Among the upper class at last," he said, and grinned.

"How do we know we should be sitting here?" Adam had followed him in.

"All seats in first class are reserved for Bournabat businessmen," said a uniformed conductor who had stepped in after them. "You'll find empty seats in second and third class compartments."

"But we are ..."

"You must make an application." The conductor moved on.

Once beyond the station in Bournabat, Adam forgot his humiliation and walked, relaxed, under giant chestnut trees lining a gently-sloping street that led to their new homes. His eyes ranged with pleasure over sprawling gardens bordering the road side, at mansions glimpsed through intricate, wrought-iron railings, and old trees. Rococo architecture, Baroque, Gothic, Ottoman and Ampir, all of it was represented in these old Levantine homes. He did not yet know who his fellow commuters were, only that one day he would make their acquaintance - as early as possible

---

for Eleni's sake. Frowning, he recalled her disappointment when she'd first seen the new house.

"This is our new home?" Her voice had faltered.

"*Chryso mou,* don't you like it?"

Adam, about to protest that he felt hard-pressed to afford any house in this suburb, said instead, "Our next move will be into a mansion, I promise you. Catching her expression, and finally provoked, added, "Look *Eleniksa,* our family has come a long way in a short time. These rich Levantines have inherited money from generations back. Really, this is a very nice little house."

"A worker's cottage," Eleni said, but put a smile on her face.

One evening some months later as he and Spiros walked through the public square where five crossroads met, he fingered a small box in his pocket, imagined Eleni's expression when he gave it to her.

"See you in the morning," he said, touching Spiros' shoulder. "Remember, when the train's whistle blows it means it's about to leave the station." He walked on, again squashing his discomfort at the cost of his new home by reminding himself he was a successful merchant, and still climbing. So, my house is a poor cousin to the neighbouring Paterson's 38 rooms, he thought, or to the Giraud's Italianate palazzo and Herbert Octavius' magnificent palace, but it's … mine.

He came from his short driveway into the glow of a sunlit garden. Eleni sat on a stone seat holding a book, her tiny figure wrapped in a bodice drawn at the waist, layers of skirts falling softly, and a daisy tucked behind one ear. Adam leaned against a stone wall, watching as she dropped her book; as her face lit up with love at the sight of a twin crawling toward her across the grass. The whole picture of her came to him then: a clever woman, tough and fragile, both innocent and shrewd, his beautiful little butterfly. Confused, humbled, he lowered his head as he walked toward her and picked up her book.

"Advanced Menu Planning?" he said, smiling. "When is our first party to be? Here, I almost forgot, something special for you *poulaki mou.*" He took her right hand, his long slim fingers caressing it and running up her arm. He closed her fingers over a small box.

Eleni quickly opened it. "A brooch? A … a black flower?" Her voice faltered. "But Adam, what is the meaning of it?"

"This *baccaro* rose, they say it's unique in the natural world. It's different and special - like you, my little flower."

"I think it looks a bit sinister," she said, but he continued pinning it to her, laughing, kissing her neck, her arms. "Now we'll have music to celebrate," and he walked indoors to switch on the gramophone. Eleni untied her braids to let her hair fall in the long rivulets Adam had first seen in the olive grove. She began moving to the music. Forgetting his financial worries, lit up with love, Adam shifted his feet in rhythm on a tiled floor still warm from the sun's slanting rays. Three-year-old Christina ran to join him, her pudgy arms outstretched. Hoisting her on his shoulders, Adam continued to dance.

***

Spiros walked another few hundred yards along the street, and thinking of Socrates Onassis and his kid Aristotle, he punched the air. "Catching up to you," he said to the trees. "I'll outsmart you yet, you bastards." And so buoyed up, he entered his house through its wide doors and continued to the kitchen, to find the bulky figure of Maria bending over the stove. She wore a heavy buttoned dress with a flounce at the bottom. On impulse he patted her broad bottom. "My Papa would crack a smile if he could see us now," he said. Ha, but the Gods will be jealous. What's that you're cooking?

"Sea-fowl eggs." Maria's eyes crinkled." Your Papa knows his family is doing well because you talk to him in your sleep."

Spiros frowned, wondering what else he said.

***

Adam and Spiros took the train to the city at seven each morning, returning at seven each night to Bournabat. Spiros confessed his longing to mingle with great Bournabat families who were members of the *Ethniki Ameni.* "We're members too," he said, "But they don't talk to us. We don't know what's going on. You're the smooth-talking one, can't you get us invitations, maybe host a party?"

But Adam felt burdened with the cost of his new house and by Eleni's extravagances. This evening he came upon her supervising the baking of honey cakes that included Persian peaches. He could not afford it. Attempting to restore his equilibrium, he walked alone about the grounds of his house and sniffed the perfumed air. Admired old trees lining the streets, the distant *Twin Brothers* glowing purple in the dusk. Each morning he felt the tug of leaving it for the chaotic waterfront where talk was of little else now but friction between Greek and Turk. It could only come to no good. But he must forget it and work … work. Maybe he should keep up the diary he'd once begun, and he searched for the notebook that also contained his poetry.

***

Eleni, happy to be removed from pungent sea front odours and noises, after some months began missing them, missed the markets and teeming waterfront. She felt isolated. She was aware of her husband's shifting moods, knew he was worried about money (overplayed, she felt); about a rising Greek-Turkish war which she hoped he'd also overplayed. She couldn't bear to think otherwise. Adam had come far in business. She was mingling with the city's wealthy people and being accepted by them as a lady. Surely nothing could interfere! And so she put aside Adam's worries and hired a serving woman to help the Nanny. She studied books on etiquette, party planning, and menus. In the evenings Adam frowned at her and mentioned money but she stopped his mouth with kisses, pushed on with her ambition to become as sophisticated as the neighbouring women who had descended from long-established families.

One late afternoon at the window of the day room, embroidery in her hands, she was startled by the sound of cackling beyond it. Looking up, she saw four old ladies passing carrying armfuls of candles.

"Adam, who are these old women?" she asked when he arrived home.

"Well, there's a whole class of them," he said, one hand in his pocket fingering a gold piece he'd purchased on credit that day. "They watch over temples and churches to protect the marble demons from being vandalized or stolen."

"Oh!" And Eleni watched for them again. One late afternoon awash in the perfume of a hundred flowers, an old woman came to her gate. Her spreading flesh was cloaked in layers of colourful cloth and about her fissured neck she had wrapped a purple sash. The parchment-like face raised to Eleni gleamed in a toothless smile and she held out her crooked hands, palms turned upward. Eleni wondered should she her food, clothing? What a ramshackle body she had, and Eleni bent her head in confusion. Abruptly her sisters' images came to mind, then Adam's mother: the bulk of her. A toothless mouth. Her skin scorched by sun and wind, and she shivered. She herself might have had a life just like that, but her mother-in-law had seemed born to it; to a life that *was* her and she was it, all in one, a many-sided, flowing thing.

"What kind of a person is that?" she asked Adam that evening. "I gave her some money – should I?"

"She looks after churches and shrines for a few coins." Adam got up from a food-laden table. "These old crones take care of God's holy places ... and often laugh at the saints. You don't have to give them money."

Eleni, discomforted, watched his retreating back.

***

Chapter 16

Smyrna, 1919

Adam sat with his notebook at a table outside the Kraemer Hotel, his mind fixed on a day in May, 1919. The great European war has ended at last, he wrote, with some kind of peace settlement made in Paris. Greece, ally of the victors, is now sending its army to occupy Smyrna – God help us all!" Aware of raised voices inside the hotel, he got up and went in to listen. Members of the *Ethniki Ameni* were hotly debating the wisdom of the events he'd just been writing about.

"Gross insensitivity," snapped a silver-haired merchant prince in disgust and blocked his ears at cannon shots fired from Allied ships in the harbour. Turning his back on the forest of blue and white flags that rose above homes and shops, the merchant strode down the promenade toward the American Colony of Paradise.

"Watch out for the Turk of tomorrow," another voice said.

Adam, looking after him, heard the words *Long live our Venizelos* ring in his ears. He got up and wandered to the quayside. He was there at the water's edge when exuberant Greek soldiers entered the city from the West with patriotic songs on their lips and immediately began looting it. Sweat broke over him. He squeezed beside a wagon, an unwilling witness to resisting Turks being roughly shoved aside and their blood spilled, until senior Greek officers rushed in to restore order.

In the days that followed he heard stories about soldiers drunk with victory celebrating in waterfront hotels and bars. About officers entertaining themselves in the newly established Greek Officers' club. Entering alone one evening, he stood ill-at-ease among the crowds,

90

absorbing the smell of smoke mingling with beer, with wine, and aniseed-flavoured *raki*. He heard talk about sumptuous dinners in Bournabat that were held in the soldiers' honour, the invitations given them for horse racing at the *Boudja* racetrack and shooting parties at Nymph Dagh. Foreboding lodged heavily in his heart as he made his way home.

As backdrop to this hectic social life, Adam and Spiros, and all Smyrna's citizens, heard rumours about violence surrounding the city. All knew that their Prime Minister Venizelos was preparing to send the Greek army deep into Anatolia to reclaim it for Greece, and a sense of disquiet smouldered. Added to the voice of the merchant prince came others opposed to Greek occupation of the city.

"The Prime Minister asks too much."

"Venizelos? Stupid, stupid. Turks, Armenians, Greeks – all of us will pay. Americans are getting out of here and the Jews too. Some have gone already."

One overcast afternoon Adam and Spiros sat in Kraemer Hotel with members of the *Ethniki Ameni* who were discussing whether they might have influence on the Greek government's decisions. Smoke rose in the air, and palpable tension.

"The Allies won the war. Now Greece thinks it should get payment for supporting them," Socrates Onassis said.

"Bloody Greeks, to be rubbing the Turks' noses in the dust. You think they'll give up their city and land without a fight? You think they'll be walking about laughing when they get Greeks for masters?"

"Our prime minister, he's smooth-talking and full of high and mighty ambitions." Homer Onassis drew hard on a twisted black cigar. "But does he really think Greece should take over the whole world?"

"No, just bring back its golden age."

"Well, damn it, why shouldn't the place be Greek? There are more of us in it than Turks."

"More Christians - and that's a good thing?" The Jew's face held a sneer.

"What about blue-eyed King Constantine who thinks to take back his throne?"

Merchants and politicians, Adam and Spiros among them, vigorously debated the return of Constantine. Spoke longingly of Greek redemption, for a restoration of its ancient glory.

"Greece, she's got a long way to go." Socrates Onassis' voice was dismissive. "A rump of a nation, poor, backward, just a shell of what she was. No different from the man who loses his lands and money and then grovels in the dirt, like some peasants we know."

"Bastard! He's poking fun at us." Spiros cracked his knuckles as the brothers walked home.

"You worry too much about that family, forget them." But Adam saw his brother increasingly resembling their father: thin, smoking and drinking too much. That anger bubbled below the surface except when he was with his beloved Maria.

"Socrates lets nobody forget him." Spiros' irritation was still rising. "He's the big man, treasurer of the *Ethniki Ameni,* he'll make noise. See his upstart son always glued to him? He's a tough kid, that one." He spat. "I'll tell you, that Onassis clan just wants to make money and don't give any damn about Greece or the Greeks." He paused suddenly and stared at his brother. "You ever think about being Greek? Do you care?"

What is it to be Greek? If it meant being related to those from the golden age, Adam did. But what did present-day ones have in common with them? As he sat down in the first-class seat reserved for him on a train home, his mind wandered over the past twelve years. Did he live differently from other people – from Jews, Armenians, Europeans? First, of course, was the church, the sanctuary of Christ. He'd hung portraits of the Holy Land on the walls of his home, baptized his children using old Greek rituals. He thought now of the times Eleni crossed herself whenever a child was hurt; the line of his children dressed for Sunday worship. Here we are, he thought, Greek peasants living among Europeans who have resided regally in the Levant for centuries and mingling with the city's merchant princes. He bowed his head in surprise and humility.

Eleni: exotic, beautiful, a woman full of mystery, he could never comprehend her. One minute, briskly she stepped about the markets, shrewd, calculating. The next, floating with tenderness, she wrapped her arms about her tiny children; about himself. Other images drifted: Eleni opening windows to catch music from mandolin, zither and harp that soared over rooftops, soothing their fretting infants. How easily she'd adopted the fashion and deportment of wealthy Bournabat wives. Waif-like so soon after the birth of the twins Melina and Christina, she shimmered in bright dresses, wore flowers in her hair. At his home-coming each evening she carried sweetmeats and cakes to the table by the window overlooking the side garden. Amazing really how she'd blossomed, a young woman fast becoming as sophisticated and dazzling as the city itself. Only Spiros turned from her.

Dusk was falling this evening as the train whistled into the station. Adam alighted and smiled up at a purplish sky, at the darkening peaks of the *Twin Brothers*. A ten minute walk along a shaded street and he was in his driveway. In the house, he followed a trail of crumbs into the living room where Eleni awaited him, the *Bacarro* rose pinned to her blouse. Clogs echoed on the floor as his children rushed to him, the word *Papa* bursting from their lips. Eleni lined up the children from oldest to youngest and each bowed before a proud father as their mother offered praise for something each had accomplished that day.

"Alekos already knows some Turkish and Greek words, and now he learns the English." Impulsively the scrawny boy turned a somersault, only to smash an earthenware jug on a nearby low table.

"Never mind," Eleni reassured him. "Nikos was a good baby as usual. The twins – Christine sat quietly beside me while I worked my embroidery. Melina, where were you today, my beautiful child? It must have taken your maid half the morning to untangle your hair." Eleni rumpled the thick coils of the child –"*Serpentine curls, just like Medusa after she turned ugly* –" an unkind neighbour had said.

"You have beautiful hair," Adam insisted, "the face of Medusa before Athena changed her." As he spoke, an image of his mother Georgia came to mind. Perhaps this extraordinary hair signified fertility, strength and potency, like Samson before Delilah got out her scissors. Because of it, one day she might do great things.

"Adam, look." Eleni had been standing by the window, a baby in her arms, staring over the street. Now she shrank back.

Adam jumped up from his chair, looked out the window, and turned, smiling, to his wife. "Well, *Eleniksa,* those are Greek soldiers. Greeks have taken over the running of the city." But a shiver ran down his spine as he spoke.

"Adam, we must get Nikos baptized, and do it soon." Eleni's voice quivered.

"Yes, of course." A shadow passed over her husband's face.

***

Chapter 17

Smyrna, 1919

Eleni sat fiddling with her teacup sipping Earl Grey tea in the shade of a lemon tree. Whenever Adam returned a ball that actually landed in the court, she clapped, but kept her ears attuned to the women's gossip – so much to learn until she was properly one of them. Tennis she didn't care about. She knew no card games. Nothing about the war between Greeks and Turks. Clothes she did – "A rare talent for colour and style." That's what Mrs. Giraud once said.

She fingered the linen skirt that reached to her knees. She had begun at last to consort with the wealthy Levantine wives of Bournabat in their mansions; today in a *fin de siècle* palace, as Mrs. Wood called it. Two stone lions spouting water stood guard on either side of the circular driveway and the air was heady with the perfume of lilacs. Aware of a sense of frivolity floating among the seven women gossiping on the Woods' terrace, she studied them, admiring their bright patterned dresses, wide belts, boleros, and fitted caps over the head - a recent craze. Too bad she couldn't imitate the styles since she was pregnant once again. Her gaze wandered to the fairytale gardens that bloomed over sloping grounds, to old stone walls and acres of roses. Seeing Mount Pagus looming darkly in the distance, she turned away.

These women might be rich and powerful, she thought, but she was the youngest and prettiest. And she heard again her father's voice*: marry a man about to rise up in the world and you will become a lady.* From a lowly goat-herder's daughter she had become the wife of still-rising merchant. But her Adam was more than a merchant of course, he was also a poet.

Voices penetrated her thoughts and she heard the words, *Turks. Christians. Armenians.* She sat up.

"... In the Gallipoli province, in the coastal towns," Mrs. Woods was saying. "They're doing it again, taking non-Turks into the desert ..."

"Not now, Hortense, for heaven's sake!" His wife's voice had reached her husband on the tennis court.

"Yes dear, I must speak. Some of us might not know." She turned back to the women and in a hushed voice told of Turkish soldiers pulling people out of bed before the sun rose and marching them into the desert. "They smash Greek hospitals and schools and no town is spared ..." her voice trailed away.

"I know. We all know." Lady Giraud signed deeply. "It's August. The heat will kill them. They'll starve."

"The Greeks already did some of these things to the Turks." Those who heard this comment ignored it.

"In the uncomfortable silence that followed, Eleni heard the rhythmic sound of water spouting from the lions' mouths, heard Mr. Wood commanding the game to continue.

A fretful voice asked, "Do you think the soldiers will come down the coast for us?"

"Well no, of course not." Mrs. Wood lowered her voice. "I mean, who will run the factories and employ all the people? Who will keep the city running and the money flowing?"

Eleni got up. She would not listen. How long had it taken her to get invitations to the great houses in Bournabat? Surely this stupid war couldn't possibly interrupt the lives of powerful people like these? She walked away.

Secret paths lead everywhere. She wandered under myrtle bowers and skirted lily ponds. She walked on to little forests of trees – so cool in the shade. Toward the back of the mansion a small pool glistened and she leaned over to look at her reflection. Voices drifted toward her and she turned. The Woods' two English nannies sat smoking under an umbrella tree. Another woman Eleni knew to be an ironer lounged in a side entrance. She knew some of the great families employed a whole retinue of servants;

that gardeners alone at the Giraud's numbered forty. Helen van der Zee had hired a bodyguard. Others employed boatmen. She sighed. One day ... one day.

"Eleni." Through the trees she heard Adam calling and retraced her steps to the terrace. The mood had changed. Men clustered and spoke in low voices while the women raised theirs with forced gaiety. Eleni stood at the edge of the group and looked up spires, turrets and domes. At the shadowed mountains beyond. She would not listen. She would not!

***

"Maria, we might be invited to a ball and I must buy new clothes." Eleni, gin-sling in hand, wandered about Maria' and Spiros' home while Maria emptied a picnic basket in silence.

"You can have your parties and balls," she said at last. "Spiros prefers picnics in the country with the children, they don't always like to be left with the maid."

"I know about the country." Eleni's voice was dismissive. "You sit in the long grass and get burned in the sun. You get stung flies when you could be one of the ladies in the garden of a mansion."

As the year slid toward its end, a vague sense of foreboding floated like a low-lying cloud. Rumours flew. Heated debates about Venizelos versus King Constantine sliced the air. Eleni continued to block her ears. In November of that year, Venizelos was defeated in general elections in favour of the king. Colonel Murphy was shot in his bed.

***

Another new baby, Adam wrote in his journal. We've named him Marcos. Five now, all of them fine children.

1921 and Smyrna still dazzles. Waterfront cafes and bars spill the music of jazz, ragtime, and classical across the waterfront. People dance. In the suburbs, sumptuous dinners still fill the summer months, and tennis matches, balls and shooting parties. Trade continues. Greek businessmen continue to wear starched white shirts to their offices. Greeks laugh and shoulder-punch in the streets.

Adam paused. *But the Turks are restless*, he added, and chewed on his lips.

Despite pleasure in his newly-established life, he felt shadows lurking, not only about money. Irritated this evening after an afternoon spent tallying his accounts, knowing he should look over a new shipment of carpets from Konya in Anatolia, he walked instead to a wooden bench at the foot of the pier to await Spiros. Rubbing his tight neck muscles, he stared over a sea coloured pink and orange by the setting sun, listened to it lap against the hulls of ships at anchor in the harbour.

"Here you are." Adam recognized his brother's anxiety by the taut coil of his body, his lips clamped tight below a ragged moustache. A barefooted boy stood in front of Adam.

"If you got a heart, Mister, give me five drachmas."

"What's your name, boy?" Adam looked down at him.

"What's it to you? I don't ask for yours. If you want to know, I'm called Alexis." The urchin gave an impudent half bow.

"Go home, Alexis. Take this to your mother." He dropped a few coins into the upturned palm. The child's insolent expression vanished as he ran off and up a sloping street, stray dogs yelping after him. Adam looked about him, aware suddenly, that gone was the cluster of old men who habitually sat laughing and cursing over their card games in the shade of a tree; that children from the alleys now hid behind their grandmothers' skirts. He detected fear, sometimes aggression, in once-familiar voices. Spiros swore at a lurking Turk, "Get away from me you old goat."

"Bloody Greek parasite," snapped the Turk. "We'll get you dogs out of our paradise yet."

"If it wasn't for Greeks you'd have no business at all." Spiros spat. A magpie added its scolding. "To hell with business. The hell with everything, I'm going home to talk to Maria."

Adam stared after his brother. He had resumed his tongue clicking and was in a perpetual state of fury. *To talk to Maria,* he'd said. Should he, Adam, try again to talk to Eleni? As he walked after him he looked at the city ranging itself on the slopes above, the late afternoon sun catching the purple-red blooms of a Judas tree. He started and turned away, trying to focus on what he should tell Eleni. The evening before, he'd relaxed with her by the window after the children had been put to bed. Had laced his fingers with hers, noting the perfect, pink-coloured nails, played with her hair, then slid his hands about her waist.

"You're a dewdrop on a rose petal," he whispered. "But I need to tell you about some things that are happening."

"What things? Adam, you look serious. If it's news about the war, don't tell me."

Adam stared at the wide eyes and trusting face turned to him. On this same face he'd seen shrewd, calculating expressions. She was smart and had to know what was happening. Maybe she just didn't want to dwell on it. "You know the European war has ended," he said, his shoulders sagging, "but a new one has begun between Greeks and Turks. The Turks don't want Greeks owning any part of Turkey. They want to get rid of every last one of them off their land, and all other nationalities too. Turkey for the Turks, they say."

Eleni's expression told him her mind had wandered. Adam said nothing else. *A nightingale silenced ... a rose that never bloomed.* How could he disturb the evening, or any evening for that matter, because he could not know how many there would be.

Instead of coming directly home from the train the following night, he walked through the public square. From there, to the Officers' Club, not failing to admire the magnificent nineteenth century village mansion as always, a place where dizzying rounds of parties, balls and games took place. He needed to talk to fellow *Ameni* members, to the Onassis brothers if they were there, to anyone who might have inside knowledge of what was going on. Only a handful of men lingered. No one bothered to talk to him.

Quickly he walked on home, to an Eleni in a yellow-flowered dress with beaded belt, an embroidered bolero slung across her shoulders. In her arms she held the mandolin she'd been learning to play. Older children ran laughing about the large rooms with Christine's piercing voice raised above the rest. Nikos, Adam's look-alike, attempting a line dance, swung his arms and accidentally struck Alekos in the chest. A small cry came from him, and Nikos laughed.

Adam shrugged off his jacket and poured himself a shot of *raki*. He picked up his pipe, trying to still the clamorous voices within. This was his life, successful by any measure – except, damn his morbid thoughts.

Eleni again took up the mandolin and struggled to play simple melodies. Getting to his feet, pushing up his sleeves, slowly Adam began dancing steps of the *Zeybek,* only abruptly to stop. He took the instrument from Eleni's arms, sat down and drew her onto his lap. He *must* talk to her.

Her smile was artless. It told him she knew he'd protect her from things Maria kept talking about, a Maria more worried now that she'd had her second baby girl. Adam forced a smile; he could not tell her.

***

Chapter 18

Smyrna, 1920 - 1921

"December 1920, and Smyrna is a different place," Adam wrote. "I shared everyone's dismay when Rahmi Bey got removed as city governor and got replaced by a fellow called Aristidis Stergiadis. This Stergiadis announced to fanfare, that his first task was to create order out of the chaos. He did, by placating the Turks. He gave them positions of authority and ruled mostly in their favour. No happy ending here.

January 1921: Rumours are flying about the Greek army that's gone deep into Anatolia. We're hearing that our soldiers are being badly beaten by the Turks on the Sakarya River. Jews still in the city are getting ready to leave...

It's spring now, but no caravans have come from Anatolia, so no imports or exports. Everyone is holding their breath. Spiros looks spooked."

The children were in bed. Eleni came to the window where Adam sat reading over an insurance claim, and as she poured him his coffee she complained about the empty fish markets. That her favourite pastry shop was shuttered and Turks stared at her with hard eyes, or even spat as she passed.

"At last you're paying attention,' he said without looking up.

"And why are black frockcoats and gold watch chains suddenly so popular? Why ever is our neighbour wearing pantaloons and Turkish slippers of the older generation?"

"I've tried to explain but you never wanted to hear." Adam sighed, put down his file and fiddled with his pipe as he stared over an empty street to the Bell house. He should tell her bluntly about trade grinding to a standstill. About Greek soldiers, having chased Turks across Anatolia, being driven back by a rising Turkish Army. Local Turks swaggering in city streets. "Eleni," he began, "put your cup down and listen to me."

At that moment Christina gave a piercing cry and flew out the door, Melina chasing her. Eleni laughed and held out her arms to both. "Oh Adam," she said, "these twins are always fighting, but really they love each other," and the next minute she was on the floor playing with them.

Adam, astonished as always by her fast-changing moods, found his moment had gone.

In late April, Eleni gave birth to their sixth child, a tiny baby they named Zoe. In dismay the parents saw she had a deformed right foot – club foot, the doctor said – adding vaguely that something could be done, but perhaps not now.

Adam, home more often because of dwindling trade, talked with neighbours on the Lane family's terrace, sometimes in the Whitall's sunlit garden. News was always the same: a Greek Army burning Turkish homes and villages, killing their inhabitants as it retreated toward the coast. Turks committing the same kind of butchery on all non-Turks as their army chased them. Greeks and remaining Armenians crossed themselves as they discussed the rise of the *Young Turks;* discussed the wisdom of the settlement made at the end of the war with its *megale* idea of a Greek super-state. No one believed it was working out the way patriot Greeks had expected, and not a man among them could possibly guess one of the world's great catastrophes was yet to befall them.

Walking home from the Lane family's mansion this evening under the shadows of Mt. Pagus, Adam longed for his father's advice. In many months he had received only short missives. The last one, Yiannis' words written by the apothecary, had said,

'Sorry that Nikos and Basil can't join you in the city. The roads are dangerous, full of bandits and hostile Turks, so few are travelling. We live quietly and keep to ourselves … I trust you are building up the business and never mind the storms of war. Always there are troubles, but no faction would be so foolish as to interfere with the commerce of Smyrna.'

Outside the gates of his home stood an old woman. With cracked voice she begged for alms. Dropping coins in her hand, Adam walked roughly past her, swearing under his breath, *'Everywhere is a garden of Satan. The devil takes the world to hell!'* At the open door to the parlour he called for Eleni and watched without smiling as she came toward him, a drink tinkling with ice cubes in one hand, a frown between her brows.

"You look worried," he said, thinking with relief that she'd listened, finally, to some of the news and he hadn't been the one to tell her. "What is it? If it's money, I'll tell you that ours is counted as one of the city's well-off families. Our children ..."

"Wear clothes of the finest cloth," Eleni recited dutifully. "Our sons go to the *Evangeliki Scholi*. We have music in the evenings and our neighbours are our friends. Well, I used to think so, but some don't talk to me now."

"Forget the neighbours. It's not safe for the children to go anywhere to play, not even next door."

"But I thought everything was becoming normal. You said there was some trading ..."

"There *is* no trading, nothing on the ships, or the trains. Nothing is normal at all." Irritated now, Adam's voice was loud. "Don't you ladies talk about what's happening? Don't you know that some of the wealthy people from around here got locked up? Enver Pasha – you heard of this fellow? He's hell-bent on making everything Turkish. Greeks have become the enemy. I'm telling you we'll go to church every day and not just on Sundays." *The rose never blooms and the nightingale doesn't sing.* Damn, the words drummed in his head, and he shook it.

"But, this is much to ask. How can I know these things if you don't tell me? How can I dress up the children to go to church so many times?" Eleni's tones became faintly accusing.

"I've tried to tell you, and I'm telling you now. We *will* go to the church!" Adam's voice rose with further roughness. "Get the boy to take down the crucifix by the window. I don't want it seen from the street. The statue of Christ and the Virgin: get it moved too. Have it put it in the bedroom overlooking the well."

Eleni, shocked, watched him walk away.

***

Events changed dramatically during the summer of 1921. Adam heard of the rise of the University of Ionia, of a victorious King Constantine landing in Smyrna. Voices about him were raised in jubilation, but others dissented. He swore as he thought, how stupid can people be!

"A bad thing he jumped in at the last minute to win the election." Spiros' voice cut into his thoughts. He stopped sweeping the warehouse and leaned on his broom. "I bet you the Allies won't be supporting Greece anymore. The damned fellow should have stayed in exile."

By the beginning of 1922, relieved merchants found trade slowly resuming. No one understood exactly why, but all collectively exhaled in relief. In the spring, barges loaded with figs and raisins arrived with the tides, porters busily loading them on steamers bound for Europe. Spring skies dawned in endless succession. Gardens bloomed, and social life picked up. Once more officers gathered in the Levantines' big houses for parties and balls.

Into the midst of these festivities came further rumours of a badly-beaten Greek Army struggling closer to the city and the coast. Well, it's the army, people said, of course it will protect us. And so the people of Smyrna sang and drank and played as they had over the centuries.

Spring passed into summer. Merchants snapped their fingers, laughed and hailed one another as railways carried carpets and cloth from the Anatolian interior. Trading geared up, and so did all the social life. Eleni and her maid took the children into the city for occasional evenings to join Adam, and the family strolled the promenade.

My children: Adam felt joy swell within him as he watched them laughing, clapping, the twins jigging to *Politakia* spilling from the from concert halls. He heard Christina's piercing voice begging to join the walking singers, Nikos saying he wanted to climb the Konak clock tower. Marcos pointed to the blood-red Turkish star and crescent flying. Only Alekos stood silent and aloof.

Just two weeks later, the Giraud family hosted a ball – 'grand enough to end all balls'– people said. On well-worn pavements they strolled, oblivious of the centuries that lay beneath their feet; of a future about to be made.

In the late days of August a splendid sun trekked its arc across the sky. From the east a ragged Greek soldier arrived on foot, then another, and another. People turned away, not wanting to know, but from sun-scorched Anatolia large numbers kept coming. Soldiers badly beaten, injured and starving dragged themselves into the city, wandering skeletons bearing tales of Turkish soldiers desecrating Greek churches, hospitals, schools and homes, of slaughtering Christians up and down the Gallipoli province. Greek soldiers, not admitting their own similar acts as they fled the advancing Turkish army.

People pointed to foreign warships at anchor in the harbour, eleven British, five French, and one Italian, and said, surely our protection? Some stocked supplies, just in case. Old men, who had returned to the quay, once more packed up their cards and moved away, *Hodjas,* their paper and pens.

Adam also put away his pen.

On a dull, rainless day Adam stood motionless in the local square, a lone sentry at the gates of the underworld. Spiros had already gone home. Adam cast quick glances about him, saw a knot of men gathered around a fountain, gesticulating wildly as they talked. *At last they're realizing they're on the brink, at a defining moment in the history of the city,* he thought, *maybe the whole of Asia Minor itself.* Watching rings of smoke from Turkish cigars envelop the huddled figures, he noted the *raki* and *ouzo* consumed. He scrubbed his cigarette butt into the tiles on which he'd been standing and walked quickly toward the train station, and home. Fear made him see lurking figures everywhere.

That night he lay sleepless.

"What is it Papa?" Nikos stood in his pajamas in a sliver of sunlight coming through a dirty kitchen window next morning. "You don't sing or dance anymore."

"And you don't laugh," Alekos' voice was mournful.

"No, Papa." Little Markos jumped in his arms for comfort.

Adam looked about him, thankful that for once Christina's piercing voice was silent. He caught sight of Zoe sucking her thumb. Damn everything to hell! Who is Greek, Turk, Armenian? Will it be my neighbour who will lay me dead, or the mighty hand of Doom for our good fortune? But how we struggled for this fortune! He studied his calloused hands with their chipped nails; walked to the oval mirror between the two bay windows and stared at himself: going on twenty-eight years and already marked by sun, wind, and worry.

In his dreams that night, a mighty fist descended from Heaven, clenched as though to crush the earth: olive trees, mansions, gardens of mimosa, the *bedesten*, ships in the bay. He awoke in a fever but his skin was cold. He and Spiros huddled together at Adam's home, took turns in going into the city to check their warehouse. Its orange paint shrieked in the greyness of closed stalls and sea and sky. The brothers listened to whispered atrocities: Turks creeping into Greek churches and mutilating worshippers, arms slashed and some even cut off. They did not believe it.

This day, under a sullen sky, the brothers sat on upturned crates outside their warehouse in a near-deserted *bedesten*.

"Look, it's all true! First the Greek army, now people are running." Spiros pointed at a ragged line of refugees stumbling down the city's slopes toward the waterfront: Old men and young, women with children trailing them; loaded carts and donkeys.

Adam's eyes followed black smoke drifting across distant valleys. Greeks. Turks. Who is setting the fires?"

"Damnable Christ!" Spiros pulled savagely at his moustache until some of it came out in his fingers.

"*Daxi, daxi.*" Adam drew his brother's hand from his face. "You're looking like a refugee yourself. Come on, we'll go home. Some of the Bournabat families have already moved into their city houses, maybe we ... damn it I don't know ..." His words were smothered as people shouted, "The Greek administration has left Smyrna!"

"Lord have mercy!" Spiros' eyes were wild.

Adam locked their warehouse door and pulled his brother through the crowds, past shops and homes and people packing. Spiros stumbled over a small boy weeping noisily on a doorstep, averted his eyes from a mother struggling with a baby in a burden of blankets.

"Can't do anything for them, come on, *come on.*"

Once home, the two families huddled together in Adam's house.

"Mama, look at all those people." Nikos pointed out the window to the road. Christina and Melina rushed to join him, to stare at the mass of people running on foot alongside donkeys that carried all their household goods: carpets, victrolas, lamp stands and radios, all haphazardly piled on wagons pulled by water buffalo and mules. Christina shrieked.

'Where can we find a boat?' came the swelling cry of people passing. 'How can we get out of here?'

"What about our family in Anatolia?" Adam swore. What will happen if the Turks rise up against them? Images of shadowy mountains and rolling wheat fields blotted out his living room walls, tables and chairs, until Spiros' curses returned him to the present.

"Damn it, how do *I* know about Mama and Papa?" Fear burned in his eyes. "Damn you God! You should look after this family. Don't we go to church every day? Don't we light candles to you?" Sweat had formed on his brow and he covered his face with his roughened hands.

"Are we really in danger?" Eleni's voice quivered. When no one answered she rushed to her bedroom and yanked off her jewelry. Shutting the door against the noise of her quarrelling children, she flung herself on her knees to pray to Saint Sophia.

"I can't think what to do." Spiros walked about cracking his knuckles. "Surely the fighting won't get to the city? You think we should go back, find out what's going on?"

Adam turned from the sight of wretched people still hurrying past his house, some driving their livestock before them. Making a sudden decision, he picked up his jacket.

"You can't leave us here and no one to look after us." Eleni had emerged from her bedroom as Adam was about to walk out the door. "See, the Turk who was our neighbour is now our enemy." She clutched him to her. "You can't leave me alone with the children. If the Turks do come, first they'll have to pass through here."

Adam turned to his diminutive wife as she stood beneath the chandelier.

"Look," he said, "I'm just going to the square, be back in a few minutes." Quickly he walked the wide, tree-lined street, fear making him jump at shadows. It lay empty, silent but for wind blowing through long grass on the roadsides. Windows in many of the great houses were shuttered. He hastened on to Bournabat's main square, to the kiosk at the centre of the five crossroads. All lay eerily empty. Adam, sweating now, sprinted back to his house.

"We should go into the city, see what's happening. You too, Spiros."

"We're all coming." Eleni spoke with finality.

The twins walked arm-in-arm, friends again. Adam carried Markos, Eleni baby Zoe, while Nikos, Alekos, and the maids trailed after them. The family joined others hurrying to the station. They remained silent for the half-hour journey. At its end, Adam pushed past women and children huddled in knots on the waterfront, stepped over bedding and makeshift households camping in the streets. Five-year-old Melina stared at a near-naked boy with his thumb in his mouth, at an old woman collapsed on a pile of sacks. Stumbling over a broken doll's house, she picked up part of its roof and held it tight.

Beneath the Konak clock tower they hung about with merchants and peasants. A bearded man raised himself above the crowds and pushed his way toward the doors of city hall. "See, there's a notice on it," he yelled. "If you all shut up, I'll read it to you." The crowd fell silent, straining to catch sight of the single sheet of white paper pinned to the door. Etched with dried blood, taped only at the top, it flapped in the wind. Alekos cried out when he saw the blood on it; cried at the set of his father's jaw.

"Convert to Islam now, or face severe consequences," Adam read slowly. "Citizens who do not, will die."

"They'll kill us who don't," said an old woman, her voice rising to a screech. "And even if we do."

Adam, catching Eleni in a near-faint, heard Christina's piercing cry, quickly joined by Melina and Markos. "Papa, Papa," became the chorus of his children as their small fists pummeled him.

"Just shut up!" Adam yelled, and each child raised an eye to him in shocked misery. "We'll die before we betray our religion. Turks, Muslims, they can all go to Hell. Christ, you can rot there too if you don't look after our family, and all the Greeks." His face twisted, and fury he did not know he possessed mounted. "We should go home again, pack up and get ready to run."

Spiros agreed, but his usual bluster deserted him, and in a faltering voice he said, "Where will we go? Won't the Greek army defend us?"

But many of the thousands of Greeks pouring into the city included Greek soldiers who, routed by the Turkish army on the *Plateau of Dumplupinar,* knowing they were vastly outnumbered, made no attempt at defending it. Shoving their way through crowds on the waterfront, they prepared to flee in any ship that would take them to Greece. Civilian Greek refugees mingling with other national groups became a swelling flood, people mutilated, ragged, exhausted and hungry; refugees with their starving horses, their rusty carts, kept coming, and coming.

"The Turkish army is headed here," became the rising cry. "They're killing all the Greeks! They're killing us. Where can we go? To the churches, the churches?"

As he grabbed his children, Adam looked out over a mocking blue sky, at a harbour dotted with ships that swung rhythmically at anchor. Merchant vessels filled the long quay alongside barges and wooden caiques. Further out in the bay, Allied war ships – American and British battleships and French destroyers – floated quietly. The sight reassured, but nobody on the quay could know that the nations represented by them were re-thinking their alliances, turning their attention to a rising new Turkish government.

Smyrna was under siege and its people in panic. Shops were shuttered and looting widespread. Adam watched as carts, prams, miserable animals loaded with sacks of flour, sugar, barrels oil, lurched past him. Men swore as they buckled under the weight of their loot. Any life still lurking about the markets included scavenging dogs, urchin boys, and bemused old men. A fat porter shouldered a bulging sack and swore profusely. Wealthy people trekked past him and headed to their private boats.

"Adam, take us away from here." Eleni had become once more the dependent wife and tears ran down her cheeks. Maria stood silently beside her husband tightly clasping each of her daughters' hands.

The brothers looked at each other. "I ... think we should get back to Bournabat and start packing." Adam's voice cracked as he spoke.

The suburban boulevards lay empty, most of its houses shuttered. The families' footsteps echoed eerily on the cobblestones as they headed home.

That night, Adam finally fell asleep, only to dream he was wandering the glittering, mercantile city known for its tolerance, for its pier that had borne witness to wealth and fortunes made, to pilgrims visiting one of the seven Biblical Churches of Asia. Walking slowly, he passed stucco-walled, orange-tiled homes with profusions of flowering balconies or high-armoured walls. From the city's upper slopes he gazed over the roofs of mansions, church spires, mosques and domes. Heading for the Armenian quarter, he passed bakery and pastry shops; passed turbaned men smoking hookah.

It was when he saw a figure crouching on a stone bench, red fez on his head, a wooden cross around his neck, his dreams turned to nightmares. With terrible premonition he saw the city about to suffer one of the largest and ugliest conflagrations in history, to be stained with the blood and body parts of thousands of citizens. At the water's edge he sensed the rumbling of an earth about to convulse; that it had already begun. Saw chaos erupting on the pier, streets running red with the blood of citizens. He couldn't bear to look ... couldn't look.

"Adam!" Eleni leaned over him where he'd fallen and begun vomiting. When finally he sat up, it was to weep and weep.

At daybreak, exhausted, drained, he slipped over to Spiros' home. "Nightmares," he explained, his voice despairing. "I saw terrible things. No point taking the family into the city, but one of us should go back, find out if my nightmares were real. You stay here."

Saturday, September 9th. Adam travelled an empty train and once in the city, wandered Smyrna's littered streets and alleys. A mass of frightened people streamed up Consulate Street hoping to find sanctuary in the American Embassy. He glimpsed dust in the distance, heard a shrill cry: "The Turks are coming! The Turkish army is here!" In the near-empty space between the American consulate and the quay he stared, seeing nothing at first but a blurred line moving, a black mass. Closer they came, and closer, until an army of mounted soldiers was clearly visible. They clattered along the quay, each one holding a long, curved sword. Citizens froze at the sight of their black-clad figures, only a red star and crescent on their fezzes to relieve it.

"Fear not, fear not!" The soldier who cried out the words raised a hand. Adam, his feet fixed to the pavement, watched as the cavalry headed in orderly procession toward the governor's palace in Konak. He let out a breath. House shutters were raised and a strange silence descended. At that moment, into his jumbled thoughts came memories of the happy mingling of Christians and Muslims on the Anatolian Plateau, of Turks, Greeks, Armenians and Jews peacefully coexisting as they had over the centuries. With vague hope in his heart, he retraced his steps to the train station, and home.

Chapter 19

Smyrna, September, 1922

The heat was merciless. The whole of the city was turned like the palm of a hand against the sun, squinting through its fingers at the sky.'

Adam recognized Spiros' hunted look when he appeared in the doorway pushing hair from his eyes. "Well? You found something to laugh about?"

"Just that the Turkish Army came in quietly." Adam grinned. "Nothing's going to happen." He slapped his brother's back, tap-danced in a circle as his wife, and sister-in-law Maria, emerged from the bedrooms. "My poor *Eleniksa*, everything's going to be all right after all."

Maria laughed. The children raised their hands, the noise of their clapping dying away as the front door banged and a neighbour's son ran in. "There's shooting on the waterfront," he cried. "My family is leaving, right now. My dad said to tell you to find a boat and get out of Smyrna, fast as you can." He ran out again.

Into the silence came Eleni's accusation, "Adam, you said everything would be all right, I think maybe you don't know anything." And she began giving orders. "You two, your membership papers in the Defense League, you better go get them or the Turks will charge you with treason."

The two families filled bags and boxes and stuffed them with what they considered most precious: small Turkish rugs, silk robes, a print of the Virgin, food, blankets, a crucifix, worry beads. Into the linings of her own and her daughters' clothes roughly Eleni stitched the gold pieces Adam had saved, her jewelry, the *Bacarro* brooch too. They rode into the city with the few Levantine women and their servants who, until now, had remained in the suburbs.

"Our men are driving the motor cars," one woman explained. Lowering her voice, she added, "Did you hear about Archbishop Chrysostom? He got lured from the Cathedral of *Photeini* by Turkish soldiers. They took him. They cut him up and killed him in front of everyone." Tears spilled from her eyes. "Our great archbishop and such a beautiful man, he only wanted to look after his flock."

Another woman said he had been offered protection in the American Embassy but had refused. If his people were going to suffer, he said, he would suffer with them.

"My husband came home one night," another offered. "He said about people fleeing to their church to find sanctuary. When they got inside they were all shot dead. Then the Turks locked the doors with the people still inside and set fire to the church."

"Stop it!" The words burst from Eleni who turned away, a hard expression on her face. Low moans rose among the travellers. A young woman fainted.

On the quayside the families were crushed among many thousands, all in panic. Adam, his nightmares now realized, could not turn himself away from the sight of corpses and soldiers kicking them; at the twisted body of a young woman, her skirt shorn off. At dead dogs and cats. His eyes riveted on the scattered remnants of peoples' lives: a clock, a broken doll, a brown shoe. He blocked his nose against the stench of rotting fish, vomit and human excrement; his ears against yelping dogs, children screaming; the laments of old men.

"*Gomoto!*" Spiros' voice rose above the noise. "Our membership papers in the League," and shoving through the crowds, he headed for the *Ethniki Ameni* offices. Vaguely he registered an absence of church bells; glimpsed irregular soldiers moving from house to house and from shop to shop, looting. He darted along the quay, past the clock tower, and on to the Defense League: more young soldiers with guns, and he flattened himself behind a cluster of bushes. Someone moved in the undergrowth beside him. He jumped, and stared into the frenzied face of Aristotle Onassis.

"Our *Ethniki Ameni* membership papers ..." Spiros' voice came out as a wheeze.

Aristotle's smile was bleak as he held up sheaf. "Got mine. Get yours and burn them. They're calling my father a traitor and will throw him in jail – if they don't kill him. *Get down*!" When the soldiers had passed, he said, "Grab your papers and get out of here."

Suddenly a shot rang out and the Defense League offices burst into flames. Ha! No building, no papers. Spiros ran back the way he'd come yelling, "*You damnable Christ! Get off your ass and do something. The Turks think they own the city and all the land but Greeks have been here all the centuries so it's our place too.*" Anger turned to pleading: "*Why can't we all live together like we always did? Get us out of here you can sit at our table, get drunk with us; dance with us.*"

But God was not listening. As green swells of the sea washed over the railway lines running from the pier, under a sky that was a sullen sheet of grey, the Turkish army began roping off all non-Turks. Orange tongues of flame, begun on the city's upper slopes, rose up against the sky. Spiros turned his eyes from it, to see a small, bare-foot boy darting from under the rope and run shrieking toward an alley. A boy soldier lifted his rifle and shot him dead. A shocked hush fell upon the crowd. Then, knowing they were damned, raised their voices as one curdling shriek.

"By God and all the Saints." Spiros' dropped his head into his hands in despair.

"Socrates was thrown in jail in the Turkish quarter." Adam's pale face was inches from his brother's. "A traitor, they said, because he was treasurer of the *Ethniki Ameni.*"

Jesus Mother of Mary, we're all traitors to the Turks. What if we can't get onto the ships? As though in answer, more gunshots were heard. On the slopes above the waterfront, Turkish soldiers strode the streets and alleyways, throwing the occupants out of their homes and shops, afterward, planting the blood-red Turkish flag with its star and crescent on each. Flames shot up behind them. Frenzied crowds pushed further onto lower streets, all heading for an already overcrowded quay.

Adam, recalling his nightmares, knew then that the earth, the city as its people knew it, was about to convulse in cataclysmic passion; that it had already begun.

Eleni, layers of cloaks covering her dress, shrieked when forced apart from Adam. A volcanic fury rose up in him as a thin soldier with menacing eyes shoved him into a roped-off area on the far side of the pier. "God strike you dead, and all your children." It was language only Spiros normally used.

Spiros had beads of sweat running down his unshaven cheeks. He spat. A savage growl gurgled in his throat and he roared as Maria and his two children were shoved together with Eleni. White-faced Alekos, almost seven years old, hid in his mother's skirts. Eleni, clutching baby Zoe, looked at her last-born child and a tiny smile stretched her bloodless lips. Five-year-old Melina thrust plump arms around her mother's legs. She stuck out her tongue at a passing soldier, and he stopped. In a harsh voice he said, "I'd keep that one out of sight if I were you." Melina's eyes were huge and wild. Her springing hair stood straight up in fat spirals from her head and the muscles of her face were twisted in ugly contortion – a Medusa indeed.

Soldiers, attempting some sort of order at the foot of the pier, separated men from the women and children into two long lines and roped them off at each side. The rough line of men fought to climb aboard waiting refugee ships that would take them to Greece, a country about which they knew nothing. They huddled, burdened with all the worldly goods they could carry, while women screamed across to them; children wailed.

Fires burned ever closer to the city's flat land as four barricades were erected and the formal searches began. Eleni shuddered, knowing what she had sewn into her own and her daughters' voluminous clothes. Heaven and the Virgin Mary help her if the soldiers found it.

"Adam. Adam!" She screamed across to him. Nikos, seeing his father at the far side of the pier, ducked from his mother's skirts, pushed through the soldiers and flitted under the belly of a run-away mule to get to him. Eleni screamed until a short soldier-boy cursed her.

"Keep your damned children with you."

Nikos would not be stopped. Marco, yet a toddler, trundled after him, then Christina, her high-pitched cry heard briefly above the din. Soldiers swore and shoved roughly against the line of women, bayonets pointed.

"Keep control over your children or you won't have any." A soldier thrust his face close to Eleni's.

Grey-black clouds scudded to blend with the sullen line of the sea. Earth and hell were one. The smell of blood thickened the air even as

Christian prayers rose upon it, prayers to the archangel Michael to send fire and brimstone to crush the enemy. On Frank Street, a wealthy pasha with a gold-tasselled fez raised his fist to a bearded Christian. A diabolical gleam entered his eyes as his knuckle struck. Near the shore, a hoary Greek lifted his face to the heavens and screamed: "You damnable God, go to the devil and take all the bloody Turks with you! You, laughing up your sleeve at us, old bastard? Maybe you sleep while we die, get off your backside and do something!"

But God continued to sleep. Swinging gently at anchor in Smyrna's bay were the Allied warships of Britain, France, Italy and the U.S., their ships' masters turning up the volume of their music to drown out the screaming that began every midnight. Themes from Humoresque, from Pagliacci by Caruso, rose in the air as Turkish soldiers raped, pillaged, and tortured those on the docks.

Many, in desperation, plunged into the sea, thinking it a better choice to drown than to perish from flame or bayonet. Some swam up to the Allied ships, confident they would be picked up. They were not. As they tried to climb up the sides, each was roughly thrust back into the seas. A boy not much bigger than Alekos grabbed a rope hanging over the side of the *Iron Duke*, a British Royal Naval ship, and tried to hoist himself up. An officer raised his boot and shoved him back into the sea.

Belatedly, in some small attempt to stem the carnage on shore, officers swept their searchlights on the docks every midnight.

Viciously people fought for places any ship that would take them to safety. Searches continued on the gangways. Turks yanked Eleni's gold ear-rings from her, and rings from her fingers. Near fainting, baby Zoe strapped to her back, she received a perfunctory search before being pushed onto a refugee ship already overcrowded with women and children. She shoved against the tide, to throw her upper body precipitously over the rail, to catch a glimpse of Adam and her other children screaming, screaming, until women grabbed her and told her to shut up. Shoved to the floor by a soldier she sat rocking her body, Zoe crushed somewhere beside her. Hugging the dirty floor she muttered to Saint Sophia to save her from tyrants and infidels.

"Don't waste your time," said a thin young woman. "The saints won't bother themselves, and God won't either. Get up and help yourself, there's my advice."

"No God, no devil." An old woman gave a maniacal laugh as she tossed a crucifix overboard. Eleni remained crouched on the floor of the refugee ship weeping tears of bitterest sorrow.

"The men, they're not letting them board!" At this shout, women's heads turned to the far end of the pier where men had been roped off. They watched as many were pushed away from the ships, away from the pier and back onto the quay. "Dear God, what are they doing with our men?"

As the ship steamed from the harbour, the sky was seen as a savage orange, the sea a copper cauldron. In the glow of a dying city, two thousand and more refugees remained jammed on the city's waterfront, huddling against the leaping flames. To escape, many threw themselves into the sea.

The ship carrying Eleni plied the Aegean Sea with its wretched human cargo. Melina shouted for her father and Eleni told her, told herself, that Adam had sailed in a different ship with the other children – Nikos, Christina and Markos.

***

The vessel with its destitute human cargo sailed to the northern part of Greece at Alexandropoulos where the refugees dispersed, some to the northern cities of Kavalla and Thessaloniki. Others went to Athens, some southwest to the Ipeiros region, and to Agrinion. Camping in the open, or in make-shift shacks, they were ignored by the locals or treated with contempt as not real Greeks. Eleni found herself caught up with several families pushing south and west, to trek across endless mountains, endless wastes, to the Gulf of Corinth, across it, and into the city of Patras in the Peloponnese. At the time, it was a poor part of Greece, a backwater.

***

Chapter 20

Toronto

Georgia

I finish this part of the gruesome story near seven in the morning; a thick headache thrumming over my face and the back of my head. Bile rises in my throat and I might even be sick. I'm not just telling a story, I think, this was real, it's history. It's what happened to people like my great grandparents Adam and Eleni, my uncle Spiros. I wander into the kitchen. Ugh, dirty ashtrays – my father's – but also butts with bright lipstick; remnants of chicken wings on dirty plates. Amalia must have been here and I hadn't heard her.

Okay. Get dressed. Take some Tylenol. Make coffee. Be at Book City by ten. But none of my busy-ness chases away the horrors of what I've been reading. I have to get out. In track pants and sweater, I step into a cool April morning and walk the short path to the street. Leaning on the gate I watch well-dressed people striding to work: mothers walking with school-age children. A teenager scuffing his shoes as he heads to school. Well-dressed people smiling, chatting, secure in their comfortable lives. I saunter a short way along the sidewalk looking for affirmation of ordinary life when my eyes fasten on dead heads of red roses from the summer before. I look, and they become splotches of blood, pooling, dripping. I suck in my breath. It's not fresh spring air I smell but human sewage and excrement. I look up at the trees for distraction, at the sun touching them, but instead see the masts of Allied ships swaying in Smyrna's harbour to mock the horror on the shore. I close my eyes. People brush past me, people who will never know about brutality and torture and death. Still feeling ill, I return to the house, to Helena in the kitchen reading a Greek newspaper and sipping the coffee I made.

"Georgie," she exclaims. "You look like you stayed out all night, but weren't you in your room? Are you ill?"

"You're not looking so good yourself." I note the dark circles under her eyes and realize she's still fragile, still not recovered properly from whatever happened to her in Patras. "Amalia was here last night, wasn't she? What does she want now, more money?"

"All the time she says I owe her because of her upbringing."

"Jesus mother of Mary isn't it time for her to ..." I stop, since there's nothing I can say I've not already said and Helena has that look in her eyes. I head toward my room, but she follows me in.

"I hear you click clicking in the night. You still writing some old story?"

Old story? It feels like it's just happened. Everything washes over me again: my great grandma Eleni's horrified face; a child's, my grandma Melina. With my head still throbbing, I flop on my bed.

"It's making you sick what you're doing. Just look at you. Look at your room."

My eyes follow hers, over ragged teddy bears, stacked dictionaries and notebooks, over pink and orange cushions jumbled with clothes lying all over.

"Well, if you don't want to see it, you can always shut my door."

She makes a face, walks over to my makeshift desk, and picking up a folder, waves it in the air. "Writing, what kind of life is this? You with all the book-learning, you should find a proper job."

Silence laps from the walls as we stare away from each other. I feel exhausted, drained. We've been down this road before.

"Mom." In sudden decision I jump off the bed, take the folder out of her hands and lock my eyes on her.

"Look, there's something I should tell you: I'm not writing little stories, I'm ... writing our family history, all of it. I've talked to *Yia Yia,* Uncle Spiros, Aunt Thalia ... and I've researched where they lived, so there."

She stands perfectly still, a mannequin frozen in place, and I wait. Then comes her familiar mantra: "Why can't you be more like Amalia? Get some friends, get proper ambition?" In agitation again she picks up papers on my desk.

"Please don't touch those! We're not talking about my sister. Listen: this is ambition, a big one. And … maybe you don't realize, but family memoirs have become the latest craze – didn't I hear you once say that people should know their stories? They should know where they come from? Mom, I'm writing our story. I'd really like it if you'd tell me what you know."

"Forget about the people already dead." She's doing a kind of dance about the room now, still moving my things about. "Just tell me why anyone would want to know how poor and miserable we were."

Impasse. I sit back on the edge of my bed, my emotions in turmoil. When I get to the part about her, I'll need her to talk to me because I can imagine only so much. Outside the window I catch a sliver of sunlight angling through thick clouds and lighting on me. Something slides through me then, through my messy room, through our small bungalow filled up with anger and betrayal and unhappiness. That sliver of light shines and expands, urging me to write our family story to its very end, and at once, almost as though my life will change once I do - a weird thought.

I try again, and in a gentle voice, say, "I heard you talk about a promise, how it's for you to redeem the family name. That means once it was – different? Better? Isn't that what your grandfather Adam and great uncle Spiros said?" I look at her hopefully, recalling what I once heard, that at some point most people have a need to confess, to tell someone about a life-altering event. Poor Helena is still carrying around an edge of sorrow, not sharp like before, but insistent. Still she wears black. One day she'll talk about it, but who to? Dad doesn't count. Amalia's not the one; Helena might praise her, and she might bask in it, but there's little mutual satisfaction. Me? But we're still antagonistic much of the time. My chaotic thoughts tumble over and over, until suddenly I make another decision.

"Mom," My voice falls casually into the silence that has enveloped us, "I'll help you more in the salon, but I'll keep writing our family story too. You can tell me things, but only if you want to, and I'll show it all to you. When I'm finished I promise I'll look for a good job or go back to school. Okay?"

Her expressions change as fast as clouds re-shape themselves. In agitation she keeps rearranging my things, then finally, without looking at me, says, "Come to me at the salon today and I'll make you a nice hair style."

"Oh! Well, I've got a split shift, but could drop in around two."

Neither of us looks at the other. She gets ready for work, and I try for half an hour's sleep. No luck.

Somehow I get through the morning, leave my boss muttering and head for the subway. From Bloor Street I walk to the salon. Helena is doing highlights near the washbasins while singing along with Grigoris Bithikotsis, one of Greece's great voices. Coming back to life at last, I think with relief. But as soon as the music stops the familiar hollow look settles back on her face.

I look down the length of the salon. A woman with bits of foil in her hair lights a cigarette. Helena says, "Please go smoke outside." New hairstylist Bonnie flits back and forth between two clients, her skimpy clothes bursting with the bulk stuffed into them. Little Isabel hums as she polishes nails. Helena's friend Leon is sitting in the shadows at the back. Whatever does he come for? If only Yiannis, Adam and Spiros could see their descendent now, what would they think? And Eleni? It's not exactly a Vidal Sassoon, a Jie Matar or Civello, and certainly not up there with all those swanky places in Yorkville, but it's special, unique even. In this narrow salon on ragged Yonge Street, Helena weaves magic; she's built a community that brings joy into other peoples' lives.

"I've heard of this place so I've come to see it for myself."

Catching the cracked tones of a very old woman, Helena wipes her hands and walks to the door to embrace the stooped old body. "Where do you come from? How do you hear of me?" She leads her new client to a vacant chair. All eyes turn to the newcomer.

"Surely everyone has heard of you." Ms Audrey looks around, her small eyes twinkling. She catches sight of Lady Godiva flying on horseback through forests of purple grapes and covers her mouth in a gasp. She says she's walked from Belmont House north on Yonge Street, hobbled to the place where a crazy Greek woman sings as she does her client's hair. "I've heard how you line up your customers and teach them to dance - I've come for the dancing lessons." A mischievous gleam lights up her old eyes and she raises the hem of her skirt.

"Dancing lessons? For you, the classes are free."

Caught up in the moment, I say, "I should join the class too." Helena gives me a face, like, maybe if you lost some weight. Ms Audrey must be ninety at least. Her bird-like legs stick out from under her skirt and I think how far they've carried her. What impulse to the future, what charm of the unknown, had beckoned that she'd pushed her bent frame this distance? Perhaps past passions provoked by spring's seductive perfumes, the promise of new life. Perhaps the recognition that her life is not yet finished. Go for it, old girl, silently I encourage her. Grab it, drink of it deeply while you still can. I move to sit beside Leon, but his cell phone rings and with a smile of apology, he rises and slips out. I remain, swinging my legs and thinking deeply on life and love and historical accident.

I'm about to head out for coffee and donuts when Helena whispers, "Don't go, see who's just come in." Helena's long-time customer Christine flounces through the door, accidentally knocking over a vase of green flowers that Leon always keeps filled. She flops into a spare chair and dumps her many Holt Renfrew shopping bags at her feet, fans herself and turns to the mirror. A blowsy recent convert to the world of the blond, she's all jingling curls and look-at-me earrings. She wears boots, even in summer.

"Oh dear, how clumsy of me." She makes no attempt to clean up the mess of the spilled flowers but examines herself in a mirror. A smile of satisfaction crinkles her fifty-year-old face. Only then does she look around.

"Do you have an appointment?" Mom calls out from the back.

"No, maybe a comb-out … and to get the local news."

For the gossip, I think.

Christine runs blue-lined eyes about the salon, then announces she's having an affair.

The instant tell-all woman, I think. "So, does your husband know or suspect?" I ask. "What did he think when you suddenly became a bombshell blond?"

"Mid-life crisis," Christina answers. "He thinks I should find something to do. But with a lover, who has the time?"

"How often do you ...?"

"See him? All the time...um...in my imagination." Christine lowers her voice, but obviously intends everyone to hear. "When my husband has sex with me, it's this man, if you know what I mean. When I buy clothes I think about what he'd like me to wear." A long sigh emits from the blood-red mouth. "I know: you'll tell me I can't go out with him in public or have him whenever I want, but where's the passion if there aren't any obstacles?" She shakes her blond head and sets her earrings jangling.

Does she wear those same outfits in her perfectly landscaped Willowdale - or is it ritzy Lawrence Park? My mind is a jumble of thoughts. She probably goes home to her scrubbed and ordered life and entertains her well-heeled friends with titillating tales of the odd and colourful people from downtown. Believes her patronage of the salon on seedy Yonge Street as a form of philanthropy.

After she's gone, I say to Helena, "I bet she thinks of herself as bold and adventurous when she leaves her safe little world for the city's main drag. The woman's a parasite. I mean, just try and imagine her getting down to the nitty gritty of owning a business like you."

"Georgie, you talking like this and you the one always feeling sorry for people?" But Helena looks pleased. "You going to write about her?"

"Certainly not." I flop in a chair, and catching my reflected image, close my eyes.

"You think too much." Helena comes up behind me and touches my hair. "These women, they got nothing else to do. Me too, I want a big house and beautiful clothes and pretty things ... and many men wanting me."

After she says this her blank expression returns. But I know she wasn't joking when she said what she did: she's a sensual woman, anyone can see. Too bad she didn't pass it on to me. When I think this, something cold and damp settles over me: I've got no love life, no one at all. And who would want me? Well, there's Jeff.

"He's a nice boy and he likes you," Helena says, "what's the matter with him?"

He's good-looking and all that, I think, but insecure and doesn't want any competition. He can have anyone he wants so goes for what he can't, something like that.

I walk out the door then, all the way up Yonge Street to St Clair, hang around in a coffee shop until my second shift starts at Book City.

My boss is sorting a stack of paperback books and mutters when he sees me.

"Let me do that." My voice sounds tired." These ones to go in the bin outside?"

"Yep, thanks." He disappears into the gloom of the shop.

My mind is not on my work that early evening but returns to themes of great love. I think of all the lovelorn figures in literature and history, the fabulous tales and fantasies woven about thwarted love. Mount Vesuvius: He fell in love with a nymph as lovely as a diamond and could think of nothing else. He lunged at her, but feeling scorched by his attentions she jumped into the ocean and became the Island of Capri. Vesuvius's sighs of fire spread until he became mountain, forever beyond the reach of his beloved.

Well, I'm unlikely to be the heroine of grand passion, and again feel envious of my mother, my sister; feel empty and passed over. My only pleasure is when I'm writing what I call *The Odyssey*.

"You're living in that world," Helena keeps saying, "but it's not your life."

But in some crazy way, it is. I feel compelled to keep writing it because of a belief that something will change, I'll somehow be different. But right now I've abandoned what's left of the family on a ship sailing from Smyrna's smoking docks.

I must get back to them.

***

Helena: An Odyssey

Part Two

Chapter 21

Patras, 1924/25

In 1922, a revolution in the Ottoman Empire resulted in the birth of modern-day Turkey. Under the Treaty of Lausanne, Greece was required to return all of the territories gained at the end of World War 1, forcing 1,250,000 Greeks from Turkey into Greece, and 400,000 Turks in Greece, into Turkey.

From Smyrna's smoking docks, Greco-Turkish refugees were ferried to Thessaloniki and Macedonian border areas. Some remained on the Island of Rhodes, while a few families trudged south across the Gulf of Corinth, and into the Peloponnese, included among them the remnants of Adam's family. The cruel journey took them across jagged mountains, across a scorched and pitiless landscape.

***

"Mama, where is our Papa? - and Christina and Nikos...?"

"Hush! Don't talk, don't talk." Wildly, Eleni looked about her as she walked, Zoe tucked under one arm. Melina's piping voice would not be stilled until a scowling Alekos told her to be quiet.

"Mama is sad because Papa and the others got left behind," he said with all the authority his eight-year-old voice could muster. "They'll find us, of course they will." The boy's anxious eyes continued to sweep the ragged lines of refugees as they dragged themselves across an unwelcoming countryside. Not finding a single familiar face, he turned his own thin white one earthward and dragged his feet.

"Mama, everything will be all right." Melina's silvery voice piped up again. "Papa will find us and we can tell him about our adventure."

A growl slid up Eleni's throat. "Stop talking!"

Frightened, hungry and sore, the children stumbled after their mother over days that turned into weeks, arriving eventually in the ancient port city of Patras, a city that gathered itself on and about the foot of a mountain, to stare over the Ionian Sea. In an old industrial area on its periphery, Greek government workers were still throwing together makeshift huts as refugees arrived. Regardless of their previous occupation in Smyrna, they were expected to farm this derelict land, some to be employed in local paper factories.

"Mama, this is not a house. It's only one room ..."

"It's got a dirt floor." Eleni's two older children stared at the rude shack assigned them, one in a line of other similar dwellings standing forlornly against railway tracks that followed the shores of the Ionian Sea.

"No kitchen?" Alekos said in horror.

"Where's the bathroom? This place stinks." Melina set up a high-pitched wail. "Do we have to sleep on the dirt? What will we eat – where's Christina?"

Eleni put Zoe down and stared at the rough-hewn walls and crude benches, then leaning up against the doorjamb, closed her eyes to her children's strained little faces. She willed herself back into her house in Smyrna, for Adam to come. He came, his sun-washed eyes smiling into hers. On his lips she heard a love song, the murmur of servants. As abruptly as they'd come, the voices and images vanished and Eleni stared stupidly at her new home. There she remained transfixed in shock and horror until herded with other refugees into lines for food and bedding distributed by government workers.

That night Eleni slept on blankets in the middle of the dirt floor, her children rolled up in blankets beside her. "Adam! Adam!" The silence of each night was pierced by her cries. Exhausted after poor sleep she got up, and dragging the children with her, trudged to the shores to watch for ships coming in. In a frayed, dirty dress and pearl-studded jacket, she wandered the strange city, her children tagging after her. Fitfully she pulled at her hair until tufts of it fell out, lifted her face to the heavens and cried out, "Adam," don't leave me here." Her voice, having risen to a shriek, subsided into suffocating sighs. The children, in awed silence, stared up at her.

Adam's absence continued to come as a new shock, and more than a year passed before Eleni accepted he was probably dead.

"Not dead," her widowed neighbour Lina said with a patient expression. "Gone to some better place, is all. In the night I hear you shouting for your Adam, and see how you search everywhere for him in the day. You should look after the children you got and your Adam will thank you for it."

Eleni looked at the older woman with swollen eyes. "I do look after my children, and my husband *will* come to me, you'll see." With terrible bitterness she saw she'd come full circle, back to her beginnings: a shack with dirt floor; squatting, knees to chin, over an open toilet. No running water. No cooking facilities but for the public ovens − the *fourno*. In half-dazed state she wandered randomly, seeing nothing of the city into which she'd been thrust: its Roman ruins, the magnificent Venetian homes on its upper slopes, spires of churches and the soaring dome of St. Andrew's cathedral.

"God is watching what you do. And your poor husband too. He trusts you to properly look after his children." Lina repeated this a week later as she pointed to a thumb-sucking Zoe sitting on the doorstep under a hot sun.

As though she'd not heard, Eleni remained in the doorway of her shack, a small woman wearing a dirty white dress, light brown hair in an untidy stream down her back. Motionless she stared over the railway tracks to a desolate beach, green with seaweed, white with the droppings of gulls, and beyond to the grey-green swells of the sea. Every bone in her body ached for what she had lost. With the immensity of it, she swayed from one door-post to the other; abruptly sat down on a packing box, head in hands on a headlong flight into her past. Eventually she gave up wearing white dresses and cloaked herself in black.

"You should look after your children properly," Lina repeated at intervals.

***

Georgia

You should look after your children: Something goes pop in my brain and I'm a child again, curled up on the end of my mother's bed, rocking, crying, hungry – always hungry. Another memory brushes me: I'm a toddler pulled roughly out of bed, clothes yanked over my head, thrust onto a chair near a fire escape and a bowl of something put in my lap.

"Stop crying. Hurry up. Eat. Don't wriggle when I put on your shoes. Hurry, hurry ..." Into rain and sleet and snow my mother Helena dragged Amalia and me around the corner to a bus stop. Rain, dirty bus shelters. Thick commuter crowds squeezing and pushing me. Someday maybe, she'll explain how all this happened. Right now I wave a hand in the air as though to wipe away the bad memories.

***

Chapter 22

Patras, 1926 - 1934

Eleni, helpless, had no idea how to get help from the Greek Government. Nor did she know how to sell her gold for Greek money. Obsessively she opened her bags, laid out the items she'd carried from Smyrna: clothes and blankets. Worry beads, a Greek dictionary, Turkish carpet, embroidered slippers and toys. She held them, fingered them, and pushed them away. Leaving Lina to watch the children, she wandered past the grey walls of tenements housing factory workers, past buildings that produced toilet and wallpaper. In broken shoes she stumbled along the railway tracks, past oil presses, forges, and the workshops of joiners and potters. She watched factory workers come and go, walked to the bleached white government buildings at the city centre seeing Adam everywhere, and nowhere. She kept the rough-hewn door of her home ajar for one day her missing family would surely come walking through.

No one came. The mean little street perpendicular to the railway tracks scuffled with the noise of hammering and digging, the whistle of engines, and swish of water from the public tap. Laments from bereaved women rose upon the air but the children were strangely silent, banished to the *Church of the Apostles* that stood between the railway tracks and the *Highway to Athens*. There they remained under the watchful eye of stout Father Meneghini.

Nine months passed. Eleni returned from the communal ovens where she'd been cooking rice and beans. She ladled it into four bowls and called to the children. Melina, drawing pictures in the dust with a stick, ran inside as rain threatened. Alekos removed himself from under a mulberry tree.

Eleni, picking up Zoe from the dust, paused to watch a storm gathering over the sea. Dogs barked and gulls wheeled noisily.

"Mama," Melina called from the window," who's that man coming?"

The family crowded the door to watch an odd-looking stranger struggle with a large sack. He stopped to ask a question and a young woman pointed to Eleni's door. Eleni stared dumbly as he collapsed onto a wooden crate inside her door and dropped the sack beside him, an apparition all jutting bones and socked-in cheeks, knuckles on his big hands like shiny marbles. Recovering from a coughing spasm, he raised eyes that were dull with suffering.

"Spiros!" Eleni's voice came as a shriek. "Where's my Adam, my other children?"

Spiros saw not the slight child-woman of yesterday, but one who had dropped abruptly into middle-aged resignation, hair disheveled, flesh already spreading. Vaguely he noted her shabby dress and dark cloak.

"Mama, who's the strange man?"

Spiros looked at yesterday's spoiled children from the golden streets of Smyrna, hair tangled and faces smudged. Tears ran down his cheeks as he swooped to pick up Zoe in his arms. "Saints in heaven woman, get me some food," he said, and after devouring mouthfuls of coarse bread, he added with sudden coldness, "So you're blaming me because I'm not Adam? That I don't pull your other children from my pocket?"

Eleni rocked on her feet, her face twisting.

"Here, you better have some of this." Spiros pulled a small bottle of brandy from his coat pocket. When the children had fallen asleep in rugs on the floor he emptied his sack: linen cloths, small Turk and Persian rugs, prints of the Anatolian landscape. He smiled then, a brief flash of sunlight in the gloom. "Here, something to cheer you," he said, and thrust one of Adam's jackets at her.

"*Oh!*" Eleni almost choked on her brandy. About to ask her burning question – what happened to the men – she saw that her brother-in-law had already fallen, twitching, into profound sleep, his head against the wall.

Awaking in the early morning, disoriented, Spiros sat on Eleni's doorstep watching rain puddles forming on the unpaved street. Eleni came up behind him and whispered urgently, "You must know about Adam, about what happened to the men."

Spiros' face closed. It remained blank until Eleni murmured, "I think nobody's there. Maybe after all, you're dead too."

Spiros got up and stepped out the door to wander X Street from its weedy eastern end to the west where it met railway lines and the *Highway to Athens*. Seating himself on a tree stump in a laneway he listened to the noise of wind and sea; watched women trudge to communal ovens, fill water jugs from the public tap. He heard their muttered laments, the unnatural quiet of the children, and thought if he put out a hand he would feel the despair that hung in the air. In the churchyard gateway stood Father Meneghini with bowed head, his soutane blowing in the wind from the sea. *I've come full circle, he thought, back to poverty, to being nobody.* Images came to him then of his boyhood in Anatolia, the back-breaking work, aching muscles and cold and wind and snow. Poverty in the early days in Smyrna.

At night he slept on the floor of Eleni's shack and dreamed he heard his father's voice, glimpsed the wrinkled face turned to him with an expression of sudden hope. Spiros had seen that look the day Adam announced he was getting married. He remembered how it had vanished as quickly as it had come, and old jealousy stirred, followed by aching loss. *Damn you Adam, where the hell are you?* Awake, Spiros felt half of himself missing, the space his brother occupied against which he'd always pushed, empty, and guilt washed over him that he'd been the one to survive. Another thought untangled itself: he would have to *be* Adam, as well as himself; earn money fast and build it up for the sake of family reputation, for Adam's children.

Energized by these resolutions he entered Mr. Stavros' rough, lean-to pub near the railway lines, hoping to find solidarity among fellow refugees, help in finding a job, even to establishing a business.

"I'm Spiros Kouvalis, successful merchant from Smyrna." His voice bounced into the smoke-filled room. Into a sudden silence came grunts, a voice saying, "Successful, weren't we all? Turkish sperm, that's us. People spit and tell us we're not real Greeks. Go find a job – if you can. Forget the merchant stuff."

But Spiros, oddly excited, knocked on local factory doors. He was turned away. Walking until he reached the city centre he approached merchants, retailers, owners of brickyards and cement factories. He'd do any job, start this minute. "I know merchandize," he insisted. "I can sell anything. You want a driver, a trucker? I do dirty jobs, any jobs."

"Too many real Greeks looking for work." With this he was dismissed. Undaunted, he went door-to-door along the streets of Patras, climbed the steps to the upper city and begged home owners, "I can clean, fix things, do anything – you try me."

He was told there was nothing. Some swore as they turned from him. Tormented by a sense of time passing, that his father was watching, he walked the long distance back to Eleni's shack. Nine-year-old Alekos sat hunched on the floor with a book loaned him from the priest. Melina, squatting in the dirt outside, called to him, "Uncle Spiros, I made a picture of you." In the dust with the point of a stick she'd drawn a thin face with slant eyes, hair scattered over a wide forehead, the mouth below a ragged moustache turned down sharply at the corners.

Spiros forced his mouth upward and patted her shoulder. Pulling the bottle of brandy from his coat pocket he poured two cups. "Talk to me," he said to a morose Eleni. But she remained mute as she pushed a needle through Melina's torn dress. Spiros himself did the talking, words spilling from him about the war, about the Onassis family with whom he'd resumed his old obsession: Socrates, treasurer of the *Ethniki Ameni* and therefore a traitor, had been jailed in Smyrna's Turkish quarter. His brother Homer had fled. Alexander executed, Basil and John sent to a concentration camp in the interior.

"Adam and I were members of that organization too," Spiros said. "It was to help the Greek army after the war to get an independent Greek area inside Turkey. So, the Turks saw we worked for the Greek Government." He gave a sigh that he had to explain these fundamentals to his brother's wife.

Darkness encircled the two of them, and stars dotted the night sky. Candlelight flickered out in the houses opposite, but Eleni had not bothered to light any.

Eventually Spiros was offered a part-time porter's job at the docks. When not working, he fixed Eleni's shack, began adding a room for himself. Evenings he dropped into Mr. Stavros' pub where he drank, played cards, and joined in other men's boasts about former glittering lives, until all subsided in drunken grunts.

Spiros, still conscious of time passing, his father's eyes on him, went hungry in order to save money. What he saved was never enough; he'd be dead before he'd accumulated a few drachmas. On a cold winter's morning he leaned up against his doorjamb, his eyes scanning the street: a line of ugly little houses. Shapeless women wandering it. Angrily he stubbed out his cigarette. He'd failed himself. Worse, he'd failed his father. Remnants of the once wealthy merchant family from Smyrna now lived in a miserable dump; they got no respect. Still the local people spat and muttered: *What do you want in our country, you sons of Turks?* Raising a fist he shouted, "Damn all you Gods and all the filthy scoundrels." He walked, kicking at neighbours straw doormats and cursing as he passed the *Church of the Apostles*, then mumbled, "Sorry," at Father Meneghini in its doorway. Feeling rejected, diminished, trying to forestall self-pity, he walked to the sea front, and kept walking right into the central city. Climbing the steps to the upper city, he ranged his eyes over its magnificent houses.

A fellow came whistling along *Kolokotroni Street,* bulging bags slung across his shoulders. Spiros raised his eyebrows. The fellow grinned and said, "Duty-free goods from Chios."

A stall, duty-free goods! An import-export business. Spiros saw again his father's face, the fierce stare of his eyes, and he blinked. *Look again, son. There's always a way to get ahead. Always opportunities for those who look for them.* Something leapt in him then, not just the knowledge that for the rest of his life, and in the next one too, his father would look to him to redeem the family name. He, Spiros, would not disappoint; he would be his father's son at last. And after him would come Adam's boy Alekos. I'll be head of this family, he vowed. I'll train up Alekos in the import-export business. Yes, and make a good marriage for Melina when she's of age. Energized by new hope and responsibility, he hurried home to X Street.

At dawn the following Saturday, Spiros sailed for the Island of Chios to purchase duty-free goods at prices he could afford. Returning, he immediately built a wooden table and set it next to *The Stone*, a phallic-shaped rock that rose up at the end of X Street where it met the railway lines. All day he stood behind it, calling, "Come see what I've got. Cheap, cheap. Better deal you get no place else."

Having lived without routine, he learned its pleasures; when rain and wind beat at him, he prized the knowledge that he had somewhere to go each day, each one born in the hope of something better. To a frowning Eleni he said, "Look, soon this will add up to something big. You – you yourself should look outside. See, we live in a city three thousand years old. It's got a castle and a theatre and a Roman fortress. From here we stare across to Italy; we got to make the most of it." But what, and how, he could not explain.

A year passed, and another and another. Eleni spent her days in a chair in the sun, smoking. She took no part in helping her brother-in-law sell jars of jam, umbrellas, ribbons and scarves; took little interest in life about her, seeing only Adam's face, the glint in his eyes, his wide smile; heard again his gentle voice ... *'my little butterfly, my wood-nymph who halts the moon in its path across the sky...'* Occasionally she walked to the *circular agora* where she sat on a stone bench, staring at people passing. She entered churches, shrines and domes searching for the face of her husband; looking for comfort in the cold sanctuary of Christ. No comfort came to her.

***

Chapter 23

Toronto

Georgia

Eleni: She should have been on Mount Olympus living among the gods who spent their delightful days shaken by no wind, drenched by no showers, and invaded by no snows.

It's four in the morning. I've been writing most of the night and feel exhausted, as though I've been the one travelling across the Greek countryside, the one suffering and fainting away in Patras. I sleep for a few hours, get up, throw on some clothes and step into the kitchen. Helena must have left in a hurry because breakfast dishes are everywhere and the cigarette tray full. I think for the hundredth time that Dad should do something, he doesn't even work. Well, did he ever? I glance in the small mirror by the front door before I dash out: Big eyes. Round saucer face. Crazy hair. When she sees me Helena will pull a face and say my hair is just like her Mother Melina's, or Musa as she was sometimes called. That I should let her do something with it or I might end up like her. I think she means my grandmother made a bad marriage. But she did too, anyone can see. I try to flatten my hair, but give up and rush to the subway.

At Book City, as I sort and stamp books and make an occasional sale, great grandmother Eleni creeps into my thoughts. After the life she'd had, how could she bear the one she got instead? After my shift I decide to brave the walk down gum-splattered Yonge Street to Helena's salon. When I get close I hear Greek music trickling out the open door. Helena is in the shadows at the back dancing, holding out her arms to an imaginary partner – definitely coming to life at last, I think, and absorb the image of her, head thrown back, voice crooning a love song. I'm still standing there when the music stops, watching her as her exuberance seeps away. Then she sees me.

"Georgie, you here today? Wait till I finish and we'll go home together."

Guessing that she'll be a couple of hours, I open up my laptop and scan through my last entries. First is the part about the Allied nations and how they felt betrayed by Greeks who voted for King Constantine to return and run their country. I wonder how they could, a Nazi sympathizer they'd already dumped once before. My mind wanders, and next thing I'm travelling eastward from Smyrna across the wide Anatolian Plateau to the ancestral heartland where Helena's great grandfather Yiannis arose. He must be my great great ... Anyway there I am in rustling wheat fields, at the edge of shallow salt lakes. I'm listening to a shepherd's pipe in the hills – whose hills are they now? Wonder what happened to Yiannis and my name-sake Georgia? By then, Yiannis must have reached the age of about fifty. But because he was a heavy hookah smoker he could have died of lung cancer, or been killed as a non-Turkish citizen, even though he'd lived mostly like a Turk. His family had grown up thinking of life as a personal thing until history smacked them in the face. This man and two of his sons had trekked to the coast to make their fortunes. Also, to have their name command respect among the elite citizens of a fabled city. Instead they were strummed about on the tides of history, and by international intrigue. I drift back to Smyrna, onto its fiery docks, to lines of men pushed away from the life-saving ships. A rumble rises up in my throat; someone leans over me.

"Georgie, wake up!" Helena is shaking me.

"What happened to them – the men?"

"What? Oh, you're back in that old story again?" she sighs and runs a hand over the tangled mass of my hair. "I keep telling you not to spend so much time in the past. Be careful or your spirit will stay there and forget to come back to you."

"But what happened to them?"

"The men – my grandfather Adam? Maybe they stayed alive somewhere in Anatolia, no one knows. The history people say they died from starvation and being tortured. Some say they got shot." Her mouth twists. "My *Yia Yia* has only three of her children with her: Melina, Zoe, and Alekos. Nikos and the other ones, they went with their Papa in a different ship. This is what the people were told, but they heard all the bad stories. *Yia Yia* cries all the time and looks for them everywhere. She gets to Patras where Uncle Spiros finds her. Still she cries. Uncle Spiros loses Maria and his little girls.

"What else? What else?" My voice sounds urgent to my own ears because last she's begun talking to me - although not yet about herself.

"Because *Yia Yia* hid gold and jewels in her clothes, she doesn't get any money from the Greek Government. Spiros sells her jewelry to buy materials to build an extra room on the shack. Poor *Yia Yia* cries for many years for Adam and her missing children."

My breath is ragged and I inhale painfully. What a mighty ruin, a shameful period in the history of a nation; all those nations. Tears slip down my cheeks as I tap my keyboard.

When at last the salon has emptied, I read out to Helena parts of what I've written. She cries too. Both of us see Eleni in her shack, the big swells of the Ionian Sea; hear trains and donkeys, gulls squawking, old men groaning under cypress trees. Children too, bunched at the feet of a priest. Framing it all is a landscape of hills, stones, mountains, and crooked mulberry trees. I wonder how much a landscape influences the lives of those who live on it, how often myths of an old world become part of a family's own legends, and I'm curious to know if there are any Kouvalis family descendants still propelled by their history. Yes, I think, my mother Helena.

My mind returns to Eleni. In frayed black cloak, the abruptly middle-aged woman shuffles across the railway lines, the Highway to Athens, and toward a sea that has risen up in fury. She lifts eyes sunken with disappointment to a shale beach once knifed from a cliff; carries an earthen jar to the public tap. Other images intrude: a young woman in Smyrna wearing Western dress, singing in the evenings, gin-sling in hand beside a tennis court.

Alekos hovers, a young man always with a book – the son of his father indeed. I can tell he'll disappoint. Beautiful Melina with crazy hair and abundant energy, there's hope for this one. Zoe, poor child with twisted foot and anxious eyes, whatever will become of her? Three refugee children coming of age under General Metaxas' dictatorship during the Greek Civil

War. After it, the Peloponnesus will become both a backwater and a Greek bastion of conservatism. Patras' redemption lies in that fact that it is an important commercial port and gateway to the West.

I'm bugged that I don't know what happened to Adam and just have to suppose he was sent with legions of other able-bodied men to the Anatolian interior. There they would have been worked under slave-like conditions for the New Turkish government, until early death. Where would he have spread out his spirit? Over the city of Smyrna, or his beloved Anatolian Plateau? Even in the after-life he probably still felt betwixt and between. Fancifully I see a jagged landscape rise up to claim the soul that had left it, and gone ... gone.

Another all-night writing binge. I watch as the sun begins its rise above the rooftops; as a few corporate-looking types pass on the street heading for the subway, and work. I go to bed.

***

Chapter 24

Patras, 1934

Melina had turned eighteen. For the family's after-dinner strolls she'd taken to draping herself in factory discards and singing love songs from a blood-red mouth. Her large brown eyes ranged over passing boys. This evening she stepped ahead of her family, walked past the factory, the school, the Church of the Apostles, and to the edge of the Highway to Athens. On its far side, Father Meneghini stood gazing over the sea. A dented truck roared up. When the driver thrust his broad grinning face out the window, Melina's hands flew up to hide her blushing face from the priest who had turned to look. The truck driver accelerated and drove on.

"A good evening to you young woman," Father Meneghini said and crossed the highway toward her. "I have some books for you."

Melina's eyes remained on the truck until it disappeared from sight. "Father," she said, "books are only for boys."

"For girls also. How else will you learn your Greek history? Come along with me."

But Melina had seen Spiros emerging from the dust kicked up by a passing car. He was   returning from the Island of Chios, shoulders bent with the weight of bulging sacks.

"Been to Chios, duty-free goods," he said, coming up. "Import and export trade, *this* is what I can do. By all the saints in Heaven – excuse me Father – I'll build up a fortune yet and show that Onassis fellow. Never will he outdo me while I've got bones still in my body."

Father Meneghini looked at him with gentle eyes and retraced his steps to the church.

"I'll get some books another time," Melina called after him. Turning to her uncle she said, "Whatever have you done now?" and relieved him of some of his burden. "I want to go with you next time."

"But this is not proper for a girl who must marry well," Eleni said when she heard.

"Are you sure it's trade you got on your mind?" Spiros gave her a sharp look. The best hope is to get you a good marriage, like to a successful merchant, you being a factory girl. Trading and the ships are not proper places for a young woman, but you got a good spirit."

"Please," Melina begged, "I've got to get away from this place. I hate it."

"You hate your home?"

"You talk about your fairytale life in Smyrna, then make us live in this horrible place."

"Melina, it's not your mother's fault." But the look Spiros gave Eleni suggested otherwise. "Next Sunday I might take you."

"By all the saints!" Eleni crossed herself and chattered about blasphemy, about all the bad things happening to people who desecrate the Lord's Day.

Melina pirouetted.

***

Spiros, slipping into the tavern one night, heard gossip about Aristotle Onassis making a fortune shipping grain and beef exports to Europe, tobacco to Cuba, Brazil and Greece. Old inferiority fell upon him. The next minute he was on his feet. "That dumb pasha, he's an upstart and I'll outdo him yet. You watch me! I'll build up my business big, big, the busiest in Patras. I'll ..."

"In your dreams. Maybe up in Heaven with St. Peter's help. You're a lowly Turk – all of us are.

"Who says? I *will* get rich yet, damn you," Spiros' voice rose in the thick air, heard above the general muttering about Greek-Turkish refugees and how none would come to any good.

Over the following six months, Spiros moved his stall close to the docks. In a wooden barrow he trundled his odd collection of duty-free goods to the ships, hawked them on the streets, and yelled until he was hoarse. With manic energy he began building a bathroom, and put finishing

141

touches to the addition he'd added to Eleni's home. The extra room along the west wall was for him.

One early morning, a vision came to him: his father nodding his head. Spiros' heart soared and he leapt out of bed. Where was Eleni? Seeing her hunched in the doorway, he felt a stab of pity.

"Still you're living in the old world," he said gently. "It's gone. But you can make another life for yourself here. The image of his father nodding returned, and his voice rose. "I'll build us up a fortune like in Smyrna and get the Kouvalis name known again. You got a son Alekos. A daughter who hangs up the washing for you and paints pictures in the dust to make little Zoe smile. I'm making our house bigger and better because your Adam, in the afterlife, trusts us to look after his children."

The thought came to him then that perhaps it was his responsibility to marry his brother's widow. But for Eleni he'd need to earn a *lot* more money than he could possibly make. Still, Spiros felt invigorated by this new feeling.

It was in the late watches of the night when shadows pressed all about, that another vision of himself appeared: a lowly hawker of duty-free goods, peddler of cheap wares yelling until he was hoarse. An ugly little man who, for all his work, earned but a paltry sum. Such a stark contrast to the successful and still-rising merchant he'd been in Smyrna. He felt old suddenly, old like a moon over a younger earth, as Adam might say. Time was passing, nothing changing. His father's voice always pressing. As always, when bitterness welled within him, he headed for the tavern.

Similar visions returned on the following evening as randomly he walked the streets of Patras. One late afternoon he caught sight of the statue of St Michael, his sword glinting golden in the sun. Saw the empty eyes of the ancient Roman Odeon staring over an orange sea, sun rays lighting up the coloured stone of Venetian homes on the city's upper slopes. *By the mother of all the saints I'll have one of those!* Spiros' heart thumped and he fell to his knees. *I swear to you Papa, what's left of your family will soon live among the upper classes in this city.* As quickly as it had come, his adrenaline ebbed. He needed a plan, and he needed help. But who? – Alekos. Time for him to wake up. Spiros' thoughts took flight. *Like his father, always got his nose in the books. Well, he can learn about business the same way. We'll be partners and make another fortune.* The irrepressible 40-year-old went in search of his nephew.

Alekos sat under a plane tree at one end of the line of little houses, his eyes closed. In his lap lay a notebook and pencil. Light hair hung below his ears, and in the dappled sunlight Spiros saw the beginnings of a moustache. Saw that he wore scrubby trousers and a patched jacket. Adam's son, so like him. But Adam had woken up. What would it take for this one?

"Hello my boy," he said. "No work today?" He watched the eyelids flutter open, the brief expression of alarm and embarrassment enter them.

"No ... not really," he said.

"You and I," Spiros said, his voice jaunty, "we're going to build up this family's fortunes and live like our families did in Smyrna. We'll travel around the southern peninsula and find us business opportunities."

"Business?" Alekos' mouth turned down at the corners. "I've been learning its history of course, but how do you know what to look for?"

"Know what your grandfather said? Look again, son, always a way to get ahead and damn fools if we don't. I got to get in you the feeling of being a proper Greek, never to forget you live at the heart of ancient Greece where Persian wars were fought. Already you know this, since your nose is always in the books. We'll go to where the Byzantine Empire once ruled, and also to the southern peninsula and the *Little Dardanelles,* find out what comes through the ports. Son, opportunities only come to those that look for them."

"And a man can always rise up above his circumstances," Alekos quoted. "Uncle, you've told me many times." His voice was flat.

***

Chapter 25

Patras, 1935

Spiros closed his stall and took Alekos with him on a journey to the south. Spiros learned only there was sporadic work in the silk industry in the south, and little else. Baffled, he saw that his nephew had no interest in girls. On his return home he headed into the tavern and ordered a glass of *Santa Helena* white wine. With it came a plate of feta cheese, tomatoes and olives, and he sighed for the days when Maria had served him shish kebab, squid or eggplant. Soon he had disappeared in reverie into his glorious past: Maria setting shrimp and stuffed capon before him, hovering over him, resting a plump hand affectionately on his shoulder. An intoxicated yet brooding Spiros returned home as the Eastern sky brightened, to sit in his doorway as the world about him came sluggishly to life; until Eleni's dark form hovered.

"Maria!" His face lit up like the sudden appearance of a tropical sun.

"What? You call me Maria?"

"Oh." Spiros' whole body crumpled. "Sorry, must have been a dream. She comes to me sometimes, you know."

Eleni touched his shoulder. "I'll make you coffee and you can tell me your news," she said.

Pleased at this, a mug of coffee in one hand, cigarette in the other, a lonely Spiros sat on a wooden bench he'd built. With surprise he noted that the little home was tidy: clothes and dishes stacked neatly against the walls and benches wiped clean. Words spilled from him. "Such bitterness still toward us refugees, not real Greeks, they say. But we were rich Greeks in

Smyrna, our city no more, Anatolia not our country. We got nothing. We are nothing."

Eleni re-filled his coffee cup and sat down beside him.

"They say about Greece," Spiros rested his head in his hands, "how it's the geographical and spiritual crossroads of the world and a bitter fate for it to suffer. I hear talk about the fellow Venizelos and his stupid mistakes. King Constantine, how he returned to his throne to avenge the wicked crime of Smyrna being burned. People ask did this *megale* idea have to come to an end? Maybe not, maybe Venizelos was too hasty."

Tired of the effort in making Eleni understand history of which she was ignorant, Spiros got up and disappeared to his still largely empty room. At times, a small flame leapt within his thin chest, a longing for affection, and he wrestled again with the thought that he should marry his brother's widow. Images of her in all her moods came to him: vibrant, cunning, sweet – and innocent in the beginning.

"Dear Eleni," he said the following night, "I've brought you some of those chic cigarettes you like. Have a smoke, and pour me a glass of wine." The two sat side-by-side at the big window in the front room. Over a light brown tunic Eleni wore a black cloak and had pulled her dull brown hair behind her ears. She puffed on a cigarette.

"Sometimes my mind wanders to the old days," he began. "I remember you, a beautiful young woman who sang sweet songs to her husband. So pretty at your dinner parties. Smart too – remember those business deals you made for Adam?"

"Adam?" Eleni's brightening eyes darkened immediately with old sorrow and she sat, pale and abstracted in the window, a ghost looking at a ghost, Spiros thought. He waited, but Eleni continued staring blankly in front of her until Spiros, mentally shrugging, got up and walked to the tavern.

That night he went to bed and dreamed of his lost wife, of his little daughters who would be little no longer. He wept while he slept, awoke and worked furiously. He crossed himself, hoped, prayed, and smoked. He slipped away to the brothel.

***

Chapter 26

Patras, 1936 -1937

Melina

Years passed. One late afternoon, Eleni, plump, dishevelled, sat mending torn sheets and jackets. On hearing Melina's singing through the open window, she got up and looked out. Her daughter, wearing bright yellow clothes, her hair pinned with ribbons, was busily painting pictures on rough paper. Sudden hope flared in Eleni's breast.

"Melina," she called "we're going to make you a good marriage, and so help restore our family's honour."

Melina looked up at her mother in astonishment. "But Mama, I want to teach – teach art." She held up the paper Father Meneghini had given her, and Eleni saw sketches of shapeless women smoking in the doorways of ramshackle houses.

Something caught in her throat, and when she could speak she said, "To teach, you must be long in school and for that we don't have the money. Soon we will dress you up and take you to the best places in this city, find for you a man who is successful in business. One day your child will become rich and famous."

"Yes, we'll do all we can to have her marry well." Spiros, silent until now, shuffled cards at the other end of the table.

Eleni looked at him: at his frayed and dirty shirt cuffs, baggy trousers hanging low over his narrow hips, and her elation subsided.

"Melina," Spiros was saying, "you must save your factory wages for your dowry. If you make a good marriage, this family will …"

"Get rich, like in Smyrna," Melina finished for him. "Everything's always about Smyrna, and my father Adam too. If I find a rich man and take you back to Smyrna, will you be happy then?"

"You poke fun at your family? You're a stupid girl and know nothing." Spiros got up, yanked at his trousers and then headed for the pub, returning only when pale light streaked the sky.

"You stay out all night," Eleni complained fretfully when she saw him. "Look at you, your face like a sun that forgot to rise."

Spiros turned his blood-shot eyes on her frayed and shabby form.

"When a Greek man sits in tavern eating and drinking and talking he gets a feeling of well-being. It rises up in him and he expresses it," he said. "So, he dances and sings. He plays cards and he smokes. This is how he forgets."

Spiros went to bed. But he could not forget. He could not sleep, could not stop his voices chattering: *How to make Melina a good marriage. What to do with Alekos? Got to get him married to a girl from a rich family.* But all about him he saw spindly-haired girls at the feet of Father Meneghini, fat girls making eyes at factory boys. Where to find one for Alekos? The young fellow wants to go to Athens. Well, let him go then.

Look to Melina instead, at once.

"She shouldn't be listening to the stuff Stavros plays in his pub," he complained to Eleni the next evening. "Or paint her face like she does. She's got that awful hair — looks like she's got slithering serpents on her head."

"She's a good girl," Eleni said, "lots of energy and good spirits."

"She got the hair from my mother Georgia." Spiros laughed suddenly and explained how African savages once worshipped the serpent; that its whole body touched the ground, so with its belly, its tail and its head, it understood all the earth's secrets.

Eleni recalled her surprise on first seeing her mother-in-law's crazy curls sprouting like weeds from a garden. Did it mean anything for her Musa? Crossing herself, she said, "By all the saints in heaven it must mean a long line of descendants with heads full of wisdom. My girl's hair is a good omen."

"Shame on you to give your child such a name," neighbour Lina said as she passed the window.

"Hush to you. I've got a child born with snakes around her head and bits of red and gold in her hair. You think I should call her Sappho? Cleis? It is to wisdom this girl is born, and it is wisdom that will make her rich and famous, never mind the name."

Melina came in the door at that moment, stuffing food in her mouth.

"My girl, you can't eat like that." Spiros frowned at her. "You must learn the manners of a lady. Learn how to cook and sew, and how to read good books like proper ladies do – did – in Smyrna. Already you can draw little pictures and sing prettily, so maybe the Fates will favour you with a good marriage."

"But can she read?" Alekos looked up from his book.

Melina made a face at him.

"You can joke," he said, "But did you learn? I never see you with a book."

"That's because Mama's always giving books to *you*. Uncle Spiros, this is the same story you told about *Yia Yia* in Anatolia and how she got books for our Papa Adam. Uncle Spiros, Mama, I told you, I want to teach."

***

Repeated scenes unfolded over the following months. Eleni accusing her daughter of dressing like a *poutana*. Melina mocking, "It's always the same old story, always the great Kouvalis name."

"Your uncle right now is looking to find you a husband. I'm serious." Eleni scrubbed harder at the clothes in the kitchen sink.

"Now?" Melina's voice was faint with dismay.

"Yes, now. We'll talk to your uncle after dinner."

On the evening's walk, Melina distanced herself from her uncle. Neighbours pointed as they passed. '*Writhing snakes*' they said and crossed themselves. "Medusa come back to haunt us. Eh, eh, may the saints preserve us." Melina walked past them, laughing.

"You must find your niece a husband, soon as possible," Eleni said.

Spiros, pushing locks of hair from his eyes, turned to his niece. "Have you learned yet who your ancestors are? Your suitor must know you come from a family that lived in wealth and splendour from the ancient days. You must always remember this."

"Yes, Uncle, you've told me many times."

"Then listen some more." Eleni, reciting the old tale of Adam, did not see Spiros' face twist. "See, anything you want you can earn for yourself, even if you are a woman."

"Really Mama, what is there to show for this once wealthy family? Bits of Turkish carpet, religious things from a place in Anatolia. A nightdress and slippers? Because of this stuff I must believe your stories?" She looked at her mother and then at her uncle: a crooked little fellow, all jutting bones and sucked-in cheeks, coughing and spitting and smoking. He drank too much and half lived in a brothel. Some famous family. Uggh!" She took to sitting on her doorstep after her factory shifts watching the sun cast orange fingers across the sky; watched for a red truck, for its driver whistling at her from his open window.

The day came when Spiros lost his job. "No work, no money," he said, kicked off his boots and picked up a bottle of *raki*. "Too many refugees, too many real Greeks looking for work."

"I've got some drachmas saved from my wages," said Melina and touched his arm in sudden pity. "I'll give it all to you."

Spiros said she should keep it for the husband he'd soon find for her, and Zoe too. "Zoe: she's plain," he said under his breath, "and she's got that crooked foot, but still I might find someone." Aloud he said, "Melina, before I find this husband for you, you will come with me to Chios in the weekends. We'll buy duty-free goods and expand our business." His shoulders lifted. "We sail at dawn, be home, maybe by nightfall."

It was an order.

***

Chapter 27

Winds whipped the sails and rocked the small boats in the harbour on the day Melina went to sea with her uncle. With red lips, red cheeks, a bright scarf to imprison her hair, she clutched at her skirt and stepped aboard a white-painted *caique*, its strake and topsides painted in vivid colours. Brown eyes darted over the chaotic scene of ships and men and merchandize.

"Uncle, my real life is just beginning," she said, laughing, and Spiros was not aware that trade was not what she had in mind.

With dusk that crept across the little houses that evening came Spiros and a sunburned, excited Melina. In her arms she clutched bulging bags of goods while Spiros pulled a wagon piled high with umbrellas and scarves, embroidered bolts of colourful cloth, brushes, combs, pottery, fabric, cards and *ouzo*. All were to be for sale on his stall, and in local shops.

Spiros dropped his of goods at the door, coughed, spat, kicked off his boots, and opened a bottle of wine. A flushed and restless Melina followed him inside. Hearing rumbling on the street, she leapt to the window, waving frantically. Spiros threw her a look of anger, or was it contempt? Eleni noticed the two ignoring each other all evening.

"My girl, what did you do to make your uncle angry?"

"I was friendly with some young men, this is all." Melina avoided her mother's eyes. "I was just having a good time."

"Young men, always the young men. Whatever you did, you've upset your uncle. Go say you're sorry."

"What makes you angry with her?" Eleni asked after Melina had gone to bed.

Spiros dropped his pack of cards. "She flirted with some wild-looking fellow and disappeared, middle of the day. I won't take her with me no more."

"No, no. Surely she can do better than sell bits of cloth and food in a grimy street market. You keep saying you will find her a husband ..." Eleni's voice trailed away.

***

Melina, having promised to behave well, returned to Chios with her uncle the following Sunday. Eleni muttered 'blasphemy' and crossed herself. In the week that followed, she noted her daughter's singing, her flushed face as she came and went from the factory. One day she arrived home with two bulging canvas bags and emptied them on the floor.

"Mama, look, we'll make the kitchen pretty with these bits of left-over wallpaper." She broke off and leaned out the window to wave to the driver of the red truck that of late parked often on the street. Oh mother of God, the fellow was whistling at her.

"Melina, keep your eyes and your ears to yourself," Eleni snapped. "Making eyes at ... a *truck driver*? You think he'll make a good husband for you?"

"He makes eyes at me. It's called flirting, Mama. Just a bit of fun." Melina turned from the window and scrambled on hands and knees. In triumph she held up colourful fragments showing trees, birds and butterflies. "See, soon you'll be living in a jungle."

Eleni watched as her bare walls blossomed. "Eh, a doll's house," and she gave her daughter a rare smile.

Next evening she saw Melina slip on a pair of Spiros' boots, pick up his shovel and begin digging by the front door. From unclaimed land behind the house she transplanted daisies and rare orchids, among them, *horta* as a salad for dinner. Before many weeks had passed, a tiny garden struggled to life beside the steps of number 24. Eleni clapped her hands in pleasure at the splash of colour, not noticing Melina raising a flushed face each time a red truck passed.

"Still I'm looking for a husband for you," Spiros said that evening. "Not a boy who works in a factory but a man who's made money from a business that sells respectable merchandize. He's older because he's got rich by his own hands."

"And not a truck driver," Eleni said.

Spiros returned from Chios alone one Sunday evening, his face pale beneath its sallowness.

"What is it – what?" Eleni cried out.

"Melina's run off," he said, and his face crumpled.

"Run off?" Eleni stared, uncomprehending.

"Run off? Where to?" Zoe echoed.

Spiros spread his hands. "We got off the boat. She told me she'd be back in a moment, and ran from my sight. Of course I don't see where she goes for all the people – the wharves are very crowded when the boats come in. She never came back. But I saw a red truck," he added as an afterthought."

"Red truck?" Eleni said the words stupidly. "No! She runs off with that man. Always he drives up and down our street and makes eyes at her. He leans out his window and whistles – to our Melina!"

"So, foolish woman, you didn't stop him? You tell me now?"

"But I did tell *her* – all the time. She laughed at me. She called it flirting, only a bit of fun." Defensiveness entered Eleni's voice.

That evening Spiros and Eleni sat side-by-side at the front window after a meal nobody ate. Gulls wheeled and trains shunted. Neighbours wandered the street full of gossip, and still they sat, brooding through that magical time where the world hangs suspended between day and night. About them drifted smells of oil, kerosene and old garbage mingled with fragrance from the orchards.

As night deepened and no footsteps tapped along the asphalt street, Eleni lit a candle. She placed it at the foot of the small, plastic archangel Michael in the corner of the living room and knelt before it, a prayer twisting her lips. Before wrapping herself in her sleeping bag, she propped the door ajar the way she'd done for Adam all the long years before.

Through three days and nights Eleni sat below the front window, not removing her apron and slippers. Hands clasped, she muttered, sighed and prayed. Spiros closed his stall and stomped the streets, searched the markets and the wharves. He swore, muttered about infidels; about lazy, ignorant people and the stupidity of the whole world. In the evenings he strode from front window to back, staring over mountains that rose dark and glowering; muttered about honour and reputation.

Zoe crept silently about the house, wiping off dust, picking up dropped vegetable peels and making tea.

Another thunderstorm burst from the heavens as workers streamed through the factory doors on the third evening of Melina's absence. Large splotches of rain fell as lightning streaked the sky. Workers fled indoors and the street gleamed wet and empty. Eleni jumped up at the sight of two figures straggling toward her door.

Melina – and God help her – the driver of the red truck! In spite of the rain, Melina's hair stood up as though pointing to the four corners of the earth. A damp skirt shrieking with gaudy colours twined itself about her legs. Out of a bright flowered blouse her breasts came close to spilling. Eleni saw her twist a cheap-looking band on her ring finger.

Fearful yet defiant, Melina looked quickly at her mother, then at Spiros who stood beside her in the doorway. Eleni's relief was followed immediately by anger and she simply folded her arms. On Spiros' face shone reproach. A flush crept up Melina's, but her expression turned quickly to one of triumph.

"Uncle Spiros, Mama, Zoe," she said prettily, "I introduce to you my husband Christos. We got married at the City Hall two days ago."

The truck driver extended a hand to Spiros, his broad face wreathed in jaunty smiles.

"A thousand years of happiness to you sir," he said with rough accent. "I tell you, God come to me one day. He says to me, this is your woman. You marry her and I bless you with seven sons." He stumbled as he bowed to Eleni, and Spiros wondered if the fellow had been drinking. He ignored the coarse and grubby hand proffered and clenched his own.

"The devil takes you both! You run away to get married and say nothing to the folks who put a roof over your head. I tell you, what you've done is … is *shameful*." Spiros' voice quivered. "Now, since you're all grown up and made your big decision, go find your own place to live." He spat, turned his back, pushed Eleni inside the house and shut the door. Zoe widened her eyes in alarm.

"But Mama, Mama, what am I supposed to do?" Melina ran to the window and called through its pane, her voice frantic. "I love Christos, so I marry him. I don't want to live like this anymore, all the crowding, all the work. What is there in this place? My Christos has a good job in construction and can get any work he wants, so we live here until we get the money for our own place. We're young, and we can get rich together." Melina moved to the door and pushed on it. Spiros blocked her.

"Stupid girl, you thought to bring your ... your *husband!*" he spat the word, "to live in our home ... *What were you thinking?"*

"But Mama," Melina ignored her uncle. "We have no place to live, and this is my home." Tears trickled from large frightened eyes.

"You just told us how you don't like your home," her mother said. "Now you want to live here, and your husband too. You didn't think of these things before you married a poor man then, with no home of his own?" But Eleni's heart softened at the thought of her daughter out in the cold with this good-time husband of hers. "I'll see if Spiros will let you stay until you find a home." But her disappointment was bitter.

"See, she marries a good-for-nothing trucker," she complained to Lina. "A man with no schooling. He's got the look of a person with a hot temper. Ach, ach, we shall see," and she took to uttering extravagant sighs.

***

Christos was a handsome man with strands of ochre in his hair, a mouth that curved upwards as though in perpetual mirth. A primal fellow, he felt the stones beneath his feet, the sun caressing his skin, the rain prickling it. He loved to laugh, to sing, to dance – and to talk. Rapid body movements accompanied his long-running tales. When not working on the city's roads, he sat under the *Stone,* quickly forming a circle of men about him to play cards. The family knew where he was by his booming laugh that echoed about the street and to the shore. Eleni learned he had run away from a violent home at the age of twelve and hitched a ride to Athens, intending to make his fortune.

"Ah, but where is the fortune?"

"My bouboulina." Christos bowed to Eleni and held out his arms. "No fortune yet, but we'll dance together and be happy. We'll sing and make music in this house."

"My princess," he said to Melina. "I got no fortune yet, but together we'll make one. We'll build us a big house. Have ourselves seven sons and *Yia Yia*, she will sing to them in their cots." Christos swung his wife in the air. He turned to Spiros and saluted. "Sir, it is my pleasure to live under your roof." Again he extended a grubby hand, but Spiros continued to refuse it.

Christos then turned to Zoe and curtsied. *"Poulaki mou,"* he said, lifting her off her feet. Zoe smiled slightly then. The tiny home had added a lively member to its number.

The following morning, Eleni sat in her doorway in the pale morning sun that followed an evening's storm, reflecting. Maybe, just maybe this Christos will make himself a rich and successful businessman as her Adam had done, Melina to help him, God willing. But her Adam had read books and educated himself and that was a big difference. Now to find a husband for Zoe. Ach, ach, what is to become of you my little one, you with your plain face and crooked foot.

Spiros, in time, did find a husband for Zoe, a small man who sat from sunrise to sunset behind a smeared window, his crooked back bent over an old sewing machine, his shop a tiny back room at the cross roads that led to the old city centre. His name was Elpenor.

"A poor tailor." Eleni looked reproachfully at Spiros, but Zoe smiled. When he was introduced, she held out her hand. "A husband, Mama. He has a kind face, and will look after me as best he can."

They married, and ever afterwards the kind little man carried Zoe in his arms through the streets, to a café, and sometimes to the sea. People laughed, but Zoe just smiled.

***

Christos dreamed of a large tribe of children. Melina too wanted children, and to find in her marriage an antidote to life's difficulties. When finally she conceived after more than a year, the pregnancy ended in miscarriage. Another year passed before she gave birth to her first child.

"I name my first daughter Thalia for one of our Muses," announced the new mother, cradling her infant.

"A girl," muttered Christos, spat and walked out the door. Several days later his voice boomed through the doorway. "So, my wise and clever Melina, we make another baby to get us a boy, eh?" His large frame filled the room. Melina looked up at him with sunken eyes.

"You make us some money, then we'll have us a boy. Why don't you ask Uncle Spiros if he needs help with his stall?" She slumped in her bed, and a sulking Christos looked for Spiros. Money he needed indeed, for his pockets were empty. Nothing for cigarettes, nothing for *ouzo*.

"No money for baby clothes." Melina's voice floated out the open window. "You promised to make a proper cradle. Where is it?"

Two years after Thalia's birth came the longed-for son. A year later, another, each bearing the names Nikos and Markos after Eleni's missing boys. Christos, proud, was not yet satisfied. "Ha my boubolina, a man can never have too many sons so we have us another boy, then another."

Eleni, sunning herself in the doorway, raised her head to look at her son-in-law. "You don't do too much to feed the ones you've already got."

Christos, restless, walked about and snapped his fingers. "More money for food? I'll go make it, you wait and see." But the only change he made was to pester Melina each night with amorous attention. "You're beautiful, beautiful. Happy is the man with a wife that gives him bonny children. We'll have us seven sons, eh, *poulaki mou?*"

But Christos' tribe was not to be. Four years after Markos was born came a tiny girl, born with difficulty. Melina, still recovering, was told she must not have any more children.

"You don't give me another boy?" The florid face contorted and Christos' booming voice was not heard for days. Had he not boasted about his third son to come, and many more? Had he not borrowed to stock up on good Turkish cigars? He refused to look at the baby girl. When eventually he did, he argued about her name.

"Georgia," said Melina, to have her grandmother remembered.

"It's not a true Greek name," argued Christos.

"Of course it is," snapped Eleni. "You've got no schooling so you know nothing."

A week passed and the baby remained nameless. One day Eleni, gazing intently at the tiny bundle, pronounced that the face of this child would hold great beauty. The world would change because of her. Many men would fight over her, and some to die for want of her love. Her name of course must be none other than Helen.

"Helena," Melina said.

"Ahh," exclaimed Eleni in a mood of exaltation. "This one will make our family famous again," and she clapped her hands. "Adam's dreams are coming true."

The infant and growing child had an olive skin, not in the best tradition of classical Greek beauty although her features were small and perfect.

"Pure Frankish blood in her veins from her grandfather Adam," Spiros said one day, but his expression twisted as he remembered his father's pride in Adam, the disdain of himself. But as Adam was dead, as he had assumed patriarchy of the truncated family, he could afford to be generous.

***

Chapter 28

Toronto

Georgia

I've just written about the birth of my mother and badly need her to talk to me. So far she's told me bits of the rest of our family's lives, but nothing about her own. I'm wondering if it frightens, or even embarrasses her. The time on my bedside clock says three. I pad into the kitchen thinking to make a hot drink and rummage in the cupboard above the sink. Coffee. Sugar. Corn starch. Where's the hot chocolate? I reach right to the back and my fingers touch paper, an envelope, and I pull it out. *Patras* is written on the front and there are photos in it. *Photos?* I tip them onto the kitchen table.

Immediately I recognize great grandmother Eleni, a woman dressed in black with a cigarette dangling between her fingers. I remember the stories, like when she had no money to buy smokes she'd find someone with the evil eye, pray for them nine times, then take her scissors and cut the air. Having cast out the evil spirits she'd be given a cigarette. My *Yia Yia* once told me on the phone that her mother often heard spirits clattering. She would panic when a shadow moved. That she heard the dead groaning and everywhere she walked was a grave ... oh, this must be Markos and Nikos when they were small. Who's this? I hold close a snapshot of a little girl standing against a stone wall, an impudent smile on her face. My mother Helena of course, her tiny figure surrounded by a city with three thousand years of history.

The photo of a rangy young man catches my eye and I look more closely. Gentle, soulful eyes, I can tell, even in the old photograph. I turn it over and there's the name Stephan written on it. Stephan! The name Mom kept saying when she came home from Greece. Thinking I can hear a noise, quickly I stuff the envelope into the back of the cupboard.

That afternoon I'm in the salon with not much to do, so I open up my laptop. Eventually Isabel leaves for the day, then Bonnie, and Silent Sylvia not long after. Absorbed in my other world I've no idea of time passing until an odd sound registers from the basement. I remember Helena had gone there to do her billing. I tiptoe down, to glimpse her in the tiny office, making whimpering sounds. She's holding a photo up close to her face and repeating a name – like Stephan. *Stephan?* My heart speeds up. Maybe now's the time ... everyone has the need to confess.

"Mom – Helena," I say softly.

"Oh, you." Her head jerks up and I see she's been crying. Hastily pushing the photo under her blotter, she wipes at her eyes. Then she turns on me. "What are you doing here? You look awful."

"*I* do?"

We stare at each other, and her expression begins to soften. She gets up to smooth my hair, but suddenly irritated I say, "What am I doing here? I work for you, remember? Something else: you might own a beauty place but everything's not always about what people look like." But still, I run my eyes over my cut-off jeans, wrinkled T-shirt, old loafers. I'm aware my face is kissed by no cosmetics and my hair bunches up like a miniature haystack.

"I get up in the night and hear you in your room doing this click click thing. You've got black under your eyes and don't brush your hair from one week into the next." Her voice has become full of complaint.

"Never mind my stupid hair." But with my hands I try to flatten it. "Something's upsetting you, and it happened in Greece; you were ... different when you came back. Why can't you just tell me?"

"You think I should tell you my private business?"

I reach over her, lift the blotter and pull out the snapshot she thrust there – the young fellow in the photo I'd seen at home. "Mum, who is this man? I heard you call him Stephan."

Suddenly her body goes rigid and she's weeping into her hands.

I repeat softly, "Who, Mom?" She wipes her eyes and grabs the photo, pressing it to her face. "Stephan,' she whispers. "Stephanos ..." And again she's choking on her tears.

"Was he a boyfriend? Did you see him when you were in Greece?" I lean over her and stare again at the lean ribbon of a young man looking back at me, someone I imagine brooding in solitary places, or perched on a stone wall gazing at the sea.

In an abrupt change of mood Helena wipes her face with her fingers then slips the photo in her purse. "Why do you want to know?" Her voice has become cold.

How on earth can I keep up with her moods? My tongue stumbles over words about catharsis and telling a love story makes it live forever and the people in it never dying. "I'm writing our family history" I say. "Remember? I really want you to tell me your part of the story – *this* part – in whatever words you want. Like I said, in it, Stephan will live forever ..."

She interrupts me with urgency in her voice, "You'll write only what I tell you? You'll show it only to me?" In the hot thick air of the office she twists her hands and grimaces.

"Of course, you can edit it. Then you, everyone in it, will have immortality."

When I say this she collapses in her chair and next thing my arms are around her, my head resting on hers. "Oh Mom ... Mom ..." We're laughing and crying and falling in and out of her old chair.

"You were always a good girl Georgie."

Those few words provoke a mixture of old memories: hunger, cold, fear, mixed up with the knowledge that she loves me – both her daughters – and always has, no matter what happened back then; no matter what Amalia says.

"The rest of this story is yours, Mom," I say, and now I'm crying too. "In it I'm calling you Helena, okay? Helena."

Later, after we've had coffee and demolished a bag of doughnuts in the empty salon, she hands me other snapshots from her desk. "I'll tell you some things," she says, "and you will show me what you write – okay?"

"First tell me about this Stephan," I beg, but that dreadful, hollow look returns and she says no, I'll have to wait.

***

160

Chapter 29

Patras, 1950

She's got fire in her eyes this one, were Melina's thoughts as she watched her youngest child wobbling on tiny feet. Like she sees far. Got small wrists too but how they grab at things, and little arms stretched out like she's wanting to ask favours of the gods.

The pudgy two-year-old wielded a hammer. When three, she grabbed a knife to cut vegetables. At five, Helena walked alone to the market to shop for her mother.

"Mischievous, just like a boy." And Christos took her with him in his truck when he carried loads of gravel, cement and shale to local farmers; when he collected rich manure from one village, delivering it to another and paid again on arrival. Father and daughter travelled south and east across hills and valleys, burned by sun and wind, their songs flung over a somnolent landscape or lost in the roar of the truck's engine.

"See how far you can jump," Christos challenged his small daughter. "See if you can climb this fence."

"I'll race you to the farmer's shed," she said, laughing up at him.

"Ha! You drive my truck? See if you can charm that old fellow into buying an extra load of my gold."

"This gold stinks, Papa." She made a face.

"It stinks? I tell you, this is manna from the heavens. The Virgin has blessed you with art and cunning, so you use it. Smile sweetly. Tell the farmer that God has sent him gold to make his fruit grow. Already he knows this, but he'll buy more if you charm him."

Christos' voice roared above the noise of his engine. By mid-afternoon when his head began nodding, his little girl sang to keep him awake. At the end of a day of dust and dirt, reeking of sweat and manure, he lifted her drowsy form from the truck, and filled with love he cradled her.

"Chugging manure from one poor farmer to another, what kind of work is that?" Eleni's fingers pushed a needle in and out of torn clothes. "What are you doing to the child? Where is the dignity for my poor Melina, and where is the future in this?"

"My husband peddles God's good earth to all its poor corners." Melina heard, and defended him. "He helps people to farm the land. He makes money …"

"But not enough for the growing family," Eleni cried. "Already we've got seven in these small rooms, and still I must sleep on the floor. Is that the way for your husband to look after your family?" She took to muttering under her breath as she scrubbed and folded clothes.

……

In time, Christos, with a now-arthritic Spiros helping when he could, added an upstairs bedroom to the house, and a small sitting area. Melina, recovered from her childbearing ordeals and still besotted with her Christos, continued her honeymoon with him upstairs. On the ground floor in one large iron bedstead slept all the children with Eleni remaining on her pile of blankets in the living room.

Christos, during those first years, swept in the door with the setting of the sun, singing, "Ha, my beautiful Mama, did you spend a fine day? I know how you sneak out to the pub for a dance and a sing-song when no one's looking. Hello Zoe, *chryso mou,* you come visiting your family today? Your husband carries you in his arms before the sun rises in the sky. Fine man, fine man. And where is my darling wife with the head full of serpents?" With elaborate ceremony he presented his pay to Melina, grabbed her arms and pulled her onto the street to dance, to sing love songs in her ear.

Melina flushed as doorways filled and faces appeared in windows. Neighbours either clapped or shook their heads. After dinner Christos pulled a bottle of wine from his pocket and with elaborate ceremony poured each of the family a glass. "The children too, they must learn how to drink properly," he said.

Melina thought of little else but of the moment Christos would come home each day. About what she would feed him, about food for their picnics at the castle or in the country. She dreamed of rollicking, sensuous nights once the children were in bed. She loved it when he praised her for the good things she prepared for him. "And you're so pretty," he'd say as he smacked his lips on hers. "You put all the women in the world to shame."

Her Christos, Melina knew, was roughly dressed and not smooth of manners. But he had a love of beautiful things, of wine, and eventually of other women. When she accused him of unfaithfulness, he laughed and said, *"'Nun chre methusthen. Nunc bibamus* – let us drink deeply: in summer to cool our thirst; in autumn, to put a bright colour on death, in winter, to warm our blood, in spring, to celebrate nature's resurrection'"* – words that might have issued from the mouth of Adam, or his grandson Alekos, who remained an enigmatic figure in Athens.

***

After two years, Christos lost held his job − to indolence and unreliability − Melina thought. He had little money. Dirt-crusted fingers played obsessively with the worry beads in his pocket. No more movies for the family. No treats, only basic food staples. His booming voice was no longer heard among chattering neighbours who, after their evening meal, strolled to the end of their street, turned left toward the *fourno* with its cluster of little shops; sometimes to cross the railway lines, the *Highway to Athens,* and to the sea.

Melina mended and re-mended the family's clothes, patched sheets, and stitched together bits of old cloth for towels. Tears fell in the night. How she disliked the poverty, the crowding, the children's ceaseless clamour. In her heart she knew her husband was a good-time man and would never make money. An idea came to her the day she saw Spiros struggling with sacks slung across his shoulders.

"Mama," she said to Eleni who was washing clothes in the sink, "I'll have to be the one to make the money, if you'll mind the children?"

Eleni continued furiously scrubbing the clothes.

***

Chapter 30

Patras: 1963 - 1965

One year passed into another and another. The family's precarious financial situation improved slightly when Thalia, at the age of twelve, brought home wages from the local paper factory, and when Nikos and Marcos joined her there on their Name Days. Helena's own Name Day fast approached, when in turn, she would be required to beg the factory owner for a job.

"You're going to the factory," a tall, thin Thalia taunted her." Going to the factory ... you'll hate it,"

The fateful morning dawned. Melina handed her daughters each a brown bag of sandwiches, then leaning close to Helena she whispered, "What you do, don't tell me."

A flash of hope lit up Helena's eyes. Dragging her feet, she walked with Thalia to the factory, to face a thin woman smoking in a side entrance doorway. "With her eyes on her feet, she stuttered, "My m ... mother is poor and has lots of children to feed. Please will you give me a job?"

"Look up at me! How do I know you're an honest girl when I don't see your face? Scrawny bit of a thing, aren't you? Go get some fat on you before you come back."

Helena stared, poked out her tongue, and fled.

***

"*Panagia*, may the saints preserve us." Melina had been preparing a picnic to take to the city centre at the end of the day when Helena flew in the door, her clothes wet, an angry light in her eyes.

"What have you done?" she cried.

164

"You said not to tell you." Helena avoided her mother's and her grandmother's wide eyes. "I won't beg anymore from that ugly *vlakos* woman, I won't!"

Melina wrung her hands. She walked from the back window to the front, muttering aloud to her husband, "My Mama said when I married you that I fell for good looks and charm, but I dreamed, *poulaki mou* ... ah, what's the use? You tell me you'll make us rich but your littlest daughter must go begging to the factory." She wiped her face and blew her nose. "Ah, Christos, you're a funny man. You make me to dance and sing and to laugh, but also to weep. You snap your fingers and think the good things will come. Already you don't find me beautiful like when we were married. I see you watching the girls go by; I hear my Mama say how stupid can this Christos be? Already he's got the best looking woman in Patras and what can he want with others? Our daughters will marry poor men and work hard all their lives; how my Papa would be ashamed! Such high hopes he had for me with my big head of wisdom and strong enough to bear a dozen children. Maybe Helena ... but what's to become of her? Christos, you'll be angry. You'll beat her and send her back to the factory."

So, too, thought Helena. She walked with her sister each morning. On reaching the factory gates she ran past, and to the sea, to stare miserably over the dirty green swells that heaved in a sullen line along the shore.

"*Yifto,* loser," Thalia said, and threatened to tell.

Helena made a face and ignored her. This day she walked back and forth across the stony beach, hands in pockets, hair flying in the wind, oblivious of a figure sitting on a rock.

The figure got up and moved toward her. "Little girl, why are you so upset?"

Helena looked briefly into the face of a thin young man. Angrily she scrubbed tears from hers. *A girl does not talk to strange men.* She ran up the beach for home.

"My silly one, don't tell your Papa about the factory," Melina said, but with alarm in her voice. "I'll explain when I give him a big breakfast. And don't *you* say anything," she added as Eleni began to speak. "Nor you," to Thalia. Sighing with fresh disappointment she pushed away fears that, like her mother, she too might disappear into depression and no longer care how she looked, or even where she was.

The sun was beginning its slow descent when Christos appeared in the doorway. "Put on the pretty clothes, we'll go to the movies." His voice boomed over the street.

"But I have a picnic ready," Melina said. "You said we'll have a picnic and go to the shops."

"Tonight we go to the movies."

Melina's mood lifted in a burst of optimism. Forgetting about the afternoon's work spent preparing a picnic, she painted her lips bright red.

"Mama, you got blood on your lips," a relieved Helena said.

"Mind your tongue. Hurry, we must dress up when Papa says we go to the *Kryptos*. He likes to see Indian movies, but you must whisper to him the subtitles. We'll hope that today he wants to see *karagiozi* so we can all have a good laugh."

Christos poured himself a large glass of wine. "We can go also to look at the shops if it makes you happy…"

"And you'll buy me something pretty?" Melina's smile was dazzling.

Christos smacked his lips after emptying his wine glass in one gulp. The light in his eyes faded. "Ah no," he said, regret in his voice. "I give you the sun in the daytime and I tell the moon to swing by your window at night, but I got no money to buy you some pretty thing."

"Then I don't want to go to the shops." Melina's joyful mood evaporated as quickly as it had come.

"We'll go to the movies. We'll get some ice cream." Christos strode ahead, with Melina just behind, the family coming after. Elpenor carried Zoe, and the bent form of Spiros traipsed after them.

***

Chapter 31

Patras, 1965 - 1966.

Helena

"You can't have your Papa know that you play about with the neighbours' hair." Melina's fretful voice rose over the clamour of hammering outdoors.

"Mama, Mama." Helena turned from washing brushes in the kitchen sink and smiled sweetly at her mother. "I'll give any drachmas I earn to Papa and he won't know where they come from."

"Eh, eh! We'll tell lies to your Papa? We hide from him how you don't go to the factory but play about with peoples' hair?" Abruptly Melina's thoughts shifted. "Where is my laughing, handsome Christos who chases other women?"

"This is what most men will do." Eleni had struggled out of her chair and leaned up against the doorframe. "You married for love, and a poor one at that. Love turns quickly to dust when there's no money. Your good-time husband finds comfort in the arms of *poutana* because ..."

"Don't tell me! You know nothing."

".... They get something they don't have at home."

"My Christos, he says he can love many women as well as his wife, but I don't feel the love how once it was." Melina's voice trembled.

With the setting of the sun that evening, she prepared a special meal for him.

"Ha, so my wife wants something." Christos' large frame filled the doorway. He threw back his head, his thick hair spinning in a tangled mass. Slipping an arm about her waist, he said, "I think we get us a flagon of wine tonight. Upon my soul, *poulaki mou,* you got something to celebrate?

You're still my pretty little woman, eh? What do you want that you feed me like a king?"

Melina held her tongue until Christos had finished his third glass of wine. "Your daughter Helena," she began. "She ran away from the factory because the woman insulted her. You know her for a girl who works hard and one day soon she'll find something better to do than this factory work, you'll see."

Christos grunted and poured himself more wine He loved his youngest daughter but right now the family was in dire need of additional income. In his warm alcoholic state, images flitted: Helena singing to him in the countryside. Charming local farmers. Dancing and laughing in the street. She'd been the sunshine of his life until he distracted himself with young women in the city. Damn the business. He belched and grunted. But what will she find to do?" he asked. "All about us are the factories, and no one else to employ her."

"You'll see." Melina's voice was soothing.

"I'll do your hair and you'll be beautiful." Helena's song-song voice drifted in from the street. "Go home and wash it, then come to me and I'll make it pretty for you."

Again Christos grunted. He watched her in the front room of the house, or outside the window, as her small hands transformed a face. He saw neighbours perched in their doorways. Others staring as they passed to and from the *fourno,* from the school and the church. Gravitating about house number 24 came young fellows. They followed her about the streets like bees in search of nectar.

"Helena, Helena, do my hair. Can you make me look pretty?"

"Do mine. I want to look *sophisticated.*"

"You should do this for money." Christos was unaware that Spiros had come up behind him. "Ask for a drachma or two. When you get good you can charge even more."

"Ohh." Helena stared wide-eyed at him, and at her uncle. "I can charge money for the hair styles?"

"*I* can tell you about hair styles." Eleni's voice floated through the open door. "In Bournabat, wealthy people did their hair in tight curls, sometimes tied on top of the head. Then came the craze to cover it with a cap, but only when they dressed up like gypsies. My girl, you need to look at women's magazines. Study hair styles and colours to see what's current."

Christos, conflicted, feeling excluded, walked away muttering, "Women's talk."

Helena stared in surprise at her *Yia Yia.* Immediately she began collecting old magazines, fastening her eyes hungrily on portraits of sleek young women with short skirts and long hair. "*Yia Yia,*" she said, "I'm going to be a famous hair stylist and make my very own images. I will be photographed wearing clothes like these, and then I'll be famous."

"So the Fates have told me." Eleni's smile lit up a generally unhappy face.

From that day Helena hung around barber shops, believing she could learn by watching and listening. Peering from the shadows, she watched Andros Papastamos set up shop under the shade of a plane tree: two buckets, and four stools. On one of them he placed special soaps and oils; slapped his cutlass-like razors and scissors onto a make-shift bench. Helena watched his busy hands, listened to the talk filling the air.

"So, little girl, what you looking at?" The barber wiped his hands on his apron and stepped toward her. "You want a haircut, or you look for a man?"

Helena fled for the city centre. Next day she hovered on the periphery of another shop and saw that a barber stood as a king in his small domain: long white apron, a cloud of white soap, razor flying, scissors snapping and lotions applied with loud slapping noise. Talking, always talking. The hairdresser king was a repository of information, fount of folk wisdom, the village Muse. While most men came for shaving and cutting, Helena saw that the most important thing was for the talk, and absorbed it all. It was this social aspect as much as any beauty she would create that she would incorporate into her professional life.

Someone else watched the square's newest entrepreneur: Stephanos, the young man who had seen her on the beach. Orphaned, but for one Aunt Johanna and a brother, he had come from across the Gulf of Corinth to find work in the factories of Patras. Like most of the workers, had made his home in a tenement, a grey wall of concrete that rose up against the small wooden dwellings around the corner from Helena's home. His lone figure was often seen beneath a tree with a magazine. In the weekends, striding toward the beach, returning shimmering with salt and seaweed.

"May the saints preserve us, no one should be swimming in that water," Melina said.

"I do, Mama." Helena laughed as she dodged her mother's hand. She became aware of Stephan and saw him everywhere: in the shade of a mulberry tree, on the steps of his tenement. She was not to know he searched for her, for a flying angel with the hair of a thousand fairies; attuned his ears to her voice that could charm the archangel Luther himself.

Summer passed with quickening changes in the air. Winds that blew from the sea brought a further chill to the drafty refugee home. Refuse and the dying leaves of plane trees blew about the street. Helena squatted in her doorway one Saturday morning waiting for business. Without a conscious decision to begin a career in hair-dressing, without realizing she had already embarked on it, she searched for clients willing to pay her something, anything, as she feared her father would order her back to the factory. She must get training, learn how to do cuts, colour, perms; styles for both thin and thick hair, for long faces and round. To know the latest fashions.

She sat this day on a rock near the shore. A figure rose out of the water and walked toward her, all clean lean limbs and glinting skin, hair streaming with bits of the Ionian Sea.

"I'm Stephan," he said with a shy smile. Helena looked up, into eyes that to her, burned like scrubbed medallions. Confused that her heart had begun hammering painfully in her chest, she jumped off the rock without speaking and ran home.

Her eyes strayed often towards Stephan's tenement after that. Lingering near the public tap early mornings and late afternoons, she watched him coming and going from the factory.

"Come here little girl. I want to talk to you." The voice was close. Startled, Helena's head jerked up. There he was beside her! Another somersault in her chest and she was speechless.

"A girl does not talk to strange men," she said, recovering.

"I'm no stranger to you. I've been your neighbour these past two years. Listen, I've got an idea ..."

"I'm not talking to you." Helena looked away from him, colour rising in her face. After a silence, suddenly she laughed. "What do you want to tell me?"

Stephan stepped closer, his voice urgent. "You're wasting your time doing this. You should learn the trade properly, then set up shop. One day you could earn good money."

"Why do you care?"

"I ... you work hard, and no time for ..." He stopped, and as his lean frame hovered above her, Helena jerked away from him, her face a furious red. Stephan moved back a pace.

"How can I set up shop?" Helena's speech returned. "My father's got no money. *I've* got no money." But an idea had been planted.

***

Her father was seated at the kitchen table, tapping out the rhythm of rain hitting the windowpane. A few more minutes and he would be working with a gang of men on the railway lines. Helena waited until he'd drained his coffee cup and lit a cigarette, and her words came out in a rush: "Papa, I want to ask you something. I want to learn hair styling and I need money to go to school."

"Money? Got no money, child." Christos blew a ring of smoke in the air. "Always we need it for this and for that, and never is there enough."

"But Papa, your uncle in Canada gave you some." Helena moved a safe distance from the reach of her father's arms, but Christos' mood was mellow.

"But Papa, you say? And this is the girl who was rude to the factory boss who pays her to work." He looked into one chocolate-brown eye imploring him, at his daughter's rippling hair that half-hid the other. Mother of all the saints she was a beauty. His mind flicked back to the time of her birth and the decision to name her Helena. Indeed she had a face to launch a thousand ... what? Why, a thousand riches of course. But this hair-dressing business? Hmm. Irritation rose within him at the thought of having to make a decision that would cost him money, but still he considered. The girl did most of the family's laundry. Her hands, so clever with women's hair, also got dirty running errands. In the evenings she helped put Eleni to bed. What would the family do without her? Damn the whole business!

171

Christos stroked his chin, rubbed a hand across his abundant hair. The ebullient man, often harsh to his children in the manner of his own upbringing, loved them with all the extravagance of his nature. Now he implored the heavens to tell him what to do. He stared out the open door. Pools of water from the rain glistened in a sudden weak sun and little boys splashed in them. Gesticulating men stood about a stalled motorcar in the middle of the street. Seeing neighbour Lina's bent frame struggling under a heavy canvas bag, he got up and lifted it onto her doorstep. Returning, he walked to the back window and looked up at the distant mountains. Abruptly he made his decision.

"By God and all the saints, my Helena will have her education," he said that evening, and plunged the family into further poverty to pay the cost of her apprenticeship in a hair salon.

In a dilapidated mansion in the Lower City, the salon lay close to a broad flight of steps leading to the city's Upper section. Helena was familiar with it, and with the owner, for it was here her father had taken his family for haircuts on Saturday morning expeditions to the city. While disliking Mr. Pousopolis, she had watched carefully, mesmerized by his flying scissors that cut and snipped; by curls magically emerging out of long, limp hair. The place shone full of mirrors, full of languid women sipping Turkish coffee, men talking. Mr. Pousopolis yelled at someone passing his door: "So, you fat pasha, what do ya do today? You got a face like a camel … Ha, I heard you lost your trousers last night."

"I'll help you," the small girl had said to Mr. Pousopolis after having her hair cut, and he'd looked at her out of his slit-like eyes as she scrambled to retrieve rollers, pins and papers from the floor.

"All the many years I bring to you my family for you to cut their hair, very good business I've given you," Christos said to him now. "I'll make a proposal: two thousand drachmas to teach my daughter all the business to do with the hair. A fair deal, for my Helena will work hard." The broad-shouldered Christos looked into the squinty eyes of a squat man with baggy trousers and a curling moustache. He struck a deal.

And so it was that in a basement room washing towels and rollers, cutting curling papers; running errands in sun and wind and rain, Helena began her career to create beautiful hair.

172

"Here, little girl, take some extra money to buy yourself an ice cream." Helena looked up into the smiling eyes of an older woman and tears welled in her own at the unexpected kindness.

"Servants don't eat at work." An irate Mr. Pousopolis looked up from his desk. "They don't keep tips and take nothing from my customers. Give that to me." He snatched a drachma from Helena's hand.

Immediately Helena began hiding tips in her brassiere. Anger built as the weeks passed, subsiding only when she was allowed upstairs to brush women's hair. The rare times when not busy, she hung about in the stairwell listening, watching and listening.

One afternoon, Mr. Pousopolis ordered her to clean his house located on a nearby street. Mutiny coursing through her blood like a fever, Helena took his keys and entered the spacious bungalow. Furiously she swept, dusted and scrubbed. When finished, she leaned against the kitchen counter, perspiring. Ha, what was that? A large grape cake sat on the counter, snowy frosting gleaming through its wrapping. Her stomach reminded her she'd not eaten since early morning. Immediately the wrapper came off and her fingers dug into it. In a brief time, half the cake disappeared. Helena wiped her sticky fingers on her dress. Serve her boss right. He'd taken her father's money, taught her nothing, and treated her like an unpaid slave. He bowed and scraped to his rich customers and ignored the poor ones - a nasty man with tiny pig's eyes.

Her stomach full, feeling avenged, she wandered into the central city of which she had seen little during her growing up years. Its lower sections had been laid out in squares to form a geometric pattern with *Georgiou 1 Square* central to it. Past the *Apollon* Theatre, the Town Hall and the Court of Justice she walked. Awed, she stared at well-dressed shoppers, at imposing buildings that sparkled under a mid-day sun.

At the foot of *Kolokotroni Street,* she stopped. Where to go? Above, a ruined castle gazed mournfully over the city. At her feet, a cobblestone path wound between buildings. She followed it, stopping at an entrance to a rectangular courtyard. A circle of tiny people stared silently up at her. She waited for their words, for them to move. They remained still and silent. "Ha," she said, laughing and clapping her hands. "It's a sculpture studio."

Two men at the courtyard's far end looked up. One seemed familiar, something about the tall, thin line of him that reminded her of Stephan. It couldn't be. She looked again but he'd bent his head to his sculpture. The other fixed her with a stare until she retreated. Here was something to tell *Yia Yia.*

Next morning, Mr. Pousopolis, his eyes as mere slits, ordered her to the basement at the same moment an elderly blond woman entered.

"Ah, Ms Mecouri, so, you've come back to me." Mr. Pousopolis' tones were instantly honeyed. "You sit right here in my chair." Gesturing Helena to get out of sight, he hustled about his American client. But Helena remained, sweeping the floor about her master's chair.

Washed, cut, and brushed with soft waves, the American woman got up, smiled in the mirror, turned to Helena and handed her an American dollar.

"For you, child," she said. "You're a good girl and have a lovely face."

Helena gaped. To her this was a fortune, American money from an American lady. She slid it down her blouse, was about to move away, when Mr. Pousopolis loomed over her.

"Give that to me."

"No. No *sir*. The customer gave it to me. You don't touch ..."

"You give it to me!" Mr. Pousopolis plunged his hand down Helena's blouse, snatched the dollar bill from between her breasts. He handed it to his idle son. A hush fell upon the salon as all eyes turned upon the owner and his newest employee.

Faces, reflected in the mirrors, stared as she shouted, "Why do you all look at me?" To her boss she said, "I won't work for you anymore. You take my Papa's money and you teach me nothing. Everybody sees how you give my tips to your son who does no work. All the time I watched to see how you do business; I learned how to do things when you weren't looking. Now I'm going to open my own salon and take your customers from you."

Some customers clapped. Others hid their smiles. Mr. Pousopolis thundered that she was rude, a no-good thief and would come to a bad end, a poor little nobody who knew nothing about hair. People would laugh at her.

Helena ran through busy traffic toward home. The prosperous old city rose up about her: neoclassical and circular marble homes that mocked, windowed eyes from Roman and Byzantine public buildings, impassive. Hawkers called to her. Sauntering shoppers dodged the flying figure. She took the overgrown path by the railway lines to reach *The Stone,* her street, and home. Rushing through the open door she went weeping to her mother and grandmother.

Nothing was said to her father that evening. Melina, fearing his anger, was not sure exactly where it would fall.

After Christos banged the door front behind him the next morning, Helena organized her salon. On the window ledge she set out one cheap bottle of shampoo and one conditioner, rollers, curling papers, brush, comb, and four folded towels. A bucket of water stood on the floor. Too young to run a retail operation, she could not advertise her business without risking the wrath of an inspector. Instead she flitted about her street and to the neighbouring ones, begging people to come to her.

"I can do your hair, a nice set. First one is free, then you pay, but only if you like what I do. *Please* come to me."

"But you're just a child," an elderly woman said.

"Please. Come and see what I can do. First one is free."

"We know what you can do. What else, a nice colour, a perm?"

Helena knew how to set and style, but not how to cut, perm or colour. Open first, and then learn, she believed. Humiliated by the injustice of her boss and general attitude toward her, she vowed to the world she *would* be somebody. She would open a fashionable salon in the square of *Psila Alonia* or *Georgiou I Square,* maybe near the Town Hall. Famous people from all over the world would come to her. Only such thoughts banished her ready tears. Begging her mother for use of part of the front room by the window she said, "I'll sew curtains for privacy, and ... please, I need some towels."

Crowding about number 24 came giggling clients dropping onto makeshift benches to await their turn. The scenes repeated: head over a basin, cold water poured from an enamel jug. Hair washed, set in rollers, the client leaving, returning in the afternoon to have the rollers removed and her hair styled.

Helena's popularity soared, clients lining up early and late. Nikos and Markos made faces through the living room window and went laughing down the street. After work Markos plopped himself into the barber's chair, as he called it, and said, "How about a pretty style for your handsome brother?"

Helena swatted him. "You think I'm a little girl playing with toys," she said in echo of her grandmother. "Watch me: soon I'll make more money than you in your ugly factory." Markos gave a mock bow and ran laughing from the room.

"Free hair style, and if you like it, the next one you pay." Once Helena had exhausted her small cul-de-sac, she called out her invitation in neighbouring streets. She saved every *drachma* until she had enough to purchase a small dryer, a chair, a plastic sink. Still she had no running water but collected a bucket at a time from a drum in the back yard.

"Watch for the inspector," old women cried. "Hide your things little girl, or he finds you and shuts down your business."

"He's coming, he's coming," chanted small children at the sight of an Inspector entering the cul-de-sac. Helena swept her tools off the window ledge. "Hide, hide," she whispered to her clients. Each obediently hid behind the back door.

"Helena, will you do my hair?" Thalia approached her one evening. "It's thin and straight – can't you make it look more like yours?"

"I ... maybe I could do it so your face looks not so long, but now you must pay me."

"Pay you!" But Thalia's outrage subsided only when she emerged with the new-wave look where ends of the hair are flipped up in a giant wave. Stephanos' brother Kostas paused as he walked by. Lean, darkly inscrutable like his brother, his eyes widened when he saw the transformed Thalia, his eyes lingering on her before turning to Helena. Arms folded, he watched the activity until local people crowded the house, only then reluctantly moving away.

"I'm not paying you," local women said. "I'm your auntie so you should do my hair for me, no money.'

"Everyone is my auntie. Please, just give me something, anything."

"Yes, why should I pay you?" echoed another voice. "What do you need money for, eh? You're too young and haven't been to school."

"Pay me something, anything, a *drachma*," Helena begged.

Days and evenings fled by. To make any profit Helena worked for many hours every day; was roused from her bed at five in the morning for a woman going to Athens, for styles requested in late evenings, and Sundays too. Older women watched, clucking, gossiping, hawk-eyes ranging ceaselessly over the street. Younger ones chattered: "Eh, do my hair, make me beautiful. You got a boyfriend yet?"

"Yeah, yeah, making eyes at Stephan. I saw her creeping out of the house when her papa wasn't looking. You go to the beach with him, huh? What do you want with him?"

"Who wants to make eyes at boys when they can make money?" And her fluted voice continued to sing out: "You can be anything you want. Sexy? Let your hair flow loose. Innocence, you braid it. For the clever look, pile it up high and tie it with a black ribbon. A woman's hair is her great beauty. A plain girl can become a beautiful one ..."

Eleni laid down her knitting, Spiros his cards. Christos, who had been sunning himself in a chair outside the door, got up, muttering, "Women's talk," and walked away.

One Saturday morning he dozed in his marriage bed while Melina busied herself in the kitchen.

"Your breakfast," she said, returning. "Sit up and I'll put it on your knees." Meekly she set a tray before her husband. Christos yawned, then spluttered at the spread before him: grapes and hymettos and honey. Black coffee, eggs, and his favourite *Papastratos* cigarette. His eyes gleamed. "You liked my singing last night? We'll do it some more, and dancing too."

Melina only smiled. She removed the tray, brought Christos his clothes, and leaning over the bulk of him, kissed him lightly on the forehead. Christos dressed, whistled as he drank more coffee in the kitchen. Melina cleared her throat and waved an arm, indicating her daughter in the doorway.

"Papa?" Helena stood beside his chair, her eyes lowered. "I've got something to ask ..."

"Not now *poulaki mou*. Your Papa is busy. Tonight you ask him what you want and I give you anything." Christos bent to his wife, gave her a perfunctory kiss and went out the door, a song on his lips. Pulling a sour face, Melina muttered about who he might be seeing, then roused herself to tell her daughter, "You try asking your papa again tonight."

"Papa, I've got something to ask you." Helena touched her father's shoulder as he stepped in the door. In his hand he held a letter. Smiling absently at her, he bent over the rocking figure of Eleni.

"*Chryso mou*, how are you? I give *ouzo* to cheer you, then you get up and dance with me." Helena, moving toward him, heard Eleni mutter, "I saw you out the window when the moon rose above the factory, I saw you with a woman on your arm, and it was not your wife."

"You're a sly old woman. You do not see anything, and don't you go saying so."

"Papa, *Papa*, I want to talk to you."

Christos suddenly raised his arm and swept the window ledge clean of her hair dressing materials. "I'm not listening," he shouted. Helena, crying, scrambled on hands and knees retrieving brushes and rollers. "Tell your grandmother to keep her old eyes inside her head. I'm going to the *taverna*." Christos left, taking his letter with him. It had been sent from Canada by a solicitor in Montreal. The brief note contained news that his mother's youngest brother there had died and left him a small amount of money. Enough for a truck – but not a new one.

Melina muttered as she scrubbed the kitchen benches. Another truck so her husband could do menial jobs for little pay. Her sense of shame remained as images mocked her: Christos as an old man chugging Greek soil from one corner of the countryside to another until age reduced him to a chair by his door. The words from his songs flying out his truck window, she thought, to be lost on the somnolent air as he roamed, careless or disappointed. Evenings spent at the local *taverna* charming passing women. He might get fat but his hair would remain abundant and curly. With his laugh and his wit he could surely seduce even the young.

Yes, the young. Melina remembered the day Christos had said, why don't you wear clothes like women in the city? Where is your laugh, your singing and dancing? Eh, eh, my wife has gone and I got this one in bed beside me. For a time, whenever she expected him home from work, she painted her lips, tamed her hair, and draped herself in bright cotton skirts.

At this moment, with thoughts of Christos in the arms of young women, of yet another truck that would soon enough break down, Melina felt a sharp stab of pain in her belly. That was the day she gave up believing she would one day be rich and live like the women in the city, that she would wear fine clothes, live in a big house and have servants – the kind of life her mother said she'd had in Smyrna. Aching disappointment gathered within her as autumn passed into winter. A moment of epiphany arrived the day Christos said his truck had broken down and where was the money to fix it?

"I'll go to the city for work on the roads," he said, spreading his broad hands in a gesture of helplessness, no song on his lips this day. Melina, chopping vegetables, saw him pour himself a double shot of *ouzo* and stand with it in the doorway, his eyes ranging restlessly up and down the street. Suddenly she wailed and sucked at a cut finger. Christos turned to her, and with an unconscious gesture, she lifted her hands to smooth the wild riot of her hair.

"Ah, *chryso mou*, put a smile on your face for we are happy, are we not? We have this good home ..."

"It belongs to Mama and Uncle Spiros."

Christos fixed a smile. "We've got your Mama, and our sons and daughters. Still we'll sing in the countryside and go to the movies same as always. Come, dance with me."

"No money to fix a stupid truck." Melina turned her face to the wall. There, facing her, were the faded, peeling remnants of forests and verdant valleys she'd once pasted on the walls when a girl. She got up and moved dizzily about the kitchen.

"Doing a crazy dance, Mama?" Nikos stood in the doorway. His mother spread her hands as though to soften a fall, then sat down hard. Familiar scenes, repeating themselves far into her future, rushed through her mind, a second broken truck representing the death of her dreams. From that day she stopped singing and began praying. Wiped off her trade-mark red lipstick and tied a black scarf over her head. She dressed herself in dark brown and grey.

"Melina, you're becoming your mother," Spiros told his niece. "You're mourning your life before you've half-lived it."

Melina did not speak to Christos for many days, refused to walk with the family in the evenings. Instead she plodded a lonely path along the shore as though to find comfort in the chaotic moods of the sea. Her cloaked form entered the *Church of the Apostles.*

"If she can't be rich, she thinks to be good, to make sure she gets into heaven," she heard Eleni mutter one evening. "I should think about getting myself in there too, *Hail Mary, full of grace.*"

179

And Melina looked at her mother. She was not to know that Eleni felt old, felt she had failed. That she had disappointed Adam, who would know his name had fallen in the dust in this distant city; that his family was poor again. "What will I say when I see him?" Eleni rocked and muttered: "Your son Alekos, he's but a dreamer like you, dear Adam. He lives in a room in Athens and keeps himself by his pen. Your Zoe is happy with her poor hunchback husband, and Melina, your daughter with her head full of serpents to make her wise, is married to a trucker who doesn't care if he's a poor nobody. And he has other women!" Her muttering ended with a sob.

"Yes, Christos, you better come to church too." With visions of her husband in the arms of other women, pain bit deep in Melina's heart.

***

Chapter 32

Toronto

Georgia

The time and place fall away: home, Book City, Yonge Street. At night I dream of that world in Patras. It floats before me when I walk, when I make sales, when I cook and clean up after dinner. Jeff comes to the door but I hardly register, seeing only gossiping women on the streets of Patras, laments for their race and their fate etched on their faces. I see my great grandmother Eleni enclosed within the walls of a makeshift house, rocking, dreaming of her glory days in Smyrna. Grandma Melina broken too. Poor Spiros still struggling with the burden of family redemption. My mother as a young girl with busy hands, songs brushing the air, her heart somersaulting at the sight of young man called Stephan.

I pick up the photos Helena has given me and will myself into them. Next thing I'm in Patras with her as a child, driving a truck in the blazing sun, singing and laughing with a father who loved her absolutely. Yes, love: I believe that for my mother it was, perhaps still is, the very elixir of life. But whatever happened to this Stephan? I think she's avoiding telling me more.

"You live back there too much." I hadn't heard her enter my room because of the maple tree knocking its branches against my window. How can I explain that I'm happy slipping among the people I've come to know there, among young fellows hanging about a plane tree; families strolling in the evenings? And Christos summoning the family. I can hear him say, 'Put on the pretty clothes for we go to the movies.' I'm with them at the *Kryptos*, among crowds watching Indian movies or popular comedy, films

181

known as *karagiozi*. Christos, on seeing the subtitles, saying, "You read to me the words." I'm imagining Helena at seven years crooning Elvis Presley love songs boomed from a roof-top radio, or hiding under the pub's espresso machine to listen.

"Get your head down, you shouldn't be here." Mr. Stavros is hissing at her, smacking his hands together. "And don't go singing out loud. These words are not for a child."

"Georgie, open your eyes!" Helena is shaking me. "You're making that strange noise. It's not normal. I keep telling you not to spend so much time on this story of yours."

"Your story, you mean." How much have I made up, dreamed, or been told? There's so much yet to pry out of her. Back to the photos. Randomly I look at them again: the family on trips to the ancient acropolis, to the temple of Artemis. Spiros in some of them, but rarely Eleni. At the docks, the broad figure of Christos leaning over the water, arms flung in mid-air. Melina pointing at something. Ships and vessels from many nations of the world, barges and caiques loaded to the gunwales. Melina laughing, her bright skirt blowing about her legs and her hair standing straight up. An earlier time, I think, a happier time.

***

Chapter 33

Patras, 1967

Stephan

"Look, I want to want to talk to you - seriously." Stephan had followed Helena to the public tap. "You're wasting your time around here. These are poor people and can never pay enough for you to earn a living. I think maybe you should be going to school in Athens to learn the hair business properly." Embarrassed after speaking so freely, he shifted his feet and looked away over the railway tracks.

"I'm not talking to you." But Helena's tone was coquettish and gave him a different message. He stole a quick glance back at her, saw her breasts rising and falling with the rhythm of her breathing; glimpsed the two perfect suns of her bosom. A profusion of images fell upon him: Golden limbs. Rivers of molten hair. A lithe little body. And he began dreaming, dreaming he could open the doors to her heart and to her shimmering universe. That he could enter the garden of her soul; listen to its songs caressing the air. When he heard her voice, he felt faint with the joy of it. While she'd said no, he felt he was being offered all the gold in the universe, a sublime happiness. He looked into her face, when able to control his voice, repeated, "You must go to Athens and get proper teaching. I'll loan you the money."

"I'm not taking anything from you." Helena's voice remained brusque.

"Why do you speak to me like this?"

"A girl does not talk nice to strange men."

"You've told me that, but I'm not a strange man." Abruptly Stephan reached out a hand to her. "Come here, little girl." He pulled her close, bent his head and kissed her. Blood roared in Helena's head and she fell against him. She wriggled herself upright, lifted a hand and slapped his cheek. Stephan sprang back, blood rushing to his face, his eyes widening in shock.

"Don't touch me again." Helena ran down the street to her door, threw herself inside and buried her face in a cushion.

Confused, and in a tumult of feelings, Helena attempted to hide from Stephan, walking the ragged paths behind the two lines of houses to avoid him. Eventually coming face-to-face with him beside the public tap, she dropped her eyes. Her face grew hot. Aware of eyes peeping from behind half-closed shutters, from doorways and balconies, she remained transfixed.

Stephan came closer. Silence engulfed the street as the two figures in the centre of it stood in silent tableau, neither looking at the other. Eventually the young man spoke.

"Look, you're wasting your time here." His voice was urgent.

"Why do you care? First I'll work to make money, then I'll go."

"I can lend it to you. Why don't we talk about it?" Expression inscrutable, Stephan's eyes bored into Helena's until almost involuntarily, he lowered them to her swelling bosom. A crimson flush flamed his neck as he allowed himself a glance at the dip between them – valleys of Paradise, honey in the desert. He saw flowered brassier straps resting on the warm tones of her skin. Quickly he averted his eyes, only to feel a thousand eyes trained on him. And into the hush on the street, a train whistled. Gulls wheeled. Sudden gusts blew coal dust about them in ragged shrouds. Now shy and embarrassed, Stephan shifted his feet and walked home.

"Stephan." Helena stood at the window, savouring the sound of his name on her tongue. "Oh, he's coming back!" But it was Stephan's look-alike brother Kostas returning from the south. The young man had taken to sauntering back and forth before number 24, and when catching Helena's eye, reluctantly moved on.

What's the matter with him? Helena swished a bucket of dirty water on the street after him, then forgot him. It was Stephan who lingered in her dreams. Covertly she watched for him, made pretense of going to the public tap, to the *Church of the Apostles,* to a neighbour's house with a tray of cookies, all in the hope of a glimpse of him. The gossip was busy that flew through the stifling air of the street.

Moodily Melina saw that Helena had already become her father's daughter, her eyes dancing at the sound of a male voice. Having no wish for her to repeat her own story, to grow old before her time and lose her husband to the arms of other women, she said, "You're always on some mad search for love, but know what I think? You're a girl just looking for some excitement."

"Pray to the mother of Jesus you don't give up your future like your mother did." Eleni added her voice.

Love: surely it was but an addiction. Melina decided it was time to talk to Christos.

***

"You must find Helena a husband."

Melina stood in the doorway of the bedroom one Saturday morning. Christos heaved his large frame up in the bed and looked at his wife in surprise.

"So, you think a fourteen year old girl should get married? She wants a career, not a boyfriend."

"She's near fifteen and can be engaged for a year, two years. She flirts with all the boys. Our neighbours see her with a fellow in the moonlight when she should be in her bed. I don't want her to ..."

"Run off and marry a rough fellow like me, eh?"

Melina twisted her fingers. "Ah, Christos, you're a funny man, and you like to have a good time. But where is the money to have nice things, for our family to have dignity?"

"You're not happy because I don't make us rich? Tell me woman, if I got us lots of money, would you laugh? Would you sing in the streets like a young girl? Would you dance?"

"What is there to be happy about?" Melina covered her face.

Angrily Christos tossed aside the bed covers, got up and flung on his clothes. "You want a husband for your daughter? – then I'll find her one."

Satisfied, Melina disappeared into the kitchen to make her husband breakfast. He would look for a rich man for his daughter if it meant money in his pocket.

But Christos maintained his usual habits. Each evening he swung through the door of his home expecting dinner. Soon after, Melina heard his voice booming from the pub, his laughter through its doors. She saw men young and old gravitate about the entertainer with the ribald mouth and laughing eyes, and took to sighing as jealousy enveloped her. Why could she not be satisfied with her husband as he was, a sudden sunbeam in the doorway, a joyous figure laughing on the hills, voice booming as he announced he'd brought home some fresh fish. Once he'd put a song in her heart, a smile on her red, red lips. A shot or two of *ouzo* and he was the funniest man in the city.

"See, you did it all to yourself." Eleni's now arthritic hands laid down her knitting needles. "Upon my soul I say it is better Helena gets help for her business. Then she'll have money and not go after the boys."

Melina brooded. Christos once loved her. Now he loved other women. She knew that in the past he'd sometimes enticed them home and made love to them when the children were in school, she was working, and Eleni at the market.

"They're cold, they're hungry, they must be fed," he'd said when she accused him. "Every woman needs to be loved. Not one should be without." She tried telling herself that her husband could love many women and it did not mean he could not also love her, same as always. But she did not feel loved the way she once had. She worried about her growing children, especially tempestuous Helena. Images ran together: Helena among other little girls playing with her dolls in the dust, dolls made from sticks and rags and stones. Papa coming home, angry about something. Picking up the dolls and throwing them, stamping on the little doll houses. Papa shouting. Helena growing up, a young girl afraid of her own sexuality. Now, it seemed, a lean young man with brooding eyes had passed her line of vision and bewitched her. Yet still she ignored him and flirted with the factory boys. What was to become of her, of them all? Would getting Helena engaged prevent her from rushing into what would become a life of misery, like her own?

***

Autumn passed abruptly into winter with its chill winds and darkness that settled across the landscape. Sudden rainstorms followed. People feared that in mud slides they would lose their dazzling elliptical houses perched on the city's upper slopes. But the famed horse-shoe-shaped and circular homes near its base first suffered in the torrents. At the wreckage, laments echoed up valleys that sprang green among relics of Frankish castles and Greek temples.

Helena's business dropped with the onset of the severe weather. Some clients objected to the increasing fee she demanded. Some stayed away for fear the rain would ruin a new style. A slow morning passed. Helena fiddled with her tools on the window ledge, heard her mother muttering, saw her motionless in the back window, the snakes of her hair twisting. Knitting needles lay still in her lap and only her lips moved. Understanding her mother's empty dreams brought tears to Helena's eyes. She had clothed her body in colourful cloth like a temple of beauty, and thought of herself as a female Apollo flying close to the sun. She sat now in a refugee house, a woman defeated. Suddenly cold, Helena hugged her arms across her chest.

"I'm going into the city, be late for dinner," she said. She snatched Nikos' boots and Markos' raincoat from a peg by the door and ran through traffic and crowded pavements toward the *Circular Agora*. Reaching Mr. Pousopolis' hair salon, she thrust her hands deep in her pockets and darted quick glances in the windows. All the stylists were strangers to her but one. Ha! A big staff turnover. No wonder, with Squinty Eyes as employer.

Shivering in the doorway, she peered down the length of the salon. Mr. Pousopolis was not in sight, so she would just slip in and no one but the thin young man at the back would know her.

"May I help you?" The receptionist asked politely. "We close in forty minutes."

"I don't want my hair done. I just want to look around. I … want a job here."

"No vacancies but help yourself." The receptionist turned back to her magazine.

Helena stood uncertainly inside the door then withdrew just outside it as a client came through, the ends of her hair swept up and behind her ears.

"Excuse me, I have a salon in my house at number 24 in X Street," she said, her voice lowered. "I'll do any style for you for a much cheaper price. Come anytime."

The client looked surprised, nodded, and continued walking.

"Come to me, I'll give you a better style and charge you less." The general response to her soliciting was a quick nodding of the head as the client passed on. Two said they would definitely come, that Mr. Pousopolis did not treat them like others because they were not rich.

But not too poor to come to him for a hair style. Come to me and give me your money.

Helena ran all the way home, guilty about trying to steal her old boss's clients. She would ask the plaster Virgin for forgiveness.

What was this? Her father sat with a strange gentleman wearing a smart naval uniform in the living room of number 24. His moustache was as thick as the hair on his head and his face folded itself in smiles.

"Ah, Helena." A thunderous expression rested briefly on Christos' face at the sight of his bedraggled daughter. Both men rose and Helena looked up – and up – at the stranger. Surely his head would bump into the doorway arch when he walked through.

"Helena, I bring this gentleman, a captain of the Greek Navy, to meet you." Christos thrust out his chest with pride in his accomplishment, not least because he had pocketed 6000 drachmas from the worthy captain with promise to him of betrothal to his beautiful daughter.

"I am Mr. Alexander Anthopoulou," the stranger said, extending his hand. "Your father tells me of his daughter and I've come to pay a call." His smile remained undimmed while Helena simply stared with bold eyes, not knowing her appearance and behaviour acted as a challenge, that the captain, as he looked at her, believed that in spite of the present mess of her, she would surely grow up to much beauty.

"Mr. Anthopoulou lives in a marble house in Patras' newest suburb, when he's not sailing with the Greek Navy," her father said. "He comes bearing gifts, and also an engagement ring."

Both men looked at Helena expectantly, and she knew they waited for the lowered eyes, the humble curtsy, the expression of gratitude.

A short silence ensued. Helena stared up into the captain's face then slowly lowered her eyes to his feet.

"I don't like your socks," she said.

Flustered, anger sharpening his tone, Christos said, "She's very young and needs time to grow up. Perhaps you will come back in ... maybe a year?"

The captain only smiled. "I'll change my socks," he said, extended a firm handshake to his would-be father-in-law, and strode confidently down the street.

Helena caught sight of Stephan hugging his scrawny form against a cypress tree, his eyes boring into the captain's broad back in fear and fury.

***

Chapter 34

Patras, 1968

The day following the Captain's visit, Stephan waited at the end of X Street until he saw Christos leave number 24, followed by Melina heading to the markets. He knew that Nikos, Markos and Thalia had long since entered the factory; that Eleni would still be in bed. Approaching the house, he lifted a hand to knock, but dropped it on seeing Helena through the front window fluffing a client's hair. Helena glanced up. "Oh – it's you!" Hair pins dropped from her mouth.

"I have to talk to you."

She retrieved her pins from the floor and from beneath the window ledge, whispered, "You must not come here. Papa is very angry – Mama too. If they see you here it will be *much* worse."

"Please, listen to me."

Helena straightened and looked at him. Eyes sparking, she asked, "What must you talk about?"

"It's ... it's just for you to hear." Stephan shuffled his feet. "Remember I promised you a loan for you to go to school in Athens? I have most of it saved."

"You – well, don't tell the whole street!"

"I'm not. I'm whispering. When you're finished, come to me so we can talk about it."

Helena continued brushing, but saw the old woman itching to get out of her chair.

She walked toward Stephan who had removed himself beyond *The Stone* to the far side of the railway lines. He turned right and headed to his

190

tenement, glancing over his shoulder to check she was following. Helena moved like one without volition, her red dress embroidered with white roses swinging about her knees, sandals squeaking on the warm asphalt. She saw heads appearing in doorways. Eyes squinted through window slats and followed her as she climbed the tenement steps to the second floor of the grey building Stephan called home.

She stood uncertainly inside the door of the apartment where she saw two iron beds with a colourful cloth thrown over each – "My brother Kostas lives here when he's not working in the south," Stephan said. She noted a wooden table and two chairs, a sink, small cooker, hand basin and large chest of drawers. On a shelf above one of the beds stood a photograph of two middle-aged women, one smiling self-consciously, her hat elaborately decorated with flowers and feathers. The other who stood bare-headed, her thin lips drawn into a tight, straight line. Prints of Saint Sophia and the Virgin Mary hung on opposing walls.

Stephan moved to straighten an imperceptible slant in the position of one of them. Helena watched the sinewy arms and the line of his buttocks as he reached. She saw the arch of his spine, the glowing skin of him, and a shudder shot through her belly. Her heart beating frantically she flung herself on him, arms grasping his arms. Fastening her hands about his neck, she pulled him toward one of the beds.

"Make love to me," she cried. "*Please* make love to me."

Rapidly-changing expressions crossed the young man's face, fleeting as clouds across the sky. He reached only for her hand.

"No," he said then. "I … I h-have too much respect." Flushed and stammering he turned from her. As he did so, a thousand Helenas swam before his eyes, streams of hair flying up from their heads to twist all about them. A multitude of Helenas whose clothes, like butterfly wings, dropped to the floor. Within his narrow chest a smoldering volcano erupted as he saw her glistening body arch toward him, breasts as two perfect suns. He fell on his knees to the floor. As a vine running wild she leapt on him, but he stayed her with an arm. Convulsed in a torment of a kind known only to self-denying virile young men, he held her from him and stared wildly out the window to the setting sun. Surprise widened his eyes as its flames burned low over the city, then moved to the glistening line of the sea beyond the railway tracks. Scratchy sounds from a gramophone trickled up the darkening air to the window. The words he would say remained on his lips, and still he held her from him, still he stared out the window.

"Not now, not now," he said, his voice hoarse. "You are but a girl with a big future to make. We must wait until things can be properly done. Now we must talk about hair-styling school. Talk to your parents about going to Athens. I'll give you the money."

"Why so much hurry?" Helena touched his arm longingly and her fingers crept up toward his neck. "If I stay, you can learn to know me better. Then things can be properly done."

Stephan said nothing, but an image of the naval captain had intruded. "I think you shouldn't wait," he said. "You can become a famous hair stylist as soon as you want."

Helena, judging the passing of two weeks after the Captain's visit enough time for her family's anger to subside, approached her mother about going to school in Athens.

"Athens!" Melina's voice rose in alarm.

"But where is the money for this?" Eleni, overhearing, roused herself out of her flitting dreams of Smyrna.

"I saved it," Helena said, avoiding her mother and grandmother's eyes.

"Athens?" Eleni had now thoroughly returned to the present. "My Adam told me that many more proper Greeks – the ones descended from the Byzantines – lived in Anatolia than in this city of Athens. Why must you go?"

"I told you, *Yia Yia*, I need to learn how to do perms and colour and different cuts so I can become famous." Helena picked up her grandmother's knitting, looked at it, and said, "Then I'll take you back to Smyrna so you can show me the places you lived." *Maybe then I'll believe all the stories about Adam and the other children, and all the riches.*

"You're good enough already," her mother said. "Besides, your father will be bringing back the Captain one day soon enough to get you engaged." This last she muttered under her breath.

At six that evening, Christos came home with a song on his lips, lifted Eleni out of her chair and pressed a rolled cigarette in her hand. "For the family matriarch. You come dance with me on the street tonight?"

Melina, mending a shirt by the fading light from a window, swivelled her chair so that her back was to him, wondering what woman had he been seeing that day.

When Eleni rolled her eyes, plaintively he said, "You see how I have no wife to hold in my arms, no wife to drink and dance with me." His mocking eyes fell on a dark-hooded Melina, her back turned to him.

"Never mind all that, your daughter has something to ask you." Melina's voice was tart. "Helena, talk to your father."

With lowered head, Helena made her request.

"Athens? You go for schooling when you already know how to do the hair? You say no to the captain to do this!" Christos' anger surfaced swiftly when he felt conflicted. Banging his glass on the table, he picked a broken piece of it and ground it under foot. "You're a bad girl. Get away from me so I don't see you."

But during the following month, Christos absorbed Helena's sing-song voice, her energizing presence about the house and street, and it occurred to him that in the big city she might grow up some more before he brought back the captain. Besides, how could he deny her? Grudgingly he agreed she could go. The autumn term having already begun, Helena enrolled for the New Year term at *L'Ecole de Paris* in Athens.

In the weeks that followed, whenever she was free from customers, Helena slipped from her home into Stephan's tenement at the end of his factory shift. She flirted with him and teased him. Eyelashes fluttering on golden cheek; near-naked breasts thrust upward, she caressed his shoulders, his arms, ran her fingers over his face, then laced them behind his neck. Still he refused her.

One late evening, half-hidden in a circle of rocks on the beach, she slipped her hands about his shoulders and frantically pulled him close. "Please, *please* kiss me." In the following silence, only the rhythmic splash of an in-coming tide was heard. Gently pushing away her hands, Stephan stammered, "Not now. Not yet."

"You don't love me!" She edged away from him. "One day soon Papa will bring back the captain and make me get engaged to him. Then you'll be sorry."

A guttural sound broke from his throat. Stephan's body shook. The words he would say remained crushed in his throat and he sat trembling as the night crept about them. Only when a rogue wave hit the rocks and soaked them both did he jump up, take her hand, and lead her to his apartment. In silence he handed towels to her, stripped off his wet clothes, and with his back to her, wrapped himself in a sheet. A naked Helena tore at it. Throwing herself on him she collapsed with him on his narrow bed, where, fumbling, groaning, he made gentle love to her.

As she left that early evening, Helena saw him frowning, heard him muttering, "Now she's mine, my woman. Nobody else can touch her."

***

Helena walked the streets wearing ribbons, a scarf, decorative belt, bright lipstick and flowers in her hair. The lovers exchanged half-hidden smiles, cryptic messages flung in the air as they passed. Furtive meetings were arranged near the shore. Stephan had recently bought a small camera and took photos of a laughing Helena. He posed for her by rocks, sea, *The Stone*, at the door to his apartment.

Gossip flew on the street, whispers on the factory floor. Helena hovered in the shade of the plane trees when the factory released its workers. Stephan bent to her, took a cloth and wiped off her lipstick. The purposeful lovers strode the pavement to its end at the shore, their feet scarcely touching it.

Kostas, returning from the south, again sauntered past number 24 mornings and late afternoons, pausing to stare in the front window. Catching sight of Helena, he stared fixedly, waited until he saw Thalia, looked her up and down, and walked on. Whatever is the matter with *him?* Again Helena threw a bucket of water out the door after him. While the weather remained warm, she crept to the beach each evening to meet Stephan. There, in a rock-guarded spot of pebble and seaweed, she flung her near-naked body over her lover's, clutched him with strength enough to crush his bones. The two made repeated, desperate love. Afterward, her fingers playing over his face, she traced the shape of his lips, brows, and cheeks, kissed the lobes of his ears, held his face in her hands. Stephan seldom spoke but a spark lit up his solemn, inscrutable expression.

"His eyes burn like the lights above the tavern," awed locals said, "and his face like a beaming sun. See how struck with him she is? She's *amirou.*"

194

The eyes and ears of the street watched and listened, and Helena felt besieged.

"Nikos, give me your shirt, your trousers, a cap, *please?*" Laughing, her brother tossed her his spare clothes. Helena tucked her hair under his cap, slipped on his jacket and trousers and a boy emerged from number 24, sauntered the street, hands in pockets, then headed for *The Stone*.

Again the street erupted with gossip. Christos heard. "You're too young for flirting with the boys," he shouted and raised an arm. Helena hid behind her grandmother.

"Not too young to marry me to a sailor." Defiance sparked in her eyes, protected as she was by her grandmother.

The trysts became difficult and Helena increasingly inventive. One evening, as dusk settled across the sea and lights flickered from windows, again disguised as a boy, she crept from number 24 and made for *The Stone*, turned the corner and walked to the beach. A solitary figure emerged from the rocks, took her hand and drew her toward a grassy cliff. There the two sat facing a darkening sea. Under a sliver of moon, Helena slipped back home with 1000.00 drachmas in her jacket pocket as a loan from Stephan, a down-payment for the purchase of salon furniture, and enough, when added to her savings, for school fees in Athens.

Two weeks passed. Dusk had already fallen when Melina set out the evening meal. The family heard footsteps, and a sharp rap on the doorframe. "Papa, there's someone at the door." Helena looked out the window, astonished to recognize one of the women in the photograph hanging in Stephan's room. In confusion, she answered the door.

"Won't you come in? Do please come into our home."

Stephan's Auntie had crossed the Gulf upon word from Stephan's brother Kostas that she might want to know the gossip about her nephew. The portly woman stood in the dust outside the door of number 24. From beneath a flowered hat she looked with hard eyes at the young girl in her doorway, a girl wearing a short skirt and swinging red ear-rings, hair hanging loose to her shoulders. Shock rearranged the stranger's features. When she found her voice, loudly she declared, "I've come to see this girl my nephew Kostas writes me about.

"*Kostas?*" exclaimed Helena, astonished.

Yes, Kostas, Stephan's brother who looks out for him. I've come to meet this girl's family." She gazed up and down the street, past Helena in the doorway to see Melina, cloaked and untidy; Eleni nodding in her chair by the back window, a tray on her lap.

"No, I will not come into your house," she said, her voice sharp. "I can see enough from the doorway. "I have heard of this ... this affair between my nephew and this *girl*. I act as my nephew's mother, God rest her soul. It is my duty to discuss this grave matter with *this girl's* family. I come for this reason, no other." The Auntie remained in the doorway flicking her eyes over Helena from head to her feet. Turning, she looked again at Melina, then Christos, who crowded himself in the narrow hallway; to Markos who stuck his head between them. A prolonged silence ensued within the house and without.

"Please do come in for tea," Melina said, her voice squeaking.

"Thank you – no," the Auntie's voice was stiff. She turned her back, to look again along the eerily silent street. Facing the waiting family, she pronounced, "This is my judgment: I will not have my Stephan marry this girl."

Helena gave a shriek but the Auntie silenced her. "You're too young, too thin. I don't like the clothes you wear and I see you will bring no dowry. My nephew will not marry you."

Christos towered mightily above the flowered hat. "My daughter is not meat for sale! I tell you: never will I have her marry your nephew – never. You leave my house and don't come near it again." To his weeping daughter he said, "You will not see that man or any of his *aliti ajizn* family again."

Helena flung herself up against the walls of the house and struck them with her fists.

"Hush, hush," soothed Eleni. "When you are eighteen you can do as you want and not your Papa nor anyone's Auntie can stop you doing anything."

"But *Yia Yia*, I'm only fifteen."

"Hush. Soon to be sixteen. You will go to school. Then come home and make the money to do what you want."

Christos, insulted, humiliated, raised his hand to his daughter but Melina stepped between them. "You don't touch her! So, she does what you've done yourself, or have you so soon forgotten?"

"She should have got engaged to the captain." Christos swore.

"She wants to go to school and have her own business," Melina said. "She can be engaged for how many years we choose. It will keep her out of trouble with the boys."

***

Chapter 35

Patras, 1968 - 1969

"Christos, you must bring back the captain." Melina spoke firmly to her husband that evening. "Never mind what Stephan's Auntie said, that boy still gets about with our Helena. You know what he's after. She'll get herself in trouble." Her hand shook as she sliced vegetables. "A whole month yet before she goes to Athens."

"*Malaka!*" Anger flamed Christos' cheek. "Damned fool girl, I'll marry her to the captain by force, see if I don't."

"Eh, eh, I didn't mean for her to be married right away, only engaged, she's still very young."

"By God she won't play around with this fellow - or any fellow. I'll get the captain back here to put that ring on her finger."

Nine months had passed since Helena had rudely refused his offer of engagement. Give her time to grow up, Christos had said. Now the captain was invited to return, and intrigued by the fiery young girl, he agreed to make another proposal.

Word flew that the captain was returning, and in a world where little changed, any impending drama quickened men's steps and raised women's heartbeats. Helena remained oblivious.

Melina sat late each night sewing, using left-over cloth from the factory. From bright reds and purples she stitched together a skirt and drafted a pattern for a bodice with tucks and ribbons to be added.

"Burning up our candle supply," Thalia complained as she hunched over a book in a tiny circle of light.

198

"Mama, suddenly you're so busy with all the sewing." Helena fingered the satin cloth. "Very pretty. Who do you make it for?"

"Well," Melina drew some pins from her mouth and said, "When the captain returns to see if the girl he intends to be his bride has grown up enough for him, she should be wearing something pretty."

"This is for me? You dress me up for the captain?" Helena gaped in horror. "I won't marry him! When ... when does this sailor-man come for me?"

"Tomorrow. I'll have this finished just in time – you'll look beautiful in it, *poulaki mou.*" Melina put down her needle. "Helena, listen to me. You're a girl from a poor refugee family. You've scarcely been to school because we can't afford the books and pencils – see how your poor sister struggles to save so she can learn to read."

Thalia looked jealously at her sister and muttered, "Not everything is always and only about you."

"You'll work in a local factory," Melina said. "Or have some little business like your hair dressing that earns you a few drachmas. Your turn will come to marry a factory boy who has no money, and no schooling either, and you will live like this." Melina lifted both hands to encompass her home and the street. "I'm telling you that when your father finds you a good man, an older one who has wealth and position, you would give it up to marry a *factory boy*?" She did not mean for contempt to enter her voice, but she'd caught sight of Stephan slipping past the plane tree and shuddered at the thought that Helena might be foolish and willful enough to give up a navy captain for this ... mute little nobody.

Helena's face paled. Turning from her mother she fled the house and was not seen until dark.

Saturday dawned fair with a brisk wind scooting white clouds across the sky. A sense of unnatural quiet hung over the street. Melina had scrubbed clean her home's new wooden floors and polished the figurines of the archangel Michael and the Virgin Mary. Next she stacked bed- clothes and linens in neat piles, and ordered Helena to pick wild flowers from the orchard.

Helena returned with a bunch of weeds.

"Flowers, I said, stupid girl," said an exasperated Melina. "Can't you tell the difference? Go get dressed – hurry." Melina retired to the bedroom to dress herself up.

As though to herald the arrival of a travelling circus, a group of youngsters ran giggling along the street from its far end. "The captain," came their chorus of voices. "He's coming, coming for you, Helena."

Helena planned on doing business as usual and had two clients waiting in the front room. She'd refused to dress in the newly-stitched clothes made for her – "I just forgot" – she'd explain afterwards. The captain would ask her to marry him, and she'd simply say no, she was already betrothed. Then surely he would just go away.

Sharply defined in crisp Navy uniform, the captain stepped confidently toward house number 24. Small children and giggling teenagers followed. Heads appeared in doorways and windows. Men who had been lounging beneath the trees near *The Stone* straightened, aware that something extraordinary was about to happen. Stephan, returning from the beach, was also in time to see the giant frame of his rival striding toward Helena's home. He hid himself under the plane tree to watch the events at number 24.

The Captain's pockets jingled with gifts for the young girl who would become engaged to him. His right hand curled about a box that contained a large diamond. Money for the father filled his wallet. He was thirty years of age, and more than two years had passed since his wife and infant son had died. Time to have another bride, a young one he could influence, and who would give him more children. His memory of this girl told him she would be a challenge. She had high spirits. She was independent, and life with her would certainly be interesting.

"Here he comes." Again a chorus of voices swelled both outside the house and indoors where Helena styled a client's hair. "Helena, Helena, the captain comes for you."

Helena looked out the window and saw the man who would marry her bearing down upon the humble family home. Courage failed her. Her heart thudded violently and she felt faint. Damn, what to do? She had less than half a minute to hide.

"Helena," Christos yelled. "The captain is here for you."

Helena looked down at her short-short skirt and half-unbuttoned blouse; touched her hair that tangled carelessly down her back. Surely the sight of her would put him off? But after the last time? No, he was not to be discouraged and she must hide. Frantically she cast about for a place. Upstairs ...the balcony ... the neighbour's roof ... hide behind the chimney.

Her father's voice bellowed about the street until its inhabitants gathered around his home, gleeful at the prospect of a scene. *'Helena. Helena, come out of your hiding place.'* The chant echoed about the street; a magpie added its scolding.

The captain stood squinting in the sun, feet astride, undaunted at this fresh display of rudeness. A chorus of muted, "Ooh, ahh," floated about him. Stifled giggles came from local girls frankly admiring the sun-tanned face and smiling eyes; the tall smart form of the captain in uniform.

Like a cornered animal, in panic, Helena slid back down the stairs to her living room, picked up a roll of carpet and wrapped herself in it. The giggling grew louder. Small children laughed as they peeked through the window. Christos strode into the room and pulled at the roll of carpet. He roared as a dishevelled Helena emerged with smudged face, bits of threads and balls of dust clinging to her hair and clothes. She stood quite still and stared at her sandaled feet.

The captain tried to hide his smile as he looked at the apparition that was his intended bride – a challenge indeed. Clearing his throat he drew the small square box from his pocket.

"It is a surprise to you that I come so suddenly," he said in a dignified voice. Helena refused to look up. "You remember your father promised you to me some time ago, do you not?" Receiving no answer he continued, his voice still-confident, "I went back to sea, waiting for you to grow up a little, but ... it's time. Come, I have something for you."

A hush fell over the house and outside it. Neighbours jostled, hoping to witness a scene. Under the plane tree Stephan's body stiffened and angrily he glanced down at his own scrawny form.

"Eh, get away from the window. Get off, all of you." Christos clapped his hands and neighbours moved back a few paces. "Come, come. Inside we will have a drink and hide from all the prying eyes."

As he spoke he led the captain toward the back of the house. Helena remained rooted to the spot in the living room, her body rigid in fear and defiance.

"So, young Helena." The captain had difficulty hiding his amusement. "I've looked forward to this day when you will promise yourself to me. You have a young person's spirit and a sense of adventure." His smile was warm. "Because you are an independent girl with your own business, I'll offer you this: when you become my wife, I will not ask you to give it up, only that you also look after me. And all our children to come, of course. Now, I've got something for you." He held out the small square box he'd been turning over and over in his hands.

Helena glimpsed Stephan's shadowy form move under the plane tree, and images of his naked body, of his urgent, fumbling hands, momentarily blotted out the giant form of the man in front of her.

The captain looked intently down at her, and even in the midst of her tumultuous emotions Helena saw kindness in his face. She saw her father's glinting eyes fixed on her; her mother's, and a crowd of inquisitive faces at the window. She glanced out the open door. Stephan had moved from under the tree's shadow and she caught a glimpse of his face: the clean lines of it, lips that so sweetly kissed her; eyes that bored with ardour into hers. But the beloved face at this moment was contorted with anguish. Helena shifted her feet and twisted her fingers. Colour rose in her cheeks. The captain was holding out the small box. The world, inside and outside the house, stood hushed.

Her voice, when she found it, bounced rough and high-pitched through the air. "I don't want it," she said. "I will not become engaged to you. I won't *ever* marry you and have your little sailor babies."

The captain's cheeks flushed and he stood a moment as though confused. Helena, looking up at him, saw his eyes harden. Saw him carefully put the proffered box back in his pocket, and turn to the door.

A ragged silence filled the room and the space outside, until broken by Christos. "*Malaka!* I'm your father. You dare to disobey me, ungrateful girl. You'll be very sorry for this. Get away from me. Get upstairs where I can't see you." His voice had risen to a thunderous roar and neighbours melted away. The family jumped out of sight, but Helena remained as a stubborn little Judas in the middle of the room, rigid with the spent force of her emotions. Christos, his voice cracking, again ordered her upstairs until he returned. Taking the captain's arm he led him from the house and along the dusty street. Voice now full of apology, he recommended that if the man would wait a little longer he would personally see to it that his wayward daughter was tamed into submission.

The captain did not answer. He smiled politely and kept walking. Awed locals followed him.

"Captain, Captain, I like you... you can give the gifts to me..."

Interspersed with the excited chatter came Melina's lament: "Eh, eh, Mother of God, you've abandoned this girl. The devil got into her ... eh, eh."

Housewives crowed triumphantly to their daughters: "See, a lesson," they said. "A Greek father must be obeyed. Melina did something wrong in bringing up that girl. Now there's to be trouble."

Melina heard all the chatter next morning and snapped, "Nonsense. But where is the girl? Get her out of bed, Thalia."

"She's not in bed, Mama. She's not here."

***

Chapter 36

Patras, 1969

Helena could not be found the day following the captain's visit. No one saw Stephan at the factory. Spiros, reliving the night Melina had run off, cursed as he stomped to his stall, Eleni's doomsday cries in his ears. Melina, red blotches on her face, twisting her hands, walked the street, to the *fourno* and shops, to the factories and back again.

Christos called loudly for Father Meneghini outside the church. Roused from his prayers, the aging priest limped to the doorway, shielding his eyes from the outdoor glare. He shook his head. No, he'd not seen Helena. Swearing, Christos strode to the beach. *By the mother of all that was holy, where is the girl's manners? Where is her gratitude? How is she to get another opportunity like this? A father's duty is to find his daughter a good husband and by God and all the Saints, it's her duty to obey!* As the hours passed, as images came of Helena laughing and singing in the street, her busy hands working with clients, his anger became mixed with confusion.

Evening was settling over the houses when a bedraggled figure crept to the door of number 24, to stand shivering inside. Melina shrieked. Christos made snapping sounds as he stepped toward his daughter, one arm raised. Slipping past him, Helena ran to hide behind her mother.

"I didn't do anything," she cried. "I didn't run away to get married like you did, Mama. "I've done nothing wrong."

"You disobeyed your father."

Christos clenched and unclenched his fists. "The captain is a good man. You refused to get engaged to him and threw away the chance of a good marriage."

"You would have had a nice life and not have to work." Tears slipped down Melina's cheeks.

"You threw away the chance to make money for this family." Spiros had come to the doorway to add his voice.

"But I *want* to work. I can make my own money."

***

Three months after the captain's ill-fated second visit, Helena still avoided her father. Thalia, feeling ignored, became silent with jealousy. Melina, dropping hints about Helena making good money with her hair business, said to her husband, "One day she'll become important, and in the New Year she goes to Athens."

Christos, this morning, sat in a wintry sun in the doorway, pipe in his mouth and a mug of thick Turkish coffee to warm his hands. Helena approached, stopping at a safe distance from him. "Papa," she wheedled, "when I go to Athens, can I stay with Auntie Maria?" Large brown eyes slid up to her father's.

"Ah, so, if you took the husband I found for you, you would not have to work." Christos grunted and fiddled with his pipe. "You disappoint your Papa and make him look bad, but you work hard. I'll tell my sister you'll come to stay. I'll give you some drachmas so you can have good times too." An unwilling rush of pride had prompted the sudden generosity he could ill-afford. To protect his self-respect he'd already expunged from his mind the humiliating scene with both the captain and the auntie. Grudgingly he noted his daughter's swelling numbers of clients, not knowing that sometimes she earned more money from her make-shift salon than he did with his truck. And he was not to know that his daughter continued sneaking off in the early mornings to Stephan's apartment.

In January of the following year, sixteen-year-old Helena Kouvalis, a girl from a refugee camp in Patras, joined students from all over Greece for the four month course at the famous *L'Oreal Ecole de Paris* in Athens.

Once she'd gone, the family collectively felt that life had been sucked out of number 24. Nikos and Markos filled it with noisy antics. Above their din, Melina heard Thalia laugh. Wiping sticky hands on her skirt she tiptoed to the door. There stood Kostas, chatting to her. Pink roses bloomed on Thalia's cheeks and the girl looked – why, she looked pretty. But in spite of the noise and activity in the house, Melina still felt the loss of some vital energy and saw that Christos felt it too.

Weeks passed. The new equilibrium established was about to change again by Helena's triumphant re-entry. To a chorus of barking dogs and women's chatter, she walked the street from its far end. Lina and Stacia got up from plastic chairs to welcome her. Men whistled at her swept-up hair style and short skirt.

Helena walked without looking. Close to her home she ran laughing through the open doorway. "Mama, see?" She held out her diploma. "Oh Mama." She flung her arms about her mother's neck then rushed and hugged her grandmother. Propping her diploma on the window ledge, she walked to the back window, not seeing trees and distant mountains, but herself with a salon in the heart of the city, in *Odis,* even in Athens itself. Women of distinction coming to her. Husbands insisting their wives go to no other than the famous Helena. She'd charge the same rate other upscale salons did; walk about in smart clothes and wear her grandmother's black flower to show her sophistication.

"Papa," she cried at his home-coming, "nobody can touch me now," and she flung her arms about him. "I'll steal Mr. Pig Eyes' customers and that will teach him."

"Mr. Pig Eyes? Ha!" Christos struck his thigh and laughed.

Within hours of her return the home felt crowded, the street noisier. Life outside number 24 thrust into higher gear as cloaked figures gathered, their scarves flapping in a breeze. Faces beamed. Voices were raised: "Ha, now you're good you can do my hair. You can give me a cut and a colour, maybe a perm. Melina, your little girl is famous."

While excited by her home-coming as a professional artist and person of importance, Helena's eyes flitted restlessly up and down the street. At the sight of Stephan leaning against the crooked cypress tree, a hand flew up to her mouth. Nothing registered from that moment but that she must be with him.

***

Over the following year, Helena did little else but work and plan how to see Stephan, easier now that Kostas had returned once more to the southern

206

peninsula. She slipped into her lover's room in the dark, returning to her own when Thalia was asleep. She deposited each earned drachma into a tin box. With her sister at the factory, she counted every one. In an occasional fit of extravagance, she spent some of it to attend local hair styling conventions in Patras.

"I have to keep up with the latest fashions, *Yia Yia,*" she called to a complaining Eleni. "My clients" – she said this with pride - "they ask me to tell them what's new in the city. I am their hair stylist. I must know these things."

***

Chapter 37

Patras, 1969

Helena heard the news first: Stephan was planning to leave Patras. The streets hung thick with gossip when locals heard. "Australia – whoever heard of it? Coal mines? The fellow should stay where he's got a good job ... who knows about a place like that ... he'll come to a bad end."

Men remembered old dreams and women sighed. The object of their interest moved from the shadows and boldly walked the street.

"Come, come," Mr. Stavros said, his round face smiling. "An honour it is to serve a young man who looks for adventure in faraway lands. To him I give free drinks for his courage and to help him on his way."

"I'm his friend – free drinks for me too?" Nikos arranged his impish face into imploring lines.

"Now you become Stephan's friend? Ah, well, let us say free drinks for all the people that raised this young man." Mr. Stavros threw open his pub doors and many in X street immediately agreed they had raised him. "Your poor *Yia Yia*, you must bring her too." The publican spread his arms.

Helena felt she was about to drop into a giant chasm, and Eleni, knowing about these things, became gentle. Christos, suspecting his passionate and stubborn daughter might sneak out to her lover, shoved his bed against the window to prevent her escape, just in case.

On her lover's last night Helena went to bed wearing the little red dress she had worn on the day of her deflowering. She waited until Thalia fell asleep. Waited until she heard her father snore then climbed over him and onto the street. Rain clouds blotted any starlight and the night was cool. Stumbling, she stifled a cry. Over a fence and through a hedge she

208

scrambled, and to Stephan's window. Reaching up with a stick, she tapped on it. After a second tap and her lover's face appeared, shadowed in the dim night light. Startled but grinning, Stephan pulled her over the window ledge, finger to his lips.

Whatever happened in that room was to burn in the minds of both for many long years. Stephan tugged at Helena's hand, moving her toward the door. "Your dress – you've lost a little red button - come, we must go." Tears slid down his cheeks as he led the weeping girl back to her home.

"I love you," he said, voice quiet but fierce, his face touching hers. "Never will I love anyone else all my life, and I promise you this with God and saints as my witnesses. I will think of you every day of my life, send you money - one pound every week until there's enough for a ticket to come to me." Ghost-like in the night his stripling form hovered, a lone sentry watching as she climbed through the window of her home and over her father's sleeping body.

Huddling in bed, Helena heard her lover's footsteps crunching the hard pavement in the still air, listened until there was only a faint echo. The time was four in the morning. Like the fury of Mount Vesuvius who, weeping fire, lunged at his beloved who lay forever beyond his reach, so Helena too, lunged, but into grief. Inconsolable in the following days, she moved about with darkly-circled eyes, until a note from Stephan arrived. Contained within the folds of a love letter was a one pound note and instructions that she save it for her voyage to him.

Christos found it and took it. He towered above her, one hand raised, when Melina said sharply, "Don't you touch her."

Helena hovered about the front door after this to intercept the postman. When the letters came she put them in her box under the bed. The day eventually arrived when she thought she had enough money for an airline ticket. That night, standing a safe distance from the reach of her father's arms, she announced that she was leaving to be with Stephan in Australia and he couldn't stop her.

Christos looked at her defiant figure framed in the front window, arms crossed, a breeze ruffling tendrils of curls about her forehead; saw the thrust of her shoulders, the lift of her chin, how she wrinkled her nose – at him? No, just a gust of wind blowing industrial waste from the shore.

"I *can* stop you." Hands thrust in his pockets, he fingered his worry beads. "You're too young; I won't sign for you to go."

Helena, about to argue, saw Eleni's hooded eyes on her. She turned away, plans already forming for her escape.

Two months passed. She had just finished giving Thalia a hair style and fresh make-up when Stephan's brother Kostas, returning from his work in the silk industry down the peninsula, strode purposefully to number 24, asking to speak to Christos –"About a serious matter," he said. An astonished Christos listened as the young man requested Helena's hand in marriage.

"I went to the south to think about it," Kostas said. "It's what I want. I know she's young but our engagement can be long. She can have her work in the salon, and have time to grow up some more."

"So both brothers want my Helena." Christos' voice boomed out the window to the street. "Let's go ask this princess what she wants."

The two men filled the entrance to the living room.

"Kostas!" The word burst from Thalia's lips and a flush crept up her neck. She lifted a hand to touch her hair, a shy smile transforming her solemn face. Kostas steepled his fingers as he looked at her. A smile formed, immediately chased by a frown. Abruptly he turned to Helena. "I've asked your father for permission to become engaged to you." His eyes held challenge.

"Oh!" the word slipped from Thalia as a cry of pain. Covering her mouth, she got up and turned her back.

"Why would I want to get engaged to you?" Helena's voice was sharp. "It's not you that I ... why would you think ..?" She broke off and looking with bold eyes at her father, added, "It's Stephan I love."

Christos' body became rigid. He clenched his fists.

"Stephan's gone," said Kostas with triumph.

"I don't care. I won't marry you. And if you give me time to grow up some more I'll like you even less." Helena's voice boomed in the small room and her eyes were cold with rejection. "I don't want to be engaged to you. I won't even want to talk to you."

Thalia bent over as though hugging herself, hands over her ears. Kostas stood fixed where he was. Slowly he lowered his eyes to Helena's breasts that moved with her sharp breathing beneath the flimsy fabric of her blouse. In his mind, the blouse fell away and her breasts stood up bold and provoking. He gasped. But when he looked up, his longing expression turned quickly to anger and he rubbed his fingers. Silence filled the small room. Christos fiddled with his worry beads and shifted his bulk from one foot to another. Changing expressions flitted across Kostas' face as rapidly as wind chasing leaves. His eyes moved from Helena and Christos, then to Thalia who had half-turned back to the room. With surprise he saw her newly-glistening hair, her cheeks warm, and his expression altered. He paced about for several minutes.

"I – it's you I really want, Thalia," he said, his voice humble. "I would like to ask for your hand in marriage, not your sister's – if you will have me, that is."

"Ohh!" Thalia's hands fluttered about her face. Lifting her eyes with a quick, shy glance, speaking barely audibly, she said, "I ... will like to marry you Kostas."

"Well, well my children." Christos, now amused, glanced from one daughter to the other. "Kostas," he said, "you can please yourself and take my older daughter away anytime." To Helena, "Ah, my little one, I think you don't know what you want." Now interested in his younger daughter's affairs of the heart

he added, "To celebrate Thalia's good fortune, and to cheer you up Helena, we'll go to the country. We'll sing songs to make us happy."

"We're going nowhere Papa. Your truck is broken down again."

***

Although she stood as second choice, Thalia bloomed, but toward Helena she remained angry and jealous. "You flirt with all the men," she accused as roughly she folded her clothes. "Kostas would never look at you but for you making eyes at him. All the time he says he wants to marry me."

"Really? Then why did he ask me first?" Helena remained before the mirror struggling with her hair.

"Only because you make eyes at him, and all the boys. Because you dress like a *poutana*. You're a flirt. Look at you: you should cover your legs, they're getting fat."

"Boys don't like skinny sticks like you."

"Kostas does."

"Stop the arguing." Eleni's fretful voice came from the back of the living room. "I was skinny once and Adam loved me for it. Then I grew fat and he liked me for this too."

"But your Adam didn't see you when you got fat because he was already dead," Melina said. Voice softening, she added, "But I'm sure if he'd seen you filled with all your soft flesh he would have loved you for it," *like he loved his own mother's mountains of flesh.*

***

Chapter 38

Patras, 1969 -70

In early 1969, Kostas and Thalia married. As a wedding present Kostas' auntie grudgingly offered them a gift of money, saying, "At least it's not the other one. The gift, together with the couple's savings, enabled them to plan their emigration to Toronto in Canada.

Letters continued to come regularly for Helena post-marked *Australia,* and in them an increasingly bold Stephan asked, "When are you coming to me, why aren't you coming?"

And it dawned on Helena that her father might allow her a visit to her sister; that this could become a stepping-stone to Australia. Immediately she agitated to go. "I can learn all the new hair styles in Toronto," she begged her father. "I'll be famous when I come home. I'll get a proper salon and make you proud."

The late spring day of Helena's departure dawned brisk and clear. Eleni looked at her granddaughter as she emerged in the doorway of her home in a short skirt and a tight knitted sweater, her hair swinging in a thick braid as her heels tapped the pavement. She hunted for something to give her from her beautiful life in Smyrna, something to remind her it was now up to her to restore the family fortunes, even though she was a girl. A sigh rose up from deep in her belly as memories of Smyrna washed over her, as increasingly they did. Spiros kept saying, "You're not living the real life that's right in front of you; still you're in the one you've left behind."

"Never did I leave it," Eleni snapped. "It was taken from me." At this moment she heard again gin-sling glasses tinkling, the murmur of servants. The snip, snip of hedge clippers, the plop of tennis balls. Adam spoke softly in her ear and a nanny scolded a child. Ah, where was she? Back in this ugly place. No luxuries; hardly all the necessities. Again came Spiros' voice: "This city is beautiful also. It too has many peoples of the world…"

"No Turks?" she said sharply.

"No, no Turks." His lips twisted.

Ah, Helena. What did she have to give her? Eleni pulled her bulk upright to locate the bag from Smyrna. The pair of embroidered slippers from Anatolia? That weird black brooch Adam had given her? Maybe it will bring the girl luck.

Melina came in from the street, a woman who constantly plucked at the air with her hands. At moments she understood she was repeating her mother's life, all joyous hope for an adventurous one having turned to nothing. She reached out to a struggling Eleni and located the embroidered slippers for her.

Helena took them and turned them over in her hands. She looked up at the figures of her mother and grandmother, saw dullness in the depths of her mother's eyes. Was it because she was leaving? Because of her lost dreams? Her skin prickled. She wouldn't, couldn't, think about that.

As she stepped onto the street among the neighbours, the gossiping over the past months rushed over her like waves running up a beach: "I see your girl creeping out your door like a thief in the night. She gets dressed like a boy so we think it's her brother. She flirts and teases the men. A bad girl to her poor mother. Now she leaves her, just like her sister." Helena turned her face from them.

"We must get to the bus *chryso mou.*" Christos came up the street from where he had parked his repaired truck. "You go learn the secrets of hair styling in Canada, then come home and set up a big salon in *Odis Ermou*. I am your father. I am proud when you are famous. Your Uncle Spiros and *Yia Yia*, they know you will bring greatness to this family." Christos' eyes filled with sudden tears and he spread his big hands. "To the neighbors he said, "My Helena has got the energy of a big army of soldiers, a face to make a thousand salons, so we are to be celebrating eh?" He clapped his hands and uncertainly, the neighbours clapped theirs too.

Markos and Nikos followed Helena down the street. Nikos dropped the bag he was carrying and flipped himself over in a somersault.

"You – you are disrespectful," Lina said.

"No, really he's not," Helena grinned at her brother. "He can't help himself. He thinks he's a clown." Turning, she hugged him tightly. Over her shoulder she saw her weeping mother and grandmother still in the doorway.

Father and daughter left to the sounds of clapping that followed them until the truck turned the corner.

Christos turned toward the docks in the District of *Siniqysmos* where Spiros had his stall. The stench of rotting fish and seaweed rose in the air. Food, dirt and oil mingled with it. Yelping dogs joined the chorus of hawkers' hoarse voices.

There behind a wooden bench a skeletal Spiros sat. Leaning on one elbow, he called out in a reedy voice, "See my fabrics – beautiful, beautiful. My fine jewelry. I sell to you my religious icons. My books in all the languages. Good prices."

Helena jumped from the truck and rushed to embrace him. "But you're so thin, Uncle! Papa must get you to the doctor. Uncle Spiros, I'm going, I have to leave now."

Spiros looked at her under the thick grey line of his brows. Extending a bony hand he said, "Indeed you do, you being the one to restore our family name, and must go where you can do it. Then you come home. Here: something for you to remember your home and your family." He held out a wood-framed oil painting of the Troglodyte landscape. "Our family once owned land that's now in the hands of the Turk – never forget this." His lips twisted.

***

On her flight to Toronto, Helena searched in her handbag for Thalia's last letter. *Come to Toronto in spring,* she'd written. But spring is beautiful right here in Patras. She heard the whistle of an approaching train, the rumble of trucks on asphalt, surf lashing the rocks. Somewhere up in the hills she imagined she heard a piper. Excitement at her upcoming air travel mingled with nostalgia for the life she was leaving. In the manner of her grandfather Adam, vivid images of her mother arose, of her father and brothers. Of bent old Uncle Spiros and the now largely silent Eleni. Of the house that had grown to a two-storey structure with several rooms and an indoor bathroom, its walls still blooming with Melina's flowered decals. At forty thousand feet above the Atlantic Ocean she could smell the trees in bud behind the house, taste sea salt in her mouth. Dozing, she heard women's voices on the street, young boys in the orchards. Heard Mr. Stavros announcing free drinks, new music, another contest; her father laughing while playing cards by *The Stone*. The future beckoned. The past beckoned. All the prying eyes, the whispering mouths and eager hands from X Street had already become a crescendo of love.

Awakening as she neared Toronto, Helena's dreams and images of Patras vanished and her lover's face appeared. Stephan, Stephan, I'm coming to you, I'm coming. We'll make lots of money then come home to Patras. In her lap she fiddled with his last letter – '*I'm in the mines in Australia and the money is good ... I'm saving it. I live waiting for the day you come to me.*' Other dreams flitted: a salon in central Patras, perhaps in Athens, even in Paris. She would learn from the best teachers in the world's capital cities and become a prominent hair stylist. But first she must earn the money to pay them. Money: something dark and damp settled over her. She had no money. She could speak no English. And Stephan was a distant figure.

***

Chapter 39

Toronto, 1994

Georgia

It's a Saturday evening in September and I'm home, setting up my notebook on a card table on the back patio. I'm up to the part about Helena in Toronto, soon to be writing about myself. Morbid fascination grips me. Who's thumping on the front door? I don't move. Footsteps come along the side of the house – can't be Dad since he's out, and Helena's somewhere at the bottom of the garden.

"Hi little-big sis, home on a Saturday night?" Amalia saunters into view pulling a large oaf of a fellow by his shirt sleeve. He must be next in line, after the one before him who was the one before him and the one before ...

"This is Arthur," Amalia says. "Called King, you know –The King." Amalia's laugh is honeysuckle-sweet. She kisses the oaf's ear lobes, the back of his neck, his chin – to impress me? Her short skirt slides up and up. Her bottle-blond hair sweeps into a bouncy ponytail, tendrils curling about her heart-shaped face. God, she's cute, and knows it. I feel Arthur staring at me, and hunch further over the card table.

"Wow, great hair," he says. "You're sure you two are sisters?"

"Unless one of us got pulled out of the garbage and shoved through the kitchen window." Amalia looks sour. "Georgie thinks she's punk, or a new type of hippie, or she's trying to be retro."

"Retro chic," I say.

"Georgie, where's Mom?" A spiked heel taps the patio stones.

"Somewhere in the garden down there." I wave my hand and turn away from King's continued appraisal of me. It's usually only in Amalia's company that I feel like a frump and beyond all that's hip, but now I glance at my frayed blue capris, at my over-sized blouse. Suddenly I hate my clothes, my round face, my big feet – and hate Amalia. She starts clawing King again so I get up and walk down the slope under the rose-covered trellis. Helena is sitting side-by-side with Leon on plastic chairs pushed up against the box hedge at the bottom of the garden. Leon's face has an expression I've seen on him before when he's with Mom, and she looks relaxed like she hardly ever does. It's then I feel a wave of depression. Amalia's always got boyfriends. She's always in love. Mom has a soul mate. Maybe Dad's got some woman stashed away somewhere. Love is everywhere; everybody's got it, except me. Amalia thinks I'm beyond hope, and I've let her think that I'd spurn love, even from a prince offering me a palace. But while I crave it, I feel totally unloved and lovable. Well, except for Jeff and he doesn't count because he wants something about me, not the actual me. I lift a hand as though to brush him away.

"Mom's not there," I say as I walk back to the patio.

"What's that you're writing?" The King steps closer and peers at my screen.

"It's called *An Odyssey.*" I snap shut my laptop. "About our brilliant family – or ordinary one – I'm letting the reader decide. When it's published you can read all about us."

He thinks I'm pulling his leg. I'd wished them gone but when they do leave, when Mom and Leon come up from the garden and disappear inside the house, I feel abandoned. There's Dad, but he never counts. I re-open my laptop and click on *An Odyssey*. It's my consolation, also my sliver of hope, no, a belief, that there will be something for me – and all of us - at the end of it.

Helena and her past comes at me then, sharp, like weapons brandished, sometimes clinging like damp clothes, fuzzy, distant. I grab it all, examine what I have, and all that I can imagine. Then from my heart I write.

***

Part Three

Chapter 40

Toronto, 1969 -1970

Into a cold late April, Helena entered a narrow street of two-storey brick houses, toes to the pavement, to leafless trees and old snow. No sun this mid-afternoon, no blooms, and little street life. Thalia, looking plump, hovered on a doorstep, Kostas beside her with his arms crossed. On seeing her sister, Thalia's mouth quickly formed into a thin line. "Your clothes," she said, "They're not decent."

"Thalia, please say you're glad to see me. Short skirts are fashionable in Patras didn't you know? Hey, I'm here, quick, let me inside, it's freezing."

"Not this door, we live upstairs." Kostas spoke without looking.

"*Mother of Mary*, so many steps." Helena struggled to a second floor with her suitcase, Kostas making no attempt to help her.

"Keep climbing," he said, "you'll be sleeping in the attic."

"Why, do you live only in the upstairs?"

"Not enough money to have a house to ourselves." Kostas twisted his fingers and turned away from the girl he once would have married.

"Aggh, the Virgin herself couldn't do it." Helena continued up a further flight of steps, to a tiny triangular space with low ceiling, a bed, small dresser, some hooks on the wall, two posters of religious scenes with their edges curled pinned to a wall. A small window gave view to a brick wall. She sank on the bed, depleted of the adrenaline that had sustained her; she was half way around the world and stuffed into an attic in a cramped upstairs house.

Sleepless that night, she switched on the lamp beside her bed. The sudden light sent an army of little creatures crawling up the walls. She screamed. A dark shape hung from the beam above her. She screamed again. Kostas, together with the landlord from the ground floor, ran upstairs; a scattering of neighbours gathered on the sidewalk.

"You woke the whole street," Kostas said accusingly. "Even if you get nightmares you must learn to be quieter."

"You live in a place with bats and bugs." But Helena's feelings next morning were a complicated mix of confusion and euphoria.

"Kostas says you made a scene in the night." Thalia moved a kettle aside to open a cupboard, re-arranged a stack of dishes so she could use the toaster. "You want some coffee, some toast?" Kostas came to doorway, looked in, and left.

Gone was the stifling world of Patras, but here was another. Helena wandered about the crowded space of this half upstairs house, its twisting passageways, stuffy rooms and sagging furniture. Faded drapes covered the windows and a small coffee table groaned under a burden of old magazines. Well, she'd make money fast and get out of this place. She was in a big city, young, pretty and free to live however she wanted.

"Kostas says soon you must find a job," Thalia said the following day, "we can't afford to keep you." Helena did not turn from the smeared kitchen window. "You live in half a house – does Kostas not do so well in his business? And you, Thalia, you also work?"

"Kostas is a brick-layer and I just found out I'm pregnant. Kostas says I must stay home. And, well, I don't mean for you to feel unwelcome, but he says when the baby comes you must find your own place."

"Your Kostas is disapproving of me." Thalia continued washing dishes without comment, but Helena persisted, "How you have blossomed with nice weight gain, but you need a new hair style, nobody sweeps up the ends of the hair up in a wave anymore – oh, see this." She had been flipping through a woman's magazine. "Here's a new look for you: *pregnant women go haute couture* – but what does that mean?"

Thalia put down her dishtowel and began moving objects about the crowded counter.

"I can give you a different style, please, let me do it." Helena reached up to re-arrange her sister's hair, but Thalia pushed her hands away.

"My hair is long out of fashion? So are your clothes, your short skirts. You should cover your legs."

"When it gets warmer here everyone will be wearing short skirts and sexy clothes – but does it ever get warm? I'd like to do for you a really nice hair style; I can make any woman beautiful and the world is a happier place for it."

Thalia succumbed.

That evening she greeted Kostas wearing a long dress. Her hair curled softly and her pink lips formed an uncertain smile. Kostas' own lips moved without sound. His face hardened and he lifted a hand – "Don't!" Helena rushed forward. Kostas lowered it and pushed his wife into the bathroom. "Wipe that stuff off your face. Take off those clothes. Wash your hair." Reminded of the young Helena from Patras who had rejected him for his brother, his voice was rough. To Helena he said, "You, you're corrupting my wife … just … go away, get out of my sight."

"Kostas says you must find a job." Thalia, her lower lip trembling, thrust a yellow pages phone book at her. "Look for Greek salons, see if they will hire you."

***

Into the Koskas salon, a small, smoky place on Parliament Street in Toronto's east end, Helena began her hair styling career. Pop songs of the early sixties played on a small radio, and soccer re-runs on a black and white television. Faded posters of the Parthenon and the Acropolis announced the owner was Greek.

"You phoned for the job? You speak the English?"

Helena nodded, but in fact all she could say was, 'how are you? It is a nice day.' To her first client she asked, "Ow doy ya loike ya hir?" in imitation of her boss. The woman waved her hands in the air and muttered unintelligibly. "Come," Helena said in Greek and motioned her toward a chair at the sink. Lifting the woman's long strands of hair, mutely she begged for some idea of what to do.

"Damn fool woman,' muttered Mr. Koskas, "just clean her up any kind, she won't care. I charge her not much and she brings some others who pay me."

Having but one other client, Helena cleaned and re-arranged hair products on a shelf, and after exhausting everything she could find to do, hung about in the doorway. She drank water from an old mug at the bathroom sink. Mr. Koskas brought her coffee at mid-afternoon, and at four, he told her to go home and return in the morning.

Jumbled images came to her as she walked the long distance to Thalia and Kostas' home: coffee shops, dollar, health food, and second-hand clothing stores. Poor people, beggars accosting her. People spitting, people drunk, but some smartly-dressed and in a hurry. Mothers with children, their heads bent against the wind. In Thalia's winter boots she kicked mounds of dirty snow as she passed houses standing gaunt under leafless chestnut trees. Strange: she'd imagined outdoor patios and the blossoms and perfumes of spring, but here she was, back to her painful beginnings.

***

Chapter 41

Toronto, 1970

Dingy salons, weird people, a dismal landscape. *None of it matters. I* will *get to the top.* Helena dragged herself though months of poverty and servitude. She wore the soles off her shoes to save transit fare. Lamplight shadows reached across the pavement as she forced herself up the steps and to Kostas and Thalia's censorious company. Needing to escape, to cover up Stephan's silence, she dropped into pubs and bars, there to sit alone and listen intently to spoken English.

One late summer day, tired of poorly-paid inner city Greek salons, she approached an upscale salon on Queen Street opposite city hall and offered to work without pay. Employment was refused because of her inadequate English.

"Thalia," she begged, "can't you help me, speak English to me?" Thalia shook her head.

"You've been here all this time and you don't ...?"

Thalia simply patted her pregnant belly.

The months slid by. Thalia and Kostas began hearing footsteps clattering to the attic, laughter floating down the stairs, and tension mounted in the upper duplex. Unspoken between husband and wife were feelings of diminishment at what they perceived as Helena's carefree lifestyle.

"You're not behaving properly," Thalia accused one evening. "You stay out late, and you wear those clothes."

"That's not fair! I work hard at poor jobs. I wash hair and cut it and sweep up and make coffee and run errands and clean all day, every day. I pay your Kostas rent. You stay home and do nothing." Angrily Helena brushed away tears and climbed the stairs to the attic.

A little voice nagged: what kind of profession is this? How can anyone be famous for doing hair? You were important in Patras but here you are right at the bottom. Nobody cares about you, not even your sister. Fretting about Stephan's silence, feeling alone and on the outside of everything, waves of homesickness slid over her for her Mama, her exuberant Papa, and even for the neighbours. After such thoughts she indulged in fantasies: herself as an artist on X Street in Patras, a person of importance. Each morning now she stood before her tiny mirror, swept up her long brown hair, brushed her cheeks and lips with cheap make-up, and ran down the stairs, repeating, I'm an artist of hair. I will make lots of money and be famous. And I will find Stephan."

Riding the streetcars when she had money, Helena realized in surprise that in this city lived people from everywhere in the world speaking its many tongues and dressing in odd clothes. Summer arrived with astonishing suddenness transforming the city with blooms, colours and tree-canopied streets; with sidewalk cafes and the music of rock 'n roll and jazz. Women wore long flowered skirts or miniskirts, sandals, beads and looped ear-rings. Sidewalks sprung with guitarists and songsters and Helena's mood lifted. Searching out second-hand shops she bought herself a flowered skirt and cheap necklace.

Fall came bringing majesty of colour, followed by a cold, sullen November.

"Kostas, do you hear from Stephan? I don't get any letters ..." Helena's voice trailed away. Months had passed and she'd had no word.

"Stephan? No, nothing."

"I don't believe you. You tell him lies about me but you know nothing!"

"I repeat, I don't hear from him." Kostas turned away.

***

Stephan's silence cast a deep shadow, and it was in a depressed mood that Helena began a new job in a Dundas Street East salon. Near noon, a tall Greek man called Alex Darousos entered, hired to do electrical repair work. His brown eyes flicked restlessly about the room, lighting on Helena as she leaned over a client at a wash basin. What Alex saw were the two golden globes of her breasts, each close to popping out of her brassiere. He ranged bulging eyes over her shining rivers of hair and short, short skirts. He swallowed as he sidled closer.

"Hi. You new here eh?" A wink accompanied a flashing smile.

Helena's depression lifted momentarily and she tried not to smile.

In the days and weeks that followed, Alex found reasons to return to the salon again and again. He trailed Helena to each successive work place, hung about in the doorway then disappeared, returning at the end of her day. While pretending to ignore him, her heart bumped at sight of his handsome face, the sensuous lips boldly smiling at her. Within weeks she allowed him to drive her to her sister's home in a dented sports car. Thalia saw them from a window, giggling as they came up the path.

Alex's attention boosted Helena's mood. Increasingly she stayed late in bars and nightclubs with him playing cards and darts. In a perpetual state of excitement, she danced over pavements; she sang under her breath while she worked. Sleep was brief. Even in the cold, her skirts were brief. She wore bright red lipstick – '*Mama's daughter,*' muttered Thalia and influenced by her husband's bitterness toward the sister who had spurned him, her disapproval grew. How very profligate Helena was in everything. Kostas, glancing at his sister-in-law, clenched his fists, forced his arms rigidly to his sides. He seldom spoke to her.

***

Often during Helena's evenings in clubs and bars, the image of Stephan hovered. She dreamed of him. He reproached her with sorrowful eyes, raised a hand – in salute, or farewell? – and turned from her.

In the kitchen the morning after this dream and with dark circles below her eyes, Helena approached Kostas again. "Still I get no letters from Stephan. I write to him to the address he gave me in Australia. Do you hear anything?"

"Yes. He moved."

"You get letters and you don't tell me? Where does he go, and what does he ask about me?"

Kostas turned away without answering. Helena asked repeatedly over the following weeks, alternately angry and beseeching. Eventually Kostas said, "Stephan does not want to hear from you, I've told him what you do." He swore at his burned toast.

"You don't know anything, I do nothing wrong. I work and save my money to go to him in Australia. Please give me his address."

"He's not there anymore. I repeat: he does not want to hear from you." Kostas left the kitchen, burned toast in hand.

"I don't believe you! He writes me letters and you hide them." Helena appealed to her sister. Thalia, please you must get them for me."

"Kostas says no."

"You can't stay here after the baby is born." Kostas had returned and stood with his back to the kitchen sink. "I ask you, when are you planning to move?"

"Well, you don't care. Soon I'll move from your attic, your poor half of a house." Helena ran her finger along the window ledge. "It's dirty, small – see my bruises where I bump into everything? You ask where I'll go – to be with Stephan. I'll find his address and go to him."

But Helena, confused and conflicted, had nowhere to go. She could love many men; dance every night in the arms of strangers, in her mind, climb mountains and soar to the heavens, as long as Stephan was somewhere, waiting for her. Without this surety all she did meant little. Nights of laughter in the attic had become nights of tears.

***

Chapter 42

Toronto.

Alex followed Helena as she moved from one salon to another. Buoyed by the attention, her melancholy slowly diminished.

One warm, early autumn day Alex parked his shiny red car outside the Dundas Street East salon and cranked up the volume of his radio. He lounged beside the vehicle, his wavy black hair tousled by the breeze, an unbuttoned shirt revealing a gold chain on his chest. Through the salon's open window Helena heard *Salsa* music playing and peeked out. Alex! Her blood grew hot. Her limbs twitched. Dropping her scissors, trance-like, she walked outside. Face shining like a sudden sun burst, she looked up at him and in a silvery voice said, "Alex, will you dance with me?"

The triumphant smile dimmed and he shook his head.

"You ...won't?"

"No. I'm not dancing with you." The handsome face contorted.

"Ohh." Helena turned to a crowd gathering on the sidewalk, wriggled her hips and said, "Come on then, I'll teach all of you to dance."

Bemused onlookers neither took up her offer nor walked away. Alex blasted his music louder, turned his back and leaned against his car.

An angry, white-trousered salon owner in the doorway ordered Helena back inside. Before shutting the door, he waved his arms as though to scatter the crowd. "What exactly is the meaning of this?"

"The music − it makes my legs to move, and my body too. I can't stop it. Maybe I can teach you to dance?" Imploring brown eyes looked into the owner's crinkled face. As customers laughed he said, "You won't be doing this again." But he spoke without conviction. Perhaps this crazy Greek girl would bring more business.

Alex, hair carefully parted, wearing a smooth white shirt and his best jeans, escorted her to the Ben Wicks pub that same night. He ordered a beer for both of them, drained his, and immediately ordered another. He looked fleetingly at Helena, only to turn quickly away, but not before she glimpsed his intense expression. Turning suddenly he picked up her long braid and released it, fluffing hair about her shoulders, smiling at her. "You must always wear it like this." Leaning his now perspiring face close to hers, he added, "Listen good, because I'm asking you something: Will you marry me?"

"Ohh!" Helena grasped the edges of her bar stool as though for support. "*Marry* you? I ... I ..." She leaned away from his hot stare, the hard light in his eyes, and stood up. "I need the bathroom." From the far end of the pub she looked back, studying Alex's handsome profile, his fine white teeth when he laughed, the expanse of his shoulders. Confused, slightly disoriented, slowly she returned to him. Face averted, she said, "Alex, first I must do things for my business – you understand?"

Alex's furious face came to her during the long night that followed, his reproachful voice somehow mixed up with Stephan's. Sleepless, images came to her of herself repeating menial part-time jobs over the accumulating years. Herself still living with relatives who wished her gone.

"Thalia," she confided next day, "I'm so tired. I hate what I do, all the grimy salons, the stupid people, and the vain ones too. They don't care about me, I'm nothing. The work is nothing. Now your Kostas won't tell me where Stephan is. I think he gets letters and hides them."

"I'm sorry about your work," Thalia said, uncomfortable, her knitting needles flying in and out of threads of blue wool, "but things are sure to get better for you. You must be patient." Face brightening, she added, "You're soon to be an auntie, maybe next week."

"Thalia!" Helena jumped to hug her sister.

But in her sleep that night, she cried for her Mama and Papa, dreamed of her brothers and the community that was X Street in Patras; again heard Stephan's voice. Confused, upset, she worked furiously. When without clients, she swept and cleaned. Most evenings she spent with Alex, her blood in a fever. Sleep was brief. Alex asked again that she marry him.

Longing flitted in his eyes, and uncharacteristic gentleness softened the handsome face.

Helena, excited, wanted to say yes, but no words came. The face bending to kiss hers became Stephan's ghostly one. "Ask me tomorrow," she said. Then to soften the answer, added, "Tonight will you come dancing with me?"

"Ask me tomorrow," Alex said, and walked away. At bars and Greek nightclubs on subsequent evenings, Alex did not dance, and his quick temper flared when Helena did so with other men. For her, the months became a blur of long walks to downtown salons, to hair management courses. Tension arose when her ambitions clashed with Alex's desires.

"This is my dream all my life," she insists. "One day I'll become a famous hair stylist and all the world will know."

Alex scowled, raised an arm, and struck at the air.

***

One cool autumn day, Helena walked from Y Street to the Convention Centre downtown, not knowing that Alex followed her. Under the name of Helena Kouvalis she had entered a city-wide hair-styling competition offering cash prizes for winners in three categories: best style, cut and colour. She felt tired after a sleepless night but pumped with adrenaline. Money was at stake. Fame all over the world – well, in Toronto at least. She was not to know that Alex had tried to gain entrance to the ballroom where the contest was being held but was denied. Jealous, not trusting, he paced the conference hallways. Through the main door he tried to catch a glimpse of his girlfriend.

Cold, wind-blown, intimidated by the sprawling, soulless spaces of the convention hall, she pushed through volunteers eager for a free hair-style, among tense stylists in search of recognition, to enter her name under best hair-style. Unaccompanied by colleague or friend, she felt alone, outside everything: these people were swinging; they were hip. Most knew each other. Her breath came in short gasps.

"Here," a voice said. "Your first model. Better get moving. Twenty minutes is all you get. Good luck to you."

Heart thudding, hands shaking, Helena muttered: "I must win this … *must* win," and willed to mind images of a glittering future.

Her first client, anxious, had long, narrow face – ha! just like Thalia's. "How do you like your hair?" Helena repeated the words she'd used at her first job. "Like you are the Boss? Like you feel sexy? Like a little girl with mischief to make, or a woman very brave?"

"I don't know. You just do it."

Daxi. Helena summoned old knowledge: very short hair – something about leaving the mother, feeling castrated, wanting to say sorry. Long, loose hair: wanting to be young, sexy and free. A style to suit the shape of the face, of course, and achieved with spindly hair. She knew styling was her particular gift, and moved her hands over the young woman's hair quickly, confidently. The young girl smiled at her transformation.

"You want to become another Vidal Sassoon," said her second model.

"I make different styles from that great man," Helena said. "I don't do his bob or his Nancy Kwan cut, and no more of the sharp, geometrical shapes like he makes. You tell me what do you like, and I'll show you what I can do. Like in Mr. Sassoon's time, we want the low-maintenance and the wash-and-the-wear. To suit your face and bouncy hair, we can have it like this."

The model exclaimed in pleasure at her reflection.

Prizes were awarded in the ballroom late in the afternoon. A tall young Italian called Luigi was awarded first prize for colour, his diminutive brother Mario, first prize for cuts. Mario bowed as he received his certificate, his eyes warm and blue as he turned to the crowded ballroom.

In the pause that followed, Helena could feel her own heartbeat.

"Helena Kouvalis, first prize for style."

"Oh, *oh!*" Her breath stopped in her throat. Her feet were stuck to the floor. She felt a hand touch her shoulder; a pair of blue eyes anxiously peer into hers. Feeling alone in the universe, she begged of the stranger, "Please will you come up and stand with me?"

The tall, red-headed conference organizer placed a large envelope into Helena's shaking hands, and smiling warmly said, "This certificate will cover your expenses for a three-day hair-styling convention in Barbados. Plus you will get an interview and photo in *Toronto Life* magazine. Well done. Your styles are original and fresh. We hope to see more of your work."

"I'm Mario," said the owner of the Mediterranean blue eyes that looked into hers. "Congratulations to you, I like what you do. Tell me, where do you work – many part-time jobs? Then maybe I can find you a chair in the *Capuzzi Salon* where I work with my brother. One day each week to start? – we'll talk about it."

"Already I say yes. Dear mother of Jesus, thank you." Helena slipped as she turned to him and Mario, thrusting out his arms to steady her, felt himself struck across the shoulders.

"That's my girl," a voice hissed in his ear. "Hands off her!" Roughly Alex grabbed Helena's arm and pulled her across the floor. The room fell silent as she yelled in Greek, "I'm going to work with this man and you can't stop me." Yanking herself free from Alex's clasp, she walked out the door alone, Alex's curses ringing in her ears. Both the red-headed woman and Mario stood there, uncertain what to do.

***

"Young Greek immigrant makes a splash in the Toronto world of hair." Helena showed this headline in *Toronto Life* magazine to Thalia, who smiled warmly. Kostas glanced at it, turned the pages and read the article without comment.

Alex boasted to his friends, but not trusting, continued to hang about the salons where Helena worked. One late afternoon, he followed her as she walked to Yorkville to explore Toronto's *Wall Street of Hair.* The day she began employment in the *Capuzzi Salon,* he loitered outside.

Helena became aware that Mario, the brother she called Mr. Mediterranean Blue Eyes, watched her while she worked; heard fragments of his words whispered to Luigi, "… a rising young star ... our philosophy ..."

"Looking good is the most you can give some people," Mario told her. "It's all they want really. You need to learn what goes on in Yorkville because in this small area there are eighty hair salons, called *Hair Salon Row.* You must find out how they specialize."

His protégé learned that *Malcolm's* offered a severe Anglo-Saxon look. *Maurice Fiorrio's,* an insouciant, sexy cut and style. *Oggi's* was known particularly as Italian. *The Touch* was to become most popular during the seventies and eighties. Throughout these years, the legacy of Vidal Sassoon remained all-persuasive. It was this name, this man, who inspired Helena. She studied what he had done and had written. Born in northern Greece, he worked first in England before arriving in Toronto to make it his North American base. Quickly he became known world-wide, achieved wealth, and a legend that he himself created.

"He worked hard," Luigi said. "He chose the geometric look as his particular style. He believed in it, and in his talent. To be successful you must have faith that you can make the world a better place because of what you do."

"Listen to this," said Mario. "Take a lawyer. He pockets your money and you see little for it. A doctor gives you bad news. An accountant tells you how much money you owe, and a psychologist says how crazy you are. But a hair stylist will make you feel good about yourself." The brothers shoulder-punched each other.

Helena emerged onto the street to Alex, who berated her for spending time with a man who would get her into bed at the first opportunity. She smiled into the handsome sulky face and kissed it, promising him another evening in a restaurant or bar. In this manner she defused each crisis.

Early autumn saw her clamouring Mario for an invitation to an exhibition of hair styling, again at the Convention Centre.

"If I get it," he said, "leave your boyfriend at home."

Helena's flamboyant personality and flying hands attracted attention. To Thalia and Kostas she showed her smiling face in *Saturday Night* and *Chatelaine* magazines; told them she had money saved to go to more conferences. To Alex she exalted, "I work in Yorkville. I'm going to Montreal." Catching the jealousy glittering in his eyes, hastily she added, "Crazy man, why don't you come with me?"

Helena's eyes feasted on Yorkville's glamour the way she imagined her grandfather Adam's eyes must have done on Smyrna. On a park bench on Cumberland Ave she watched as people passed: the clothes, the make-up. Soon these women would be walking into the *Capuzzi Salon* to ask for her. Hungrily her eyes gazed into boutique windows, into the faces of diners on patio restaurants. What confidence they had.

"But I am poor and have not been to school," she wailed to Mario and Luigi. "How can I have my own salon when I haven't been to school?"

"You'll go when you finish your work – in the evenings," Mario said. "You'll learn from your books instead of going to church. You struggle and work days and nights for many years and all the time you think of little things to give to your customers they don't know they want."

Mario's own hands were never still, nor his voice or his laugh. At this moment he walked to the window and looked down on Yorkville Avenue. "This place, it sure does scare off potential customers," he said, his eyes twinkling. "One day I found a way to overcome it: I confessed to some of my clients about my roots in … what is the word – obscurity? – before I won customers by word of mouth."

"You know that some people sneeze at a stylist like they are a servant," Luigi said. "They call the work a trade, but it's art, something creative. Helena, you must study the anatomy and physiology of the body and how it affects the hair – which is a living thing, it keeps on growing even after a person is dead…"

"So it has immortality in it," Mario finishes. "It's true, don't laugh."

***

"You came home drunk last night." Kostas, furious, waved a slice of buttered bagel in the air. "You woke the whole neighbourhood with your noise. I'm ordering you to leave my house – today."

Helena, still in her pajama's, looked at him, shocked. "To...today? You know I can't find somewhere to live just like that."

Go live with that Alex you hang around with." Kostas poured milk into his instant coffee. "I wrote to my brother how you go about in the night with a fellow. You're not a good woman and to forget you."

"That's a lie! I haven't got into bed with anyone. You tell me where Stephan is."

"He doesn't want to hear from you. He won't interfere … he said he doesn't care what you do." Kostas devoured his bagel in large bites.

"When I find him I'll tell him you lie about me – all lies. I'm happy to leave your horrible house on this horrible street. *I hate you*." Helena ran upstairs and collected her possessions in furious haste. Thalia watched from a window as her sister dragged a suitcase and box along an empty pavement. Watched, unhappily, until she turned the corner.

Helena found lodging in a rooming house near the Danforth, the Greek-populated area of Toronto. In her bare, rectangular-shaped room facing a patch of grass at the back, she sat on a lumpy bed, opened a tin box, and from it withdrew her photos of Stephan. Holding one, then another, she gazed with wet eyes at her old lover. "Where are you?" she cried. "I love you. I'll never forget you – never!" She fell on the bed in a paroxysm of weeping. Stephan might be a distant, shadowy figure, yet he remained her Muse. Belief in him allowed her to do all the things she did. In her heart, she believed she was faithful to him, even while she had met and fallen in love with dashing Alex.

In the following months, her skirts crept higher, her hair longer. She laughed, flirted, stayed out late many nights with Alex. By eight in the morning she was at work in a salon.

One day Alex entered a small Queen Street salon near the Eaton Centre where Helena worked. In one hand he held a blood-red rose, in the other, a ring in a tiny blue box. Helena, bending over a client, felt the hair dryer taken from her hand. Alex, in a smart dark suit, his thick hair carefully combed, grabbed her shoulders and turned her to face him. Astonished, she stood motionless in the middle for the salon. Dropping to his knees among the hair clippings, again he asked her to marry him. "You won't say no to me," he said into the sudden stillness of the salon.

Excited, in love with the scene and its audience, Helena was about to say yes when she clutched her throat. In a strangled voice she cried out, "Oh, oh," and wildly gazed about her. The fleeting ghost of Stephan had wafted sorrowfully past her line of vision.

"Oh, oh," she cried out again, "I can't breathe, I need some air," and fell into Alex's outstretched arms.

Had she not been so unceremoniously dumped onto the street, she thought long afterward, if she'd had any – *any* – contact with Stephan, she might not have fallen so readily into marriage with Alex, an immature twenty-two year-old man besotted with ... and with new insight, she saw herself: a beautiful Greek girl who flirted who taunted and teased him.

"Yes, I will marry you," she said, and her voice caught in her throat.

On the evenings that followed, Alex boasted that his girl was *amirou.* He laughed loudly and drank too much. His voice boomed about the walls of the Ben Wicks Pub on Parliament Street as he told how his girl worked in a place where the rich folks went to have their hair done – "Yorkville – you know the place? Ha, one day my girl will be the boss there."

Preparations began for the wedding.

***

Chapter 43

Toronto, 1972

Two weeks before Christmas in 1972, Christos and Melina arrived in Toronto for Helena's wedding. Severe cold lay over the city and snow threatened. The city glittered in Christmas lights. The couple, disoriented, were welcomed into Kostas and Thalia's recently-purchased bungalow. Thalia emerged into the tiny white living room wearing patterned blue wool pants and blue sweater. In her arms squirmed a swaddled baby, on her face, an expression that said, *Papa, Mama, at last I've done something to make you proud.*

Kostas set out chairs before a gas fire.

"Papa, how you have got fat." A laughing Helena arrived. She hugged her parents, tweaked her father's jowly cheeks.

"Eh, show respect to your father! My little rascal, you get some nice fat on your bones, and pretty pink cheeks too." Christos beamed. "But I don't laugh when I look at your mother."

Into an awkward silence Helena said, "Mama, still you're hiding yourself under a big brown scarf. Where is the Mama I used to know with the beautiful serpent's hair and smiling face?"

Melina drew her brows together. Then she smiled. "We have a special guest to come," she announced as though offering a gift, "Alekos, from Athens."

"Ohh ... ohh. What about Nikos and Markos?"

"Pah. Your factory boy brothers – too lazy to save the money," Christos said. "I say to them when at the last they beg to come, you stupid boys, do you think I've got the money to pay for your tickets? They say,

236

but you must have some money, Papa. I tell them, where's your own? But I know what they do: they throw it away on girls and smokes and drinks. Nikos's girl – got a head full of noodles. She plays cards and loses his money."

"Never mind your brothers," Melina said. "They're good boys."

Helena's thoughts, returning to Alekos, remembered what she'd heard: favoured first-born with privileges. A spindly boy under a tree with books. A man, having done little to help the family, had gone to Athens.

***

Alekos arrived, pale and stooping. Melina fussed over him.

"I think it is a younger Uncle Spiros who has come to us," Helena exclaimed, and Alekos blinked beneath shaggy brows.

"Eh, Spiros is not well." The corners of Melina's mouth sagged. "Looks like a stalk o

f dry grass. I try to get him to eat and stop all the smoking. What's to become of him I don't know, still he thinks he'll be a rich man like that Aristotle Onassis he always mutters about."

In the days that followed, Kostas, filled with importance, took an aloof and abstracted Alekos about Toronto's Greek neighbourhood, while Christos moved his bulk about Thalia's small home exclaiming, "Nice house, nice house." A spark appeared in Thalia's solemn grey-brown eyes.

After visits to the priest who would conduct the wedding, after preparations had been made for a reception afterwards, Melina said, "Helena, why don't we meet your Alex where he lives?"

Helena frowned. Alex had never taken her home.

"And we must visit your salon."

"Mama, it's not my salon."

"Ah, still she works for somebody else." Christos rubbed his hands. "But one day she'll have her very own, we'll see. Now we'll visit the one where she works."

Christos, in the glittering space of the *Capuzzi Salon,* was awed into silence. Unsure where to place his bulk, he ranged his eyes over clients; over attendants who cut, styled and coloured; at skinny mannequin-like young men and women who washed, swept and made coffee. He noted the girls who hung up coats and took money. In a far corner he saw others who

237

waxed and plucked and smoothed. Music unfamiliar to him drifted throughout.

Next he inspected the famous men who worked in this place: the blue-eyed one who laughed as he looked into the face of each client and asked, "How *are* you? Will you have coffee, some water, a magazine to read?" The brother Luigi in the colour department — a young Apollo. Aloud he said, "Such dignity these men have, I think it is different from my day."

"Papa, will we do your hair to cover up the grey?"

"Ah, I'm getting to be an old man now and I should look like one, eh my Helena? But see what I have for my wife? What is a man to do? You colour my hair and I look like a young fellow, but I have on my arm this old woman."

Melina clicked her teeth in the manner of Spiros and got up abruptly. "Helena, when you finish your work, please take us to the place where you will live after your wedding."

Alex's flat in Cabbagetown — for Helena, alarm bells rang. "First I must help Mario to finish here," she said, "then I'll phone Alex and ask him to meet us at his place."

In the late afternoon, by subway and street-car she took her parents east of Yonge Street to Cabbagetown. She smiled as her mother exclaimed in wonder at the pretty streetscapes, at their beautiful Victorian houses and tiny front gardens.

On Berkeley Street near Gerrard she stood under a giant horse chestnut tree admiring the four-storey red brick building where Alex lived. The family waited on the sidewalk, and waited. Helena's anxiety grew. An old man came out, sat on the building's cement steps, and lit a cigarette. "Who you waiting for?" he asked.

"Alex Darousos," Helena said.

"He ain't there. Third floor. He don't lock it."

Helena's admiration turned quickly to shame as she took them up three floors of a damp, dark staircase and entered Alex's one bedroom flat. Once having focused in the dim interior she saw a cramped place with a fire escape running immediately outside the one window to block the light, a place of peeling paint, chipped walls, a dirty linoleum floor. Searching further she saw saucers spilling ashes. Clothes flung over the two armchairs. Dirty dishes in a cracked kitchen sink.

Her hands flew up to cover her face. At that moment Alex walked in, heard her give a small cry; heard Melina exclaim, "*Panagia mou!*" He looked about him, saw Melina staring him, and at the gold chain about his neck. Christos was fixing a smile, extending a hand and saying. "You are this Alex we hear about, soon to be married to our beautiful daughter. A thousand years of happiness to you my boy."

Alex glanced at the diminutive couple. Forcing a smile, he returned Christos' handshake. "I ... did you have good travel? Do you like Toronto?"

"Beautiful, yes, yes." Christos rubbed his hands together. "Helena tells me you get lots of good work. One day soon you'll be a rich man, eh, and buy a nice little house?"

"Uh, uh. I'm living here to save money." Alex nodded toward Helena in a half-hearted apology. He filled an uncomfortable silence by tapping a boot on the floor. "I need cigarettes," he said. And fingering the gold chain about his neck as he headed toward the stairs.

Melina stared with hard eyes at her daughter. "I think you fall for the good looks and charm, same as I did," she said and ran her hands through her hair until it stood up in spirals. "This Alex of yours with the gold chains on his neck, already I can tell he won't do you no good. Before many moons cross the sky he'll turn his face to other women. You will work while he plays, and all your dreams will fly out the door. Grandpapa Adam in his grave will be disappointed and in the after-life will be asking, who's to make this family famous - who?" She sucked in her cheeks and crossed herself.

Helena, equally shocked, saw that Alex would bring her to a poorly-lit, one-bedroom flat in a rooming house on Berkeley Street. Humiliated, she turned on her mother. "Once *you* had no running water. You washed your clothes in a dirty stream. What about Thalia and Kostas? They live in a poor half house that had mice and cockroaches in it."

Melina scrubbed at her colourless lips and turned her back.

Into a silence that fell, Helena heard another voice and a hand flew to her mouth: The voice was Stephan's, his words faint falling faintly, their very gentleness renewing her anger and she shouted, "You know nothing about *anything*."

"My daughter with all the talent," Melina was wailing now, "you the one to make the family name respected and you marry a man who takes you to live in a slum."

In Alex she'd caught glimpse of a man much like her own husband, a fellow who liked a good time, but no responsibility, a fellow who didn't care about success and moving upward. He thought himself handsome. This son-in-law would laugh, drink and play cards. Like her Christos, he would probably have other women.

***

Christos, who had loved his youngest child above his others and saved hard for this journey, intended to celebrate Helena's wedding in exuberant Greek manner. His beautiful daughter was about to marry a handsome, charming man and her father would dance at the festival. He'd teach this Greek community the *Kalamatianos*, and other dances too: the *Zeybek, Tsamik, the Syrtaki*. He rubbed his hands together in anticipation.

"The *Syrtaki* was originally a Turkish dance," Alekos said.

"Yes, yes, but the Greeks made it their own. Helena *poulaki mou*, I'll sing for you," and in a raspy voice Christos began crooning a love song.

"You'll get drunk and make a fool of yourself," Melina muttered.

"You the fool, damned woman!" said Christos under his breath.

In preparation for the big event, Christos, in Kostas and Thalia's home, held out his arms to an imaginary partner. Slowly his feet began moving to a rhythm only he could hear. A shadow dropped across his path as Melina walked outdoors to see what grew in the cold, and anger washed over him. Like a widow she was, no joy in her, all because he had loved other women; because he had not become a rich man. *Gomoto!*

Later in the evening the family headed for *Zorba*'s restaurant on the Danforth. "Authentic Greek food," Kostas said.

"And cheap," Thalia muttered. "*Avli's* or *Pantheon* is where we should go."

Melina felt people bustling past her on the street. She scuffed remnants of old snow. When she exclaimed in delight at the lights, Christos glanced hopefully at her. "So many Greek signs," she said, "I think we must be back home," and she smiled.

Inside *Zorba*'s, a long table had been prepared for them, and the dishes came, one after another. Alekos rose at the table and cleared his throat.

"I have news that will make you both happy and sad," he said. "I've researched the family's genealogy as best I could," and explained he'd found little else but subsistence farmers in the family stretching back over the generations. A poet here and there. An occasional artist who created watercolor portraits of the Troglodyte landscape. "I looked everywhere for descendants of Yiannis and Georgia's family in Anatolia," he said, "but no Greeks remain there, all are Turkish Muslims. One or two have the name Kouvalis, men who work in the carpet factories outside Bunyan and Kayseri. They know nothing about any Greek origins."

"Ohh." Melina's face puckered. Helena wondered fleetingly if she cared where she came from. Surely only the present mattered. The future, each person could make for themselves.

"Uncle, what was our family famous for?" Thalia sat thin and upright in her chair. "How did they make their money all those years ago?"

"And how did they lose it?" asked Kostas.

Alekos fidgeted. "I ... well, it's something we may never know. But I do believe our family had aristocratic origins so we, their descendants, must live in dignity."

Silence followed, punctuated by many sighs; grunts from Christos. Melina's tears spilled for Adam and Eleni, for herself, and for the daughter on who had been imposed an impossible burden −for what?

"This is not the end." Authority entered Alekos' voice. "We tell ourselves stories to make sense of the world and our place in it. Grandfather Yiannis needed to believe his family once had a glorious past, like the golden age of Alpha, and maybe they did. But we need new stories for our children. Think of a tree: never mind the great trunk and its old roots: it's time to grow new branches. "In an undertone to Helena he added, "Please put the Kouvalis name above your store when the time comes. It is what your great grandfather would have wanted. If you do, he will salute you from his grave."

But this is more of the old story?

Christos got up and crushed his daughters to him. "Ha so, this family, it is not the famous one we thought. We must make a toast so to think about what we heard." He grabbed Helena's arm and drew her into the lobby. "I got something to tell you and for nobody else to hear: I saved up money for your salon and gold coins from your *Yia Yia*. She also knows you for a good girl. For your salon, you hear? Or hard times if they come. This you not tell to anybody, eh?" He rubbed his large belly and belched.

"Tell my *Yia Yia* I thank her from the bottom of my heart." Helena touched her father's arm. "I'll keep her gold coins safe. I'm sorry I don't write to her, but you – please tell me about her."

"Ah now, she doesn't leave her bed anymore. But I'm almost forgetting: she wants you to have the black brooch Adam gave her and to wear it on your wedding day." Out of his pocket Christos pulled the *Bacarro* rose brooch, its colour such a deep blood-red that it appeared black. Helena looked at it, and shivered. "I know you say how it makes special the person who wears it." Reluctantly she took it. "But I'm not sure, I don't know what it really means. *Yia Yia* kept it all these years and what did it do for her?" She was sure the rose was ominous, and because of it, someone was going to die. Familiar hysterical emotions swelled.

"Never mind the brooch, you coming home again? Your hair brushes and shampooing things sit on the window ledge and the people ask for you." Christos crushed his daughter to him.

Helena felt the large soft belly, looked into the florid face, and thought how much she had both loved and feared her father. Now she need only love him. Half-formed thoughts tumbled, that although often a disappointed man, her father loved life exuberantly, fiercely, his vision of it an intense and weighty one. Still he could laugh, dance, and be purely happy for a moment, for a day, two days. He heard the songs of the wind, felt the sun warm his skin, the tickle of grass beneath his feet. His wife: Helena glimpsed her mother through open lobby door. There was a disappointed woman who knew little pleasure. Perhaps too many expectations had been put upon her, while life had stacked much against her. Perhaps she had stacked it against herself. Helena's jumbled thoughts raced on until tired, she tossed them aside. She whispered in her father's ear the one question that burned in her brain: "Do you hear of Stephan?"

"Stephan? Ah yes..."

"Shh, Papa. Talk softly."

"You don't know from Kostas, his own brother? Well, let me see: I hear he got married. A girl she was really, the younger of him. He brought her to Patras and after, they went to live in England. Where? I don't know. Some say the girl looks like you."

Strangled sounds escaped Helena's mouth. Her life was about to begin, but at this moment she felt it had just ended. *How could he be married to anyone but her?*

She acted as one in a stupor for the remainder of the evening, and next morning her pillow was soaked with her tears.

***

The morning of the wedding, Helena, Melina, Thalia and Alekos trekked to the *Capuzzi Salon* to have their hair styled. Melina took much persuasion. "Why should I look like my life is good and I am a happy woman? Always I am in sorrow for my life."

"Shh, Mama. This is my wedding. For this day you will be beautiful. You will be happy. Then comes another day and you will be happy again. Go sit over there while I do Alekos' hair. He's to be my *koumbara* so he needs it to be fixed up." Helena combed out her uncle's spindly strands, then went to work on her father's. "Would you like me to colour it too, Papa?"

Christos patted his exuberant crown of grey, then his belly. He laughed and said no, the women did not look at him anymore. But his eyes roved over all the little nymphets who washed and cleaned and brushed as they waited on the customers. He absorbed the sunlit space afloat with soft music, punctuated by the tap tapping of the bobbing, stiletto-heeled mannequins.

"How many ways to cut the hair?" Christos asked his question of the whole room. The skinny young mannequins raised their heads, stared, smiled briefly and turned away.

"How high can you count?" A sassy brunette was stacking glossy magazines into a neat pile, then held one up. "Hey old man, want one of these? Can you read?" Into the pause that followed came Mario's polite but firm voice ordering her to the back of the salon. Christos sank into silence, subdued but for a moment. The glamour of the place again washed over him: the muted voices, soft footfalls on the polished floors, glitzy wall hangings and elegant prints. "Ah, my Helena works in a place like this, and soon she will have one of her very own." He looked about for her.

"Mama, I'll do your hair now," Helena was saying as she removed her mother's black scarf. She heard someone clapping, heard Mario exclaim, "Snakes alive, I never did see such a wonder!"

Melina's hair, once her source of both joy and exasperation, had long been covered in shame and sorrow. Helena fought the writhing coils of still-rich brown hair and arranged them in pretty ringlets. She saw her mother glance quickly at herself in the mirror and smile briefly, heard her father say, "Ah, my wife, she is smiling. We wait now for Mario to do your hair, my Helena." He was beaming.

***

Chapter 44

1972-1973

Hard white snowflakes hit the pavement as Helena's taxi cruised toward the intersection of Yonge and Dundas Streets. She shivered in her flimsy shawl and stared at the dark night. Street lights rocked drunkenly in the wind. Christmas decorations flickered on trees and roof tops. She heard her mother exclaim and point at streets crowded with shoppers, at dazzling window displays, at billboards glittering above a giant Christmas tree.

Helena stepped from a limousine in front of a St. George's church softly lit with candles. She floated, an evening's princess in casings of white muslin, tufts of white tulle trailing her like the hair of a snow goddess. In her arms she carried a bouquet of white carnations, and the single *Baccaro* rose forced upon her by Melina. Thalia, emerging behind her, made little oh, oh sounds, and Helena turned in time to see her sister trip over her train. That moment a savage gust of wind blew Helena's crown of roses sideways and she threw up her hands to grab it. People crossed themselves, and again on glimpsing the single dark bloom in her bouquet.

Inside the church, the priest's voice emerged hoarse from a recent cold. Alekos kept forgetting his role – "*still dreaming*," Helena heard her mother mutter – and Alex, some of his lines. Helena, about to say, "I do," suddenly uttered a strangled cry and pointed to the church door. It had swung ajar with a creak. There, silhouetted in candlelight under the Romanesque entranceway, she saw the shadowy figure of Stephan, his arms hanging loose. He looked helplessly at the bride with a sad little smile. All heads swivelled to look and the priest, annoyed, said, "I don't see anyone. Do we continue with the vows?"

Helena covered her eyes and shook her head, then whispered 'yes.' Her face gleamed ghostly white.

"Very well. It is my duty to say this: A woman must tremble before the man. She must fear him and obey him in everything." To Helena: "Will you hold your husband in fear, and obey him all your life?"

Helena uttered, "I do," again in strangled tones. Alekos, acting as *Koumbara*, exchanged the white crowns on the bridal couples' heads three times then led a slow dance around the perimeter of the church. Afterward the guests showered the bridal couple with flower petals. Alex strode down the aisle, leaving Helena alone at the altar. Fragments of yesterday's conversation came to her, Alex saying he would refuse to marry her if she insisted on the new Greek custom where the bride stood on the bridegroom's foot to symbolize their equality. He was the man, the boss. He would tell her what to do. Now, as one in a trance, she followed after him, Alekos ambling behind. Melina, in the background, crossed herself and muttered a prayer to the Holy Mother of God. Christos fingered the worry beads in his pocket.

At the conclusion of Mass, after the enactment of all the old Greek wedding rituals, came the wedding celebration. Helena waited for Alex to come to her for the ritual bridal dance, but he remained fixed in his seat in a dim corner of the ballroom, a cigar burning in his fingers.

"He won't dance. He doesn't know how," his best man hissed in her ear.

Mother of all saints, I've married a man who can't dance. Helena stared stupidly at her new husband, anger and dismay rising together like bile in her throat.

"You … can't dance?" She stared stupidly at him. "Then *you* dance with me." She grabbed the best man's hands and pulled him onto the dance floor. The young fellow hesitated, glancing quickly at Alex. Hesitantly he put his arms about her, and Helena began dancing with abandon. When the music stopped she picked up a wine glass, leaned against a wall and drained it in one gulp. Someone had begun clapping and she looked about her, to see her mother jump up and begin dancing with the same abandon as she had. Haunting little cries came from her lips.

Helena saw her father's eyes grow large – *he believes his wife is laughing* – heard him cry out: "I have my wife come back to me, my wife." In grand gesture, he strode out to her, swept her in his arms and slowly began the *Kalamatiano* dance with her.

The wedding reception was in full swing, Helena floating with all the wine she had swallowed. Recovering from the shock of learning that Alex did not dance, she was aware only that she had snared the handsomest man in the Greek community. Her Alex was charming, funny, and made people laugh. Fleeting moments occurred when she stilled a faint voice inside her. Ignoring Alekos' quizzical glances, her laughter grew louder. Her feet tapped the dance floor in faster tempo, and faster, her arms aching from all the men she held, mind and body exhausted with the extravagance of emotion she expressed in voice and eyes and feet.

Late in the night she looked about for her father. Heard him muttering as he sank heavily into a chair: "Ah, I am getting to be an old man. I tell you Christ, if you look after my daughter and her new husband, if you give them happiness and many sons, you can sit at this table and feast with us." Helena was not to know he was echoing the very words of Adam, of Yiannis before the burning of Smyrna.

***

Chapter 45

Toronto

Georgia

My mother married a man much like her father but with a meaner temper, I think. I'm at the kitchen table sifting through wedding photos while Helena chops vegetables for dinner. She's got dark circles under her eyes, her shoulders are slumped, and she's making weird little ugh, ugh sounds. Suddenly she stops chopping and glares at me. Is it me? The mess of the living room? Has she sneaked a look at what I've been writing?

I turn back to the photos, struck by Dad's triumphant expression, almost the smile of a conqueror. In one snapshot, Helena's hand is on his shoulder but she's looking at someone behind her with an expression of astonishment, even dismay. Ignoring the mood she's in right now, I show her the photo. "Whatever were you looking at, Mom? Did something scare you?"

She puts the knife down and stares right past me. Half-whispering, she says, "I saw Stephan looking in at me. Like a ghost, he haunted me, even on my honeymoon night." Her voice rising in sudden indignation, she adds, "He got married himself and never told me! But this is private and not for the story, okay?"

A thrill zings up my nerves. Keeping my voice casual, I say, "What happened to both of you?" But it's too late, she's closing up, although I'm sure part of her really wants to tell. My thoughts slide off to some of fiction's great love stories, and fancifully I think of her as a Cathy to her Heathcliff.

"Okay," I say. Taking the vegetable knife that dangles in her hand, I change the subject. "What about the Bacarro rose? Such an odd thing to pass on in a family. I looked it up and guess what? It's a freak of nature, a kind of unicorn of the plant world because it goes against biology - something improbable, even unattainable in the natural world. And there's more: the black flower is said to attract obsession and passion ..." I interrupt myself, struck by the thought that these might be the qualities held by those attracted to it. Aloud I say, "Some say it symbolizes hate and revenge, and not love and friendship. Obviously great grandfather Adam would not have known any of this when he gave the brooch to Eleni, and none of us would ever question it."

"You should let me read more of the story." Helena's voice has a sudden edge. "You do all this writing, what kind of things do you put in it?" She takes the vegetable knife from my hand. "Give it to me to read now."

Whoa! Taken by surprise, I stutter, "Well, um, not yet Mom. I mean it's not finished." I'd completely forgotten about my audience and have made up stuff she won't like - or the family either. What to do? I'll just say that even if parts of it might seem personal, they speak of universal truths and who's to decide what's real and what's mythical anyway? My characters have emerged out of fragments of memory, out of hearsay, and I can't always control them. It's Helena in the story, but not her. What will I do when it's published and anyone can read it? I push these thoughts aside as the old compulsion to finish it pulls at me again. An epic story, I think, beginning with Yiannis and his belief in a myth, and because of it, a burden he imposes onto Adam and Eleni, to Melina, to my Mom – and to me? Not likely, but get rid of that thought. Many people are driven to raise their standard of living, I think, but few inherit the mantle of having to resurrect a supposedly glorious past. Then, why the need to have importance other than what reality gives you, or that you make for yourself? Some ideal to motivate perhaps, make you feel better about yourself and your place in the world? For a Greek – well, I won't go there.

Another thought nags me: no one in the family seems to have appreciated the extent of Helena's achievements. Her knowledge of hair and how it was – maybe still is – a woman's greatest weapon, transforming her, giving illusions of beauty. Helena had learned all the secrets of how to

249

do it, worked on *Hair Salon Row* with the best stylists in the city, surely a position many aspiring stylists would die for. She'd travelled to conferences, won awards, taken business courses in Montreal. Hair, and the business of it, came first in her life even before her love affairs −if she had any−before her marriage, even before Amalia and me. Clattering images hit me: Helena's furious striving to rise up in her profession, not only to make money, but to be known among people who count. "But who's to notice a hair dresser?" I once asked her.

"You ever hear the name Vidal Sassoon? Jie Matar?" she said. "The rich follow them around the world."

'Okay, what's with the name Kouvalis?"

"Think, Georgie. If you got a name like Onassis, or Kennedy, you'd want to live up to it, wouldn't you? If your family once owned lands and titles and lost it all, you'd want to get it back, wouldn't you?"

Returning to the subject of hair, my fingers fly across my keyboard. 'Hindu, Buddhist, Catholic and Jewish faiths all give significance to it, and relate it to the Divine – well, of course, its sex appeal is the very reason major religions insist that women cover it. Hair, and hair styles, go to the core of a person's very identity, beautiful hair the major item in a woman's seductive armory ...' Oh Mother of Jesus. I rush to small mirror in my bedroom. What does my hair say about me? You're a slob. You don't believe in yourself. You don't care. Forget it, forget it! I struggle to concentrate. The colour, texture and scent of hair: 'Comb it away from the forehead in a nun-like fashion and you get sexual repression− or elegance− depending on your interpretation. Do it in ringlets and you have cute or sensual.

I think how intuitively Helena understands all this. Another thought hits me and I write: 'But then, like Narcissus, she looked into the oval mirror one day and fell in love with her beauty and its promise.'

Ah, Beauty is merciless
You do not look at it.
It looks at you and does not forgive.

It's one in the morning, I should get to bed. First I wander into the kitchen to look for something to drink. Surprise – Dad's at the table surrounded by empty beer bottles and overflowing ash-trays. When he looks up, I'm struck by the sadness in his face.

"Something wrong, Dad?"

"When a man has a wife, he should sleep in the same bed with her." He looks at Mom's closed bedroom door. "She makes me sleep in the basement."

Ohh. I'm not getting into that. "Just talk to her," I say. That's when he suddenly looks me up and down.

"You looking better these days Georgie. Losing some fat off you– got a boyfriend? What's with sitting up half the night?"

I tell him I'm writing a story.

"That right? What's it called?"

"Ugh, well, I just call it *An Odyssey*."

"What's it all about?"

"Well, a family from Turkey believes they descended from Ancient Byzantine Greeks and were once rich and famous. They keep trying to get it back– their wealth and reputation, that is."

"So do they?"

"I ... they haven't got to that part yet."

I lie sleepless that night, thinking about my dad lying alone in a small basement bed while his wife lies in the matrimonial one upstairs. Why do they stay married? Next evening is Wednesday and Dad will be at his gun club. On impulse I decide to drop in to talk to him since I can't do it at home.

In a sports bar on the Danforth east of Pape Avenue I find him. Still a handsome man, still wearing a gold chain about his neck, a little jowly now, but with thick dark hair scarcely touched by grey. He's lounging in the card room with his friends, baggy beige trousers, open-necked striped shirt, brown loafers. The number of empty beer bottles scattered on the table indicate a lot of drinking. When Dad sees me he actually gets up and puts a hand on my shoulder, beaming when the men whistle. I don't mind. I look much better now that I'm slimmer, (it's thanks to *An Odyssey* I really do forget to eat when I'm into writing it – well, living it.) Sometimes I take trouble with my hair. Having men's eyes on me is a new experience.

"My Georgia is a clever girl," my father boasts. "She writes little stories. One day she'll write a big, fat book and become famous for it."

"Dad, can we go somewhere and talk?"

His eyes flicker briefly over mine.

"Aw, Georgie, we can talk anytime..."

"No, really Dad, I never get a chance to be alone with you. Last night it was too late." I draw him toward two cracked leather chairs in a dim corner of the room and fix my eyes on him. "I'm your daughter and we never have real conversations."

"You want talk? Okay, you talk." He drums his fingers.

"Well, I'd like you to ... tell me things about the past. I'm curious about you and Mom: what made you fall in love?"

A flicker of anger, suspicion, and confusion crosses his broad face and he shuffles his feet under his chair. "I don't know, don't know. Go ask her."

"Dad, I really do want to know more about you."

"My Georgie, my gentle girl." I can tell he's surprised. "Go on, ask your question."

"Well, it's ... do you still love Mom?"

"Woman's talk." Irritation enters his voice.

"Please Dad, tell me something, anything."

"None of your damn business. Ask your mother. Ask her why she locks me out of the bedroom." His anger lasts only a few seconds. Again he shifts his feet, looks back to the table, and says, "Not tonight Georgie. Not any night. It's all in the past. It's gone. Done. Anyhow, you can see I'm busy."

***

Now to write about my own birth and early life. My family, when, or if, they read it, might quarrel about the truth of my account and my objectivity, but it's what I understand. It's what I feel in my heart.

***

Chapter 46

Toronto, 1973 - 1980

Alex whistled in the street, brought home Greek wines and crates of Molson beer. He made love to his wife every night. From the tiny window by the fire escape Helena watched his handsome solid figure walking along Gerrard Street past the library to the streetcar stop. No doubts, no ghostly appearances clouded the joy of those early weeks. But after some months, exhausted after his nightly exertions, Alex began getting up late and coming home early.

"But your work, won't you get in trouble?" Helena put down her hair-brush and looked at him still tangled in the bed clothes. Alex grunted and rolled over.

Helena ran down the stairs into a cold early morning. You're young, you don't need sleep, an inner voice said. You keep learning the stupid English. Watch. Listen to everything. Read all the hair magazines. Don't care about sweeping floors and scrubbing basins and making coffee. All the poor work is just for now ... just for now.

Each night she climbed the stairs to the cockroach-infested flat in Cabbagetown, squashing disappointment by remembering Thalia's early beginnings. Who cares if there's a prize at the end? *I'm almost twenty. I've married the handsomest Greek man in the city; one day I will open my own salon.*

***

One year slipped by, and at the beginning of another, Helena brought her first baby home to the flat on Berkeley Street.

"A girl!" Alex cursed as he walked out. The following day, ignoring the flat's clutter, he sat in his usual chair by the window and asked, "What's for dinner?" Only briefly did he glance at his infant child before fiddling with the radio in search of sports news.

"Let me introduce you to Amalia," Helena muttered, her eyes half shut.

A second baby girl was born one year after the first, named Georgia in honour of her distant forebear in Anatolia. When the little girls were but two and three years of age, an exhausted Helena took them to her sister, asking would she look after them for a few days each week while she worked – "for the sake of my career," she said, avoiding her sister's eyes. "I'll pay you, of course."

"Why must you work?" Thalia drew the little girls through the door, Amalia sullen, Georgia sucking her thumb. "I must tell you: when Kostas was coming home from work last week he saw Alex in a sporty-looking car on the Don Valley Parkway. Where does he get the money?"

Sports car? Helena stared. "He just needs to grow up some more," she said, and avoiding her sister's eyes, added, "He's used to having what he wants and hates hearing babies crying. I'll pick them up from you by five, for two, maybe three days each week, okay? I'll pay you."

Whatever money Helena earned she spent food, children's clothes, babysitting. Alex worked in short bursts and paid the rent. When at home, he gave scant attention to the children, indulged in bouts of drinking, afterward slapped his wife around until the two rooms echoed with crying children, a crying Helena, and an Alex throwing objects about.

"You're not the girl I married," he accused. "You don't take care of yourself."

"I don't have money to buy nice clothes or make-up," she cried. "All of it is for food, and to put clothes on *your* little girls."

When Alex was absent, Helena unlocked the box she'd hidden in the kitchen and counted *Yia Yia's* gold coins, sliding them through her fingers. *For my salon, for my future.*

***

As her home life deteriorated, Helena's silent conversations with Stephan increased, although she'd not heard from him since she'd arrived in Canada. Knowing in her heart it was futile, still she begged him to intercede with the Virgin for her. One evening after a fight between husband and wife, Alex walked out, and for Helena a time of darkness of body and soul ensued. In the chill of early mornings she dragged herself out of sleep, scrubbed her face, dressed herself hurriedly and tied up her hair. Roughly she pulled her tiny children out of bed, yanked on their clothes and sat them at a small table by the fire escape.

"Stop crying. Hurry up and eat. Don't wriggle when I put on your shoes. Hurry, hurry..." Into rain and sleet and snow she dragged each sniffling child by the hand, around the corner and to the bus stop on a Parliament Street where she had begun her first hair-styling job. Within the bus shelter they huddled. Up the steps of the street-car she yanked them, and through commuter crowds, squeezing their tiny bodies against throngs of dull-faced workers. Except for her two days at the *Capuzzi Salon*, she continued her long days of servitude: sweeping, cleaning, making coffee, and running errands in between cuts and styles and perms. Feebly she cried out to Stephan. Still she told herself that he would rescue her.

On a bitter February day when snow and sleet slanted piled high against the Dundas Street salon where she first met Alex, a ragged figure appeared in the doorway. Helena's heart jumped at the familiar shape of him leaning against the doorframe flicking snow from his eyelashes.

"Alex!" she hissed. "You come back? What do you want?" As she walked to the door she smoothed the skirt that strained against her flesh, flicked strands of hair from her face. Hands on hips, she glared at him, jumbled thoughts chasing about in her mind: He's missing his kids. He feels dishonoured in the Greek community. He's run out of money. Perhaps his affairs are not satisfying.

"I'm a Greek man." Alex spoke at last. "A Greek man should get respect in his own house." His expression changed rapidly from uncertainty to insolence.

Helena stared at her wayward husband in the doorway, turned and glanced down the salon. One client at a wash-basin, one under a hair dryer and another awaiting her turn. The salon owner lounged against his office wall. All were hushed and expectant. Suddenly an unbidden image of Stephan floated, and she told herself she must just be patient. There stood Alex, in his own way, was saying he was sorry. Fleetingly she considered her position as a Greek woman with an absent husband: no one to take her to community events; the object of fear for other women – *watch your own husband.* She knew some of the things said about her: a no-good wife, a seductress, words spoken in whispers, eyes full of dislike for the discarded woman who might steal other women's husbands. Alex still leaned against the salon doorframe denying he'd had affairs.

Helena, her face inches from Alex's, spoke fiercely in an undertone, "If you come home, you work every day and help pay for everything. You look after your family." With a swish of her skirt she turned from him.

At home, hands on hips, she accused him: "You, a Greek man, leave your family to go hungry and you don't care. You chase other women and make love to them. These *poutana,* they are ugly. They're nothing. You tell them to go and never see them again."

Alex, looking subdued, denied he'd had affairs. He remained home most evenings playing cards, watching sports programs. He went out to work each day – where, Helena did not know. On occasional Saturdays, he took the children to the Riverdale Park to see the animals, to local school playgrounds, and on warm days, for ice cream. Relieved, Helena cleaned the flat and baked pastries. She styled her hair.

***

After seven years of marriage, Helena gave birth to a still-born baby boy.

"By the blood of Christ I'm a cursed man!" Alex spat the words at his near-comatose wife. With Helena's and his daughters' cries ringing in his ears, he walked from the flat. The time was eleven in the morning on the day his wife had returned from the hospital.

"Amalia, come to me," Helena called feebly to her seven-year old. "Mama needs you to help. I know you're hungry, but you must feed yourself. Please don't cry, Mama will be better soon. Tomorrow I'll get up and buy you some nice things – ice cream, chocolates?"

Amalia sat at the end of the bed, examining her fingers, spreading them out as though to check they were all there. "I'm not hungry," she said, stuck a thumb in her mouth and began rocking back and forth on the bed.

"Oh baby, please go and see what Georgia's doing, ask her if she wants to eat." But Amalia buried her face in the blankets and continued rocking.

Alex did not return the next day, or the one after. Helena, weak and depressed, hushed her daughters who lay on the end of her bed, whining

256

when they weren't fighting. The flat was cold. There was little food. She had no energy to go shopping and no money to pay for it anyway. *We'll starve,* she thought, too depressed even to cry.

Mother and children dozed away their despair. When Helena awoke she saw the early darkness of a late October afternoon already descending. Saw her small girls sucking their thumbs as they lay curled in fetal position still on the end of her bed. *Damn Alex, damn him to hell! I must get up ... have to work ... need money. But I've still got Yia Yia's gold coins!* She got up, picked up a rubber band and tied up her hair. In a floppy T-shirt and baggy sweat pants she padded into the kitchen, reached behind a radiator and pulled out a rusted tin box. After picking up some coins and rubbing them against her cheek, she counted them. She struggled with herself. *They're for my salon,* and firmly closing the lid, she returned the box to its hiding place. Searching through her cupboards she found stale bread, a half-empty box of Cheerios, some smelly feta cheese.

Georgia's pudgy hands were pulling at her trousers and roughly she said, "Here, eat these," as she tipped the Cheerios out of their box onto plates on the kitchen table. *No money. Got to get back to work. What to do?* Thalia, maybe she could help. But how could she confess, even to a sister, what had happened? Or to Mario and Luigi? What to do with the children? Next morning with sudden decision she got her daughters up and dressed, gave them cherrios to eat, and took them out into a rainy morning to the *Capuzzi Salon.*

Mario frowned as he looked up at a disturbance in the doorway.

"Sorry, you can't bring them in here," he heard his receptionist say. A loud exclamation followed, and a child's cry. He strode across the room.

"I said we can't have children in ..." began the young woman with long blond hair.

"I'll take care of this."

All eyes in the mirrored salon stared at the group in the doorway. Mario saw Helena's shapeless brown coat, wet from the rain, eyes with dark circles beneath. One child standing aloof in wet slippers, the other clinging to her mother, a thumb in her mouth. Each child looked up at him with large eyes. He took their hands and said in an undertone to Helena, "Let's get you dry."

He led them to small change rooms at the end of a short corridor. "Dry the kids off," he said, and tossed a pile of towels to her. To the children: "Are you hungry? Of course you are." To his receptionist he said, "See what you can find in the fridge for the kids."

"I've got no money." Helena stood with her head lowered. "My husband is … away. My babysitter can't look after the children. If you let them stay here I can work. Truly they'll sit quietly. They are not any trouble." Tears of despair slid down her cheeks.

Neither Mario and Luigi spoke for a moment. Mario cleared his throat. Expression inscrutable, he said, "There is always a chair for you." He ruffled the hair of Georgia while Luigi picked up elder daughter Amalia and made her solemn little face smile. "Your children – well, we can try it and see. Maybe you should wear a gown while you work."

Helena, spirits reviving, went to work. The children cut up woman's magazines and drew pictures with paper and pencils. As she left that afternoon Mario gave her an advance sufficient to cover babysitting expenses for two weeks.

Thalia reluctantly agreed that she would again look after the children. Helena dressed herself carefully for her days at the Francesco Salon, pinning the Bacarro rose brooch to her jacket to bring her luck.

On a warm September day during Toronto's Film Festival when Yorkville bustled with the hip and well-dressed, a tall woman bearing an elegant air entered the *Capuzzi Salon*. Mario looked up from his client to see the actress smiling in the doorway. "Ms Smith!" His exclamation was followed by a sweep of his hand and a bow.

"Oh, call me Maggie," she said with a big smile. "You know I can't miss a visit here when I'm in Toronto - film Festival, you know. I need a trim and some colouring – you'll know best." Her laugh was warm and tinkling. Mario hovered, saw that his next client had already been waiting fifteen minutes, and hesitated. Then he nodded toward Helena.

"I've got one of the hottest stylists in the city working for me," he said. "She'll take expert care of you. Helena, make Ms Cruz real happy – okay?" He winked, and turned back to his own client.

"Thank you, thank you," Helena whispered.

Chapter 47

Toronto, 1980 - 1986

When Alex returned home after four week's absence, his erratic behaviour continued. He went out unshaven, returning later drunk and abusive. Ignoring his children, he pushed his wife into the bedroom and forced himself upon her each night until she dreaded both the nights and days.

Dismissing the fact of Stephan's marriage, Helena prayed to her old lover as to a saint. She saw his face, heard his voice. In her dreams, the years and all they had accumulated rolled away: marriage, children, furniture, unpaid bills; work in grungy hair salons. She was back in Patras once more, on the beach, at the bend in the road where it ran to the sea, stripped of all that had come since. She was a young girl in the throes of passionate love, the joy of life in her blood.

Rudely yanked back into the present, she worked, cooked, cleaned. She learned that Toronto's Greek community thought Alex handsome and charming. Being a man, he could do no wrong.

"He goes away for business," she explained when she had to, and told none of her unhappiness, not even to her mother, knowing what she would hear: *you married a no-good man with good looks and charm. Love flies away when the good times don't come.*

Alex is not all bad, she argued with herself, he's only taking a long time to grow up. She knew he'd been fired from work for arriving late and leaving early, for taking too many smoke breaks. All he could get now were brief, contract jobs. She understood that he hated his life because he had little money, lived in an ugly flat and had produced no sons; an immature man who, to console himself for his disappointments, used whatever money he earned on a sports car that he financed on credit, flashy clothes, gold chains around his neck and expensive wine. She knew he found her pudgy and uninterested in sex and, as his father-in-law had done before him, he began having affairs. None of it matters she told herself, and held fast to the dream almost consuming her: recognition as an artist in a salon of her own.

***

A year passed, and then another. Helena, struggling with the children and her work, registered that Alex was at home more often. Were his love affairs disappointing? The food better at home? Because he could get his laundry done? Certainly he liked that little Georgia made a fuss of him. Occasionally he plunked a stack of bills on the table and she took them without comment; slipped some into her tin box.

One bright spring Sunday morning, Alex, on a whim, took the girls to church. Alone in the flat, Helena pulled the box from its hiding place and counted up all she'd saved. Exultant at the sum, she decided she could soon afford to rent some little space for a salon. She began columns for expenses and estimated an income. Fluctuating between exaltation and doubt, she confided in Thalia.

"Why would you take this on?" Her sister paused in her scrubbing of toys in the kitchen sink. "You've got a job, owning a business will only bring you trouble."

"But Thalia, remember when you worked for the factory boss? You hated it and wanted something more – something better."

"I never wanted my own business."

"Well, *I* do. You – are you happy? Always cleaning, cleaning. Give yourself a break."

The following day Helena at the Capuzzi Salon she asked Mario why he had chosen hair for a business, why he had set up his own salon and not just worked in somebody else's.

"This is a long story." Mario rubbed his hands together. Having finished with a client, he poured two coffees and led her to his small office. Pushing his chair in front of his desk he leaned back in it, his black denim trousers riding up over his socks. "My father wanted me to be a lawyer," he said. "Enough with the hands in the dirt and sweat on the back; enough of slinging tools, coming home at sunset all worn out." Intensity burned more deeply the blue of his eyes.

"My dad boasted to his friends that his sons would use their brains to become doctors or lawyers. That made it hard for Luigi and me because we *wanted* to work with our hands – to do hair. Give a great haircut, we believed, and a person feels lifted up; everyone feels better for it." He sighed deeply. "We had to disappoint our father. We told him we must have our own business so we could make a difference for all the people in it, build up respect for everyone: the floor sweeper, the errand-person, the receptionist. In old age homes too —we do the hair of old people out of respect for them."

Helena held a sudden vision the brothers as masters of ceremonies trying to orchestrate a kinder, gentler place for the people who came to them; men whose love for people made the world a better place.

They can do it, I can do it. I *will* become famous. Helena's inner voice incessantly chattered. What had Spiros said? There's always a way get ahead. But what about your daughters? came the voice. Okay, what about them? They know I love them but I must tell them again.

At home, Georgia's big eyes smiled up at her, a pudgy hand patted her. "My angel, my little peace-maker." Helena bent down to kiss her, then looked around for Amalia. Her older daughter only challenged her with a stare and turned her back.

Fame means money and that means I can give them good things, Helena argued with herself. I can send them to college - unless they want to work with their hands like Mario and Luigi. Then came her *Yia Yia's* voice. *You were given training that your sister and brothers didn't get so it's your duty to restore our family's good name. You must get your own salon and put above it the name Kouvalis.*

Always the name. Always duty, duty, duty.

***

On a dull, rainless late spring day, fourteen years after her arrival in Toronto, Helena opened her own salon. A narrow building on teeming Yonge Street, it wandered crookedly from creaky front door to rusting iron at the back. Her savings, and her grandmother's gold coins, paid for basic furniture and products, for the hiring of hair stylist Bonnie. Alex was not told where the money came from. Helena, wearing her *Baccaro* rose, supervised tradesmen in the setting up of her physical space, placed advertisements in the *Toronto Star, Toronto Voice* and *The Bulletin* community newspapers. She made appointments for clients sent by Mario and Luigi. Beside the door geraniums bloomed in large pots and a blue and white banner floated above. Music from *Dionysus Stavropoulos* drifted to the street. Indoors, a friend of Alex's painted one wall in blood-red colours on which he added grape vines and flowering meadows. Georgia helped paint a figure resembling Lady Godiva riding among them, her hair streaming out behind her. On the opposite wall winged chariots raced over an azure-blue sky.

The city's newest entrepreneur moved about in a rainbow of colours: sling-back red shoes, and a low-cut bodice tucked into a red-patterned skirt with gold filaments trimming it. About her near-naked shoulders swung rivers of glossy hair. Passing pedestrians were given leaflets offering a two-for-one deal. Eyes brimming, Helena moved like a person flying close to the sun.

The long days that followed were pent in solitude. Having few or no customers, Helena sent Bonnie home, remaining to stare out her open door, willing clients to come. People looked in and passed on, or passed without looking at all.

Spring passed turned quietly into summer. On Yonge Street's melting, gum-splattered sidewalks, locals and tourists traipsed. They entered Country Donuts, Sushi and Thai restaurants, Roberts Gallery, McDonald's, the Panasonic theatre – and The House of Lords salon opposite. Still nobody paused at her door and a cry rose up in her throat. It was all so far from her dreams.

Dreams: and time wound itself backwards, to a bottle of shampoo on a window ledge, a bucket of water on a living room floor. Her scrawny self, running the narrow streets calling for clients. The piggy eyes of Mr. Pousopolis dismissing her. Back further, her mother's laments over her disappointments. Her grandmother's sighing over a lost Smyrna, Spiros, over the glories of a receding Byzantium ... Helena closed her empty appointment book.

***

Summer gathered itself up and departed tempestuously. The salon remained empty. Then slowly, in the autumnal days that followed, one client entered, then another with a friend, two friends, until, as with the barber under the mulberry tree in Patras, people gathered. On word of mouth they came for hair-styles, cuts and colour; for companionship, entertainment and gossip. Mingling with the well-to-do and middle class were the poor whom Helena served at no cost.

A proud Alex strutted, beaming and expansive.

"Why this part of Yonge Street?" asked a young woman as she scanned the ragged streetscape.

"It's close to the subway, and everybody knows Yonge Street. See the people who walk by all the time? Some of them come in."

Hard work for Helena was just beginning, long days and humble tasks. After school and on Saturdays she brought eight-year-old Amalia and seven-year-old Georgia with her, doughnuts and fries for their supper. Amalia sat importantly at her mother's desk staring at pedestrians passing, sometimes playing with her lank, light hair before a mirror. When the door closed at last, Georgia helped clean the wash-basins and line up hair brushes while her mother scrubbed the floor.

"You're a good girl to your mother," Helena said. "Look, I'm going downstairs. You stay in one of these chairs, have doughnut, okay?" Georgia happily reached for the bag.

"Fat face, pumpkin face." Amalia was teasing her hair.

"Squinty eyes." Georgia flapped her hands behind her ears.

"Yifto. Loser."

"Stop it." Helena's voice came up the basement stairs. "One of you sit at the back, one in the front, and don't even talk to each other." She returned to the space she called her office. For her desk, she'd nailed a board to stretch across a narrow space between two walls, and on them pinned photos of Patras. Money would be in short supply for some time, she knew, and everything would be a struggle. But it was her very own place. Remembering Alekos' injunction, she called it simply, *Helena Kouvalis, Hair Salon.*

***

With her daughters in school, in the quiet of early mornings, Helena sat alone, updating her accounts, reckoning her successes and failures. Feelings of triumph – "I've done it Mama, Papa, I've done it, Alex" – were mixed with a sense that something had slipped from her grasp. What? Alex hung about, smiling at passers-by, inviting them in. Ha, that was it: Stephan should be the one sharing this moment; he'd been the one to propel her on this path. An urgent desire to see him swelled within her like a fever. No Stephan, only Alex who was happy she earned money, happy she was becoming important in the city's Greek community, but angry that her name, and not his, was inscribed above her salon.

This day, Helena's eyes wandered to a photograph on the wall above her desk. In it, Eleni was sitting in a wicker chair outside the door on X

Street, someone in the background. She peered closer. Stephan! He'd been captured unawares striding the street in shorts, towel slung over a shoulder. Funny she'd never noticed it before. Pulling it off the wall, she held it close, willing old memories to mind. As images tumbled in the stifling air, she sensed a creeping spirit. She waited, eyes squeezed shut, silently begging Stephan to come to her, now wishing that her *Voices would* talk to her. Like the soft rustling of willow branches, like a quiet sea running up warm stones, she heard his voice but did not understand the words. She saw his face, but his expression remained inscrutable. He held something in his hands – what was it?

Please don't go, she begged, but the image faded. In chill nights in the flat when the children were in bed, she tossed in her own, dreaming again of him: Stephan leaning over her telling her to be careful, placing a hand over his heart then drifting away. During another dream on another night, Stephan was trying to tell her something and she awoke with a sense of foreboding. His spirit faded and in the days and weeks that followed, it was her grandmother's that haunted. *What is it, Yia Yia, what is it?"*

***

After all his part-time work, Alex eventually gained regular contract work with Rogers Cable and increased his contribution to household expenses.

"I'm making some profit," Helena told him, "lots of customers who keep coming back," and that evening she sang. Catching an expression on her husband's face she'd seen before, she smoothed his sulky brow, and when the children were asleep, drew him to the matrimonial bed.

"Mom, I'm coming to the salon after school," ten-year-old Amalia announced next morning. "Aunt Thalia doesn't have to babysit me anymore."

"Then Georgia will have to come too, and you must bring your homework."

Amalia made a face.

At home one late one Saturday, Alex stood in the needle of sunlight that angled through the fire escape window, rubbing his hands. "Listen now," he said. "We're going to buy us a house."

In the small glittering silence that followed, Helena's hand flew to her mouth. She stammered, but couldn't form the words she would say. Behind her eyelids danced images of lace-curtained windows opening to gardens of trees. Violets and wild roses perfuming the air. Bedrooms with white coverings, a sparkling kitchen and bathroom. She laughed, clapped her hands and said, "Dear Alex, I love you so much. When do we buy our new house?"

***

Chapter 48

Toronto

Georgia

"'Dear Alex, I love you so much. When do we buy our new house?'" Helena is leaning over my shoulder, her voice rasping. "You put words in my mouth – like this?"

"I told you: I make up the things I don't know." I lean away from her.

"And just look at the state of you." She straightens, folds her arms and glares at me.

I stare right back at her. "Look," I say, this is a good story, an important one. When I'm writing it, it's like ... like I'm someone else. Stop worrying about it, and about me. When I get to the end I'll be ... different." I don't say it, but I also believe that when I'm finished, so will the burden Yiannis put on to his family: Eleni, Spiros, Melina, Helena, will be free of it. Me too – if I ever felt it. And who knows, I might really be different. The sliver of hope returns that something important will be waiting for me at the end.

"Where are your friends?" Fretfulness enters Helena's voice. "You should be more like your sister and go out more, do things."

Same old mantra. I can never compete with Amalia – or with my mother – so don't even try. Amalia is always the successful one, pretty and clever. She got student loans, went to college and studied dress design. She has her own place. Although part of me always envied her, I thought that it was good riddance when she left home because she added to all the things that upset Mom – and all of us.

"My little peacemaker." Helena seems already sorry for her words. "You need something better than reading and writing and taking money for old books. What kind of career is that?"

This old line surprises me because I'd thought she'd come to approve of my reading, of 'getting yourself educated in your own way.' And she's the one who passed on to me information about Adam and Alekos and how they loved books.

I clear the table for dinner, tell myself to forget about everything except *'An Odyssey.'* From the beginning it has alternately elated and depressed me, taken off and gone outside my control. It's not the exact truth of my Mom's life or all the others before her, of course not, I can't possibly know everything, but I believe it captures the essence. I've no idea how I'll explain it to her and so I put off the thought.

The next few weeks the world outside dims and almost disappears as I read and type and live among the people in my story, characters so insistent they get right into my pores, my brain, my heart. At four this morning my fingers are still poised above my keyboard. Reluctantly I shut it down: my laptop, my Greek *Laika* music, and get into bed.

Dragging myself out at eight, I pull on an undershirt, a blue sweater, and jeans that are becoming loose about my waist, and without stopping for coffee, slip on winter boots, a woollen cap, Amalia's cast-off pea jacket, and head for Second Cup, then to the salon. The cold stings my nostrils and tips of my ears. I enter carrying two steaming cups of coffee.

"Bet you won't get many customers today." I hand Helena a cup. She's dressed in brown slacks and a pale green sweater that emphasizes her mid-riff bulk, but her face is carefully made-up. No other stylist has yet arrived.

"Customers book, but they don't come," she complains.

"Can I just sit and flick through your magazines?"

"Sure," she looks surprised. "What are you looking for?"

"Oh, just some information about the history of hair."

"I can tell you anything."

"Well, not all the things I want to know." I flick through the heavily thumbed pages of 'The Curl Wants Out. Convoluted Tresses. The Irascible Curl. Woven Strands. Hair Flip…' I intend to visit a bunch of salons and find out what goes on in the world of hair dressing. Helena will think I'm going overboard but I don't care.

Snow squalls threaten as I prepare for my salonary expedition. First to the House of Lords diagonally across the street from Helena's, a lovely Spanish-style building and an important piece of Toronto architecture. I stand uncertainly in the doorway, my ears assaulted by a cacophony of noise.

"Shut the door, will ya?"

"Oh, sorry." My eyes travel over rows of bobbing young people attending very young, hip clients. Their lean ribbons of flesh are pierced everywhere with slivers of silver, tattooed, jangling with gold and silver at neck, ankles and wrists. Magazines lie haphazardly on tables.

"Do you look after anyone older than … twenty?" I ask the receptionist.

"Well, not really. S'pose you can tell by the music."

I stick my fingers in my ears and leave.

Next, to Yorkville, to the ridiculously expensive place called *Salon Jie* owned by Jie Matar, considered by some to be the new Vidal Sassoon. I wonder if it would ever be possible for Helena to achieve what he had, this Paris-trained Lebanese man who had swept the whole country to become the idol of the rich and famous. Okay, Mr. Jie, I think, you've generated all your own hype with shameless self-promotion. You've even called yourself, *the god of hair*, so let's find out about you.

Mr. Jie presents himself twenty minutes after I've asked for him and fixes me with an interrogative stare. Assuming a deliberate pose of elegance, I stretch one booted leg over the other. I mention the weather, admire his décor, then ask who makes up his clientele.

He tosses off names with a careless air, naming politicians, celebrities, prominent lawyers and cosmetic surgeons. "I give them a silhouette that goes with their shadow," he says, "but they must have the right kind of personality."

"Oh. Have I got the right kind?"

He shrugs as he runs an eye over the length of me. "Can you afford me?"

"I think I … don't want to afford you. Thanks for your time."

I trek next to Robert Gage, 'Mr. Glitter' and his salon, beautiful, elegant, and also expensive. Okay, enough of that, and I head for a streetcar that will take me to Little Italy. Tomorrow, to China Town, to Forest Hill Village. After that, North York, The Beach. In each salon I ask for a trim, or advice about hair colour and styles, surreptitiously making notes about large salons and small, the super glamorous, and the grungy little outfits like the ones Helena once worked in. There's mystical atmosphere, New-Age music, Art Deco. I think of Helena's salon with its apparent chaos, its clients and staff singing and dancing, and I laugh out loud.

I'm back on Yonge Street in the salon doorway, feeling again the exhilaration that comes from the sun, the moon and the Greek Muses shining from its walls; from Aphrodite watching Apollo flit over the old hills of the Peloponnesus, Lady Godiva still streaking across one wall. I think how clients must feel they are floating beyond the earth-bound toward the celestial. This place is about hair, yes, but also a gathering place for gossip in the manner of the post mistress or village store of yesteryear – like the barber shop in Patras. Helena has created a place where people can be happy for a moment, for many moments. Admiration that has been gathering within me swells as I look around for her.

***

"Helena, listen." I burst in the door at home one evening to find Amalia slouching in a living room chair. A sullen expression distorts her pretty face and her eyes are wet. She's wearing a short skirt, black woollen sweater and knee-high leather boots that drip melting snow onto the carpet. Helena ignores it and hovers about her. When Amalia sees me her familiar assessing, judging expression returns.

"So, little sis." Her voice is a drawl. "Losing some fat, eh? Want to snare a boyfriend? What's with calling Mom Helena?"

"Amalia just lost her apartment," Helena tells me in her Amalia-placating voice. "And her boyfriend too." She replenishes Amalia's empty wine glass.

"That King guy?" I ask.

"Such a jerk!" My sister's face twitches. "A stupid nobody going nowhere. Lots of guys waiting in line for me so what do I care. What are you up to Georgie? Mom says you're researching stuff for a book." I hear dismissal in her voice.

"Nothing you'd be interested in." I'm bursting to tell Helena what I've learned, but not in front of Amalia. "Why don't I get a glass and have a drink with you?"

"I'm talking privately to Mom."

"O...kay." As I slide off into the bedroom we once shared, I hear Helena give her the familiar line about sisters making an effort to get along.

"What's she doing still living at home? Isn't it time she got a full-time job and a life of her own?"

Irritated, I walk straight back into the living room. "I live here and you don't, so quit telling me what to do." Immediately I see I've upset Helena. Then, with a sudden strong wish to impress Amalia, I say, "Let me tell you a story." I pick up the wine bottle, pour the small amount left into a glass, and settle myself in Dad's armchair.

"It's about the power of long hair. Clovis is a 6th century Merovingian ruler. He dies and leaves behind his wife Clothilde and two sons. But it's the grandsons who are to inherit the throne, with Queen Clothilde as their guardian. The queen's second son gets jealous. He sends a message to the Queen to say he's planning the coronation of the grandsons and please send them to their uncle. When the young princes arrive, they're seized and held captive. A note is sent to the Queen. With it comes a sword and pair of scissors. Does she prefer to see her grandsons live with their hair cut short, or would she rather see them die? The Queen chooses the sword.

"A grandmother murders her grandsons – don't tell me," Helena cries out. "This is terrible! You put something like that in your story?"

Even Amalia looks shocked.

"Yes, a terrible story. But see how it illustrates the myths about long hair? Like it was once a symbol of the sun's radiant power, and maybe still is. Just yesterday I read about ancient sun gods and solar heroes from India to Ireland. All of them had long hair. Apollo too, he never allowed his to be touched by a razor. Think of hair's symbolism: Eve's shame, Samson's power, Lady Godiva using hers to cover her nakedness ..."

You've left something out." Amalia, unwillingly captivated, interrupts. "Hair means love and permanence. Lovers exchange locks of their hair because it's like if I can't have you, let me carry away a strand of your hair. Hey, something else: you can sell your hair and get money for it."

"Yes." Hair and its power, erotic or otherwise. Sudden, unbidden images float before me: my mother as an owner a famous hair salon. Clients lining up to get inside. A hundred staff. Coffee tables stacked with magazines, their front covers graced with her photo. Another image follows this: a handsome man on her arm and big diamonds on her fingers. My mind flits to the Captain and how he would have funded her business. But what Helena's got she's achieved all by herself. Obviously she's had an inner voice that has commanded, has suggested great things to come if she obeyed it.

I hear clattering on the basement stairs and Amalia, who had been smiling, interested, jumps up, kisses Helena on the cheek and heads to the front door for her boots and coat just as Dad emerges from the basement.

"Do stay and say hello to your father," Helena implores.

"My father does not want to say hello to me." Amalia is only half into her coat as she steps out the door and shuts it firmly behind her.

"We're talking about hair, Dad," I hurry to say. He lumbers to his chair by the gas fire. "It's amazing how powerful it was, like the cutting a girl's hair in medieval war to use as catapult ropes. And remember Rapunzel? Hair, It's also got fetishist qualities that both attract and repel. It's immortal ..."

"So, the plump daughter comes home and the skinny one flies away." Dad flicks one hand in the air as though to brush something off him.

"Georgie is not so plump anymore," Helena says.

"What's eating our Amalia?"

I want to tell my father that it's him, but say instead, "Don't worry Dad, Amalia always sorts herself out. Before you came upstairs I was telling Mom about some research I'm doing. I've got one more salon to visit, then I'm going to put what I've learned into '*An Odyssey.*'"

"*An Odyssey?*" Okay. Woman talk." Dad gets up and pads about kitchen, but I know he's still listening.

"Oh, I almost forgot." I drop my voice. "I went to see Mario and Luigi's new salon on Bloor Street near Runnymede. Nice setup they've got. A big space now, and big prices to go with it. I asked Mario if he lost any customers after he raised his. Know what he said? People think they're getting the very best when the price is high. A place with low prices can't be very good. He lost some customers, but got others."

"You must know where your clients come from," Helena says. "Christine, she could pay Mario's prices and lots more, but many people can't, so you have small prices to help them, and sometimes do it for free."

"I think you're great, you know that?" Impulsively I rush to give her a hug.

"Ah Georgie." Helena's smile is both warm and tired, and suddenly my heart aches for her, for all her heart-breaking work. I see her lizard-like eyes snapping open to issue an order or remonstrance. Eyes penetrating to every corner of her salon, noting everyone who comes in. Given to faints and hysteria, she's a woman who knows no contentment, I think, only ecstasy or sorrow. I marvel that she can run a business that requires sustained concentration and dedication to menial tasks. To book-keeping, negotiating with suppliers and landlords, knowledge of advertising and managing of employees, and all of it self-taught. What a long way she's come from a small girl in Patras. Some old superstition intrudes and I worry what will jump out at her next – other than Dad.

***

Chapter 49

Toronto

Life hummed along in a pattern with Helena's calendar filled every hour. Her hands danced over clients' hair, her feet to the rhythms of Greek music. One bright summer morning she wandered outside to dead head the geraniums beside her door; crossed the street to Roberts Gallery. Turning back, seeing sun rays lighting on the words, Helena Kouvalis, Hair Salon, she was struck by a sense of defeat. 'You're forgetting your ambition,' said a little voice. 'Nobody important comes to the Kouvalis Salon. If your name is the best, nobody knows it.'

Always the name. This message, inculcated since childhood, was a part of her. She could no more change it than she could change the shape of her nose, her mouth. Her vision that early morning was of years stretching before her, one following another and another, all the same: Alex the same, strutting or jealous, promising to fix things but doing nothing.

The day the letter came she was at her desk, day-dreaming of Stephan, his sinewy figure leaning over her. His lips moved but she couldn't make out the words. She ripped open the envelope Bonnie handed her, and some minutes later, jumped up and stared wildly about her, a wordless howl in her eyes. Silence lapped around the salon walls. Nobody moved, until a sympathetic Bonnie took the crumpled letter from her and read:

'My beloved granddaughter, I am ill, and I know you can't come to me, so I tell you this for you to remember after I'm gone: The greatest success in life is finding a little joy to make you to smile. You have a big heart and must always fill it with love, for what else is there? Only our family name. My Adam first made it to be respected. Now it is for you to...'

Helena snatched the letter and walked out the door.

The phone was ringing when she arrived home. She picked it up, to hear her mother's voice: "Helena *chryso mou*, your *Yia Yia* has died. Yes, at last she's put away the burden of all her years, and happy in her last days because she thought she was back in Smyrna with all her children. Before she closed her eyes for the last time she whispered about the Virgin coming to take her to Adam – please don't make such a big noise with all your crying. Your *Yia Yia* knew it was her time and was happy to go. We are not to be sad, only to miss her."

"Don't go yet Mama." Helena felt an intense longing for her home. "Don't go. Tell me more, more and about Papa and Uncle Spiros too."

"Your Papa is good, but your uncle, what's to become of him I don't know." Melina sighed deeply.

"Mama, I want to come home."

Silence weighed on the line. "What I can do is send you some photos," and her mother sighed again.

***

That night, Helena, in memory, wandered with her mother, uncle and grandmother on X Street in Patras. She gathered within her their aching disappointments. *Yia Yia:* a life cut off in full bloom, and grinding slowly to nothing. Her mother Melina: an artistic child who had wanted to teach. She'd made a bad marriage, but Helena wouldn't, couldn't, think about that. Shivering on this warm summer evening, she picked through snapshots she received, fastening on familiar faces: Uncle Spiros hunched in a chair, sparse white hair combed carefully across his scalp, his burned-out eyes glaring the camera. Nikos making faces. Old neighbours Lina and Stacia hunched under layered shawls. Publican Stavros leaning in the doorway of number 24 holding a bunch of white chrysanthemums. Homesick again, Helena reached for the phone. To her astonishment, Mr. Stavros picked it up.

"I mourn your grandmother for her sad life," the publican said. "And your uncle Spiros, I don't know …"

"What about him?"

"He's not well, not well."

Helena listened to an account of her uncle's sad life, his obsession with the Onassis family, his boasting he could outdo Aristotle even yet, insisting, "That family always rises up from the ashes, and so too will this one."

Poor Uncle Spiros: Helena recalled images of a little man feverishly working to restore what he'd lost. Then the thought came that if he hadn't had the Onassis obsession to drive him he might have been worse off.

"Mr. Stavros," she said suddenly, "Do you remember Stephan? Or know where he lives? I ... I need to find him. Is he in Patras?"

The publican, surprised, paused before saying, "Stephan, the young man who sailed for Australia to make his fortune – I heard he made no fortune. He got married and went to England."

"England! Why does he live in England?"

"I'm not saying he does. Others saw him once, here in the city. They say his wife left him. It's all I can tell you."

***

Chapter 50

Toronto

Alex purchased a small bungalow on a slope in the Upper Beach: five tiny rooms, one bathroom, an overgrown garden. When Helena clapped a hand to her mouth to stifle a wail, a flash of anger passed over Alex's face. With effort he said, "We'll fix it all up and make the garden look nice – see over here." Walking to an enclosure at the end of the elongated back yard he pointed to a pond half-hidden in the grass. "See, we'll clean it, get some fish in it. You and me, we'll sit here when the sun sets and have us a beer." He rested a hand on her shoulder, touched her hair. Helena recognized then the Alex she'd first known, and hope flickered like a wan shaft of sunlight

"See, I'll build a trellis for roses to climb over and an archway for you to walk under." Alex's words came fast. "I'll paint all the walls, put something nice on the floors."

"You'll do all that? But no pond, the children might fall in it. When … when do you start all this fixing?"

For the first few weeks after their move, Alex was busy with broom and paint-brush. But all too soon he started getting up late, going out, returning a few hours later. Sometimes he came home in the early morning hours reeking of smoke and beer. Helena had no idea where he went, what he did, or even if he worked, and dared not ask. At times she saw him pull wads of cash from his jeans pocket and plunk it on the kitchen table; heard him whistling, heard beer cans opening, the television blaring. Other late evenings he walked in, said nothing, and stared at the television without turning it on.

It was she who cleaned floors and painted walls, weeded and cleaned out the garden.

On a hot August day Helena was on her knees weeding when Thalia arrived, white blouse tucked into blue jeans, her hair tied back. Helena jumped up, smearing dirt across her forehead as she brushed hair from her eyes. "Looking good, eh?" she said, and her sister stared in astonishment at the transformation of the formerly weedy patch of ground in front of the bungalow, at a reclaimed backyard that wandered to a rotting wooden fence against which a line of daisies bloomed.

"I never see Alex here? Oh here you are, Amalia. Such nice clothes, but your Mama lets you wear lipstick?"

"She just likes to play dress-up. Tell Georgie to come out and say hello to her auntie."

Georgia came slowly through the door a sketch-pad in hand. Wearing a shapeless dress in red and browns, her hair spilling from a rubber band, she said without looking, "Hello Aunt Thalia."

"My girl, she likes to write little stories, and she can draw pictures too. Alex? He works outside the city most days." Helena wiped her perspiring face. "So I do the garden ..."

"And the housework, and earn the money. Where does Alex work? Why not in the city where lots of it can be found?"

"He likes this work. It brings more money."

"Well, little you see of it." Thalia looked at her sister closely and Helena knew what she saw: dark circles, blotchy skin, hair like a hurricane blowing through it. Her desire to confide warred with her need to save face against the dreaded, 'I told you so.' Who better than a sister to tell simply that Alex was having affairs? About the strange women who phoned asking for him. Last week's humiliation burned afresh.

"Is Alex there?"

"No, who is this?" The phone had gone dead. The same afternoon a woman with bouffant red hair wearing a swinging short skirt and stiletto heels appeared and lounged insouciantly in the salon doorway.

"Who are you? What do you want?"

"You think you can do my hair? No, you're not so good." The woman fluffed her own and blew a large puff of smoke in the air.

"Go smoke outside. You want me to do your hair? So why do you tell me I'm no good? What do you want?"

"Does your husband like you to do this poor work? You make any money? Is he happy in his home and his bed?"

The silence in the salon shattered when Helena dropped her curling iron, and hands on hips, strode to the woman, thrust her face inches from hers and said, "*Poutana*! Get out of my shop. Never come here again."

To Alex that evening she'd said, "You give up these other women or you go. I earn the money and don't need you. I'll tell everyone how you treat your wife. I'll shame you!"

Alex's momentary embarrassment turned quickly to anger. "You're damned fool stupid," he said, "You're fat." He stepped close and pinched a skinfold of her belly. "I go to the arms of other women because my wife is no use to me, no good in bed." He struck his hands together in the air and Helena slipped past him, threatening to call Kostas to throw him out.

Alex packed a bag and left home and Helena found herself at the dawn of another dark age. Like ghosts whispering she heard the sneers of the red-headed woman: *you're fat. You don't look after your husband. No good in bed.*

A month after this Helena received news of her Aunt Zena's death, followed not long after by her hunchback husband Elpenor.

"He couldn't live without his wife," Melina said on the phone. "Your poor auntie, but such a beautiful love."

In a threadbare voice Helena said, "Mama, I'd come home for my auntie but we don't have the money. My salon is very busy, and Alex goes away for his work." Her voice faded.

"I think your Alex has other women," her mother said after a silence. "I saw the look of him, and men will do this. My girl, you look after your home the way a good Greek woman must? You take care of Alex in bed?"

"Oh Mama." Helena's sigh rose up from the bottom of her feet to mingle with shadows that crept from the walls. "Mama, you don't know, I try, and I don't forget the family name."

"Never mind that now." Melina's voice was sharp. "It gives trouble. You must look to your family; what you owe your husband and children."

"Mama, I remember those times when Papa loved other women and you covered your head in shame. Now you're telling me different?"

"Listen to me: You must decide if your husband and children are to be your life's work. Your Papa is good, good, the most important person in my life now even if it is in our later years and never mind the money. We've learned to be happy with each other. This is what I'm telling you."

Helena heard again her father's laugh, the songs on his lips, remembered his dancing in the streets. Tears welled in her eyes.

Thalia was still standing in the garden, questioning, concerned, her eyes ranging over her exhausted-looking sister. Helena said simply that she worked hard because she had to help Alex support the family while still holding onto her dream of having the name Kouvalis known among the important people in the city. Success: what was its definition? She had a salon full of paying clients. Her name appeared in trade magazines, had been profiled in *Toronto Life,* mentioned in *Saturday Night Magazine.* She had won competitions. But at what cost? Would her marriage have ever worked, even if she'd spent more energy on it …"Sorry, what did you say?"

"Amalia's thirteen and looks like a tart," her sister repeated. "Your Georgia sits around scribbling; you don't spend enough time with them."

Helena sat down suddenly on a plastic garden chair, her head in her hands. In Alex's absence, obsessively she'd chased down weeds, scrubbed floors, washed and re-washed curtains, sheets, her family's clothes, swept the pathway to the street. At the salon, she'd cleaned floors, counters and washbasins, re-arranged trolleys of rollers and brushes, all after clients and staff had gone. She had arrived home late, exhausted. How had she fitted her daughters into all this?

"If Alex is still not home to take you to the ball, will you look after our children?" Thalia still hovered.

"Of course." Helena struggled to bring a smile to her lips. "I'll do your hair and make you look beautiful."

"Alex doesn't come home at all, does he?"

"Sometimes." Helena's voice sounded hollow to her own ears. "He's got work that takes him away."

"I hear things. About Alex with other women – just like Papa…"

"I'll do your hair, look after your children. You go and dance all night."

***

279

Chapter 51

Toronto

Georgia

"Ah Georgie."

Helena comes upon me over the slope of the back garden. I'm sitting in a Muskoka chair in the shade of a dogwood, a book in my hand. "We've got a visitor– know who he is?"

I don't recognize the whispery man peering at me over a pair of wire glasses. He's dressed in a buttoned-up shirt, brown trousers, his sparse grey hair combed carefully over his balding head.

"This is your uncle Alekos from Athens."

Wow, I think, this is super cool. I get to meet one of my semi-fictional characters and find out he's not fictional after all. At last I might finally learn what happened to Helena on her last visit to Patras.

We sit on chairs arranged near the hedge where fingers of late afternoon sun reaches us. After getting-acquainted talk, with Helena in mind, I turn to the conversation to love and ambition. "Are they compatible?" I ask. "Take Aristotle Onassis for a start. Ari is alone in his sumptuous yacht among the Greek Islands after his guests have gone home. What then? He's only got himself to talk to, no one to share gossip with about people, politics, the love affairs of friends and the famous. Forsake love for ambition, they say, and you've got empty arms and an empty heart at the end of it."

I hear Helena mutter, 'ah, Georgie,' but I'm not finished. "What about women who gave up everything because of their irrational love of a man who they put on a pedestal, one not nearly good enough for them? Women, they think men's lives are superior to their own. It's not cool."

Alekos looks bemused. Helena repeats, "Ah Georgie," and pats me on the shoulder. Shadows lengthen, and the air cools, so we move indoors. Helena turns on her MP3 player that spills laika music into the living room. Next thing she's moving, dancing, lost in the rhythms. I'm watching her, thinking how prolific are her emotions, how extravagant her gestures, and wonder what my uncle thinks of her.

"Uncle Alekos," I say, "you said you went to Anatolia looking for Kouvalis family members. Did you find any? (I'm anxious to know if any family footprints remain.)

Helena has collapsed in a chair. Dad wanders through the front door, is introduced, then immediately ignored. Feeling sorry for him, I offer him a beer and potato chips.

Alekos, pleased with my question, pulls on his scruffy beard. As he talks, images flit: Adam as a young man dreaming among the family's vegetable and tobacco fields, roaming an ancient plateau among salt lakes and dry riverbeds. If he'd had a choice, would he have remained to work the land his family had owned since primordial times instead of going to Smyrna?

"Surely some relatives must remember old Georgia," I insist, and suddenly recall my own words about the matriarch, my namesake: massive flesh, missing teeth, wayward hair. A fixture in a wooden chair by her kitchen door; staring across the plain to distant mountains. What I've largely imagined has, for me, become true.

"They might all have been killed by the Turks in 1922 and 1923 – or even accidentally by Greek officers chasing the Turkish army," I continue, "so there would be no one to remember anyone. Did you meet anybody who survived those wars? Something else: I've always wondered about the descendants of Hellenistic Greeks: were they Greek, or Turk? If one ethnic group lives among another, and lives like them, if they speak their language and keep most of their customs regardless of their own heritage, are they not the same? Can you become someone other than what you once were and, you know, take on someone else's heritage?"

Alekos' eyes are closed. Helena leans forward, her expression intense. When her uncle re-opens his eyes he explains he's always believed there must have been something to his family's claim of former wealth and status, something to have prompted his Uncle Vasilis to make the trek to his brother Yiannis' home near Boldavin. "I kept searching," he says.

"Well, do you know?" My fingers tap the coffee table.

Alekos looks about the room but I can tell he sees nothing of it. "Yes," he says, "Yiannis' great grandfather was once a close advisor to the Caliphate in Constantinople."

"What! A Greek man?"

"Yes, in those days. He must have been a clever fellow, and for his excellent service would have been granted lands and titles, until – well, nobody knows what happened. Maybe someone was jealous of him and set him up. All we know is that he got exiled and lost everything."

"Oh sweet Jesus." Helena's hands shake as she pours more wine. It's when Dad has gone downstairs, Helena to bed leaving me alone with Uncle Alekos, I show him the snapshot of Stephan I'd taken from Helena's office wall. "Do you know this man?" I ask.

"Well, yes, I did meet him, as it happens. He stopped me in the street when I was visiting Melina. He asked about your mother."

"Really! What else?" I twist my hands.

"I told him what I knew." Alekos gives me a penetrating stare. "Even if her marriage were okay, I think she looks for... more excitement, am I right? But I must apologize, I should not be asking this of her daughter even if she is a very mature young lady." The smile he gives me shows a row of crooked teeth and I think, what an odd fellow.

"It's okay," I say. "I do love my Mom and want her to be happy. She's had quite a hard life over here, and ... I don't know, she's got a right to be happy after everything that's happened."

"After your dad happened," Alekos says this under his breath, then adds, "but in the end, she did choose him."

"Everyone has a right to be the happiest they can be," I insist, and Alekos laughs and says something about youthful idealism. "Just so you know, Helena will ask you about Stephan," I add. "She's carried the idea of him around with her all these years, especially when times were bad for her. He's her fantasy man, her rescuer – her saint if you like. Dad, well, he wasn't reliable for a long time, let's put it that way."

"For a young woman, daughter to the man you're talking about, you are indeed mature. Tell me, what will she do with this Stephan when she finds him?"

"Tell herself she's still in love him and try to put back the clock. Pretend all the years since she was seventeen haven't happened. Whatever we think, uncle, she – this relationship– needs closure."

"I hear all this whispering." Helena appears in her bedroom doorway (Alex still sleeps downstairs.) She's wearing a blue nylon dressing gown and her hair hangs like thick curtains about her face. "What's all this talking? Alekos, did you say you'd find out where Stephan lives?"

A quick look flits between the two of us. Alekos shifts in his chair. "I think you need to tell me first how it was that you did not keep in contact. But first, your wonderful daughter should be going to bed."

"Georgia knows this story," Helena says, "she's been writing it since she was a child. If you know where he lives, please give me his address."

"Well, I can look."

A lump rises in my throat when I see the mixture of pleasure and longing on her face. When she's gone back to bed I tell Alekos, "It all wasn't fair. Why did everyone have to interfere in my Mom's life? Put onto her this ridiculous thing about the family's reputation? I mean, who cares, why keep telling the old story about Yiannis and Georgia and all the others?"

After I've spoken I feel sorry for him. After my outburst he looks away from me out the darkened window, fidgets with his wine glass, then says he must get back to Thalia's, and to bed.

The next afternoon, Thalia brings Alekos to the salon. He claps his hands when he sees the sign above it, remains arrested in the doorway listening to Greek music spill from it. Venturing in, he absorbs a place brimming with laughing, chattering clients, a Greek mythical world springing from its walls: Aphrodite, Artemis – and surely not Lady Godiva streaking across one wall? He blinks as his eyes fall upon a Silent Sylvia's ponderous breasts, on tiny Isabel's skinny legs skipping from one client to another. His eyes range over etchings of exuberant Greek figures, over the embroidered cushions, a vase of green flowers, a black rose rising from it. He looks at last at Helena, a large woman with plump cheeks and dark eyes snapping, at her busy hands, her feet tapping to her music. Thalia pats him on the shoulder and leaves.

At the close of the afternoon, Alekos watches Helena fly about with broom and cleaning rags; line up chairs, hair dryers, jars of hair-brushes and shampoo. So many sides to this woman.

***

Chapter 52

Toronto, 1992- 1993

Alex finishes work early on Yonge Street one mid-summer day and drops by the salon. Through the open door he hears his wife crooning a love song, sees her sunlit face, her hair tied up with yellow ribbons. He punches the air and keeps walking. That evening he slams kitchen cupboards, complains there's no food in the house; that his wife never sings at home. "You got something makes you happy when you're someplace else?"

Helena, scrubbing down the kitchen table, stops, astonished at the aggression in his voice. "Yes, dear Alex, if you help me sometimes, I might sing in the night too."

"Aghh!" Alex slams out the door.

***

"Letters for you," Isabel says, handing Helena two white envelopes. "Postmark says Patras. Funny you get one when your uncle was just here. Didn't he bring you all the news from home?"

Helena, while opening one, says, "Uncle Alekos lives in Athens so he doesn't know everything ... oh, from my Uncle Spiros. Here Georgie, you read it."

I walk from the back of the salon, pick up the second letter and scan it before reading it aloud.

My dear child Helena,
A surprise for you to get your old Uncle's spidery handwriting, but God's scrawny servant did learn how to do it.

285

Helena: An Odyssey

My time is coming to an end and I see the devil's teeth in the night, my old bones scattered in the shadow of Mt. Argeus. When I see my Papa's face I have a great ache that never leaves me, all because of that business about restoring the family name. So disappointed he'll be to learn all that's happened.

More and more I live in the old days. In my dreams I see toothy headlands and rows of cypress trees, huge skies and summer suns. Little boys in the orchard. Rocks and salt lakes and waving wheat fields. Strong smells of earth and sky wash over me. Then comes the devil's face grinning in the dark, but the old serpent has not got me yet. He laughs horribly as he wanders the streets of Smyrna after flames.

Then comes the blackness and nothing exists anymore, like the dreams and hopes we had for this family. I tell you child, when not many days stretch out before you, all the ones that came before jump up, voices and faces from long ago. Maria and my daughters come to me now. But more than any other, my Mama and Papa. Enough of all that. I write also to say that just last week I saw your Stephan's Auntie. She looks old but still she has a high-and-mighty air. Remember how she came to our door and swore her nephew would never marry you? She's looking for Stephan who, they say, has come back to Patras, but not in our village. I have not seen him but there's talk: no wife anymore and no children with him.

Dear Helena, never forget your family and how it too can rise up like the Onassis one. But remember that what rises up also comes tumbling down. All Ari's love affairs come to nothing, not even getting married to Jackie Kennedy, and sad news about his daughter Christina. See, our family will do better than this, so I ask, when do you come home to Patras to be a famous hair designer? One day, my child, you will restore our fortunes."

I just finish reading when the phone rings. Helena picks it up, and from where I'm standing I hear my *Yia Yia* sobbing across the distance, hear her saying that this morning Uncle Spiros refused to wake up from his sleep. Helena's shriek silences the whir of hair-dryers and the hum of many conversations. No one moves. She jumps up and says she must go to Patras at once and see her uncle's grave, to say some prayers for him. She thrusts the phone at me.

"My Mom's coming home," I say into it. "Mom?" But Helena makes weird oh, oh sounds and prepares to walk out the door. I run after her.

"Helena, I'll give you my savings if it will help you get to Patras."

"I've got my own money, *poulaki mou.*" Helena stops, hugs me tightly, then into my ear whispers, "I'll find my Stephan too; he's waiting for me there, I just know it."

'Helena's was a love that was fierce, a harsh fire that consumed others in its cindery path', I write later. 'Smoke and flames and combustion. Passion that scorched both itself and others in its path.' She would stoke those old fires whose embers never died, take the red-hot flame of her love to the pale, wan man with the bruised and vacant heart, a heart that had been emptied all those years before with the annihilation of his early passion.

Where will all this end?

***

Helena is bent over the stove frying onions when Alex comes in. In a rush she says she must go to Patras to Uncle Spiros' funeral and say prayers for him. Alex, whose jealousy has continued as an undercurrent, dips his chin at an angle that indicates rising anger.

"Say your prayers here. Talk to your parents on the phone." He switches on the radio and turns up the volume.

Helena swings around, still holding the frying pan, but before she speaks, Alex adds, "Who will look after your shop, your daughters?"

I hear all this through my open bedroom door, watch as Helena puts the frying pan back on the stove and slumps her shoulders. That evening she takes photographs from Patras, some of Smyrna before the fire that Alekos once sent, and props them on a shelf in front of her cook- books. For the next two days she moves about listlessly.

"Helena," I say when we're alone, "invite him to go with you, but you know he won't."

Alex, stupefied, hears himself invited to Patras. Two days later he comes home with a new travel bag. "You go," he says off-handedly. "I'll look after things, fix everything up."

Helena rushes to hug him looking both relieved and guilty. She tries to hide her excitement– or is it agitation? – and I remember she hasn't seen Stephan since she was eighteen and he, twenty-four.

"He's had his life and nothing to do with me," she confides later, "he's lived in other places and done things I don't know about. He might not want me to disturb everything … my God … maybe he's still got a wife lurking somewhere nearby, or a girlfriend!"

Amalia supports our mother's new adventure when Dad's not around – *however did she find out?* – but I dread what the consequences might be, and know I'm getting close to what happened on that last visit.

"Yo, Mama, bet your old boyfriend's forgotten how to do it and you get to teach him." Amalia, standing tall in high heels, laughs, ha ha. "Go for it, Mama. Your younger daughter'll go to church for you and get the Ten Commandments re-written just so you don't do any mortal sin – eh, Georgie?"

"Big Guy won't care what Mom does," I say to match my sister's mood. "And *you* won't care." I watch as Amalia unbuttons her expensive navy blue blazer while staring at herself in a mirror. "Yucky clothes." But my voice holds envy. "Whose car is the red one parked on street? What do you do to get a car like that?" I give Amalia a sudden hard stare.

"I borrow the money, is all." Amalia tosses her long hair and pirouettes. "You're jealous."

"You're not to talk to each other like that." Helena repeats this as a matter of course, but her mind is elsewhere. Visions of Stephan must be haunting her and I remember what I've already written: his stripling form and hungry eyes, his slim brown arms reaching for her, his smooth brown body making beautiful love to her the way he did all those years before. *Oh dear, am I getting fixated on him too?*

On a cool early autumn day, Helena flies to Greece.

***

Chapter 53

Patras, 1993

Stephan: The voice that compelled and sustained my mother in place of the old inner voice of the patriarchs; Stephan, her one great love who had lived in her pores, her heart, her bones. A love she had destroyed all by herself, and was now in a fever to get it back.

I'm writing this long after it happened. I've pieced together what took place on Helena's last visit to Patras, and used my imagination for the rest.

As she flies through the sky, Helena's images of Patras come tumbling: The door to number 24 wide open, her *Yia Yia* sitting in it. Weeds straggling up among the geraniums on each side of its steps. Trains shunting and sea gulls wheeling. The sharp, sweet-sour tang of the sea. She hears her father's voice, teasing, plaintive, or raw with anger. Her brothers' laughing voices mixed up with housewives calling to one another. The spindly form of Spiros slumped over his stall.

Stephan's face appears, his eyes as dark plums, and a choke rises in her throat. He's in Patras, and she'll find him – she *will*. They'll love each other as they'd done all those years before, everything beautiful and perfect. What will he look like? The same, of course. Sudden alarm arises as she thinks of herself, so different from the girl he'd known. A wail escapes her and she draws in her stomach. The passenger squeezed beside her chuckles. "Whoever you want to impress will just have more of you. It doesn't have to be a bad thing."

"Oh, oh." Helena lets out her breath.

Nikos, at the airport, pinches her arm and rolls his eyes. "You do get fat," he says.

"Well, you look like a dead fig tree." She punches him on the shoulder. "How are Mama and Papa?"

"*Kala, kala.* You're in for a surprise."

"You hear anything of Stephan?"

"Stephan?" Nikos stares. "What do you want with him?"

"I'm just asking."

"*Daxi.*"

Nikos enters X Street and parks his truck outside number 24. On newly-painted front steps flanked by purple summer phlox stand Christos and Melina, faces raised expectantly. Helena, about to rush forward, stops. What's this? Her mother is wearing a fitted crimson dress, her hair springing in tumultuous riot about a smiling face. Christos' crisp white shirt crackles when he moves.

See," he says proudly and puts an arm about Melina's shoulders, "it's my wife come back to me."

An astonished Helena remembers the phone conversation with her mother after Alex left home the second time. "You must decide if your husband and children are to be your life's work. I now make your Papa the most important person in my life, even if it is in our later years and never mind the money. We have learned to be happy with each other."

Well. After all the misery, all the affairs. Jolted by this display of marital accord, Helena looks at the new paint, the new windows; wherever did the money come from?

Christos wins at card games, she learns, and earns small amounts doing odd jobs for Mr. Stavros. Melina does fine needlework and sells it. As for her brothers, they still work in factories at the far end of the street. Nikos, having run wild with girls over all the years, is at last to be married, and Melina has set herself to sewing.

Disoriented, Helena wanders about the house. A new bathroom has been built by her brothers. A deck behind the house. A wide balcony upstairs. In the kitchen, fresh flowered decals grace the walls to replace those her mother had stuck on when a young girl. And there on the front window ledge sit bottles of shampoo and conditioner, a jar filled with brushes and combs. Memories flood her, visions of long ago. But the once shimmering path beckoning her into the future has faded, smudged with work, heartbreak and poverty.

She returns outdoors and stands with her feet planted in the middle of street. Gardens bloom beside every door. The road to *The Stone* is paved and beside the old public tap stands a fountain decorated at its base by mosaic tiles.

"*Kala.* Now you're home." She jumps at the rasping voice. Neighbour Stacia is in her doorway holding a plate of cookies. As though at a signal, old women swarm toward her, gesticulating, smirking. "Ha, so you come home again. You going to stay? You famous yet? Where is your husband, your children?"

"Where's your Stephan?" The voice holds a sneer.

"Ask me tomorrow, ask me next week." Helena shrugs and continues walking toward Stephan's tenement, watching the faces she passes. But what's this? In place of the old tenement stands a gleaming new concrete high-rise, clean pavement surrounding it, boxes of yellow daisies along its west wall. To the strangers who come through its door she asks, "Do you know of a Stephan Konialidis?" Most shake their heads. Someone says he might have seen him in the city centre, that maybe he's come to live back in Patras, but not in the district.

"Got married and had a child," another says. "No wife living with him anymore."

Helena stares at the new building, her heart beating frantically as she wills her beloved to appear from within as in days of old. At the factory gates she watches strange faces pass as though expecting to see Stephan's among them. When the doors close she wanders the old enchanted places, her eyesight blurred with her tears.

***

Anxiously Melina studies her daughter: the forlorn expression and dull eyes; the hours spent in the doorway scanning people passing. "You cry for your uncle?" she asks. "He had a sad life for most of it because he came from nothing. He worked to be a merchant prince in Smyrna and in the snap of a finger, it was taken from him."

"I do cry for him." But Helena's sorrow is also for herself, but how can she explain it? On impulse she ways, "I'm going into the city to see old man Pousopolis. He must be very old, maybe he's not there anymore. I want to see what they do with hair. When I come home, Mama, I'll make you a nice style."

Melina smiles, relieved.

Excited by her secret mission to find Stephan, Helena dresses in colourful clothes, half-unbuttons a scarlet blouse, slips her feet into studded sandals and paints her face.

"You dress like a *poutana.* You dishonour yourself." Melina draws her lips tightly together. "You do all this to impress old Mr. Pousopolis?"

"You mean, why do I dress like a *hetaira?*"

"Don't you go saying such things!"

"I dress just for me." Helena gives her mother a quick kiss and wanders outdoors. Ha, *Mr. Pig Eyes* – wonder does he still own the salon? Or his creepy son? What kind of hair-styles are in fashion here? Sandals clicking in the dust, she saunters the street, nodding to old women in their doorways, then heads for the short-cut she'd taken long ago; along *Ayiou Street* toward *Georgio 1 Square*– the ice cream shop still there. Along *Paliovouna Street,* the movie house, the monument to the Greek revolution. Narrow streets are lined by low-rise apartment blocks, balconies leaning crookedly over them. Sidewalks are pitted, graffiti everywhere, but indoors, shops are upscale, the shoppers well-dressed. At last she reaches the *Yiogaraki* stairs to old Patras in the upper city, and climbs *Panahikon Mountain.* Wind-blown and cold, she looks over the city and a rippling Ionian Sea.

Half way down the steps on her return, a sign catches her eye: *Sculpture Studio.* She remembers it from long ago. With a slight push its gate swings open and she wanders into a secluded concrete rectangle surrounded by the crumbling walls of old commercial buildings. It remains as she recollects it, but with many more stone figures, all looking eerily alive, their feet apart as though about to walk toward her. Expressions range from happy, to solemn, to pensive. Scattered among them are small animals, gnomes, pixies, as well as faces of the Green Man. Helena moves from one to another, touching them lightly. Strange no one is about, don't their owners worry someone might steal these things? How peaceful, a place for angels to walk. She lets out a long breath and steps in further. A slight figure moves in the shadows by the far wall, oblivious to her presence. Moving closer, she watches his hands moving over a stone sculpture. Tripping, she swears under her breath, and the sculptor jumps up.

"What is it? Who is it? I didn't know someone ... why are you here?"

The voice! Helena's nerves jump with shock. Confused, her eyes rake over the lean, lined with face and receding hair-line. "I think maybe I know you." Her heart beats wildly. "*Please* tell me your name."

"I ... don't think I know *you.*" The sculptor echoes Helena's confusion. "But because you ask, I am Stephan."

"Stephan!" Helena's one word rises as a shriek in the still air to bounce about the concrete walls. Her body jerks forward and she flings out an arm to grasp his stone maiden for support.

"Don't you touch her! Nobody must touch her."

"Oh, oh, *ohhh.*" All the figures in the garden swim together as Helena sways between two sculptures. The whistle of someone's breath touches her cheek, an arm supports her. In her ear a voice whispers, "Are you all right? What can I get you, what can I do?"

Stephan leads her to a rough stone seat and lowers her onto it. She looks into the face close to hers. The eyes! When she can speak, she cries out again. "It's you ... I've found you at last."

Stephan jumps back a step, looking again at the plump woman in a rainbow of colours: hot red apples against purple skies, and he shades his eyes. Who is this woman? He retreats further from the arms stretched out to him, takes a sharp intake of breath at sight of her mascara-rimmed eyes now smudged with tears, the paint on her cheeks, her lips. He lowers his eyes, only to see the strange woman's blouse plunging to all but reveal the two half-moons of her breasts, to glimpse plump feet spread between the straps of glittering sandals.

"Stephan ... Stephan." As the woman repeats the name a half whistle comes from him. His mouth twists, but no words come.

"You don't know me," Helena cries. "Can't you see? I'm your Helena ... *Helena.*" She struggles up, moves to throw her arms about the slight figure. He steps back, offering no embrace, only a hand held out to shake hers.

"Oh, oh." Helena sinks back onto a stone seat.

"You're not well." Stephan looks helplessly about him. "Is somebody with you? I ... I could take you to my home not far from here," but doubt has entered his voice.

"Oh please, take me to your home."

Stephan leads her down the steps to the lower city, through the crush of people and traffic, past old concrete walls and ever-narrower streets. A cool wind whips about them and dark clouds gather over the mountain. Eventually Stephan reaches a graffiti-covered building and inserts a key into a stained grey door. It creaks as it opens. His apartment is on the second floor and Helena's first glance is of a small space with a Spartan interior.

Stephan doesn't speak as he indicates a chair for her and hurries to make tea. On a small table a crocheted cloth appear along with tea two cups. A paper napkin, a plate with buttered biscuits. Helena looks about, hugging her arms and shivering. His home is cold, bare, as dismal inside as it has become outdoors. Stephan, disoriented, repeatedly raises his eyes to her, only to look quickly away.

Helena jumps up and throws herself on him, but he remains with arms rigidly at his sides. "How can you not know me?" she cries and stares up at his crumpling face. She cannot interpret it, cannot know he finds her loud and vulgar, has an urge to take a jacket and cover her up, to wipe off her make-up. She looks up at him, and down at herself. Then it hits her: Stephan had last known her as a young girl in short skirts, with rivers of hair and a shining young body. Her face had been clean of make-up. Lipstick, yes, but he'd always wiped it off. Her jagged thoughts made her feel ill and she sits heavily back onto the stone seat.

Outdoors the sky darkens. A rising wind howls through cracks around the windows, and rain threatens. Helena must go home. After extracting promises of future meetings, trembling with confused emotion, she begins the long trek.

That evening she confesses to her mother she's seen Stephan.

"Stephan? How did you find that boy, and what do you want from him? Don't you go meddling. And don't tell this to your father." Melina's mind at that moment is flooded with images of a flirtatious Helena running about with Stephan to *The Stone,* the beach, the orchard. Of refusing the navy captain's offer of marriage, because of this … this nobody.

"Mama," Helena says now. "He's poor and doesn't look well. I must help him." Her voice trails away at her mother's cold stare.

"If you want to help him, then bring him here for dinner with your family and his old neighbours."

"First I must go to him," Helena repeats.

"I never knew Stephan to be in any need of help. But I suppose you'll do what you want, like always." Melina draws her lips into a straight line. "I'll tell you this: it's much better you never see him. Oh, I know you, how you always ran about with the boys and never could you leave them alone. Listen to me. Leave Stephan alone. I'm sure he's had hard times, but he doesn't need you." She repeated with emphasis, "You leave him alone. If you want something to do, make nice hair styles for the neighbours."

The following afternoon, holding an umbrella against a cold drizzle, Helena sets off for the sculpture garden.

"Here you are again." Stephan's tone is flat.

"It's too wet, you're all wet, why don't we go to your home and make dinner?"

"My place is small and not comfortable. I'm sure you are used to nice things."

"I don't care about nice things."

At Stephan's flat the two put together a pasta dinner and eat it largely in silence. Then Helena asks to see where he sleeps.

"This one is the spare," he says of the first small bedroom, and Helena looks at a single bed pulled tight with yellowed sheets, nothing on the walls but a faded seaside print.

"Where do you sleep?"

Stephan steps across a narrow corridor into a similar small room. A single bed, a chest of drawers, a night-stand and white-shaded lamp. A print of the Virgin and another of Christ on the Cross hang over the bed, faded photographs propped on the chest. Helena draws closer to look. The same photo of the two aunties remains, the one peering out from under a flowered hat, the other with her mouth drawn tight. The faces of Kostas, Thalia and their children look self-consciously at the camera, while a young woman who bears some vague resemblance to herself, stands, unsmiling, a small boy clutching her skirt.

"Who is this?"

"My wife, and my son Dimitri," he says, not looking.

"Where is your wife, your son?"

"Dimitri works in Athens for a printer, also in an art shop. My wife, she went with somebody else, and lives in Athens too. But this man, he left her and … and now you see I have not much money because I send it to them to help."

Stephan opens a dresser drawer. "My boy Dimitri when he was sixteen," he says with sudden pride, "but not a boy anymore."

Helena picks up the photo. Why, the face looking back at her could be the young Stephan! When he has returned to the kitchen she slips it in her pocket.

Stephan fills and refills their tea cups, captive to Helena's voice flowing fast over the stones of their past. "Don't you remember?" she cries many times. "How can you forget?"

Stephan apologizes, repeats that his memory is mostly empty of the times and places of which Helena speaks so passionately.

Frustrated, she bursts into tears.

"Wait," Stephan begs. "Don't cry."

She takes his hands in hers. "Do I look the same to you? No, I know I've changed."

"You do not look like I remembered." Stephan removes his hands. "You were so small and always running about, so busy."

"You think I'm too fat? You don't like what you see, but I'm the same Helena as before."

"Hush, hush. We'll get to know each other again and everything will be better."

Another evening in Stephan's home. Helena's words run together as quickly she recreates the past as though any minute it might disappear. "The rocks, the beach, the orchards past *The Stone* – you *must* remember. And the beautiful love we made on the sand, how it got in our clothes."

Stephan, fingers twitching in his lap, in a dull voice says, "I'm sorry I don't remember much." Standing up, hands in his pockets, he walks back and forth in the small living room.

"I carried you around in my heart all the years." Helena's voice has dropped to a whisper. "You came to me in my dreams, you talked to me; helped me in all my bad times. Now you leave me before you even come back." Dropping her head in her hands she rocks in her chair.

Awkwardly Stephan puts thin arms about her. "It's nine o'clock," he says. "I go to bed at nine o'clock. You should be home. Tomorrow will be a fresh day and you will feel better."

Helena struggles up and to the window where a thin moon hangs in a darkening sky.

"It's too late for me to go home and I can sleep in your spare bedroom." Right in front of him she begins to unbutton her blouse.

Stephan walks to his own bedroom and closes the door.

The threat of annihilation of her first love carries a pain so great Helena lies fully dressed and sleepless. First love is the greatest, the most shattering love that exists, she believes. That Stephan scarcely remembers their trysts, their passion, feels like a weight enough to crush her, and during the long night she begins to doubt her own memories. She sleeps fitfully, awaking with fresh determination to rescue herself from the humiliation of the evening before. She won't go home until she's retrieved her lost love.

She sees at once that Stephan too, has slept poorly. In the tiny white bathroom, she washes off yesterday's make-up and enters the living room. A glance out the window reveals a clear sky and a pale sun touching old city buildings.

Stephan hovers in the kitchen with a cup of tea for her, a slice of toast with goat cheese. Walking up to him she offers him a kiss. "We'll go somewhere today and have fun the way we used to?"

Stephan nods as he pours the tea. "I can take you back to the sculpture garden," he suggests.

***

Chapter 54

Patras, 1993

Stephan unlocks the gate to the sculpture studio and walks to his stone maiden. His lips move, but no sound comes as he runs his hands over her. The sensuality of his caress shocks Helena who comprehends that Stephan spurns her, a real live woman of hot flesh and blood, in favour of this cold stone maiden.

As he stands back, as his manner of someone lost and confused returns, Helena realizes that his virginal, flawless sculpture is a replica of herself when young. Had he fallen in love with this stone girl and, as Georgia would later explain, developed a fetish for her, a maiden he believed more perfect than any living woman?

"She looks like you when you were a girl, do you think?"

Helena understands his message.

"I'll make another one of how you look now." He slides an arm tentatively about her.

"This time I cry only for happiness."

The answering kindness in his face resembles expressions of long ago, giving Helena sudden hope.

"I work in the studio for pleasure," he says. "But sometimes on a commission to earn some money. "We'll go to have coffee, or tea if you like."

In a small coffee shop Helena makes further reference to their past, anxious to unfold it, to hold on to these few warmed moments. "You came to me. You said you'd saved enough money for me to go school in Athens." Anxiously she looks into his eyes.

Recognition dawns, a fragment of memory that brings a shaft of sunlight into his eyes. Again Helena recounts trysts at the edge of the Ionian Sea, among trees in the orchard. Laughing suddenly, she tells of the occasions she'd slipped out of number 24 dressed in Nikos' clothes.

"The day when you left, remember I crept into your flat and into your bed?" Helena grips Stephan's hand as she stares into the past. "You *must* remember. You promised to send me money for me to come to you in Australia. It came in a letter, but my father told me, 'You don't go. You're too young.' When Thalia married Kostas and went to Toronto, my father let me go to them. This is exactly what happened."

Changing expressions cross Stephan's face, one chasing the other like flitting shadows. At last, with an edge of bitterness in his voice, he says. "But you did not come to me. My brother told me things about you, how you went with other men. You forgot me. You married someone else." The hurt flickering in his eyes is followed immediately by a careful expression of neutrality, and surreptitiously he crosses himself.

"But all the time I loved you." Helena speaks rapidly. "In my heart I carried you with me. I told you everything. When I had bad times I talked to you; you came to me in my dreams. Then I remembered – those times I'm now telling you about." How can she explain her abiding belief that he would protect her in the end, even while she had flings with other men, even while she married Alex? That when she made love it was always and only to him, his face she saw, his eyes adoring her, no one else's. He was her God, her saint. Throughout her husband's betrayals she'd clung to the belief that in the end he'd save her from the man she'd married, from the ignominy of her position. Trembling now, she clutches the edges of the stone bench.

She cannot know that Stephan's emotions and memories have shrivelled, so long has he been drawn in upon himself. That he has repressed what does remain to him, and with their revival, feels frightened; Helena's recounting of their shared past is so rich, *so extravagant,* it diminishes his present even further. Each stares at the other, only to look quickly away. A giant chasm yawns between them.

"I'll visit you tomorrow," Helena says into the silence. "We can go to the beach like we used to…"

"Tomorrow is Sunday and I go to church." Stephan's voice is timid. "Every Sunday."

"Then I'll come with you."

On Sunday afternoon, after attending the *Church of the Apostles* where a bent, very old Father Meneghini still presides over his flock, Helena walks the long distance to the city centre and on to Stephan's home. The perfumes of flowering gardens are blown on a gusting wind. Starlings chatter in the blackening sky. City lights twinkle as dusk approaches, and the sound of traffic dims. After a light *souvlaki* dinner that Stephan prepares, Helena pulls him into his tiny bedroom and seats herself on the edge of his bed. Her eyes glitter with restless passion and with a small cry, she moves toward him, covering his mouth with kisses, all the while hugging him tight to her bosom. A flush creeps up Stephan's face and in his eyes a strange light shines. His arms creep about her.

"I love you, even when I make love to another man," Helena whispers. Her fingers trace the outline of his lips. Unbuttoning his shirt, she places the palm of her hand on his chest. Her fingers slide over his nipples, his navel, caressing and probing. She unfastens his belt.

"It's always your face I see." Her voice sings in his ear. "I pretend it is to you I make love. When I cry in the night, you come to me."

She pulls his trousers over his hips. Her fingers play with him, massage him. With quick movement his body arches toward her, not because of his old love or any memories of it, but because the quivering flesh touching him is hot and urgent, the owner of it passionately offering herself to him.

And so begins Stephan's gradual reawakening. The two make love on the tight white sheets of his bed. The love does not resemble the old, but tenderness is mixed with longing, the whole of it suffused with sweet sorrow at the passing of a passion that once held promise of endless love.

"But you're married," Stephan says. He has quickly drawn on his trousers and buttons his shirt. "What do you want with me?"

"Don't think about that. Just now we love each other."

Without thought for the unfolding of the future, or to the place in her life he would assume - a life that is already crowded with others - Helena leaves Stephan with declarations of future visits and a promise to love him forever. Disappointment at his lack of confident stature, his ill-fitting clothes and poor manner of living is banished, although a faint smile lurks as she imagines what Georgia will write about him: an anorexic soul inspiring little admiration. Yet within the form of him remain faint remnants of the young Stephan, little bits of him peeping out from long-dulled eyes.

***

Helena peers from the window as her aircraft circles over Toronto. Its flatness spreads out over a vast, indecipherable landscape of highways and streets snaking everywhere; over moving people toward loved ones, or away from them. Yes, loved ones: before her float the faces of her husband, her daughters. Leon too, with his ready smile for her.

In the airport taxi, on impulse she gives Leon's address. She might see him, maybe raking leaves in his front yard. The driver stops before a large red brick house with its garden fenced with iron railings, and craning her neck, Helena glimpses through the large front window a scene of happy tumult: Leon's wife watching children tumble. Leon throwing one of them in the air. The many generations of family members doing what families do best. A chill strikes her. She's on the outside looking in. Where does she belong - with Stephan? They share a past but he scarcely remembers it. In Patras? Uncle Spiros and *Yia Yia* are gone; her parents are aging. Alex? Mostly at home now, he sometimes expresses rough tenderness; helps in the garden. With a scrambling of confused feelings, Helena tells the driver to take her home.

***

Chapter 55

Toronto, 1993

Georgia

I'm rushing about the kitchen, my face hot and perspiring in the steam rising from the stove. Helena! She's at the door already. I leap to her, my arms outstretched, words running out my mouth: "Welcome home Mom, you okay? I can't wait to hear about what's happened but you look so tired."

"My Georgie, my good girl." Helena drops her bags and hugs me tightly. With a finger she wipes away trickles of sweat from my cheeks, tucks a tendril of hair into the rubber band tying it. She hugs me again then drops into her chair by the gas fire, only then noticing Alex. "So," her voice holds surprise, "you're home?"

Alex smiles lazily. He remains with his feet on the coffee table, his Greek newspapers tossed on the floor. "Your parents are good, your brothers? You had a nice time? Now you're back I can get some good food."

"Dad, I've been cooking you good meals!" I give him a playful punch.

"Where's Amalia?" Helena asks.

I shrug and say she must be racing about in her new car. Alex spreads his hands to indicate he doesn't know.

"New car? Where does she get money?"

"You'll have to ask her." I feel uncomfortable. "Oh, here she is now."

The door swings open Amalia, out-of-breath, rushes through it. "Hi Mom, I tried to get here before you. Have a good trip?" After giving her mother noisy kisses, she shrugs off a leather jacket and drops onto the sofa.

"Amalia, such a pretty sight, beautiful." Pleasure shines in Helena's eyes as they range over her daughter's clinging, cream-coloured sweater and leather skirt, at leather boots that reach to her knees. Flipping long hair over her shoulders, Amalia gives me a triumphant smile. "So, sis, couldn't even get yourself dressed up for your mother when she comes home?"

"Everything's not always about what a person looks like. Anyway, I'm not competing." I bang dishes about.

Helena's eyes, when she looks at me, hold a brief flicker of disappointment but all she says is, "Georgie's been doing other things."

Amalia laughs. "Yeah, like what?"

And suddenly I hate her. Suddenly I can't help myself. "Mom," I say, but watch Amalia, "I agree my sister has beautiful clothes, but haven't you ever wondered how she earns all her money to buy them and have her own sports car?"

"What are you trying to tell me?"

"Well, it's that Amalia's got another career she hasn't told you about."

Amalia's eyes snap wide. I feel another flush staining my cheeks but can't stop myself now, don't want to. "She's an escort girl, *that's* how she makes her money."

Melina a prostitute! Immediately Helena knows it's true and her mouth hangs open. I imagine what her first thoughts are: Does anyone else know – Alex, Leon? What about Thalia and Kostas? The make-up, the clothes: why hadn't she ever wondered how her daughter had so much money to spend? I sense her humiliation, her anger with herself. But she turns it on me. "You knew, and didn't tell me? Didn't you think I had a right to know?" A growl comes up her throat.

"Look, I'm not my sister's keeper. What do you want from me?" I cover my face with my hands. "I work, look after the house. I write all your story, and you talk to me like this." But immediately I'm remorseful at the sight of her crumpled face. "I'm so sorry." I start fiddling with cutlery on the table, "I shouldn't have ..."

"Bitch!" Amalia spits out the word. "Couldn't wait to tell, could you, you *yifto*. You're losers, all of you!" Hands on her hips, she swivels to Mom but points at Dad. "Why didn't you kick that man out years ago? What's he ever done but live off you?"

"Kick him out? He's *family*. Always you look after family." Helena wrings her hands.

"Only stupid Greeks think that."

Mother of all the saints, now what's to be done? Dad, looking truly shocked, gets up and heads for the basement.

The silence, hanging in the air, shatters when the front door bangs after Amalia.

Helena remains leaning against the kitchen doorframe, her lips moving. I put a tentative arm about her shoulders and draw her to the table. "So sorry, so sorry," I mumble. "You would have found out some time, but I shouldn't have told you just now. Look, I made lamb stew. Have some and go to bed. In the morning you can tell me about your visit − everything."

***

Worried about my mother − because of Amalia who remains absent and silent, and because of some crazy thing she might do about Stephan − I stay at home when I'm not working, or hang about the salon. I know her restless thoughts keep returning to him, and to all the exhausted years in Patras. She has long-distant conversations with her old lover in the early mornings and tells it all to me afterwards. He asks what she's wearing, how she does her hair, what she's doing. The day comes when he tells her he's saving for a visit to Toronto. She says she has a sudden snapshot of her life: Alex in the background, a security blanket − *better to have a husband than not* − Leon a faithful companion, like a puppy dog, a different kind of security blanket. That Stephan, having finally resurrected his past, wants it back.

I know she's both confused and excited by her infatuation. She pins the *Bacarro* rose to her blouse as a sign of her private passion, takes the snapshot of Dimitri from her purse and slips it in her bedside drawer. She's begun going to church every Sunday, but only because Stephan does.

One year after her return from Greece, she receives a brief letter from Dimitri. In it he expresses both his pleasure that her visit has lifted his father's spirits but has left him restless and dissatisfied with his life. What exactly are Helena's intentions regarding him?

In shock, again she confides in me. "You've been encouraging him to believe you intend offering something that I don't think you mean," I say. "His son This Dimitri, tell me about him."

"Dimitri?" Her thoughts shift. "His father says he's been to college. He works in a print shop to make money but he likes art. Here, I've got a photo." She pulls the photo of Stephan's son from her drawer. "See," she says, "exactly like his father."

"That's why you keep it?" I look, and a tingling feeling runs up my spine. Dimitri gazes at me with large black-brown eyes, like two burned suns, I think, eyes filled up with ache and longing exactly how she − or I? − had described his father. Now I'm falling into them. Mesmerized, I want to keep falling. "Is his personality the same as his father? Tell me Mom, if you could go back in time, would you have married Stephan and been happy with him? If you lined him up alongside the captain, alongside Dad, and Leon, let's not leave him out, who would you choose?"

"So many questions." An irritable note enters Helena's voice. "Let me ask you: have you ever looked at a man? When you choose one, and after you live with him for a while, let me know if you learn to be happy with him."

I've stopped listening because my mind is on Dimitri, on my idea of him: A young man looking out for his father. Working hard to make a living. Interested in art. I look again at his photo. Yes, just like his father, romantic eyes seeing beautiful things. Beautiful things? Feeling Dimitri's eyes on me, I raise a hand to dampen my unruly hair, smooth my rumpled sweatshirt. Helena's voice comes to me as though from far away and distracted as I am, I can hear its studied nonchalance. "Stephan tells me he's saving up to come to Canada. He'd like it even better if I could go back to him. He gives no hint of any unhappiness − what was it Dimitri said? But the son, what does he know?"

Her voice trails away in uncertainty.

***

Chapter 56

Toronto, 1994 -1995

Georgia

Almost two years pass. The flame of Helena's early love exists now as smoldering coals, I think, an undercurrent of excitement that she elevates when life in all its frightening ordinariness threatens. Rarely does she acknowledge to herself what an artificial creation it is, fixed as it is in the past. It's a slow Monday and she's persuaded me to have my hair done. Stephan phones. When the call is over I ask what they talked about. "Well?"

"Not much really." she shrugs. "He tells me he loves me and remembers more of our past every day. His stone maiden is finished and looks just like me."

I watch her hands flit quick and sure over my hair, see her absorption, and realize again how doing hair, making people feel good about themselves, gives her fathomless joy.

"You like it?" Instead of looking I jump up and give her a hug. "You truly are an artist, you know. I love you so much Mom –Helena."

"See, when you arrange your curls on top it gives length to your face and makes it not so round." Helena continues to fluff and pat stray ends of my hair. "Any woman can be made beautiful with the right cut and style to their hair."

"I feel beautiful already. But back to Stephan: would you really want to spend more time with him, like, live with him? Would you have been better off marrying him instead of Alex?"

"You've asked me these silly questions before. If I'd married him, you wouldn't be you."

"Yes, well, I'd be somebody else, wouldn't I, someone cleverer, prettier ..."

"Don't go saying these things! You, you're looking much better, much slimmer and nice clothes." Suspicion enters her voice. "Who are you dressing up for? You getting together with that poor Jeff after all?"

"No, just fixing myself up for me." Seeing the snapshot of Dimitri has inspired me. I don't understand it, so what can I say?

A shadow crosses Helena's face. "Amalia hardly comes home anymore, and never if you're here. Georgie, why don't you call her, say you're sorry?"

"I will, Mom, of course I will." I mean it.

***

One memorable day three months after this, Helena is in her garden by the hedge, staking summer phlox bent by recent winds. *(I'm writing all this afterwards.)* The phone rings. She's prepared to let it, but on hearing a familiar voice, rushes to grab it before Alex comes upstairs. It's Stephan telling her he's saved enough money for a visit to her.

"You should only phone me at the salon. When do you come?"

"Two weeks. Two weeks I'm coming."

Helena rubs her damp palms over her cheeks as if to cool the rush of blood staining them. As she does when confronted with any hard decision, she pushes aside the difficulties his arrival will cause by refusing to think about it.

Damp-mopping the salon floor one early morning twelve days later she picks up the phone to hear an oddly detached voice she recognizes as Dimitri's. What lecture will he give her now? Preparing to tell him her relationship with her father is not his business, she hears muffled tears.

"My father has had an accident in his car." The words spill harshly into the salon. "He crashed it on his way to the airport to see you."

***

Georgia

Finally I learn that Helena's last visit to Greece had been to her lover's funeral. I'm lying across my bed, brooding, imagining her on the street

307

where she grew up, staring about her bewildered as though by a place unfamiliar; seeing Stephan on the beach, sloping to and from the factory, leaning against the walls of his tenement. I imagine her running out the door of number 24 toward the *Stone*, across the railway lines, past the church and to the beach, weeping until exhausted. I conjure images of my grandparents and how they must have aged. Next thing my mind is flying and I'm right there, watching the sombre figures of my family entering the Church of the Apostles; seeing Father Meneghini, now so bent he requires a stool to see over his lectern. Dimitri is flanked by a scattering of relatives from across the Gulf of Corinth. My mother Helena stares at the young man, gasps and falls backwards. Markos catches her and says in a harsh whisper, "Pull yourself together, this is not your show. So what that the son looks like the father?" To Dimitri, "We are local people who lived alongside your father. We come to pay our respects. This is my sister Helena."

Penetrating eyes stare into Helena's. In a voice hoarse with grief, Dimitri says, "It was better you never came to see my father. All the years you didn't exist for him, not that I ever heard. After your visit, he wasn't the same, he ..."

An anguished cry escaping her, Helena runs weeping from the church, straight to the secluded spot where she and Stephan had made their desperate, doomed love. Crouching in its womb-like crevices among pebbles and seaweed, she howls her grief into the on-coming night.

Through it, she hears Markos' voice calling her. Past *The Stone* she creeps, deserted now, past leafless trees in an overgrown orchard. How can she be in Patras with no Stephan in it? And no parents, for surely they would not be far off following him to the grave. The magic of the place has gone, her memories of it painful. The streets lie drear and empty. Nothing means anything anymore. Grey slabs of buildings rise up about the line of little houses, new ones to replace the old. Dark-cloaked women still gossip about streets that are now choked with traffic and people hurrying. What is her heart but a vacant thing that keeps on beating, for what?

In the crowded living room of her parents' home, Markos, and Nikos with his wife, drift in and out, saying little. Someone asks about Alekos and surely he should have come.

"He sent his sorrowful regrets," Melina says. "He's not a strong man you know, and didn't feel up to travelling."

Christos sits in a chair near the back window, a spectre of his former self. Shrivelled but for a pendulous belly, motionless he gazes over the old orchard. He turns to his younger daughter and gives her a wrinkled smile.

"I'll tell you stories to cheer you up my Helena," he says. "Stories from long ago and you a little girl. You come with me in my truck and I say to you, eh, Helena, see if you can jump this fence. You remember this? I race you to the farmer's shed, but you run the faster. I say, can you drive my truck? One day I tell you to charm an old fellow into buying an extra load of my gold..."

"And I said, 'This gold stinks, Papa.'"

"Ah, but I tell you that this gold, it is *mana* from the heavens." Animation fills Christos' voice. "I say how the Virgin has blessed you with art and cunning and so you must use it, you remember this?"

Helena's heart lightens at her father's chuckle.

"Eh *chryso mou*, always you made me laugh." Christos chuckles again. "I smile at all the good times when I remember them." A shaft of sunlight through the window lights up his stubbly face.

Helena's own smile fades as she looks at her once ebullient father, a roaring lion, pride of the wild. He was fast entering his old age.

"Papa, my Papa." She throws her arms about his neck and hugs him frantically. But Christos is deep into memory and wants to talk. "You were always my blessed child and sang to keep me awake." His face brims with love for her, but why is she laughing and crying so much? "You weep for us? Then I say this to you: Your mother and I are getting old. We're coming up for eighty years and soon will come our time. God gives us life, and he takes it away. Do not weep so, *psychi mou*. You are my good, my hardworking, faithful girl."

Faithful, her father has called her. At this moment Helena feels she's never been faithful to anyone or to anything. In tears, she repeats the word to her mother until Melina says, "Hush my child. Always you were faithful to your work and your salon. Never mind being famous for what good does that bring to you? You are important to the people who come to you. You make women to feel beautiful, and give love to many. Being alive in this world is about the giving of love. Now you tell me you want to be good.

309

You must go to church like you did as a child. You pray to the Virgin to be forgiven for your sins."

"I do go to church sometimes, Mama."

In the days following, Helena wanders to the place where Spiros had his stall, then continues her lonely path to the sea. In her hands she holds a bunch of wild irises, some daisies. She throws them into the water, watches them bob on the surface. A shaft of memory comes to her, something about her grandfather Adam and how, on entering Smyrna, he'd gazed over the Aegean Sea. With joy and hope in his heart he'd given his wife Eleni a black rose as promise of good fortune. Well, it had given her no fortune and done nothing for her mother Melina; nothing for her. From her skirt pocket she pulls out the Bacarro rose she'd carried with her and savagely stamps it into the sand.

Returning to number 24, she puts a scarf over her head and visits the *Church of the Apostles*. On entering its solid stone portal she crosses herself, kneels, and prays for her sins to be forgiven, in particular, for her part in Stephan's death. Had she not gone to him he would not have been travelling to visit her. Forgiveness for not being a good wife to Alex, the way a Greek woman should. For encouraging Leon to spend time away from his wife.

You must have love, and love is what you give. Her grandmother's words return to her. Well, she had once loved Alex, given him a home and stability. To Leon she'd offered deep friendship. To Stephan, her heart. As Dimitri had said, she'd brought sunlight into the gloom of his life at the end. A lump rises up in her throat and she feels sick. Tears fall in a torrent as the faces of the men she has loved float about as though to taunt her.

After confessing everything, a sense of peace quiets her soul. Her chattering *Voices* are stilled at last. The Virgin has listened, and answered her. What must she do now? Where must she go?

Dimitri knocks on the door of number 24 three days after Stephan's funeral and asks for Helena.

"I'm sorry for the words I used to you at the Church," he says. "I'm sure you brought my father happiness, even if for such a little time."

"We were so happy for those days," and impulsively she throws her arms about him. As the son of his father, she'll love him.

310

"I'd like to give you my father's sculpture if you can find a way to get it to Toronto," he says as he steps back from her embrace. "If you'd like it, that is. My Dad said once that it's likeness of a young girl he'd known in Patras, so he must have meant you. I'm sure he'd want you to have it. You brought sunlight into his life near its end, and for this, again I say thank you."

"I adopt you!" Helena cries. "I take you home with me. You must talk to my daughter. She's writing our story with your father in it." She laughs and grips his hand. Dimitri turns a gentle yet enigmatic smile upon her, and steps away.

* * *

Chapter 57

Toronto, 1995

Georgia

'After the euphoria of finding Dimitri fades, the full impact of her loss hits Helena,' I write afterward. 'Stephan, her first and only great love, had lived in her pores, her heart, her bones; his voice had sustained her through her adult life. How would she sustain herself now? No wonder, when back home, she'd fallen into bed in grateful oblivion.'

When finally I feel she's ready for all my questions, I ask Helena about Dimitri, and does she have more photos.

She runs her eyes over my slinky skirt wrapped about my slimmed-down hips, my low-cut blouse, my hair I've arranged to fall in ringlets.

"Ah, Georgie, you're beautiful. Beautiful after all. Who are you dressing up for?"

"Just me."

"Photos of Dimitri? Whatever for?"

I just ... well, do you?"

Astonished, she rummages in her bedside drawer for the snapshots. "Here, you keep them, one day I'll tell you everything, one day ..."

I wait. One evening, after she finishes a bottle of red wine while watching a love story on television, thinking herself alone, I hear her talking aloud to her Voices. 'My ambition has come to this ...thinking only about love ... what about fame? Just an ordinary, middle-sized salon like hundreds of others ... not much to show for the hard work. A husband not really a husband, a daughter a prostitute. A soul mate who prefers his grandchildren. My young idol dead. The family name?'

***

Georgia

It's back to the beginning, near the end of *'An Odyssey'* and want to get it finished.

"Why so much hurry," Helena asks me, but I don't know. Often I take out Dimitri's photo and look at him, the strong jaw, the wide, sensuous-looking mouth. I stare into his copper-coloured eyes, and feel like I'm falling right into them. Like a noon-day sun burnishing the Anatolian earth, fancifully I think. Okay, 'An Odyssey': where, and how, is it going to end? Dimitri's father, my mother's first love, is dead. My mother still works, same as always, at her middle-sized salon, still pursues her fantasies of hair designer fame. Still shacks up with a man who has never really been a husband.

"Georgie, won't you be late for work?"

That evening I rustle about setting up a candlelit table and serve up mousaka and rice. Afterward it I say, "Helena, when you've got time, I need you to tell me a few more things for *'An Odyssey.'* And I want to know more about Dimitri.

"Dimitri? Whatever for?"

"I don't know. I'm thinking maybe ..." I break off, then boldly add, "I want to go meet him ..."

"Well!" Helena's one word cuts me off. Surprise and bewilderment flit over her face. "You're a good girl and looking so nice now, who wouldn't fall in love with you. But Dimitri, whatever could you want with him?" Becoming business-like she says, "You must give me *'An Odyssey'* to read. You've been promising me."

Mother of Jesus. I've given little thought to what will happen at the end. Helena won't like it. She'll complain it's too personal; too many private things that only the family should know, and not all of them either. I've called it a novel, but she'll still fear people will find out that Helena is her. Part of her will want them to, of course.

"When you read it," I begin carefully, "you must remember I've made up lots of it. I had to, because I didn't know all the details."

"Then it's not a true story," she says at once. "You said you'd write the true family story."

"I think fiction can be more powerful, more truthful than truth," I say, my thoughts racing. "In the end it's the big things that count, the big ideas, the big dreams and myths that influence people to do what they do. The little things, well, I have the essence of the people and the history of what happened. Remember what Uncle Alekos said in his letter? I've still got it somewhere."

Helena reaches for a bottle of ouzo while I hunt for it.

'Your great, great grandfather had indeed been a wealthy man,' I read. 'He was an advisor to the Caliphate and an important man in Constantinople. To him was given land in Anatolia, money, titles. What happened to it all? Somebody was jealous of him and told the Caliphate he was with a Turkish Muslim girl, that he visited bordellos, and perhaps met the girl there. I've often thought Yiannis' story was a myth, something necessary to believe in to get respect when little was coming. But it's an old story. Helena, tell it to your children and grandchildren, then forget it. Begin a new one. Never mind the old tree and its roots, it's time for new branches."

A new story? A spark flickers in Helena's eyes and she makes a series of little oh oh sounds. She's comprehending something larger than what she's known, I think; wondering what new tale she'll tell.

"Write this for me." At the command in her voice, I open up my new laptop.

'Helena, the girl with a face to redeem the family name, leaves her native Patras for Toronto in the New World to build once more the family wealth and reputation. She starts from nothing. In a cockroach-infested flat on Berkeley Street is where all the struggles begin, poverty, hard work, long hours, the bad dreams and weeping in the night. Many long years later she opens her own salon created all by herself. She wins contests, prizes, travels to conferences, and never once lets go of her dream.'

"Helena, this is more of the old story."

"I'm not finished. 'She forgets about the name and her dreams of being famous. Instead she builds a place where everyone can come and be happy. She offers them love. Makes them look beautiful. They go out into the world feeling good about themselves ...'"

Helena. My mother. Always conflicted, always suffering through lost love and marital miseries. Proud of her glorious Greek heritage but burdened by it, and by her own profligate personality. At the salon next morning, I stand on the pavement looking up at the name Kouvalis, one letter missing. What would Yiannis, Adam and Eleni say if they could see their descendent? Certainly she'd touched a lot of lives; had embraced the world with profligate warmth, with love. Love: that was the important part. I recall the trembling hope, the little sliver of something I believed might be waiting for me at the end of this story. From my purse I take Dimitri's photo. I hold it close. The eyes: fancifully I fantasize love in them. Also echoes of pain, poverty and struggle. Well, was this not the whole history of Greeks smacked down by history, yet not destroyed?

Dimitri, I'm coming to Patras and want to get to know you. I want to get to know my grandparents and uncles too. To learn more about Greeks and Turks: I want to know the history. The beauty among the violence. I'll travel to Smyrna, in fact, all the way back to the beginning, to where everything started in Anatolia – or should I say, Byzantium?

***

Helena: An Odyssey

Acknowledgements:

My grateful thanks to the following people for their interest, assistance and expertise during my long journey creating this novel:

Kiki Kostakyriakos for inspiring me, for sharing her own and her family's story.
Frank and Claudio Pascuzzo for giving me unique insights into the world of hair, Frank, his personal philosophy.
Sarah Mayor for tireless re-reading and feedback, and to the Parliament Street Writers Group
Michael Redhill for his excellent input and editing
Victor Ostapchuk, Associate Professor, Middle Eastern Studies, University of Toronto for assistance with research
Judy Sandbrook for reading, editing, and input
Maia Ono for assistance and advice
Caroline Finkel for her encouragement and belief in my project
Gemma Hooper for feedback and proofing
Giles Milton for copy-editing

And Gordon Watts for everything!

Please visit Carolyn Taylor-Watts at: www.carolyntaylorwatts.ca.

Made in the USA
Charleston, SC
26 October 2014